The Darkest Swarm
Written by Jake Durrance

The first in the Ascendium Series
From the minds of Matt McArdle and Jake Durrance

[handwritten signature]

12-20 '17

Cover art by Sabrina Mine
CreateSpace Independent Publishing Platform

Contents

Prologue

His eyes sprang open, peering into the black of the night. The clock on the nightstand read two-fifteen AM, casting its dull red hue all around the bedroom. There was no sound, except the slow, soft breathing of his sleeping wife and the distant humming of an unseen car. Something was wrong.

"Hello, Victor." His eyes turned in the direction of the voice, trying to cut through the reddish night. There, in the room with him, stood a man in a black suit. He was staring out the window, his pale, smiling face reflected in the glass. Victor's heart skipped a beat at the sight. A burglar. The intruder carried himself with a confident demeanor. He stood straight, with his pale hands clasped aristocratically around his back.

"Who are you?" he growled, "What are you doing in my home?"

The intruder turned around. He was a tall man of maybe thirty years, with dark, well-kept hair and sculpted features. Even through the almost impenetrable shroud of night, Victor could make out the smile on his face. And those eyes – they were blue, but there was something else about them as well. Were they... glowing? The man opened his mouth for a moment, and then hesitated, as if deciding on his words before finally saying, "April seventh, 2033." His voice was bathed in a thick English accent, with a hint of something else – something Victor couldn't figure out.

"What the hell?"

"On that day," the intruder continued, "I want you to get out of Boston." His voice was so carefree and nonchalant, but nevertheless hitting with an unmistakable air of authority. His demand made no sense. Still, for some reason Victor couldn't help but feel this man wasn't delusional, nor was he there to make off with anything valuable. In fact, he actually had to stop himself from feeling some bizarre sense of trust in this invader. He couldn't explain it. It was as if something had come over him as soon as they made eye contact, but this apparent spell didn't keep him from reacting with fear.

"Yeah, no." Victor retorted, "I'm calling the cops." He was ready to leap out of bed if the trespasser took a single step forward.

"Oh, I'm afraid that would not be in your best interest."

"Are you threatening me?"

"Heavens, no." The interloper pulled his hand out from behind, holding it up with his palm forward. At once, Victor felt drawn to this trespasser's words, as if what he was saying held some vital importance. He listened with care to the man's next words, "Consider this as more of a warning. A friendly piece of advice, really. Next year, on the seventh of April, I want you to leave Boston. In fact, it may be best to avoid cities in general. I hear there are some gorgeous rural areas in western Massachusetts. Go take your family. Maybe bring a close friend along for the ride. You will not regret it."

Victor was struggling to find words to say. He tried to get up, only to realize that he could no longer move. "What? Why?"

The man with the piercing blue eyes took a step towards him, "All will be clear in time, Victor. That, I promise you. Many things are about to change, my friend. Many things – and I hope to see you through it all. But for now, go back to sleep." The intruder's hand stretched outward.

"Get away from me." Victor meant to yell his words, but could only manage to voice a stiff groan. He tried to say it again, but it was of no use. He was powerless. The intruder's finger touched his forehead and then... he woke up.

He was still in his bed, but the blue-eyed man was gone and the sun was shining through the window. Victor sat up and looked around. What had just happened? Was he dreaming? He glanced over to Marceline, who was now beginning to stir next to him, "Morning, honey."

"Morning, dear." he returned, albeit absentmindedly. It was a dream. The whole thing. It must have been in his mind, but it felt so real.

Chapter 1

"Everything alright, Vic?" Marceline looked up from her fried eggs, waiting for his answer. Her gaze held a look of idle curiosity and a hint of concern.

Victor was sitting at the kitchen table, lost in a reminiscent daze. He couldn't stop thinking about last night, but hearing Marceline say his name snapped him back into reality, "Yeah, I'm fine. Why?"

"Well, it's just that you've barely touched your food." Marceline said, starting to go back to her meal, "And you've been so quiet – quieter than normal."

"I just had a weird dream last night." Victor answered, "That's all. Guess it stuck with me." He kept staring off into empty space, reviewing the previous night in his head over and over again. The man. Those eyes. Those glowing, blue eyes. In truth, he couldn't tell if it was a dream or not. It felt so real.

"Did Daddy have a nightmare?" a little brown-haired girl blurted out from the edge of the table. At eight and a half years, Samantha was the older of their two children. She was finishing a bowl of cereal and had stained milk all over her face. For a young girl, she had the manners of a small boy. Her big, hazel eyes stared wildly at her father, waiting for some kind of answer.

"I guess you could say that." Victor replied, sinking back into his thoughts.

"I had a nightmare, too!" Sammy began, bellowing in the way that young children often do, "Last week! There were spiders everywhere! They crawled all over me and in my mouth and-"

"Mom…" Zack whined as he put his little hands to his ears, "Make her stop."

"Sam," their mother intervened, "you know your brother doesn't like bugs."

The girl's arms flailed, "I was just talking about a dream! They're not real!"

"Just please don't talk about bugs in front of him, sweetie. He'll get nightmares, too."

Sam sighed, "Okay…"

"Now go get ready." Marceline said to her daughter, "You have school soon."

"I know. I know." Reluctant to move, Sam was told once more before handing her empty bowl to her mother and trotting off to her room.

Marceline turned to her husband, who was still off in his own world. "I'm gonna go get Zack dressed." she said, "You should get to work soon."

"What?" Victor looked up at her, finding himself back in reality.

"Vic, it's almost eight." She pointed at the clock with her fork, "You need to go to work now."

He blinked a few times before pulling himself out of his seat, "Oh, right. Right." He rushed over to grab his tie and jacket from the bedroom, putting them on as he made his way to the door.

"Oh no, you're doing it all wrong." Marceline dropped the fork on her plate and beckoned him over. With practiced grace, she adjusted his tie to perfection, "There you go."

"Where would I be without you, Marci?"

"Probably dead in a ditch somewhere." They kissed each other goodbye and Victor was off. He made his way through the apartment hallway, down the flight of stairs and out of the building. As he got to the sidewalk, he heard her call out to him through an opened window, "You'd better not zone out like that at work!"

"Yes, Mom!" Victor called back, taking care to drench his words in as much sarcasm as possible.

However, he didn't even make it to the train station before the questions came back. It must have been his most realistic dream to date. A thought came to him. Didn't weird dreams often have hidden meanings behind them? If so, then what was the meaning of this? He racked his brain over it, but couldn't think of any subconscious message that it could symbolize.

The whole subject was starting to stress him out. He let out a low sigh and muttered, "I need a drink." Catching himself on the last syllable, he immediately regretted even considering letting that sentence leave his mouth. It had been three months. Marceline was so proud of him. She would be heartbroken if he relapsed again. Or worse, she would take him back to couple's therapy. He never wanted to go back there, and resolved to stay on the wagon no matter how hard it would be.

This was Victor Roberts: parent, husband, native New Englander. He was far too young to be the father of two kids. At twenty-nine years old, he had yet to do much in life besides drink and regret. In fact, it would have been safe to say he gave up on his aspirations long ago. Instead, he grew accustomed to a low-wage job and a habit that had numbed him to a life without goals. In the past, he'd made three other attempts, all in vain, to kick his addiction. None of them had lasted this long. By all accounts, three full months was a new record.

Trying to get his mind off booze, Victor looked around the train car. All around were working class people, each on their own commute, occupied with their own thoughts or books or music. He peered straight ahead and saw his reflection in the window – a murky, smudged double staring back at him across the aisle. In physical terms, Victor was nothing special. At five feet and ten inches tall, he had a solid frame that sat somewhere between toned and pudgy. He had pine green eyes and fair skin that showed off the Italian side of his heritage. His wavy, chestnut hair was cut short around his head. A trimmed beard outlined the lower half of his face.

In his own eyes, he was about as ordinary as could be.

Now his wife, Victor thought, was anything but ordinary in any way. Marceline was four inches shorter than him and a good deal paler. Long, brown curls of hair draped around her face, bringing out her beautiful, hazel eyes and framing her enchanting smile. Victor knew no one who could ever compare to her, for as beautiful as she was, it was her mind that he fell in love with. She was, by far, the most unique woman he had ever met. She possessed a kind of energy that he both adored and envied. She shared his love for everything from various sciences to the literature to musical tastes, yet she did so with a wild passion that he could never match.

His drinking was the one thing Marceline didn't have a passion for. She despised it – and not only that, she despised him when he drank. Whenever Victor came home smelling like alcohol, Marceline refused to speak to him. She knew what it was like to grow up with an alcoholic father and she wouldn't allow the same for their children. Victor understood. However, saying that he would stop was quite different from stopping, and this day was proving to be difficult.

* * *

The children had been dropped off at school and, by now, Victor was at work. It was time for Marceline to do the same. That is, if work was what she called it. They often said that, if you enjoyed what you did, then you never worked a day in your life. While she didn't agree to the letter, she was still relieved to be in her favored line of work. Before she went back to college, Marceline had been in the same office as her husband. Answering phone calls, filing paperwork, data entry. It was about as compatible for her as it was for Victor. The only difference was that she got out. After returning to complete her degree, Marceline began to work in toxicology at a local hospital. It wasn't the most exciting job, but it was better than where she'd been before. The people were nicer and more focused on making a difference, however little that difference may have been. Meanwhile, Victor was going on nine years at the office, where dreams went to die. Perhaps that was part of why he never went back to school.

Victor. He'd been acting so strange this morning. Was it really a dream that had him so aloof? He'd always had moments of peculiarity, for sure. These episodes always got to their worst when he'd fallen off the wagon, but that couldn't explain what she saw this morning. He was sober and, in all their years of marriage, she'd never known him to be this far off in his own world.

Thinking of him like this brought forth unwelcome feelings. Feelings that she didn't want to feel again. Victor was so much more than his flaws. He was sweet and charming and so caring when he had the mind to be. She loved him for his strength, for his loyalty, for his courage. She loved him because of his love for her. The only times their partnership fell into any drama was when he drank...

With a sigh, Marceline switched on the old van's auto pilot and stared out the window. People walked up and down the busy sidewalk on their way to who-knows-where. A homeless man held up a cardboard sign in a plea for food. A group of children strolled by on their way to school. One of them looked, in her eyes, like an older Zack. He was holding hands with a blonde-haired girl, a heart-melting look on his face. She couldn't help but smile back from her view in the rickety van. Perhaps this was going to be a good day, after all.

* * *

"It's true. I couldn't make this up if I tried." Victor shouted to his friend, Dan. They were sitting together in a bar as he tried to yell over the sound of music and other voices. He was telling his friend about the dream that he couldn't get out of his head. After a long day of pondering, Victor couldn't handle keeping it to himself anymore. If there was anyone in this world he was going to tell, it was Dan. After all, they had been inseparable since elementary school. He knew Victor even better than Marceline did.

Daniel Emerson was, in a way, a beast of a man. At well over six feet tall, he towered over everyone else in the bar. However, despite his great size, Dan was quite the gentle giant. Unlike his counterpart, he was the kind of person who preferred to focus on the moment and live for the fun times. He was a child at heart, always prepared with a new game or a painful joke of some sort. In truth, his carefree attitude was why he and Victor became so close.

Dan looked at Victor with a face full of intrigue, "His eyes were glowing? Like a robot or like something out of a horror movie?"

"Full-on horror movie style, man."

"And he was just standing over you?"

"Yeah. At first, I thought the guy was gonna kill me, but then he started saying all this stuff. And then when he reached out to me, I couldn't move to stop him."

"Maybe it was sleep paralysis? You know, when you wake up but you can't move and you see things that aren't there. I've heard of some pretty messed up stuff happening to people when they go through it."

"I don't know. Maybe that's what it was." Victor swallowed down some of his beer and continued, talking over the crowd while gesturing with his free hand, "It just felt so real."

"Well what do you think it means?" Dan leaned in closer, "A dream as weird as that has to mean something."

"I have no clue."

"What about the date? Does April seventh have any meaning to you? Or the year 2033?"

Victor took a long sip of beer before shaking his head, "Nothing. It's just a random day next year, for all I know."

"So why should you leave Boston that day?"

"How should I know?"

"I don't know. It's your dream."

Victor looked at his friend's inquisitive face. His pine

green eyes met Dan Emerson's icy blue stare. They were silent for a moment, giving the former an opportunity to finish his drink and order another one.

"So uh," Dan started. His voice was hesitant, but not without purpose, "If you don't mind me asking... does Marci know you're here?"

Victor shook his head, reluctant to admit to his fault, "Not a clue. And it's going to stay that way. I texted her saying I had to stay late at work. That's the story and there's nothing else to it. She'll get home from the office and go about her night, because nothing abnormal is happening. Right, Danny?"

"Of course." his friend agreed, "I just wanted to make sure. Last I checked, you were still trying to stay sober." Victor nodded but said nothing, so Dan went on, "And I heard she was really happy for you. And proud."

"That's enough, Daniel." Victor turned to face him, but stubbornly avoided his eyes, "You don't want me to be both drunk and depressed, now do you?"

"I just don't want to see something bad happen to you, Vic. Or your family."

"Yeah, well Marceline won't ever know I was even here. I'll make sure of it."

"How?" Dan looked at him with perplexity, "You smell like this bar and your speech is wonky."

Victor raised a finger towards him, "It's called breath mints and acting, my friend."

"Yeah, let me know how that works out for you."

"Will do, Danny Boy. Will do."

Dan groaned at the sound of his nickname, "You know I hate it when you call me that. I'm not even that Irish."

To that, Victor smirked and looked at him, "Danny Boy."

"Yeah, you're drunk."

"Shh!" Victor held a finger up to his lips, "Don't tell my wife!"

A while later, Victor and Dan departed for their

respective homes. Despite his friend's urgings, Victor insisted on taking the train home by himself. By the time he got back to the apartment, he had gone through half of a pack of breath mints. He walked up the steps as well as he could, turned his key in the door and crept inside. The silence rang like music in his ears. Everyone was asleep. No one was going to catch him. He thought he had won until he passed by the living room.

"It's ten thirty at night."

Victor jumped. His wife was sitting on the couch, her eyes fixated on him. Her arms were folded and her legs were crossed. A look of quiet fury had fixed itself upon her face. "Oh hey, Marci." he called out, "I'm sorry, my boss kept me at work late and-"

"No, Vic." Marceline began, standing up and taking a step towards him, "Let's skip the part where you make some brainless excuse. And keep your voice down. The kids are sleeping."

"But-"

"Dan told me where you were."

"He did?" Victor stood there, open mouthed, shocked at this betrayal.

"He texted me right after you asked him to meet you there. I had him make sure that you would stay safe. But I see the idiot still let you go home alone."

"Well... he wanted to drive me." he conceded, a slight slur to his words, "I just refused."

"That's not the point, Victor."

"Okay, then what is the point?"

"The point?" Marceline fumed, trying to maintain a whisper so as to not wake the children, "You were over three months sober. All that work – all that progress – gone. Are you proud of it?"

"No, I'm not!" Victor cried, throwing his hands up into the air, "But at least it's better than when I was drinking every day."

"Do you want your kids to grow up with an alcoholic in

13

the house? You know what it's like. I know what it's like. Do you really want that for Zack and Sam?"

"I'm not constantly hammered like your dad. I'm not violent like mine. What I do is totally different."

"Be quiet." Marceline warned, "Don't wake the kids."

"What I do is totally different." Victor repeated, "These were my first drinks in months. Months! You're making this seem so much worse than it really is."

"You know I'm not. You know if I let you keep falling off the wagon, one day you'll never get back on." Victor was silent. He wanted to deny it – to scream that she was wrong and that he would be fine – but deep inside, he knew she was right. Marceline, having just won her latest victory, stormed off to bed and left her drunken husband alone in the living room. Left with nothing but his own intoxicated thoughts, he plopped himself on the couch. He fumbled for the remote control and switched on the television, letting the mindless entertainment clear his head. He fell asleep not long after, still dressed for work and thick with the stench of a cheap bar.

Chapter 2

"We have now arrived at Philadelphia International Airport. Please remain seated until the flight attendants allow you to grab your luggage. I hope you enjoy your stay in the good old Keystone State of Pennsylvania."

"I need to stretch my legs." groaned a young, slender man from the back of the plane, "Five and a half hours of flying don't exactly feel good on the arse, either."

An equally young, auburn-haired woman sat by his side. She turned to him with a look of annoyance, "Oh come on, Travis." she said, "There's children here."

The man sighed, "All I said was arse."

"Well right now, you're being an arse."

He smiled and stared back until her face of disapproval faded into a reflection of his. "I just don't like being confined, is all. You know that." The man went quiet, but his companion could still sense the uneasiness growing within him.

The claustrophobic man's name was Travis Norwich. He was a twenty-two-year-old London resident who had just sat through an uncomfortably long flight to the States. In honesty, he was fine with staying in England. Yet his girlfriend, Jane, insisted that he should tag along.

Jane Greene was the auburn-haired woman beside him. Although a native to Pennsylvania herself, she had lived in London with Travis for the better part of three years now. Since then, she had only come back to America twice. The first time was to attend her grandfather's funeral, and then for a two-week vacation during the summer of '32. It was during this eventful summer that her family at last met Travis. Some

15

of them adored him for his peculiar words and his quirky ways. They thought he was a gentleman, a true icon of modern chivalry, or at least an exotic curiosity. Others didn't take such a liking to him. In particular, her father found him to be rather annoying and far too liberal for his taste. More than once, Mister Greene had put him on the spot or made a scene, questioning everything from his intelligence to his sexuality. Ever since, Travis had dreaded ever coming back to see Jane's family. It was unfortunate for him, then, that it was time again to meet and discuss and be gawked at by the small-town family.

Her sister, Olivia, was getting married. Jane would have died before she let him skip out on the wedding. She told him it would "mean a lot to the family" if he came, adding that he might "make a few friends". He didn't believe her, but it didn't matter in the slightest. She had bought the tickets, so he was going.

It was another forty minutes before they got off the plane and through airport security. In his short list of trips outside his native England, Travis learned to despise the tedious process of airport security. It was the kind of thing that only a post-9/11 world, as they called it, could justify. Every time he had to travel, it seemed as if the rules became stricter. Fewer items were allowed onboard. Lines got longer. Everybody had to bring further proof of identity. It wasn't until the past year that the last part had been rescinded.

At last, the couple was granted the freedom to pick up their luggage. Without delay, they grabbed their stuff and made their way to the parking lot. There, Jane's uncle, Tom, was going to pick them up. Thomas Greene was older than his brother, Jane's father, yet he still retained much of his youth. He was far too wild and eccentric for a man in his fifties. His eyes glistened with boundless energy for life. He carried himself in a strong, untested fashion that never hinted at his many weary decades spent in this world. Even in those long-outdated clothes, he looked some twenty years younger than he had any right to.

Near the exit, Travis took a quick look around to see the time. A nearby overhead screen told him it was eleven-forty-six in the morning on Thursday, April seventh, 2033. Almost noon. That would give him and Jane plenty of time to get to the wedding.

* * *

This was the day he'd been warned of – the day where he needed to leave Boston. For Victor Roberts, though, it was like any other day. To be honest, he had almost forgotten about the dream. After all, that strange night took place a full six months ago. Now that the mentioned date had arrived, the dreamed warning was nothing but an unintelligible whisper in the back of his mind.

It was just after five o'clock and Victor was riding the train home from the office. He was half listening to a couple of men talking a few seats over. They were marveling over some nonsense about a faulty transmitter at an army garrison in Devens. He didn't know how they knew or why they cared. Perhaps they knew somebody there.

Victor was far too occupied with his own thoughts to care, though. He wanted a drink to help him wind down after a long day of menial labor and repetitive tasks. This time, however, he wouldn't break. After close to a month of sobriety, he wasn't about to ruin his progress again.

To get his mind off of it, Victor tried to look forward to the evening that lay ahead. Dan was coming over for dinner and was preparing quite the feast. Of course, Victor was going to help cook when he got home, or at least do what little he could. He may have loved food with a passion, but he was a terrible chef. It was his daughter, Sammy, who was talented beyond her years. She may have been less than nine years old, but she had the skill and discipline of someone twice her age. Victor wondered if she would help get things ready tonight, as she often did when they had company over.

The doors of the train spread open, letting a herd of passengers spill through like animals packing into a pen. Not that it was out of the ordinary in any way. This particular station was in the financial district, and it was the time of day when many workers were on their way home. Still, an odd feeling was rising within Victor. A sudden desire took hold - a biting need to know every detail of his surroundings. He made a long scan of the boarded crowd. Brokers and agents stood around, either talking on their phones or amongst each other. Teenagers stared out the windows, their earbuds helping to block out the chaos of the world. A white-haired woman sat at the end of the car, engrossed in some romance or detective novel on her tablet. Nothing seemed out of the ordinary.

Then, at once, something caught his eye. In the midst of the rabble was a man in formal attire. Against the background of movement and clamor, he was an island of stillness. He looked familiar, but Victor couldn't recognize him with the first cursory glance. Everyone was walking, moving up and down the aisle, clustering around, trying to find a place to stand or sit. Everyone, that is, except this man. He went for a long double take of his finding. In the river of motion, he stood like a rock. The man must have somehow sensed Victor's gaze, as he at once answered with a look of his own. Their eyes locked in a cold, knowing stare. Just before the train doors closed, Victor saw something that nearly made him jump out of his skin. The stranger blinked. He blinked, and his eyes glowed with a piercing blue aura. Then, just as quickly as they lit up, his otherworldly gaze faded back to normal. With that, the stranger gave an icy smile and the slightest nod before turning and disappearing into the crowd. Victor bolted from his seat, ready to pursue, but the blue-eyed man was nowhere to be found.

* * *

"And here we are." Tom declared. His car rolled by a

large white building with a tall steeple, "That's the church where Olivia and Jordan are gonna get married." Travis gazed at the structure in disapproval, deciding that whoever worked there was trying far too hard to make the place seem appealing. The paint was fresh – a few months old, at the most. A garden surrounded the main building with a colorful assortment of flowers. Even the sign out in front looked to be polished with obsessive care. It stood with dominance as plaster statues surrounded it, acting out different scenes from the Bible. Travis wondered why someone would try so hard to impress people. After all, shouldn't a church be more about what's on the inside?

Frustrated by his own train of thought, Travis turned his attention to the radio. The news was on, with a disembodied voice feigning care over some national story, "And now it appears that the Tobyhanna Army Depot has joined the ever-growing list. The US military has now lost contact with more than fifty military installations across the eastern seaboard alone. The depot, established in 1953, is a logistics center for the US Department of Defense."

Travis furrowed his brow. Another one? That's all he had been hearing about since he and Jane had landed. There had been report after report of these military centers losing contact with the outside world.

"Meanwhile, the team sent to Fort Indiantown Gap, better known to locals as the Gap, still hasn't returned to update us on the situation."

"Oi, Tom." said Travis, "Could you change the station? I'm getting a bit sick of this rambling."

Tom shook his head, "I tried to find something else. It's on every station."

"Then turn the radio off." Jane suggested, "I'm tired of it, too. They're making a big deal out of some stupid communications error."

Tom turned it off, but not before teasing the young couple about their inability to handle real news. A few minutes of welcomed silence later, Tom pulled into the parking lot of a small motel. The lot was surprisingly full for such a small town. Travis figured that the other cars must have been there for the wedding as well.

The trio was forced to park the car in an old garage beside the building. The aged structure was dark and stingy. Coating the walls and ceiling were some strange mesh of metal. It reminded Travis of a bird cage. Power tools and spare parts were everywhere. He figured this garage must have been where the motel's employees fixed cars that had broken down.

Between the time that they drove past the church and when they got to the motel, there was nothing but farmland, dirt roads and the occasional tree. Everything was so dull and quiet. Travis was not at all used to small, rural towns like this. He was more comfortable with the bustling streets and towering buildings back in London. Jane, though, was in her element. She had grown up here, attended the same church that Travis wanted to lambaste, and even been to many of the farms that they had passed by. She was at home amongst the trees and fields that decorated her childhood, but Travis didn't find the place to be so heartwarming. Still, the glowing, ear-to-ear smile from his girlfriend's face was more than enough to keep him quiet about how he truly felt.

The three pulled themselves from the car and got to work unloading the luggage. Only one of the suitcases belonged to Travis. The other two were Jane's. As the couple followed Tom, he turned to tell them, "You're reserved in room two-twelve. I'm in one-oh-nine, but I already unpacked before I picked you two up."

"Thanks, Uncle Tommy." said Jane.

After about twenty minutes, they had finished unloading the car and unpacking all that they'd brought. Now it was time to get dressed and head for the church. Tom had arrived in his suit, which was famous among the family due to its pure white color. After all his years of wearing it, the outfit never seemed to grow worn or dirty. Already dressed, he disappeared into his own room to relax while the others made themselves ready. Travis had just finished wrestling with his bow-tie when he heard his girlfriend call for him. He hurried over to the bathroom to find her struggling to close the back of her dress. "Could you get this for me?" Travis took the strings of the dress and tied them well across her back.

"I don't know why you insist on changing in the bathroom." he said, "I can help you more quickly if you're near me."

"Well I need the mirror for my makeup."

"And since when does Jane Nicole Greene need makeup? You're beautiful as is and you know it."

Jane's face pulled into a wide grin. "Well everyone else is wearing it today."

"I'm not." Travis answered with a sly wink.

She gave a playful push, "You know what I mean." Travis took her arm and leaned in to kiss her. They both stood there for a moment, eyes closed and lips touching. When he pulled away, he smiled and looked into her soft, blue eyes. He was about to tell her how much he loved her, but a sudden darkness cut him off. The two of them looked around. Not a single light in the motel room was on. "The power must be out." Jane concluded.

"We should go." Travis motioned toward the door.

"You think?"

The couple left the motel room and made their way for the end of the parking lot. There, they saw Tom opening the garage's wired door and retrieving his car. As they looked through the windows of other rooms, they saw that the power outage wasn't just limited to them. Indeed, every other room was stuck in the same unexpected darkness as theirs. Tom noticed them approaching, climbing into his car and backing out to meet them. As he got to them, he stopped and lowered his window, "You guys ready?"

"Did you see what just happened to the lights?" asked Jane.

"What do you mean?"

"The power just went out." Travis told him.

As Tom pulled the car out of the garage, he twisted his neck around to see the building. "In the whole motel?"

"Yep." Jane answered.

"Well let's just hope that the power comes back on before we get back here. Otherwise, we might want to find a different place."

* * *

Victor sprinted like a madman, getting from the train station to his apartment in record time. He raced up the steps, bolted through the hallway and made his way to his door. Then he stopped. He stood in the doorway like a statue, trying to make sense of the thoughts in his racing mind. Then at once he turned the key, opened the door and cut into a brisk stride. Dan and Sammy were tending to a pot of pasta. The former looked up and smiled, "Hey, Vic. Dinner will be-" Victor ignored him, walking past the kitchen and through the apartment's main hallway. Dan tilted his head, "Vic?"

Marceline was sitting on the couch with their son. Looking up from the television, she at once noticed that something wasn't right. "Hey, Vic." she called, "What's going on?" Victor was silent as he walked right by and disappeared into the master bedroom.

From the living room, he could hear Sammy ask, "Is something wrong with Daddy?" Part of him wanted to answer, to say that he was fine, but not a word left his mouth.

Victor looked around, unable to keep his body from shaking. He needed to pack some of his belongings. But how much would he need? He didn't know how long they would be away from home. At last, he grabbed his old gym duffle bag from the closet, emptied it onto the floor and dumped a few days' worth of clothes into it. Then a knock on the door frame broke his concentration. Victor turned around and saw Dan standing there. He looked somewhat unnerved, his eyes scanning Victor from head to toe, "Hey, Vic." he started,

"What's going on? What are you packing for?"

Victor looked at the duffle bag in his hand, and then back at his friend in the doorway, "We have to get out of Boston." he announced. His voice was shaky, scared, yet confident in his words.

Dan looked at him, even more confused, "What are you talking about? Is something going on?" Then his face changed, a sudden realization washing over him, "Oh, this is about the dream, isn't it? Today's the day that the guy talked about." While he was speaking, Victor had begun packing again. "It was just a dream, Victor." Dan reminded him, "The guy isn't real."

"That guy. That guy with the glowing eyes. I saw him."

"You saw him in a dream."

Victor's deep voice rose to a shout, "No, Dan. I saw him twenty minutes ago!"

Daniel's eyes widened, "What? What are you-"

"I saw him again. On my way home from work. He was there on the goddamn train."

"What do you mean? How do you know it was him?"

"The eyes! I saw his eyes and they were glowing, just like in my dream." Victor took a step back, shaking his head, "No, no. It wasn't a dream. That guy is real. He's real and he wants me to get you all out of Boston."

At that point, Marceline came to join them. A look of deep concern had etched was etched across her face, "What's going on?"

"Victor saw the man again." Daniel told her.

"What man?"

"Some guy that visited him at night a few months ago. He had glowing blue eyes."

"Wasn't that just a dream?" Marceline looked at Dan as if she were questioning his sanity.

"It wasn't a dream!" Victor roared, "And you're missing the point. He told me to leave Boston today, and now he's showing up on the exact day he told me about. There's no way that's a coincidence."

Marceline took a step towards him, holding her arms out as if offering a wife's embrace, "Victor, sweetie, have you been drinking again?"

"I haven't had a drop all month." he growled, "I know how crazy this sounds, but I swear I'm telling the truth. He was there. He wants us to get out of the city."

There was a pause. Nothing sounded, nothing moved. The tension in the air was almost tangible. The children scurried over from the kitchen and the living room, curiosity having overcome them. They waited by the doorway, quiet as mice, hoping for the next part of the drama to unfold.

It was Dan who broke the silence, "You know how crazy this sounds, right?"

"You think I don't know?" Victor countered. Then his voice, losing its energized fury, took on more of a pleading tone, "Please, both of you just listen to me. We have to get out of Boston. Right now. That guy wouldn't have broken into this home if nothing was going to happen. Something bad is going on. Something very bad. And I don't know what it is, but I don't want us to be here when it goes down." There was another moment of silence while the other two were collecting their thoughts.

"I think we should do it." Dan said at last.

Marceline looked at him, astonished, "What?"

"Marci, I know Vic. I know that he's telling the truth. He really saw that guy. And if Blue-Eyes wants us out of the city this bad, then we should go. Maybe something's gonna happen, after all."

"If you're wrong," Marceline warned, "and nothing happens, I'm going to assume that you're drinking again. Or on drugs. Or just totally crazy. Either way, I'll seriously be considering a divorce."

Victor considered her words for a moment. He had to be sure of what he saw. If he was wrong, it would be the end of his family – but if he was right and he did nothing, it would be even worse. At last, he nodded, "Okay." Then, in a full voice, he said, "Let's just get the hell out of Boston."

Travis and the others hadn't gotten far before they caught sight of something peculiar. At the side of the road was a maroon-colored sedan. Beside it stood a man and a woman. They were perhaps a couple of years older than Jane and Travis. The man was clothed in a fine white shirt and jet-black pants. He was working under the hood of the car, his sleeves rolled up and his hands full of filth. The woman was in a small, violet dress that flattered her curvy frame. In one hand she held a black coat that could only have been her partner's. In the other hand was a cell phone, pressed tightly against her ear. As the car drew closer, the frustration on their faces became as clear as day. The woman seemed to notice Tom's car, looking up and waving the black coat in the air.

"She's signaling us." Travis said, "Should we help them?" He looked to the others for an answer.

"Look at what they're wearing." Jane pointed, "They're probably here for the wedding, just like us."

"Yep," Tom nodded, "I know that girl. She's Olivia's friend. I'm stopping."

When Tom pulled up behind the stranded car, the woman rushed over to meet him at the door. She had pale skin accompanied with long, reddish curls of hair and a face full of freckles. As Tom rolled his window down, she began to speak frantically, "Thank you so much for stopping. My boyfriend and I were on our way to a wedding and – Oh, you're Olivia's uncle, aren't you? Tom, is it?" He replied in the affirmative and she peered further into the car, "And you must be Jane! Oh, it's so good to finally meet you. Olivia's told me so much about her little sister. How's London been? Is that your boyfriend in the back seat?"

"The car, Beth!" her partner cried, still under the hood of his maroon sedan.

"Oh, sorry." cried the red-haired woman.

"What happened?" Tom asked, leaning his head out of

25

the window to better direct his voice.

The man dislodged himself from under the hood and straightened himself out before walking over. He had short, golden brown hair and a small beard that suited his face well. "Our car just died out of nowhere." He wiped his blackened, greasy hands together.

"Need a hand with it?"

"I don't think that would help, but thanks. I can't figure out what's wrong with it. It's like somebody just... I don't know, hit a button and turned it off."

Tom's brow furrowed, "That couldn't really be what happened, though."

"I don't know." said the man, "All I know is that I know my way around cars and I, for the life of me, cannot find something wrong with it. Nothing at all, besides maybe the battery. Maybe the circuits inside. But the car had been running fine with autopilot for over an hour. I doubt it just died."

"Do you two have a ride to the wedding?" Jane asked.

Beth gestured to her cell phone, "I was trying to call one of the other bridesmaids to see if they could come give us a ride. My phone died, though. I don't know how, because, I mean I just charged it before we got in the car. But I guess that's what we get with phones these days. Right? I mean, if this thing actually decided to work for a change, we could have had Christie or Rosie over her by now. But oh well. Technology, right?"

Jane blinked, "So... you're stranded."

"Well that's a way to put it, yeah."

"We can give you a ride, if you want." Tom offered them, pointing his thumb to the back of his sedan.

"Hey, it beats walking." said the boyfriend, "And maybe I could get something for my hands, too?" He lifted his arms to show off the grease and oil that painted him up to his forearms.

"I think I have a water bottle and some napkins in my purse." said Jane.

"Oh, thank you, thank you, thank you." Beth repeated, "You have no idea how much this means to me. Thank you all so much."

A moment later, both were sitting with Travis in the back of Tom's car. He had made it a point to stay quiet earlier, already being uncomfortable with going to the wedding in the first place. Of course, he didn't want to attract any unnecessary attention to himself. Now that Beth was sitting next to him, he was forced to deal with her barrage of over-worded questions and irritating remarks. Still, he was able to find some solace in the fact that her boyfriend looked to be as annoyed by her yammering as he felt.

"If you don't mind me asking," Jane began, looking to Beth, "if you're one of the bridesmaids, then shouldn't you have already been at the church? Why are you just getting there now?" Travis had the feeling that she only asked this to get Beth's attention away from him. God, he loved that woman.

"Well we were planning on getting there early to help set up, but we kind of took too long getting ready."

"She took too long." her boyfriend clarified.

"Oh, whatever. I'm a woman. I get to take too long." Tom gave a laugh and Beth continued, "So we didn't even get on the road until like an hour ago. It was only supposed to be a half-hour drive, so we figured there'd still be plenty of time. But then my genius boyfriend's car broke down. And then my phone decided not to work, so we couldn't call for help. The whole thing was a gigantic mess until you guys showed up."

As she finished her story, the car pulled into the church's parking lot. The five of them got out of the car and Travis found himself surrounded by the same over-decorated yard that he wanted to laugh at. They hurried inside and found the place crawling with family, friends and all kinds of socialites. Even in the church, all the lights were out. Travis wondered how far this blackout went. Would be fixed by the time they got back to the motel?

People crowded around in small groups, chatting with each other in the way that extended relatives often do. By the altar, he saw Jane's parents talking to a young priest. To his complete dismay, she dragged him along to join them.

"Do we have to?" he groaned.

"They're my parents, Travis." Jane insisted. She gave him a comforting kiss and smiled, "Come on, sweetie. It'll be fine."

"If you say so."

Jane locked her arm with her boyfriend's and together they approached her parents. When Jane's mother saw the young couple, she dashed over as fast as her dress and heels would allow, grabbing her daughter by the arm and calling, "Oh, there she is. Father Joseph, I'd like you to meet my other daughter, Jane."

"What happened to Father Richard?" Jane asked, "I thought Olivia was going to have him marry her off."

"He's still around, don't worry." answered the priest, "That old man still has another few years left in him. God bless him. He's just out sick, so I've been filling in for his duties. I've only been working here for a couple of years and I hear that you haven't been around these parts for a while. You probably haven't seen me before." He extended his hand to Jane, "I'm Father Joseph."

"Jane Greene." she said, taking his hand, "And this is my boyfriend, Travis."

"I was wondering who this fine young man was." Father Joseph smiled as he shook Travis' hesitant hand, "You don't talk much, do you?"

"He's just shy." Jane explained, "Don't worry about him."

"Ah, okay. Well, I'd better get back to my duties. How about I give your parents some time to chat with you?"

"Thank you, Father." Jane gave a smile and Travis hid a grimace.

When the priest was gone, her parents came up and hugged her, "We've missed you so much." her mother exclaimed, "How's London?"

"It's so exciting. And it's so different than Pennsylvania. I love it there, but I missed home. I'm so glad to be back here for a few days."

"Well, of course." Her father chimed in, "You're a small-town girl. You're not meant for big cities."

"I didn't mean it like that, Dad. I love London. And besides, Travis is from there."

"Right." Mister Greene peered over at the Englishman, "Speaking of, he doesn't look too good right now. Are you okay, boy?"

"Yeah, I'm fine." Travis stuttered, "Fabulous. Never better."

"You look nervous. Is this your first wedding or something?"

Travis shook his head, "No, I went to my parents' wedding when I was little."

Mister Greene raised an eyebrow at the young man, "Is that so?" Travis silently cursed himself. Mister Greene was a traditional man. He wouldn't want his daughter to be with an open bastard. "Let's hope that the apple fell far enough from that tree." he said.

"Don't be mean, Dad." Jane insisted. The Englishman wished that he didn't love her so much. He could have refused to go with her. This night was already starting off awkward and miserable, and Travis was dreading every moment of it.

* * *

"Where are we going?" Sammy shouted from the living room. Her father and Uncle Danny were loading Marceline's van with anything they figured they'd need. Her mother was by the doorway, tying Zack's sneakers and fitting him into his spring jacket.

"I'll explain later, sweetie." she answered, giving her best effort to hide the creeping fear in her voice.

Dan barged into the living room, still panting from his trips back and forth to the van, "Okay, we're packed. Let's get out of here."

Marceline took Zack's little hand and called for Sammy to follow. As they headed to her van, Zack looked up and asked, "Mommy, what's going on?"

She didn't know how to answer, at last coming up with, "We're just going for a ride. Okay? That's all." Zack then asked why, but she didn't answer. They looked out the window and saw Victor, who sat impatiently in the driver's seat of the van. "He'd better know what he's doing." She muttered just loud enough for Dan to hear, "For his own sake."

"For everyone's sake." Dan added without looking at her.

The horn wailed and Victor cried out, "Come on!" The group climbed in and they took off. Marceline was in the front passenger seat, leaving Dan in the back with the children. The drive was dark, the only light being from the van. Dusk had crept by, pulling the world into an unfettered darkness. None of them spoke of it, but they all noticed that none of the street lights in the neighborhood were on. Neither were any lights in any of the apartments they passed. No sounds of traffic or music filled the streets. Everything seemed dead. It was an absence that everyone noticed, but nobody wanted to acknowledge.

After a few minutes of sitting in complete silence, Marceline felt that she'd had enough. "Do you know where we're going?"

Victor nodded, "We're taking the back roads to ninety and following it out west."

"But won't we have to go further into Boston to get there?" asked Dan, "If the point is to get us out of the city, then –"

"Once we get there, it'll take us directly out west. That's what we need to do."

"But ninety is a toll road." Marceline warned, "There'll

be so much congestion."

"Then where should we go?" Victor was losing his patience, "Do you have any better ideas?"

"What about ninety-five?"

"That'll take us straight into Providence." Victor barked, "We need to get away from all cities."

"I thought you said it was just Boston."

"He said that it would be best to avoid cities in general."

"Then route two." Marceline shot her hands out in frustration, "No tolls. No congestion. It'll be smooth sailing out west."

Their argument was forgotten when they turned onto one of the main roads. They came into view of a peculiar cluster of cars blocking their path. They had all stopped together, resting in the road at random angles. Some vehicles had rear-ended the ones in front of them or had careened onto the sidewalk. Marceline looked around at the crowds of people standing by their dead machines. Some were arguing with each other or surveying damage. Others were trying to use their phones.

Victor managed to drive around a few of them, but had to stop when he was confronted by a truck that had stopped sideways, taking up most of the street and blocking their path. He lowered the window and shouted, "Come on, get out of the road!"

A woman stepped out from around the other side of the truck. She called back, "Hey, dumb ass, does it look like I can move?" She was large, with dark skin, chestnut hair and a look of fury in her eyes.

"What do you mean?" asked Victor, looking around. From what he could see, nothing was blocking her from moving.

A young man began to approach the driver's side of the van. He shook his head as if Victor didn't understand, "Our cars just stopped working."

"All of them?" Dan asked, more to himself than anyone else.

"Have you tried calling tow trucks?"

"Yeah," the woman nodded, "but none of us could get through to them."

"So, your cars all broke down at the same time and your towing people won't pick up their phones?"

"No, I mean our phones aren't working." she clarified.

"None of them." the other man added. By now, he was only a couple of feet from Victor's window.

Marceline leaned over her husband, "Do you want to borrow one of ours?"

"Sure."

Marceline reached into her pocket and took out her phone. She pressed the "unlock" button on it, but nothing happened. Figuring that it must have turned off in her pocket somehow, she held the button down to reboot it. Again, nothing happened. "Vic, Dan, check your phones. Mine isn't working, either." The two men tested their own phones, only to find that the same thing was happening to them, too.

"This is getting kind of creepy." Dan commented.

"Maybe something's going on, after all." Marceline muttered. She looked at the man by the window with apologetic eyes, "I'm sorry, but our phones aren't working either."

"At least your car works." he answered.

The large woman called out to them, "I can move my truck, if you guys need to get by. My son and I can put it in neutral and push it off the road."

"Yes, thank you." Victor called back, "We would really love that."

As they continued along the street, they saw that many other people had begun to do the same. Countless cars and trucks were rolling away from the middle of the road, clearing a path. It seemed to them that, somehow, the Roberts family had the only working automobile in the city. Seeing all of this had chipped away at the skepticism of the group. With the cars and the phones and the lights, it was becoming clear that something was happening after all.

"Oh, you two look so adorable." It was one of Jane's relatives. She was a heavy-set woman who appeared to be in her late forties or early fifties. Curly brown hair framed her round face, and her stocky limbs made her seem even smaller than she was. Travis couldn't remember her name or her place in Jane's family, but he kept his ignorance to himself. The woman grabbed her phone from her purse and tried to turn it on, ready to take a picture of him with Jane. "Get ready to smile."

Jane grabbed hold of her partner and smiled, kicking one of her legs into the air behind her in a sort of pose. The couple waited for the relative, who just stood there, staring at her phone with growing annoyance, "Are you kidding me? Mine doesn't work, either."

"Is something wrong?" Jane asked, taking her arms off of Travis and walking over to see the phone's screen.

"You'd better check your phone, too. Everybody's has been acting up, today."

Jane reached into her purse and tried her cell phone, only to be met with the same stubborn black screen.

"When exactly did all your phones stop working?" asked Travis.

The relative looked up at him, "Oh, I don't know, dear. Around the same time that the lights went out, I think."

"This is weird." Jane looked at the blank lights above their heads.

"I know, dear. And how are we supposed to take pictures of the wedding without cameras or good lighting?"

Jane nodded, "I don't know, but this won't stop Olivia. She's not the kind of girl to freak out over small things. Besides, people came here from all over. The wedding kind of has to be tonight, or tomorrow at the latest."

A half an hour later, they were ready for the ceremony. The crowd gathered in the rows of pews. It seemed that the church's extravagance wasn't limited to the outside decorations. Their pews were made of a dark, rose-colored wood and padded with royal purple cushioning. Even in the shade of darkness, Travis could make out the ornate carvings in the seats. It was far too comfortable and pristine for an organization that should pride itself on modesty. At least, that was what Travis thought. He looked around at everyone's quiet excitement. "I can barely contain myself." Jane whispered, who was sitting just to his left, "My big sister is getting married."

Her mother leaned over from her spot and added, "And think, someday it'll be you up there. Maybe someday soon."

"Oh, Mom." Jane blushed. Although he pretended to be oblivious, Travis saw Missus Greene glance at him. She then whispered something to her daughter through a cupped hand. Jane, in turn, whispered back into her mother's ear, giving a slight shake of her head as she did so.

Music faded in as the strings and the organ beside the altar came to life. All eyes turned to the far end of the room. A line of beautiful young women, all in violet dresses, stepped out from around the corner and into the aisle. One by one, they passed by, Beth among them. Travis recognized her as soon as she came into view, purely by her red curls and freckled face. He watched as she strode down the aisle, stopping once to wave to her boyfriend.

At last, the one whom they had all been waiting for came into view. Olivia Greene was nothing short of stunning in her strapless, white wedding gown that hovered just above the floor. Simplistic yet effective, it made clear the beauty in her that everyone had already adored. A nervous but ecstatic smile told the crowd that this had been the day that she had been waiting her entire life for. Even Travis, who desired nothing more than to be gone from this place, couldn't resist feeling a sense of happiness for her. She was radiant with joy. No, she was more than that. She was in love. Maybe someday he would get to see Jane walking down the aisle too, with a smile just like that.

34

* * *

Victor drove on for hours. In his hyper focus, concepts of rest and speech and even blinking failed him. Once he got onto route two he made his way west through the dark, endless river of dead metal. None of them had ever seen anything like this before. Victor wondered how every car in Massachusetts could have broken down at the same time. Every single one, it seemed, except for theirs. It wasn't limited to cars, vans and trucks, either. Street lights and toll booths also had also fallen victim to this strange blackout. No matter how much he racked his brain, he couldn't think of a single reason as to why or how this could happen. All he knew was that the blue-eyed man was right. Something was going on – something that he and his family couldn't be around for.

He adjusted the rearview mirror to check on the children. They were asleep in the back with Dan. The latter raised his head, answering Victor's reflected gaze with a tired wave.

"We need to stop." Marceline told him. The unexpected voice made Victor jump in his seat.

"Why? We need to keep going."

"It's been hours, Vic."

"At least turn on the autopilot."

"I tried. It doesn't work."

"I'm sure that everyone here has to use the bathroom. Even you."

"I can hold it."

Marceline gestured towards the dashboard, "We're almost out of gas."

Victor's eyes darted to the fuel gauge. They were on their last eighth of a tank. "Damn it." he cursed under his breath, "Okay, we'll stop. Just a few more miles."

"Promise me that we can take a break at the next rest stop."

Victor gave a slight nod, "Sure. Not a long one, but sure."

"And maybe I could take over with driving for a bit?" When her husband didn't answer, she added, "You've just been so tense. There's no way this is good for you." Still no response. His face had become rigid and stoic, unlike anything she had seen before. Fear had turned her husband into a focused machine.

Victor kept to his word and they finally did pull into a nearby rest stop. He got out of the van to fill the gas tank, but Marceline took the pump from his hand, "I'll do it. Go walk around a bit. Stretch your legs. Clear your head." Victor hesitated, taking a moment to process her words before nodding in concession.

"I'm taking the kids inside." said Dan, "We're gonna find a restroom and get some food. He can tag along."

"Good idea. Why don't you go with Dan?"

"Sure." Victor answered, "Good idea."

He followed them into the rest stop's main building. Even in there, it appeared that nothing that used electricity was working. The lights were all out and the air had the unaltered chill of an April evening. Victor soon realized that the employees must have left after the power went out. The whole place stood deserted.

Sammy led Zack off to the bathrooms, leaving the adults alone in the hallway between the lavatories to the food court. They remained there for a time, waiting in complete silence. Victor stood motionless, shoulders slumped and head turning this way and that. Dan leaned against the wall across from him, studying his friend with intensity. Even when the kids came out and walked back to the van, they just stood there, one staring at the other. After what seemed like a small eternity, one of them had to speak.

"So, what now?" Dan asked.

"What?"

"Vic, we're as far west as we can get and still be in the Commonwealth. We're miles from anything even remotely resembling a city. We did what Blue-Eyes said. So now what?"

"I don't know."

"But you have to know, Vic."

"Why do I have to know?"

"Because you brought us into this. We kind of need something a bit better than blind faith."

Victor sighed, "Something is going to happen in Boston and we have to be out west. That's all I know."

"What about all the cars out there? I swear that we have the only working wheels in the state. I'm willing to bet money on it. And everything else that's electronic is broken, too. Lights, air conditioners, cell phones, toll booths… What's up with that?"

"You're acting like I have all the answers, Danny. But I don't. I just don't. I've told you everything that I know. Okay? All I know is-"

"Yeah. Boston is a no-no and farms are prettier in the dark. I know, Vic."

"Then why do you keep asking?" Victor stood there, arms outstretched in exasperation, waiting for Dan to answer him. When no response came he turned back around to leave, only to stop again after a couple of steps. He turned, looking around at the various booths and restaurant chains in the empty food court. After a moment of deliberation, he strode off towards a burger kiosk.

"What are you doing?" Dan asked.

"Looking around." Victor told him, "Who knows? Maybe we can stay here tonight."

"We're in a rest stop, Vic. Not a motel. We can't just stay here."

"Why not? It's abandoned. And they probably still have food. Maybe even some booze."

Dan groaned. He was looking for something to drink. At a time like this, when everyone needed him more than ever, Victor was trying to wash the world away. The thought made him sick.

* * *

Travis Norwich sat alone, slumped in a chair at one of the corner dining tables, watching the celebration before him. Olivia was dancing with her new husband. Jane was off in a crowd, talking gossip with the bridesmaids. Her parents were amusing themselves with other relatives that Travis couldn't say he knew. He only remembered them well enough to understand their less-than-friendly disposition towards him. In truth, he was much more comfortable as a fly on the wall, rather than as an active member of the celebration. He would have been even more content, though, if he had missed the event altogether. The young Brit felt that he didn't belong anywhere near this place. It was the private gathering of a family that was not his own. He had no place among these strangers. As he understood it, many of them didn't even want him there anyway.

He grew even more uncomfortable at the sound of a chair screeching next to him. Out of curiosity, he looked over. He wanted to see if he knew the face of whoever interrupted his contemplation. To his surprise, he could. It was Beth's boyfriend. Travis had admittedly forgotten all about the man. Without so much as a glance in his direction, the newcomer took a seat beside him and muttered, "Some party."

By instinct, Travis wanted to pretend that he was enjoying himself. However, he saw that the man at his side felt at least as out of place as he was. Travis turned to him, "I can't wait for it to be over."

"Oh, so you are British."

"And you're American."

"I'm Canadian, actually. I just came to America when I was ten."

"What for?"

The man tilted his head and made a face, "Eh, my parents divorced. I went to live with my dad and he had to move here for work."

"That's... interesting." Travis couldn't think of a response, "I don't believe that I got your name, by the way."

"It's Luke. And you're Travis, right?"

"That's me." There was a lull in conversation, but Travis didn't want it to end. As weird as it was, he felt that he'd found someone worth talking to. So, he spent half a minute pondering over what to say next. He needed some kind of topic that they could both relate to, "My parents divorced, too. I was nine."

"Were you?" Luke sat up in his seat, "Tell me then, Travis. How long do you think Olivia's going to last with this guy?"

"I'm sorry?" Travis was wide-eyed, not hiding his confusion over Luke's question.

"It's just a thing that I do. When I see a newly married couple, I try to figure out how long they'll last before they go the same way as my parents. Or yours."

Travis raised an eyebrow in confusion, "Not all marriages end in divorce, though."

"Maybe not," Luke conceded, "but from what I've seen, people just get sick of each other."

"That's a rather cynical way of looking at things."

"I guess you're right. Beth says I'm a pessimist."

"Can't blame her, now can we?"

Luke smiled. For a time, they were quiet again. Travis took the moment to gaze at his beloved. She was still on the other side of the room, conversing with a random group of relatives. "I could never get bored of Jane, though." He said.

"Oh, you'll see." said Luke, "Before you know it, she'll be gone."

"Care to bet on that?"

Luke let out a short, stuttered laugh, "I'm not going to take your money. Pounds are no good in the States, anyway."

* * *

Dan wanted to follow Victor, to confront him and put a stop to this, but he decided against it. Instead, he went to find Marceline. After all, out of the two of them, she had always been the best at keeping Victor's problem in line.

He pushed open the glass door and stepped into the outside world, only to stop in his tracks. Far overhead, he could make out a faint red streak moving across the sky. To him, it looked like a great spark inching by, high in the air. Below it was another, fainter but still present. "What the hell?" he muttered. Anxious, he collected himself again and made his way to the van.

"Where's Vic?" Marceline asked him.

"He's, uh, inside. Listen, I have something important that we need to talk about."

Sammy jumped up and pointed at the sky, exclaiming, "Mommy, look at the lights!"

"They're very pretty, dear." said Marceline. She pet her daughter on the head before turning her attention back to Dan, "What's so important? Is it about Victor?"

"Uh, well yes." Dan stammered, "But at the moment, I'm actually kind of more worried about the lights."

Marceline looked up at the red streaks as they marked their way across the sky. They almost looked as if they were burning. Gradually, both of them began to come to the same conclusion. They exchanged glances, gazing upon each other's growing terror. Marceline began to shake, "What direction are they going in?"

Dan's heart was pounding. He didn't want to admit it, but he forced himself to say, "East, I think."

"Towards Boston?"

"I'd say so."

"Get inside!" Victor's voice rang throughout the lot, making everybody jump. They turned the main building. He was standing just outside the glass doors, pointing at the sky with one hand and gesturing to them with the other.

Hearing the panic in his voice, Dan and Marceline didn't hesitate. Victor held the door as they took the children and rushed back into the food court. As Dan passed him, he asked, "What are those things up there?"

Victor stared him down with a dour expression, "I know missiles when I see them." There was a grim feeling to his voice, "But I don't know how big they are or how far they're going. So, find some cover. Now."

Chapter 3

Travis Norwich rolled in his bed. He'd expected Jane to still be asleep, but when he opened his eyes, his gaze was met by her lovely blue stare. "Morning, dear." he mumbled.

They were in their motel bed, still wrapped in the darkness of the power outage. When the wedding celebrations had died down, everybody needed a ride back to their respective homes. Since Tom had the only working vehicle, he spent half the night driving people this way and that. That was a job that Travis was more than grateful to not be a part of. He greatly preferred having a good night's sleep and waking up the next morning, refreshed and ready. Though it would have been easier if their key card worked. With the blackout, the front desk lent them a physical key to get into their room. The relic, that thing was.

While they waited for the hand of drowsiness to loosen its grip, Travis and Jane laid together in bed, wrapped in each other's arms. Without a working television or cell phone, they had nothing but each other – not that they at all minded. When they finally did get dressed, they then trotted over to room one-oh-nine to wake Tom. They were relieved to know that today was to be more casual, with the three going to visit her parents. Travis wasn't looking forward to it, but he wanted to greet the situation with at least a veneer of optimism.

When their copy of his key card didn't work, Jane knocked at the door. She and Travis hoped for an answer, but were met with expected silence.

"He might still be asleep." Travis mumbled, still rather tired.

"That's what I'm thinking, too." Jane agreed, "And with no electricity, he couldn't have even set an alarm."

"So, are we stuck out here 'til he wakes on his own?"

"Or until our knocking wakes him up." Jane knocked again, this time harder. "Wake up, Uncle." she said, "It's time to go to Mom and Dad's."

At last, a muffled response, "Do you have any idea how late I was up last night?" A moment later, they heard the latch and the door creaked open. Tom stood before them, rubbing his eye, shrunken by his exhaustion, "Because I don't. I kind of lost track after the seventh trip. Or was it the eighth?"

"I can drive, if you want." Jane offered, "And I'm sure that there'll be a place for you to sleep there, if they haven't repurposed my old room yet."

"Oh, they have." Her uncle mumbled, "It's an exercise room now. For your mother. And sometimes your dad, when he's not being lazy."

"Well that makes sense. She does look a bit thinner."

"She's been trying, for sure. Not your father, though. He's still got that good ol' beer belly." Tom and Jane laughed. Travis was silent.

Once the humor subsided, Jane cleared her throat, "So, are you coming along?"

Tom nodded, "Let me brush my teeth and get dressed. You two go wait by the car. And don't expect me to be awake at all today."

It was at least half an hour before they got to their destination. It was a two-story hilltop estate, fairly large compared to other homes around the small town. The place was painted a dull mustard color, save for the white porch and matching windowsills. A driveway cut into the side of the shallow hill, ending at a small garage that seemed too full of rubbish to even hold Tom's little sedan.

The trio clambered out of the car and worked their way up a series of steps that led from the driveway, up the hill and to the porch. Jane's mother, Anna, answered the door and invited them in, "Sorry about the lack of light." She said,

"The power still hasn't come back on yet."

"Same with the motel." Jane told her.

"That's because it's not a power-outage." Called a voice from the other room. At once, Mister Russell Greene strode in to meet with his family. He hugged his half-asleep brother and gave his daughter a kiss on the cheek. Then he turned to Travis and extended his hand. "Nice of you to show up."

"Leave him alone, Dad." Jane groaned.

"Sure." Russell nodded, giving her boyfriend a disparaging look. With a gesture of his hand, he beckoned the group to the living room. When everyone had a seat of their own, he continued, "Anyway, as I was saying, this is no power-outage. Anyone who's calling it that is a moron."

His wife waved a hand at his remark, "Oh, there he goes again. He hasn't shut up about this all morning. Don't listen to him. You'll just encourage his conspiracy theories."

"It's true, Anna." he said, "I can understand all the lights going out, but what kind of power-outage stops cameras from working? Or phones? And I'll bet money that Tommy's got the only working car in the county. How did that end up happening, anyway?"

Tom blinked a few times before answering, "You seem to be the expert on this stuff. You tell me."

"I mean, why is any of this happening?" Travis asked in a shy voice, "If this isn't a normal outage, then what is it?"

Russell Greene leaned forward in his seat, directly across from the Englishman, "Think about it, boy. What else can take out everything with a circuit in an entire town?"

"Besides one car?"

Russell ignored Travis' remark and continued, "It has to be an EMP. Electromagnetic pulse. It's a side effect of lighting off a nuke a few miles in the air." If all eyes weren't on him before, they were now. Even the ones glazing over in Tom's half-sleeping head were wide and trained on his brother.

"So, what does that mean for us?" Jane asked.

"It means that the 'power outage' isn't limited to here.

It's probably all over the northeast. Maybe even further."

"But if an EMP is supposed to take out all electronics," asked Tom, "then how come my car is still working?"

Russell was quiet for a small moment, thinking his words over before answering with a question of his own, "Where was your car when all the lights went out?"

"Just in some garage."

"What was the garage made of, though? Some metal structures can block an EMP."

"It was just a normal garage." said Tom. Then he seemed to have had a small epiphany, "Except for... Well it had a kind of metal mesh all around the insides of it."

Russell adjusted in his seat, "That garage must have acted as a faraday cage."

"A what?"

"A faraday cage. Come on, Tom! Didn't you pay attention during science class?"

His brother waved a hand of dismissal, "That was decades ago, Rus. I forget most of that bull."

With that, the room went quiet. Everybody, save for Jane's father, wanted to discuss something else – something a bit less farfetched and bone-chilling. But no one could keep their thoughts away from what Russell had said. Had they really been attacked? By nuclear bombs?

Travis wrestled with his words, "But... if someone... actually did nuke us-"

"Then we are at war." Russell stated plainly.

"But with who?" Jane asked. Her eyes were wild, darting from face to face, looking for a knowing expression. Travis saw that she was uncomfortable, so he put a reassuring arm around her.

"See, that's the part that I haven't figured out, yet." her father answered, adjusting in his seat.

"All this talk about nukes and war – it's all speculation." His wife stated in an obvious attempt to calm people's nerves, "We don't know anything for sure, yet. But I'm sure that, as soon as everything starts working again, it'll all be

45

explained. And I'm telling you all that it won't be nearly as bad as Russell here is making it out to be."

* * *

"Do you think it's safe to come out?" Marceline peered around the side of the counter, careful not to slip on the shattered glass.

"I don't know." Victor answered. All through the night, they had taken cover inside a fast food booth, their backs against the counter and their heads between their knees. They hid from the havoc they knew was coming. At once, the darkness of the building had been pierced by a series of flashing lights. The walls in front of them lit up, illuminated again and again by the distant blasts. The little ones, Sammy and Zack, mistook the glaring brightness for lightning, but the adults knew better. Afterwards came the terrible, crashing booms of the shockwaves. The building itself seemed to vibrate in place, shaking the windows apart and knocking around anything that wasn't bolted to the floor. The kids cried and whimpered, retreating to their mother. She, in turn, held them in a tight embrace and assured them that everything would be alright. Even Dan, who was never one to let fear take hold of him, seemed terrified beyond measure. He and Victor knew the sort of bombs at work. Only nuclear weaponry could display such power from so far away.

While the others were calming the children and waiting for death, Victor was thinking. Analyzing. Calculating. He measured the time between the flashes and the shockwaves. The great delay meant to him that the blasts were coming from far off. Maybe the bombs fell on Worcester. Perhaps they came all the way from Boston or Providence. He kept it to himself for the time being, but he had no doubt in his mind that at least one of those cities had just been wiped from the face of the Earth. A question came to mind. Would bombs going off so far away have caused such effects so nearby, or were some of them dropped closer? Victor decided

46

that it was worthless to guess or worry, and that only time would answer his questions. Anything that was hit was already obliterated. The people who had once lived there were already dead. His knowledge of the subject didn't matter to them.

A more pressing concern was the radiation. Were they far enough away to not be affected? Once again, only time would tell. However, they weren't dead yet and that was sufficient enough for him. In the meantime, he was trying not to recall the horror stories he grew up with. The ones of men and women reduced to husks by radiation's poisonous sting.

"We can't stay here, that's for sure." With care, Victor rose from his spot behind the counter. As he got to his feet and peered over his cover, he stretched his limbs and felt all of the soreness of the previous night. It was only then that he noticed how uncomfortable a position he had been in for all those hours – hunched over, sitting in a fashion akin to that of a cowering child, grasping his legs and curled into a ball, sitting with his back against stone-hard counter.

Signaling with his hand for the others to stay behind, he made his way out from around the counter and further into the trashed food court. Shards of glittering glass littered the floor, reflecting the few rays of light that were beginning to penetrate the building. Behind him, he could hear Sammy asking where her father was going. "I'm just taking a look around, sweetie." He told her.

"Can I join?"

"Sorry, sweetie." Ignoring her protests, Victor crept alone towards the shattered glass door that led him into a shimmering, warped corridor that, in turn, led to the outside. The crystalline shards cracked under his feet, making any attempt at stealth impossible. As he surveyed the area around him, he realized the sheer pointlessness of his efforts. Nothing was alive outside. Off in the parking lot were several vehicles, Marceline's old van among them. In the far distance, he met the sight of towering smoke, each column rising miles into the air. There were two or three that he could spot with ease, but there were hints of several others just beyond the horizon. Victor couldn't tell for sure though, since the distant sky was growing hazy. The light of the sun was somewhat hampered by the dark, scorching clouds erupting from these sites of death. There was no immediate danger, though. Victor felt the weight of a world lift itself from his small frame. "We're clear." He said, motioning for the others to join him.

Marceline gasped at the dark, burning horizon before her, "Oh my God."

"What's that, Mommy?" little Zack asked, tugging at her sleeve.

When she didn't respond, Victor answered for her, "It's,,, just smoke."

"That's a lot of smoke."

"Yes, it is." Dan agreed, "What now, Vic?"

Victor thought for a moment, taking in the situation before answering. He took a long breath and peered off at the horizon, "We need to keep going west. North west, south west – it doesn't matter."

"Into New York, you mean?" asked Marceline.

Her husband nodded, "Upstate New York is mostly farmland, right? Small populations, open countryside, not a likely target for…" With a hand, he motioned to the ash clouds, "For that. Maybe we should head for there. But as of right now, we just need to get out of here as soon as possible. Those bombs might have dropped far enough away for us to be safe from fatal amounts of radiation, but we shouldn't wait around and soak it up until it gets painful." Something had changed in him. The others around him could see it as clear as day. He was calmer, more focused, like when they were on the road the night before.

"Come on." he said, taking the lead as they walked to the van. Their vehicle hadn't been spared from the shockwave. Glass littered the seats and would have to be cleared away, and it was safe to assume that there were a dozen other new problems that only time would uncover.

"I wasn't able to fill the tank." Marceline warned as they got close, "The pumps don't have electricity. I don't think I can get gas without it."

Victor glanced at the cars and trucks in the parking lot, then back at the van, "Those cars look old enough to still use gas, like ours. We'll siphon from them."

Marceline's face twisted into a look of disapproval, "But that's stealing."

"They won't miss it." He stated, not even making so much as a glance toward her. He was preoccupied with scanning the area for anything useful and thinking over their route of travel.

Marceline, not to be silenced, moved within inches of her husband and whispered harshly, "What will this tell the kids? That stealing is okay?"

This time, Victor looked at his wife and said in a low, hushed tone, "It'll keep them alive."

She fell silent after all. Although she didn't want to admit it, this situation was dire. Something tragic and dangerous was befalling the North East. Her first priority was to her children. And as much as she so desperately wanted to keep them set on the right path, none of that would matter if they were dead. She had to listen to Victor.

Marceline took the children inside to use the restroom one last time. Victor and Dan found a few items in the surrounding cars and managed to siphon a few gallons into their tank. When the crew reunited, they cleared the broken glass out of the van and set off to New York. They were hungry, scared, sore and tired – but most of all, they were alive.

* * *

Ever since Anna denounced her husband's insane theories, everyone tried to occupy their minds with anything else. The family often let their thoughts and words lead into random tangents, where new, more distracting conversations could arise. All of them joined in, except for Tom who fell asleep in the next room over. They spoke of Anna's new sedan and all of its crazy features, of life in the United Kingdom, of Jane and Travis' flight to Pennsylvania, and of the wedding.

During this long stream of collective consciousness, Travis learned the name of Olivia Greene's newfound husband. He was a fellow named Jordan Drummond. Jordan was a native to this small town and had attended the same high school as the sisters. Although he was a grade ahead of Olivia and three ahead of Jane, he became a close friend of the Greene family. He had even won the favor of their father, who spoke very proudly of his eldest daughter's choice in partnership.

Eventually, there was a lull in discussion. Everybody drifted from thought to thought, attempting to find another topic; as people often do in these awkward family reunions. Travis was about to venture out of his shell and ask about some of the people he had seen the night before, but a peculiar sound stole their attention away.

It started off small and distant, as if the smallest gust of wind could blow the noise away. As it grew closer, it took the form of a meek voice. Travis peered around and saw that the others were taking notice as well. All heads turned to the nearest window. "You hear that?" Jane asked.

The sound grew louder and clearer, and soon Travis was able to make out the words, "Anybody? Is anybody here?" The lands beyond the house were full of fields, wooden fences and the occasional tree. Without many tall structures to block his vision, Travis could to see for miles. He could make out an oddly-colored cloud formation roosting along the horizon. Against this backdrop was a figure, too far away to be seen with detail, but slowly advancing towards the house.

Mister Greene made his way to the door, the others following close behind. As they stepped outside, they saw that the man was riding up to the house on a bicycle. "You, there!" he cried, "You have to listen to me!"

"What's going on, here?" asked Mister Greene, equal parts annoyed and curious.

The man on the bicycle came to a stop, "Don't go near Pittsburgh." This rider looked to be younger than Travis, and somehow even scrawnier. He was panting, drenched through his shirt with sweat. He must have been riding all morning, "Don't go into the city." He repeated, "Something's happened. Something bad."

Missus Greene stepped forward, gripping her husband's arm, "Tell us what happened." She looked at him with an almost sorrowful expression.

The man shook his head. He was still panting, but forced words out between dry breaths, "There's smoke. Smoke coming from the city. A huge cloud of it."

"It's Pittsburgh, kid." Mister Greene grumbled, "There's always smoke coming from there. What's your point?"

"You don't understand, sir. I saw something come out of the sky and hit the city." There was a noticeable change in the group. The rider went on, "Some kind of objects were making these long streaks across the sky."

"Missiles." The words echoed in every ear. Everyone looked at Mister Greene, their faces holding a mixture of confusion and fear.

"That's what I thought, too." The rider nodded, "But I have to go. I've been warning people since before dawn. I can't stop now."

The man tried to start on again, but Missus Greene rushed forward and grabbed hold of the handlebars, "No, honey. You look like you need some rest. Come inside for a while."

"What? No." her husband objected.

"But I have to go warn people."

"You need to rehydrate. Look at you. You're about to pass out. Your eyes are glazing over."

Russell tried once again to object, "I did not agree to this. We can't just randomly bring some stranger into our house; especially with all that's been going on."

"The kid looks like he has heat exhaustion." said his wife.

"Anna-"

"I don't want to hear your excuses, Russell. Or yours." She looked back at the young man on the bicycle, "It's my house and I'm not letting this poor boy kill himself on this bike."

Once they returned inside with the rider and got settled in, Mister Greene went to work on some kind of project, moving briskly about the house and collecting various items. Among them were binoculars, old rags and cloths, an assortment of knives, a shovel from the outside shed and even an old Geiger counter that he'd fished from an old box in the attic. Over and over, he called it "preparing", but his wife's words followed his closely, naming it "lunacy". As far as Travis was concerned, the man was delusional. Of course, no one would attack the United States. People had been threatening it for years, but nobody could have been stupid enough to go through with it.

"I was on the roof of my apartment building when it happened." Their guest began his spiel, taking several breaks to down some water, "Maybe seven or eight miles from the inner city. I was on the roof because, well, that's always kind of been a meeting spot for the people that live there. We go there whenever there's something big to talk about or a celebration or something. Don't ask me why. I don't know how that whole tradition started. Anyway, I couldn't believe what I was seeing, but I knew what those things in the sky were as soon as I looked at them. Then... then it happened. One second, it was all there. And then the next, boom." He raised his arms, spilling some of his drink onto the couch, "Oh, sorry. I'll get that. But anyway, I looked away when it hit. I just turned around out of instinct, or maybe as a reflex or something. Then there was this light – this huge light that just made everything so white. I had turned away, I had my eyes closed, and I was covering them with my hands. But when that light hit, it was so bright that I swear I could see the bones in my own hands." He shuddered. Then after a moment, he took a long drink and continued, "After it all ended and Pittsburgh was… you know… I just got on my bike and I rode. I wasn't thinking anything through, but I felt like I had to get as far away from that scene as I could. Every time I saw somebody on the road, I told them to stay away from Pittsburgh. Eventually, it kind of just turned into a mission – warning people about what just happened. There's no internet or tv to spread the word, so I decided to do it myself."

"That's so…" Jane appeared to be at a loss for words, "You mean Pittsburgh is gone?"

"At least a good part of it." The rider answered. Travis couldn't believe what he was hearing. The three of them were quiet as the rider let the news sink in. He took advantage of the lull in conversation to take another long sip of water. It had only been a few minutes, but he was beginning to look more alive.

From around the corner, they could hear Jane's parents arguing. Missus Greene was scolding her husband for making "such a fuss" about nothing.

"It's just a power outage." she cried, "Maybe something bigger is going on, but you don't need to be acting like this. The world isn't coming to an end, Russell. You don't have to barricade the whole damn house!"

"Haven't I been saying that this would happen? For years, I've been saying it. It was only a matter of time."

"What the hell are you talking about? Nothing is going on. It's a power outage."

"It's an EMP! Look around, Anna! An outage doesn't stop a car from working. Or cell phones."

"And why the hell do you think that someone would hit us with one of those? It's Pennsylvania. We're not the Pentagon."

"There's a lot of people in this state, and a lot of military. They hit us like this to make us defenseless. I'm telling you, this is an invasion plan. They take away our technology – our high-tech weapons, our transportation – and they just march in and take control. And with us knocked back to before the Industrial Revolution, we can't do a damn thing to stop it."

"I can't believe you. You're delusional."

Back in the living room, Travis leaned into Jane and whispered in her ear, "Hey, could I talk to you in private for a moment?"

"Sure, hon." The two excused themselves and walked into the adjacent hallway, leaving the rider alone on the couch, "What is it?"

Travis spoke with the softness of a concerned partner, choosing his words with the upmost care, "It's just that, with all that's going on, maybe it isn't a good idea to stay here."

"You want to leave?"

"Yes. Well sort of. I don't know if the motel would be far enough. Or even the next town, for that matter."

Jane put her hands on her hips, but her voice held itself in steady neutrality, "Is this about Pittsburgh or my dad?"

"This isn't about your dad."

"Good, because he's really starting to warm up to you. I can tell. And he's not crazy. He's just-"

"Jane, will you please focus?" Travis' voice gave away his growing impatience, "Listen. Everything electrical except for one car has stopped working, and that car is only still running because it was in a metal cage thing. Also, a good portion of Pittsburgh has apparently turned into a hole in the ground."

"So, you think we should... what? Leave the country? Go back to England?"

"In my perfect reality, that's what we'd do. Yes."

Travis tried to read her face, but Jane kept whatever feelings she had secret. She thought it over for a moment, then put a hand on his shoulder, "Travis, don't get me wrong. I know how dangerous things are right now. I just know that panicking about it won't solve anything."

54

"I'm not panicking." he snapped.

"Yes, you are. You're saying that we should just pack up and leave the whole continent. But that just can't happen."

"And why the hell not?"

"Think, Travis. If nothing electrical is working, do you really think that a plane will be any different?"

Travis' eyes dropped to feet, "Maybe."

Jane's thumb rubbed up and down his shoulder. She looked into his eyes, forcing him to stare back at hers. They stood there for a time, silent, eyes locked, "I'm sorry, but it looks like we're stuck here for now. But we'll try to stay safe until we can get back home. Okay?"

Travis nodded, "Okay. But I'd like it if we could at least get away from Mister Conspiracy Theory for a while."

"Maybe later today or tomorrow, we could go see the Lewis family down the road." She said, "They might have an idea of what's going on."

"Sounds like a plan." said Travis, forcing an awkward smile.

* * *

"I'm hungry." Zack groaned in the back seat, "When are we gonna have lunch?" The young boy was growing more stir-crazy by the moment, confined in his car seat. On top of that, he was becoming more famished by the minute. None of them had eaten since before the mad dash out of Boston. Even Victor, who was too absorbed by his own thoughts to feel the pain of hunger, remembered that his last meal was nearly a full day ago.

"We'll stop soon." Victor told him, "We just have to find a good spot, first."

"Just hang in there, sweetie." Marceline added. She then turned to her husband and leaned in close, "I know it's a long shot, but do you know if there's a food place open nearby?"

"Probably not."

"Then what food did we pack with us?"

"I don't remember. Danny and I just grabbed random cans out of the cabinets. I don't think we looked at many of their labels. I know that we have some beans, canned bread, corn… stuff like that. We'll find something they'll eat."

"We'd better." said Marceline, "Or it'll be you who raids a farm for a cow. They love burgers, especially Sammy." By the serious tone of her voice, Victor wondered if she was entirely joking.

"Since when does Zack eat burgers? He's five years old. When I was that age, I wouldn't go near anything like that."

"There's a lot that you'd know about our kids if you paid more attention."

"I guess so." He agreed, trying to ignore the burning of Marceline's words.

After another mile or two, it became clear that they wouldn't find another rest stop for some time. The van took an exit at random and found its way into open country. Although they were passing through mountains, the world around them seemed to open up, with fewer trees and more open farmland. They were deep into the rural countryside of upstate New York, the land with the promise of relief from the radiation. At a glance, this place looked to be untouched by the devastation that had overcome the east. In this serene landscape before them, they felt at peace. It was as if they could, for but a moment, forget the sheer enormity of their troubles. This was where they finally decided to break for a meal.

Dan got the portable stove working. The kids, Sammy and Zack, hounded down three cans of noodles between them, while the adults each took a can of baked beans or clam chowder. They ate straight from their cans with spoons. Forgetting to bring plates or bowls wouldn't stop them from savoring every delectable mouthful of their meal. They talked little and, when they did, they spoke only of where they were going next. After all, they had made it to their destination unhindered. The broken glass and melted steel was far to the east, but they still needed some place to actually go. They needed some kind of civilization, not just open fields of wheat and corn. Eventually, the adults decided to move southwest. Perhaps a small-town motel or turning back to the highway to find another rest stop could do them some good.

When they had eaten their fill and had gotten some time to stretch their legs, the group ruefully clamored back into the van and went on their way. However, as the group rode along, Marceline came to notice a column of smoke rising beside the road. It was comparatively much smaller than the clouds of nuclear debris that she had seen the skies over Massachusetts, but it was still enough to leave her unsettled. "Vic," she muttered, getting her husband's attention, "do you see that?"

"Yeah, I do." He answered.

Behind them, they could hear Dan stir from his nap, "Smoke. It looks too small to be from… you know."

"But it's still pretty suspicious." said Victor.

"And scary." Marceline added.

"I think I can see what it's coming from." Victor told them. They were closer now, only a few hundred feet away, "It's a barn. A barn is on fire!"

"Oh my God." His wife gasped, "We have to do something. We have to help."

They pulled over and saw that two buildings had been set aflame. One, a two-story house with several windows and a long porch, was already collapsing into itself. The other was the barn. It was being consumed in an ever-growing column of fire and smoke, but hadn't yet begun to fall in like the other structure.

"Save the animals!" the kids cried from the back, "Daddy, save them!"

"It's too late for the house." Victor exclaimed as he leapt from the vehicle, "Whoever lived there either got out or is already dead, but we still might be able to save the animals. Come on, Dan! Marci, you stay behind with the kids. Make sure they stay by the van."

Without any further exchange, Marceline gathered the

kids by her van and Dan followed his friend into the barn. Smoke stung their eyes and nostrils, and the scorching air made breathing difficult. Soot and small debris peppered their skin, singeing anything they touched. However, this further added to their determination. They couldn't let some defenseless animal suffocate and burn to death because of some foolish accident on their owners' part.

Meanwhile, Marceline was left with time to look around and ponder. Victor had said that the owners of the house were either safe or already dead. By the look of the razed building in front of her, she couldn't argue that. No one could have survived being trapped in there. They would have needed to get outside, but… but then why didn't she see the family around the property? She was alone with her children, with no one else in sight.

Back in the barn, the young men lifted their shirts over their noses to mask their airways from the smoke. Wooden walls and bales of hay had ignited all around the place. A line of large animal pens stood before them, one side veering off around a corner on their left and another on their right. The corner to the right led to a plywood staircase that, in turn, led to a second floor. The upper level acted like a sort of elevated walkway around the barn, with a sturdy railing in place to keep people from falling through. Through the roar of the flame and the crackle of wood and hay, there was one thing they hadn't heard – animals. There were no cries or caws of any sort. The men looked at each other, dumbfounded by the realization. Maybe the animals had suffocated or burned?

Dan took it upon himself to make the first move. Keeping his massive frame low to the ground, he raced around a corner and rammed into the door of the nearest animal pen. He had expected to find a horse or perhaps a large pig, either ready to bolt or passed out from the fumes. However, as the door gave into his great force, he found himself falling face-first into a more horrific sight. The animal that lay beneath him was dead. It had died, not from smoke inhalation or the raging firestorm around it, but from a deep

58

cut to the throat. The poor beast was sprawled in a pool of its own drying blood. What's more, it looked as if chunks of flesh had been taken from its sides and neck. Dan leapt off of the creature like a mouse scurrying from a cat. His first instinct was to gasp, but a lung's worth of smoke and heat turned it into a wrenching cough.

"It's dead!" he cried, hacking through the poisoned air.

Victor ran over to help his friend to his feet, but jumped when he caught sight of the corpse. He looked around. Through the smoke, he could see above the door of another nearby pen. Something was hanging on the other side, dangling from the ceiling by a thick rope. The end of the rope, in turn, was tied to the sturdy railing of the walkway above. He kicked the door in, yelped, and fell back onto a patch of smoldering hay. There in the stall was the farm's owner. He was hung upside down by a leg, with his limp, bloody hands dragging along the ground. His throat was slit deep, almost to the bone. Several gashes and rips along his body had removed enormous chunks flesh.

They hadn't gotten far from the barn when Victor stooped over. Before Dan could ask why, he emptied his lunch on his own feet. He then doubled over, whimpering as he coughed up the poison from the smoke. Tears were beginning to form around his reddened eyes. Dan wrapped a great arm around his friend, almost carrying him back to the van.

"What happened?" Marceline shrieked. Sammy and little Zack were about to run up to them, but thought against it when they noticed the coat of blood covering Dan's clothes and face.

"Get the kids in the van." Dan answered through labored breath, "We have a lot to talk about, but not in front of them."

* * *

After the incident in the barn, nothing in this world

would get the Roberts family to stop again for some time. With Marceline driving, they moved onward, taking a series of unpopulated mountain roads until night fell over the state of New York. By this point, they were seeing fewer farms, replacing the sight with more open wilderness and the occasional small town.

Neither of the men could keep from reliving what happened. The image of the man hanging from the rope was seared into Victor's mind. He couldn't so much as close his eyes without seeing that vision painted across the blackness of his eyelids. Even without sharing a word of it, they had all come to the same general conclusion. That farmer was murdered. The animals, too. Someone or something killed them all, and then set the place afire to destroy any evidence.

Marceline parked the van in a plot of gravel at the side of the road. They were concealed by trees on three sides, only visible from the road itself. Once they got settled in, they were able to stretch their legs and get their space for the first time in hours. The kids were the most grateful to be out of that confounded metal cage. That night's dinner consisted of a few cans of chicken noodle soup, heated on the portable stove. The adults didn't think it wise to light a proper campfire, despite the children's wishes. After all, whatever burned down the barn could have followed them. Indeed, they already felt as if something was leering at them from afar, unseen in the shadows of night.

Once the little ones had expelled their energy and were ready to rest, Marceline took them back into the van. Without enough room in there for everybody to sleep with comfort, Victor and Dan were forced outside with only a couple of blankets for comfort. They didn't mind, though. The two of them laid awake for what seemed like hours, watching the sky and making idle conversation. Out of the correct context, they looked less like adults who needed space to sleep and more like overgrown children at a slumber party – something that didn't escape Victor's observation.

"Hey, Dan." Victor whispered, "Does this kind of

remind you of when we were kids?"

"You mean with us laying out here like this?" Dan asked.

"Well, yeah. It's like those old sleepovers that we used to have. It's weird, and I know that I shouldn't be thinking so randomly at a time like this, but being out here really brings back memories."

"Yeah." Dan agreed, not quite knowing how to respond.

"It kind of makes me feel young again."

"Vic, you're twenty-nine. You're young."

They turned their attention upwards. Dark clouds had covered parts of the sky, but many celestial lights still shone through the patches. "Look at that." said Dan, pointing at the sky, "A shooting star."

Victor found the figure, following it with his eyes, "I see it." He announced, grinning like a school kid, "Make a wish." As he said that, the dot in the sky curved its way across the sky, drawing an arch that led back to where it came from. It then continued on in the sky, apparently content with its new path.

"I wish it was a real shooting star." Dan mumbled. At this point, neither of them were shocked. After all that they had seen in the past twenty-four hours, something as small as this couldn't hope to faze them.

After some time, the realm of sleep and dreams came to Dan and he began to pass in and out of consciousness. Victor, in turn, was left awake and alone. A noise in the darkness – a wild chirping of sorts – would not let him feel the comfort of sleep. All else was silent, save for the piercing shrieks of those accursed insects. They rang worse than sirens in his ears, growing in intensity with every passing minute.

When he could no longer handle it, Victor turned his head and whispered to his drowsy friend, "Are you hearing this, too?"

Dan stirred next to him, "Just a few crickets and some guy who needs to let me sleep."

"Those must be some big crickets, then."

"Go to sleep, Vic."

"Yes, sir. Right away, sir."

* * *

Travis awoke with a start to a loud bang. His body shot into a sitting position, his wide eyes darting around the room. Listening with rigid intent, he could make out the sounds of shouts and quick footsteps coming from the outside.

He was on the second floor of the Greene household, in the guest bedroom. After the news about Pittsburgh, Russell had refused to let his youngest daughter stay another night in the motel. He said it was too filthy and defenseless for her and insisted that the house was better. To be fair, it was safer now that Russell had prepared the place. Jane and Travis still couldn't see why all of this was necessary, but they decided to go along with his antics anyway.

The room around him was unfamiliar, making the sounds outside even more unnerving. How he longed for his small apartment back in London, far from all of this chaos and ominous mystery. However, for the moment he was trapped here. He had to act. With quiet care, Travis got out of bed and followed the noises to his window.

"Come back to bed." Jane mumbled, stirring slightly from her reposed state.

"I'm just checking out whatever's going on. I'll be right back." He pushed the window open, bent on getting a better sense of what was happening. At first, all he heard was a distant chirping from what sounded like crickets – though not from any kind of cricket that he had ever heard of – or maybe some other insect that lived around there. Then he heard the voice again. The howls came from Jane's father. Travis couldn't see past the black world of night, but from the direction of the voice, he figured that Mister Greene was several yards beyond the house, towards the edge of the lawn and moving further away.

"Where do you think you're going?" Mister Greene's voice bellowed, "That's right, run away! Run and tell your bastard friends not to screw with us!" Two more earsplitting bangs sounded off in the night, each one shooting a small flash of light into the darkness. These dots along the black canvas of night told Travis exactly where to find his deranged host. He was just under the window, perhaps ten feet beyond the porch. Each flash betrayed a glimpse of his rugged, wild frame and the weapon perched in his arms.

Travis heard a screen door slam underneath him, followed by the hurried patter of footsteps and Anna's shrill voice, "Russell, what the hell are you doing? Get back inside!"

"I shot the bastard, Anna! One of those bastards was sneaking around and I got him right in the chest!"

"Get the hell inside! Damn it, Russell, you'll kill somebody! Get rid of that rifle and get in here! If the phones worked, I'd call the police on you myself!"

Travis pulled the window closed. He didn't want to hear any more of Mister Greene's lunacy. The man must have seen some kind of animal and had taken it for some intruder.

He retreated back under the covers of the bed and fell into Jane's warm embrace, "What's up with your father?" he asked.

"He's always been sort of a conspiracy theorist. No one but him is proud of it. I remember when I was growing up, he would always tell me and Olivia all of these stories about how terrorists and socialists were planning to attack. They were coming for us in our own homes, apparently. Sometimes, even our own government was out to get us."

Travis furrowed his brow, though no one could perceive it in the dark, "So he was always like this?"

"Well he's never been this bad, but I guess hearing about Pittsburgh really set him off. He really is just trying to protect us, though. Really. He's crazy, but he's also caring. He wants to protect all of us. Even you."

"From what?" asked Travis, "I mean, do we even know for certain that Pittsburgh really is gone? None of us have actually seen it for ourselves."

"You heard what that guy from the street said." Jane answered, "I don't see why he'd be lying."

"Maybe to get a rise out of us. Make us scared, have a good laugh at our expense."

"Are you sure about that? He practically killed himself on that bike, trying to warn people. My mom even looked him over. How does someone fake heat exhaustion?"

"I guess." Travis turned onto his back, staring up at the ceiling, "Everything just seems too strange to be true. I mean, how could this really be happening? All the tech stops working, Pittsburgh is gone, and now there's an invasion or something." They laid there on the bed in silence. Then Travis sat up, turning on his side to face his partner, "And the worst part?" he said, "I have a feeling that things are going to get a lot weirder before all this is over."

Chapter 4

The cloudy, damp morning of April ninth marked the beginning of the group's second full day on the road. A day and a night ago, they had witnessed nuclear fire disintegrate all that they had known. By now, the reality of what happened was beginning to sink in. What's more, they had no idea of where they were going. Their van was low on gas and their energy had been sapped from sleep deprivation. Dan and Victor, who had spent the night outside, awoke now with the morning dew sprinkled over them like a cold blanket. Their skin was red and irritated where it met the air, but neither of them cared to complain. They were famished, and as such were too occupied with getting their portable grill working.

Gasoline wasn't the only thing they were running low on. The family had already gone through half of their canned food. With reluctance, the three eldest agreed that they would only share two cans of the least appetizing food that they had. That way, they could save the best and most filling goods for the young ones. So it was that the children dined to their fill on noodles, while the grownups had kidney beans. They ate in silence, for the most part, since none of them had much energy for needless conversation. Nor was there anything worth talking about. Nothing positive, at least. Anything that went through any of their minds had to do solely with this pessimistic situation at hand.

Soon, the children had finished their food and were begging for a bathroom. Marceline took them into the woods beside the road, leaving Victor and Dan alone together. They didn't talk at first – neither of them wanted to – but the silence eventually became too unbearable. Besides, there was something that had to be said.

"Do you ever feel like you're being watched?" Dan asked, being the first to break the insufferable silence.

Victor pulled his head up from his share of the beans, raising a curious eyebrow at his friend, "Am I gonna like where this conversation's going?"

"No, but I think it needs to be said." Dan straightened himself where he sat and took a long breath as he thought through his choice of words, "I keep seeing... these things. These random shapes moving out of the corner of my eye."

"Dan, is this one of your bad jokes?" asked Victor, a stern tone coming over his voice, "Because it's not funny."

"I wish I was joking, Vic. I'll think that I saw something, I'll turn, and it'll be gone. But I just can't shake the feeling that someone's out there. Watching."

The men were quiet as Victor processed what his friend said. At last, he spoke, "How long has this been happening? How long have you been seeing these... things?"

"Since the barn. Maybe a little after. I've seen it all over the mountains." Dan averted his eyes, uneasy with his own answer.

A moment of contemplation passed before Victor made his response, "Let's not tell Marci about this."

"Agreed."

Before long, the group was back on the road. It was still early in the day when the mountains began to recede into the backdrop with rolling, forested hills and gray ponds taking their place. They saw no sign of civilization, save for the pavement they drove on and the occasional road sign. Indeed, they were relieved to be this deep in the wilderness, where they needn't have to worry about whatever was befalling the cities. The group even felt safe enough to stop for a rationed lunch in the middle of the road, instead of finding somewhere along the side to park. Still, while they were satisfied with the distance they had made, none of them forgot why they were there. They still recalled the burning clouds to the east and

66

south. No one dared to disregard what the men saw yesterday, either. Such horror. Something so inhumane could never and should never be forgotten. For now though, they were relieved. Not safe, but relieved.

Their mood quickly changed after lunch, when the van rolled to a long-expected stop by the side of the road. Victor turned the key, switching the vehicle on and off again. He tried the pedal, but to no avail. They'd run out of gas.

Marceline looked over at the fuel gauge when her husband broke the news. "So, what now?"

Victor gripped the steering wheel, thinking hard. He turned to view occupants of the van, the ones that he loved and had to keep safe. Then he looked outward, down the road. As long as they stayed there, they were sitting ducks for whatever came to pass. He knew this. And if Dan was right and someone was watching them, then they needed some protection. Victor had actually begun to feel it too, as if some unknown entity was peering from the trees and rocks and shadows around them. He couldn't explain it, but nor could he shake this intuition. They could not stay here. But what could they do? Slowly, an answer came to him, "Danny and I will go out ahead and see what's out there, down the road."

"We are?" Dan blurted from the back seat.

"But what do you think is out there?" asked Marceline.

"I don't know." answered Victor, "A broken-down car? A house, maybe?"

"We haven't passed a house in over half an hour. There probably isn't anything around here for miles. You wanted to get away from civilization, Vic. Remember?"

Daniel's voice rose again from the back seat, "Wait. Could I possibly get a say in what I'm signed up for?"

Victor turned in his seat to face him, "What? Do you want to stay behind with the kids?"

"After the barn, yes. I'd like that very much."

Victor groaned and turned back to face the dashboard. He could not go out there without some kind of company. After all, who knew what was out there? He needed support, just in case something was to come up.

Just then, a hand came to rest on his shoulder. It was the soft assurance of his wife, "I'll go with you, Vic." she said, "There probably isn't anything out there, but it's worth checking."

"Are you sure?" he asked.

"Of course. Come on."

* * *

The morning rays cut through the blinds of the window, casting an optimistic light into the room. Travis heard a knock at the door. As he brought himself to a sitting position in the bed, the knock sounded again. This time, Tom's voice followed, "Morning, love birds. Jane, your mom wants you two downstairs for breakfast."

The couple came to life and stretched away the stiffness of sleep. The idea of impending food brought them both to their feet. They were hungry, but the weight of an unwelcome morning hour kept them from much expression. With delay, they traversed the second-floor hallway, down the staircase, and into the kitchen where an assortment of pancakes and waffles awaited them.

"How did you do this?" Jane asked, when Missus Greene entered the room, "I thought the power was still out."

"It is." answered her mother, "I got a portable stove running."

"We have a portable stove?"

"It was part of your dad's survival gear."

Travis took a close look, sniffed the air, and felt his stomach grumble. A short laugh came over him, "Praise be to conspiracy theorists." The couple sat at the kitchen counter and grabbed for some food. They hadn't realized until now how hungry that they were. It was as if they had been starved for days. When they realized that they'd forgotten to eat for most of yesterday, it all made more sense.

After breakfast, the family and Travis made their way to the yard. They were growing stir-crazy in the hilltop house. Fresh air was becoming a necessity. When they got past the screen door, Travis saw that Mister Greene was already outside. The man was on the porch, sitting stout in a worn rocking chair. At his side was an old hunting rifle, the stock laying against the ground and the barrel held firmly in his hand. The man looked troubled, as if something had kept him from sleep all night. His feet were bare and eyes were glazed over, staring off into their own plane of reality.

Tom looked at his brother, astonished, "How long have you been out here?"

It took a moment for Mister Greene to register the question. He let out a long sigh and answered, "All night, it seems."

"It seems?"

"There was something out here last night. Over there." He pointed off towards the edge of the property, "I chased it off with my rifle, then just… sat here. Waited for it to come back. Never did, though."

"Yeah," Jane nodded, "Travis and I heard you shoot it a few times to scare that guy off."

"That guy." her father repeated, more to himself than to the others.

"Have you left that chair at all?" asked his wife.

"I don't think so. No."

"That's…" Travis attempted to find a word that would fit the situation, "worrisome."

Tom nodded in concerned agreement, "Yeah, it is. Rus, maybe you should go lay down for a moment. Inside, I mean."

"Maybe." Russell spoke the word, but did not move from his seat. He sat there, his glazed, bloodshot eyes staring off into nothing. It was of no use trying to talk any sense into him.

The group tried to occupy themselves in different ways. Missus Greene, worried for her husband, spent her time trying to get him to come inside. Tom and Jane went for a walk to shake off some extra energy and see if anything interesting was going on around town. The Greene family's mustard-colored estate was far from any other buildings or civilization in general. Aside from the rider that went by yesterday, news was bound to travel slowly without internet. For all they knew, "Jesus could have come back, and we would have no idea." That's what Tom said, at least.

Travis spent his time getting better acquainted with the landscape. The farms and pastures of rural Pennsylvania was nothing like the sprawling city of London back home. Still, as much as he disliked being outside his zone of comfort, he wanted to at least come to terms with the change of scenery. Jane was in love with this place, so why couldn't he be?

He walked around the house to survey the back yard. A few yards of grass and dirt were framed by a thin line of trees. Beyond that, he could see field upon field of crops, dotted every now and again with a small farm house. Everything was so distant. Everyone lived their lives so far from each other.

When he'd at last gotten his fill, he strolled around to the front of the house. As he walked, he realized that he was nearing the area where Mister Greene had chased off that intruder. His mind went back to last night. The yelling. The gunshots. His curiosity got the better of him, and he started to look around for something – some sign or evidence of what had happened.

"Hey, Mister Greene." Travis spoke with a hint of hesitation, "Didn't you say that you shot an intruder or something last night?"

"Yep." he answered, sternness in his voice, "Right over there, where you are. Why?"

"I think we may have found something."

Mister Russell Greene gave the boy an odd look, as if considering his words, "Well, let's see." He stepped from the porch, walking with bare feet and stoic purpose to the sight of interest. Soaked into the stretch of lawn was a pool of some dried liquid. As he observed, Mister Greene noticed that it led away from the property in a long trail, taking the form of tiny black droplets.

"What do you suppose that is?" Travis asked.

"Blood, probably."

"Black blood?"

"Then maybe it's something else. I don't know, kid. I don't got all the answers."

Travis knelt beside the coagulated pool, catching a glimpse of solid forms in the dried blackness. He reached out and pulled one of the objects from its place. Was it a rock? As he held it up to his eye and rubbed some of the dried flakes of ooze away, he could see that it wasn't so. To his eyes, it looked somewhat like a piece of an egg shell, though much darker in color than any bird's and much stronger as well. He pressed on it with his fingertips, but it wouldn't break. With its jagged edges, this thing had the uncanny appearance of a mere fragment – a shard of something larger.

"What do you make of this?" he asked Mister Greene.

"What'cha got there?" The man knelt to consider the boy's hand, then answered his own question, "Well I have no idea." His face was stretched into what looked like concern, but his tone was as complacent as ever.

"Looks like it came from whatever you shot."

"Then I don't know what I shot."

* * *

Jane and her uncle at last found themselves coming up on a neighboring house, almost half a mile up the road from the Greene family's residence. It was the small, worn-wooded home of the Lewis family. These fine folk had been part of this small town's close-knit community for a couple of generations now. Jane and Olivia had actually gone to school with two of the Lewis' children: Robert and Marie. Rob was in Olivia's grade, and kept a close friendship with her all throughout high school. He had come over for dinner a few times in their junior year, and some of the Greene family even wondered if something more was going on between them. Evidently though, this theory turned out to be far from the truth. When he came out in his senior year, he made a point of addressing that bit of gossip. His sister, Marie graduated a year after Jane. Not much can be said about her, other than that she was silent in the classroom and that she left Pennsylvania as soon as she got the chance.

With Tom following a few paces behind, Jane walked up the driveway and approached the front door. She knocked. A few seconds passed with no answer, so she knocked again and called out, "Hello? Mister and Missus Lewis? It's Jane Greene. Olivia's sister. Are you home?"

Tom glanced at the silver sedan in the driveway, "It's not like they could just drive off, right? They have to be here."

Jane tried the door knob, but it was locked, "Hello? Is anyone home?"

Her uncle shielded the sunlight from his eyes and peered into one of the windows. He wanted to see if family was inside and simply ignoring them. After a moment, he lifted his head from the glass. His mood had drastically changed. He turned to his niece with a look of distress, "Jane, get away from the door." His voice was hard, like nothing that Jane had ever heard from him before.

"Why?" she asked, "What do you see?" She took a curious step towards him.

"No, don't go near the window either. Just back away from the house."

* * *

A short time later, Jane and Tom returned to the mustard-yellow house. Travis saw the two working their way back along the road and walked out to meet up with them. He was relieved to see his girlfriend back so soon, but she did not seem to feel the same. Her face was twisted into a look of utter shock and horror. As Travis got close enough to notice, his pace slowed to a stop. "What's wrong?" he asked.

She ran to him, grabbing him in a tight embrace that made him take a step back. Tears soaked their way into his shirt. He was surprised. Scared, even. He had never seen her like this before. She was always the strong one, the resilient one that could handle anything. Her sobs hit him with the force of a freight train. All that he could do was wrap his arms around her and feel powerless. His mind raced through countless scenarios, trying to guess at what could have made Jane appear so… devastated. There was no other word that could describe her expression. She was devastated.

"We need to talk." Tom warned, "Something… happened to one of our neighbors."

"What happened?"

Jane lifted her face from his shoulder, "The Lewis family…" Red eyes and drenched cheeks told him the story. Something had happened and the Lewis family. These people, who he'd personally never met but Jane was so close to, had died.

"Why the hell is my daughter crying?" roared Mister Greene as he and his wife ran over. The rifle was grasped firmly in his hands, carried with the stock against his shoulder. He looked ready for battle. Why? Only he knew.

Tom took his time recounting the story, as if still in disbelief at his own memories, "Jane and I went to the Lewis house to see if they knew anything. They wouldn't answer the door, so we looked through one of the windows. They were… It was bad."

"They were what?" Mister Greene blurted, "Dead?"

At the last word, Jane dug her nails into Travis' arm, forcing him to stifle a groan. Her mother put a hand on her shoulder, "I'm sorry that you had to see that; that both of you had to see it. Come on. Let's go inside. I'll get you two whatever you want."

* * *

Victor and Marceline Roberts traipsed along the abandoned New York road for quite some time, searching for any source of gas. They had the materials to siphon it, but the road seemed completely devoid of vehicles to loot. Every once in a while, they would spot something peculiar off in the distance. Whenever that happened, they would stop at once and scout the site with a pair of binoculars. Often times though, it was only a fallen tree or a sign, and not something helpful. At one point, they actually came across another van – a pine green one of Japanese design. The doors were wide open, revealing that nobody was inside. Still, the couple approached with caution. Blankets decorated with childish designs were tossed around the back seats. A stuffed animal had fallen onto the road, coming to a rest beside the rear left tire. They too seemed to have run out of fuel. At least, that's what the couple had hoped. Victor didn't see blood, so he kept a mild optimism for the missing family. To be sure though, he checked the gas tank for fuel. Nothing. Not a drop.

The sky was dreary. The wisps of fog that had greeted them in the morning had turned into a colorless haze that pulled both light and warmth from the world around. Victor was still burdened by a lingering stinging that refused to leave him. He wondered to himself if there was something in the morning dew that was burning him; if the droplets had absorbed some of the chemicals or radiation from the east. It seemed entirely possible, in his mind at least.

Perhaps another quarter of a mile past the empty van, something else came into view. It was large, with bright shades of color enveloping its form. Victor grabbed the binoculars and peered off down the stretch of pavement. There, hidden behind a bend of branches and leaves, was what appeared to be an old school bus. "Do you see that?" Victor handed the binoculars to his wife and pointed.

"I see a bus." confirmed Marceline, "But how is that supposed to help? Don't buses take a different kind of gas than vans?"

74

Victor was not deterred by her words, for he had another, entirely different plan in mind, "We can't take the gas," he said, "but maybe we can take the bus."

"You mean we can steal the bus."

"Marci-"

"You want to steal that thing? What the hell, Victor?"

"We need something to ride in."

"But we're not criminals. We don't just steal things. Is this what you want our kids to learn? That stealing is okay?"

"I'll tell you what." He began, "We'll go check it out, at least. If it seems like it's abandoned, then we'll take it. If not, then we'll leave it alone."

"And what qualifies as 'seeming abandoned'?" asked Marceline.

"I don't know." Victor answered, "We'll see when we get there." It was clear that he was losing patience. They had been away from the others for too long. By now, any number of things could have happened to them. The sooner he and Marceline got back to them, the better.

At last, they got to their item of interest. They were standing at the back of the vehicle, which seemed to be in decent shape for a machine of its age. Indeed, it looked to be at least a couple of decades old. Why a school bus from the turn of the century was still in service, they could not understand. Nobody was around to answer. No one was around at all. Victor made his way around to the front end. There, he found the first clue that something was amiss. The doors on the side of the bus, the narrow ones that were meant to fold open and shut to let passengers on and off, had been ripped from their hinges. They laid in the grass between the pavement and the trees. Broken glass littered the ground.

"My God." Marceline held a hand to her mouth, disbelief and concern taking shape in her heart, "What could rip the doors off like that?"

Victor shook his head, "No idea. But whatever it was, it was pretty damn strong."

"Is that blood?"

75

Victor followed her finger under the stairs of the bus, where the doors used to reside over. The spot was dark, as if something had stained it. He knelt down for a closer look, touched a finger to the bottom stair, and then drew it back. It was sticky. Coagulated.

Marceline approached the bus and called out, "Is anybody here? You can come out. We're here to help."

"You're not gonna get a response." said Victor, "Whatever happened to these people, they're gone now." Rising to his feet, he took a careful step onto the bus. The dried residue stuck to his shoe, tugging on his feet as he climbed each step.

"What are you doing?"

"I'm gonna see if this thing still works." He sat in the driver's seat and looked to the ignition. There was no key.

"But we haven't seen a working vehicle since Boston."

"That was two days ago." He said, "The blood is relatively fresh. Whatever happened to stop this bus must have taken place a day ago, at the most."

Marceline looked down at the dark pool. Something made this happen – something dangerous – and she could not let her children to be the next targets. She resolved to get them far away from here, no matter what the means, even if it included taking this bus for themselves. "So, we can get it to work?"

"If you can help me find the key." Victor answered. He searched the inside of the vehicle while Marceline took the perimeter. The interior of the bus hadn't fared much better than the doors. The seats were filthy, covered in pen ink and nameless stains. Some of them had been torn open, bleeding bits of pale cushioning onto the floor. More shards of glass littered the floor, along with empty soda cans and wrappers. A few items of discarded clothing, mostly socks and a couple of shirts, were strewn about in the back seats. The whole place reeked of iron and burnt rubber. Marceline eventually found a ring of keys outside, not far from the bent frames of the doors. Victor tried them all, until one fit into the ignition.

When he turned it, the ancient machine stuttered and then roared to life. They had found a working vehicle.

* * *

Travis spent most of the day consoling his girlfriend. She had stopped crying after an hour or two, but a cold, vacant stare had come to replace the tears. To Travis, this was no better. He wanted to see her smile, to laugh, to sleep – anything else besides this grief. He was powerless. After what she had seen, nothing could be of use to ease her mind. She felt the burden of images that he could never imagine, nor would he ever want to. Tom explained to Travis that he had tried to keep her from looking through the window. If only she had listened.

At last, in a low whisper, she spoke. Her words came out in a mumbled, hushed voice, "We need to go."

Travis' eyes widened, at first because she had spoken so abruptly after over an hour of silence, and then because of the nature of her words, "Are you sure?"

Jane nodded, "It's not safe here, like you said."

Travis hadn't a clue how to respond, finally coming up with, "I'll pack the car and come back for you."

"Okay." Jane answered, giving a slight nod. Her face was so blank, her mind so distant. He kissed her on the forehead and got to work.

When everything was packed, Travis made his way out into the hall. He kept to slow, light footsteps, which were not easy to keep with luggage in his arms. Even at his slow pace, it wasn't more than half a minute before he got to the top of the staircase. After glancing around to ensure that he was indeed unseen, he took a slow step onto the top stair. The old board beneath his shoe struggled with the weight, letting out a long, pained sigh. Travis, eager to keep to his stealth, fought the urge to curse under his breath and carefully continued down the flight. It took him several minutes and endless concentration, but at last Travis got down the stairs.

Soundless, he worked his way through the main corridor of the house. Now, the one solitary thing that stood between him and his goal was the section of hallway that passed by the living room. Travis figured that nobody would be in there. He'd heard no sound from there, and concluded from the time of night that everyone would be asleep in their respective bedrooms. Just to be safe, he kept to his most silent pace as he walked out into the open, through the room.

"Where are you going, kid?" Travis froze. He'd been spotted. Mister Greene peered from his recliner in the corner of the living room. His speech was slurred and he smelled of whiskey.

Caught in the middle of his escape, Travis could only stand his ground and try to explain himself. He placed the cases of luggage on the ground, stood straight, and turned to face his interrogator, "Jane and I need to go. Now's as good a time as any."

Looking at him now, Travis could see the shape of the man through the orange hue of a half dozen candles scattered throughout the room. He was sitting upright in the recliner, with his old rifle in his lap and an empty bottle at his feet. "You're not going off in the dark. Not with my daughter." The combination of booze and firepower made Travis fearful, but he knew that he had to continue. For Jane.

"And why not?" he asked, "We're both adults. She's not some young girl sneaking off on a school night."

"It's too dangerous. Something's out there – something evil – and it'll find you. You'll both be dead before dawn."

"Oh, another one of your conspiracy theories? Now we've got monsters in the dark? What's next? Little green men?"

Mister Greene's voice grew stern, "They ain't conspiracies. I'm telling you that I know what I'm talking about. Something's out there."

An air came over Travis. From then, he was dauntless, "And how exactly do you know this? Mister Greene, you've been acting weird ever since the power went out, and even weirder since we heard that laughable story about Pittsburgh. It's just a story, Mister Greene. That guy on the bike made it up to scare us. It's not true. Nothing happened to Pittsburgh, but you obviously think that something big is going down. Did you ever stop and think that maybe it's all in your head?"

"A story? It's not a story, Travis. Pittsburgh is gone. I know it is."

"Then I want answers. Why are you acting like this? Goddamn, if you think that you know something, then just say it already."

The crazed man hesitated. When he spoke, it was in a near whisper, "You wouldn't believe me if I told you, son." He sounded almost afraid. This sudden change caught Travis off guard.

"Try me." Of course, he would never believe a word out of the man's mouth, but he at least wanted to give him a chance to be sane. Travis felt he at least owed him this much.

Mister Greene went quiet. Then, surely enough, he gave in and tried his best to recount his story, "At first, I just thought it was some crazy dream – something that my mind made up. But everything that the guy said…" His voice trailed off as he tried to figure out an explanation.

"Oh yeah? What guy?"

"The guy…" Russell racked his brain, trying to think of a way to describe this mysterious figure, but Travis was losing patience.

"What guy, Mister Greene?"

"The guy with blue eyes." said the man at last, silencing Travis. He went on, "Half a year ago, I was… visited in the night by this guy with these bold blue eyes. Almost looked like they were glowing." His hand went to his face, feeling the skin around his own eye, "He told me to watch out for next April. He said something was going to happen and I had to be prepared. But what he said was too weird – it didn't make sense. He said that the first sign would be a power outage – bigger than any that I've known before. One so big that even our vehicles wouldn't work."

"The EMP." Travis' aggression had faded. He was listening with intent, a growing sense of concern coming over him.

"Exactly. Listen, I thought that the visit was just some dream. I wrote it off as something that my brain made up. I know that I can be nutty – believe me, I do – so I figured it was just me rising to a whole new level of crazy." He shifted in his seat, "But then everything that he said started to come true."

"What else did he say?"

"He said that something's coming after us. Something evil. Whatever it is, it wants what we have and it's coming fast. He said it would start with the power, and then we'd hear about our own weapons attacking our own cities. That's why, when that guy came by and said that Pittsburgh was gone, I knew that it was missiles. Our own American missiles. By that point, I knew for sure that the guy with blue eyes wasn't just my imagination. He was real and he had given me a warning.

"So now two of his warnings came true and I'm stuck here waiting for the third one. And I don't want you and Jane to leave here. You'll both get caught in the middle of it. I can't let that happen to my daughter."

"Just tell me what it is, Mister Greene." Travis insisted, "What did he say? What'll happen next?"

"He said that..." Mister Greene paused to collect his thoughts, "He said that the shit kicked up by all the bombs is going to blot out the sun a bit. Not enough for a complete nuclear winter or anything, but enough to make things a little colder and darker for a while. Then he said that when the sun starts to dim from the dust... they'll come out in full force. They like the dark, and when it comes they'll be everywhere. And if they catch us, we'll end up like the Lewis family down the road."

"So those things... They killed the Lewis'?"

"I'm damn sure of it. The way that Tom and Jane found them – that's a lot like how those things kill their prey. They cut them up for fun and…" He stopped, his words too unholy to finish.

Travis was horrified. Mister Greene's face was honest. It sounded so terrible, but could it be true? Could something that sounds so insane be fact? Besides this, one other question came to his mind that he felt as though he had to ask, "What are those things? Did he say?"

"He didn't say exactly what they were, but he called them minitia."

"Minitia." Travis tried the word on his English tongue.

"I know how crazy this all sounds, Travis. I thought I actually was insane for a while. My wife doesn't know. Didn't tell her. Didn't tell anyone 'til now. But this is why I've been so big on keeping this place fortified and keeping you all safe and close by. When these minitia come, it sounds like they're going to bring hell with them. So please, I can't let my daughter get caught in that. I'm asking you, please don't take Jane and leave. Not during the night. If you really do have to go, then try the daytime. Just not after dark."

"We have to leave, Mister Greene." Travis thought for a moment. Should he consider this man's tale? What he was saying sounded completely insane, even worthy of being admitted to a psych ward. Was there any chance that it could have been true? He needed to make his choice, "But I guess we could wait until morning."

* * *

It was almost nighttime before the Roberts family stopped again. Throughout the afternoon, they made their way south through the winding forest roads of New York, rising and falling through the mountains like a ship on the waves. The passengers were travelers with nowhere to go. Only one goal drove them onward – to stay far away from people.

The others had a cold dinner, while Victor drove. When they decided that it was time to stop for the night, he brought

81

the bus to a halt at the side of the empty, tired road. It seemed like as good a place as any. It was quiet, dark, surrounded by trees – just like every other road they had seen that day.

Marceline took the children for a short walk to let them stretch their legs. She didn't want to take Victor's pocket knife with her, but he insisted. The dark made him especially paranoid. After all, who knew what could have been lurking around there?

While they were gone, Victor and Dan stepped off the bus for some fresh air. It had been so long since either of them had stepped outside the bus, and it was a wonderful feeling to be able to move freely.

"So, the van runs out of gas and you find us a bus." Dan commented between stretches, "Gotta say, I didn't see that coming."

"Marci wasn't too happy about it." Victor admitted, leaning his back against the massive yellow machine, "She thought it belonged to someone."

"Understandable." Dan was quiet for a moment. It was clear that he was trying to find a way to bring something up. Something uncomfortable, but a subject that he felt was necessary. Eventually, he seemed to have found his words, "About the other night... Just before the bombs fell, you were-"

Victor wasted no time, cutting him off at once, "It won't happen again." He gave a reassuring smile. One that he hoped was convincing enough for his longtime friend.

"I'd hope not. We need you here in the moment with us, not off in your own hammered little world."

"Don't worry."

"No, I do worry. I worry a lot. Listen, Vic. You're the only one here who's had some kind of head's up about all that's been going on. Whether you like it or not, we're all looking to you for guidance."

Victor shook his head, "I only knew to get out of Boston. That's it."

"I don't believe that. Maybe that's all that you remember Mister Blue-Eyes telling you, but that's not all you know. I can see it every time I look at you."

"What do you mean?" asked Victor.

"You're always focused, calculating, figuring things out. You're always trying to stay a step ahead of whatever's going on. I've never seen you like this before."

Victor's voice took on a defensive tone, "I'm just trying to keep us alive."

"And it's working!" Dan blurted, almost shouting. Victor tried shushing him, but he kept going, "Bombs fell on our homes and you got us out of the way. Something's going around destroying cities, killing people and burning homes, and somehow they haven't gotten us yet. Whatever it is that you're doing, it's working." The conversation paused. Victor was about to make his response when Dan cut him off, "Just please don't drink anymore. We need you to keep doing what you're doing."

"Well I don't exactly have anything to drink anyway, but…" Victor looked at the dark, nighttime silhouette of his friend, focusing on where he suspected his icy blue gaze to be. He thought about his family, "Yeah, sure. I'll stay away from the stuff. Even if we come across some, I'll look the other way."

"Thank you."

After a long, uncomfortable silence, Dan got back onto the bus and got to work setting up places for everyone to sleep. Who knew what time it was, anyway? None of them had a working phone with which to check the time. For all they knew, it could have been close to midnight. In that case, the children especially needed some rest. Victor, however, remained outside for a time. He looked up at the blank, starless sky and tried to make out the shapes of the ill-colored clouds. It was far too dark to see anything. He thought of what Dan had said. Of course, Victor wanted something to drink. More than anything else in the world, he wanted to be back at the bar with a friend or two and an open tab. But that wish could never come true. Not as long as Boston was gone, along with most of his friends back there. Not as long as they were on the road, going in circles in the middle of nowhere. He wondered if they really needed him as much as Dan had claimed. Surely, they could survive without him from here on out. He wasn't important. It wasn't like anything was out there, trying to hurt them. Was there? Dan was acting like the people who ruined the barn were following them. Could he have been right? There was also the way that Victor and Marceline had found the bus. Whoever or whatever attacked the previous owners could have easily been the same thing that was responsible for the barn. This thought chilled Victor to the bone. Suddenly, he found the world outside the bus too unwelcoming. With haste, he got to his feet and went back inside, where he at least felt protected by the creaky, metal frame.

Not long after the men set up the blankets and pillows, Marceline came back with the kids. They seemed distressed for some reason. When Victor asked what was wrong, Zack said that there were bugs outside. He hadn't seen them, but he claimed to have heard them everywhere. Sammy heard them too. She commented on how loud they were, saying that they were like people whispering in the dark. It seemed that she was the only one who failed to understand the horror of what she just said. Victor's listened close to the world outside. Indeed, he could plainly hear the chirping of insects, namely crickets, in the trees and underbrush around them. There was something else out there, too. As he listened more closely, he could make out another noise – some kind of clicking. It was the same clicking that had kept him awake the night before. This time, however, it sounded much more forceful, if that made any sense. What's more, the sound seemed to be getting louder, little by little. A cracking sound echoed out – perhaps a small branch snapping in the woods by the bus.

"Do you hear that?" asked Dan. Before Victor could answer, he was stopped by what felt like an earthquake. The bus rocked sharply, as if shoved by some unseen force. Everyone inside shouted in surprise, holding onto their seats to keep from falling. Then there was silence. Complete silence. No crickets, no clicking. Nothing but the frantic breathing of the passengers.

"What the hell?" cursed Victor.

The bus shook again. Violently, it thrashed from side to side. The family feared that it would turn over. They clung to the seats and to each other for dear life. Cold screams and guttural shrieks broke through the pitch blackness. Metal whined, glass shattered around them and they soon heard a terrible scraping along the walls. Victor grabbed the little body of one of his kids, though he couldn't see which it was. That was when it happened: the vehicle buckled harshly, paused briefly in the air, and then came crashing down onto its side. It did not stop there. Soon the invisible bodies pressed on the bus again, even harder than before. Glass crackled and metal skidded as the vehicle scraped along the ground, moving towards the center of the road. The great machine then lifted at one end again and rolled until it rested upside down.

Once again, everything fell to silence. Victor found himself resting against the frame of a broken window. The cold air bit at his wounds. Shards of glass had cut him badly all over, but it didn't matter. Was his child okay? "Daddy?" cried the small body in his arms. It was Sammy. Victor was about to answer her, to ask if she was alright, to tell her that everything was going to work out, when he felt something grab at him from behind. Sharp, crooked talons groped at his back and seized his arms, pulling them sharply apart. He yelled as the claws pinned him from behind against the window. Sammy crawled to safety while her father fought the creature's hold. The hideous clicking behind him changed at once to a fast-paced, even-pitched rhythm. Terror filled every ounce of his being.

Through the dark, Victor saw a figure inside the bus come scrambling forward. A leg launched forth, striking the beast that held him back. A low-pitched grunt revealed the shape to be Daniel, whose attack only managed to increase the resolve of whatever was holding onto Victor. It latched on tighter, digging its talons into his right shoulder and making him yell out in pain. The beast only let go when Dan kicked shattered glass at its horrid red eyes. Victor fell forward and crawled on top of unseen shards, desperate to get away. They cut into him, slipping into his skin with every move he made, but he didn't care. He had to escape. In seconds, he was at the other side of the bus, but by now the terrible clicking and screeches could be heard all around. He knew that going outside meant instant death, and staying in the metal cage wouldn't keep these monsters away for long. There were too many, and they were far too strong to resist. Whatever befell the original owners of this bus, whatever had killed the people and the animals in the barn, was now coming for them in force. They were surrounded and outmatched. Helplessness seized him.

What happened next was a blur. The horrible talons that seized him were pulled away. Bright bolts of light pierced the darkness with thunderous ferocity. Harsh shrieks and wails sounded from all around. There was the frantic patter of running, and every few seconds another bolt shot through night's veil. A torrent of smaller blasts and shots buzzed through the air, making small, momentary openings in the blackness. Then the chaos fell at once into silence. Complete, motionless silence, as if the entire world had simply stopped. Victor looked around, still unable to see anything. He slowly became aware of his own panting, as well as the whimpers of two small voices.

Suddenly, he felt something grab at his chest, catching him by the shoulder and pulling him clear out of the window and to his feet. The hand was firm but nothing like the jagged claws that had just come after them. It was more... human. He opened his mouth to ask who had grabbed onto him. Was it Marceline? No, she was by no means strong enough to lift him so easily. It was a single hand that brought him to his feet. Danny? No, Victor could still hear his voice whispering to the children inside the bus. He was scared, but all fear dissipated when he saw something appear through the darkness in front of him. Victor realized that he had come face to face with a pair of glowing blue eyes.

Chapter 5

Victor's eyes shot open, his view filled with the metal ceiling over him. All around, he heard voices – hurried whispers and mumbled exchanges. What were they saying? Most of it was indecipherable, but he could make out a few words and small phrases… "She might need an IV.".… "When are we gonna stop again?"… "Mommy! MOMMY!"… He made an effort to sit up, noticing through his movements that there was a soft, binding pressure around his arms. His hands moved to feel his limbs and chest, at once recognizing the texture of bandages. He'd been wounded, but someone had helped him. Who, though? Someone in this room, perhaps. His green eyes narrowed, studying his surroundings with extreme scrutiny. People dressed in ragged clothes and crimson bandages, much like his own, laid on metal beds – the kind that one could find in a doctor's office or a hospital. Gurneys. Yes, that's what they were called. He was in one, too.

These people. Long, awkward slashes marked many of their faces and bodies. They were talking amongst themselves – at least the ones who could speak. Some of them possessed more than minor injuries. Eyes and ears and hands and legs were missing from many of their bodies. Dark gauze wrapped around wounds that refused to stop seeping. The stink of their blood was thick in the air. Victor couldn't help but feel bad for them. They probably wouldn't survive. Everything was so gruesome. The whole scene appeared to be out of a scene from some graphic war movie. Bloody and chaotic and dark. If it weren't for the droplets of natural light poking through the walls, he wouldn't have been able to see a thing.

Even still, the faintest of lights were welcome after last night.

Last night. What had happened after he'd met those piercing blue eyes? He couldn't recall the faintest detail, but whatever took place had ended with him lying here in this room, in these bandages, surrounded by these people. Was this even a room? The rumble of a distant engine was slowly emerging over the general commotion around him.

He looked over to his right, his gaze meeting that of a familiar, welcoming face. Daniel Emerson sat hunched over, with a warm smile blanketing his face, "You're awake." His left arm was covered in patches of rust-colored gauze. Those icy blue eyes of his sat above two dark circles of exhaustion. He must have been there through the night, not sleeping for even a moment.

"Hey, Danny Boy." Victor answered. His words stung in his dry mouth, "Do you have any water?"

Dan looked at him for a second before answering, as though he were lost in contemplation, "Oh, yeah, I do." He grabbed a plastic bottle from his side handing it to his friend in the gurney, "Just don't drink all of it. It's all I'll have until the afternoon."

"So, it's morning?" Victor asked him, after guzzling down a good half of the miraculous, life-giving elixir.

"Easy, dude." Dan warned him as he took the bottle back, "And yeah, it's morning. A little after nine thirty. April tenth, if you really need to know."

Victor nodded, "And this may sound like a stupid question, but where exactly are we?"

"We're safe, Vic."

"No, but like, what is this place?"

"Oh, that. It's just the back of some semi-truck these people repurposed. They have a few of them."

Victor took notice of Dan's implications. They had been picked up by a group of people – probably other survivors, like them. "They got a semi to work?"

"Apparently." Dan paused, as if he was forcing himself to decide on how much to give away, "There's a lot for you to get caught up on. Blue-Eyes had you knocked out for a while."

"Blue-Eyes?" Victor's face changed from a somber relief to that of total shock, "He's really here?"

"Unless there's someone else in the world with glowing blue eyes, yeah."

"What about Marci? And the kids? Are they okay?"

Before an answer could come, the clanking of determined footsteps caught Victor's attention. A brunette woman in a nurse outfit was fast approaching them. Her face, round and fair-toned, held a mixture of weariness and cautious relief in a forced, courteous smile. "Glad to see that your friend has finally woken up." She raised a hand to feel Victor's forehead.

"What is this?" he asked, "Where are we?"

"It's a military convoy. You're in the infirmary truck. Do you remember what happened to you?"

"My friend and I – we were attacked by these... things."

"You're both very lucky. Most people don't survive an encounter with the minitia."

Minitia? What were minitia? Victor wanted to know, but a far greater question was searing inside him, burning away at his core with every beat of his heart, "I was travelling with my wife and two kids." he said, "A small boy and a girl."

"They're fine." Dan interjected, "They're in another truck, waiting for us."

Victor was quiet for a moment while the nurse checked his blood pressure. When he had sufficiently calmed, the unknown word crept its way back into his mind, "Minitia?"

"That's what they're called." she answered, rather nonchalantly. It occurred to him that she had probably given this speech many times over the past few days.

"But what exactly are they?"

"There've been a lot of guesses." the nurse told him, "I've heard everything from them being aliens to, well, huge mutated insect people." Her voice stayed weary and uncaring, with little concern to taint it. Content with Victor's blood pressure, she grabbed a small syringe from a pocket and drew some blood from an exposed section of his arm. She then emptied the red fluid into a vial, shook it, and added a thin, papery strip to the concoction.

"And what story do you buy into?" asked Victor.

The nurse's face wrinkled as she stared at the strip, "Well they're not mutants. At least, I don't think so. Honestly, I have no idea. Maybe the higher-ups here know. But if they do, they're not telling anyone."

Their conversation temporarily came to a halt as the nurse noticed something in the blood-soaked, papery strip. She gave a light smile, placing the vial onto a small metal table beside them, "Well it looks like you've got some radiation exposure, but you'll probably be fine. Just an increased risk of cancer for, say, the next few years or so. Nothing definite."

Victor nodded, not knowing how to feel about her statement. Still, a lingering question haunted his mind. He could tell that she was preparing to leave them, so he had to bring it up now, "Hey, can I ask something? It might sound crazy, but I have to ask."

"Of course, hon." she returned.

"Is there a guy here in this convoy that, well… Sorry, I don't know how to describe him well."

"If you're looking for someone, then you'll want to talk to Colonel Abrams. He's-"

"No, you don't understand. There's no mistaking this guy. You'd know if you saw him. He, well, he was tall, pale, brown hair, and he had these really blue eyes – almost like they were glowing."

The nurse gave him a strange look, "Were they 'almost' glowing, or were his eyes glowing?"

Victor almost couldn't believe it, "You know who I'm talking about, don't you?"

The nurse stared at him with curious, somewhat unnerved eyes, "What does Athriel want with you?" she asked. Her gaze locked with his for a moment, and then, as if pushing away an intrusive though, she shook her head, "No, never mind. It's not my business. Does he want to see you? Should I send word that you're awake?"

Clueless as to how he should respond, Victor peered at his friend in a silent plea for suggestion. Finding none, he turned back and gave a tentative nod, "Well if he's not too busy, I'd like to talk with him. Yes."

* * *

"Air strikes are impersonal?" The shouting came from Commander Jason Pullano, commanding officer of the First Northeastern Military Convoy. In front of him was a scrawny lieutenant who all but cowered as his voice rang in the steel walls of the semi-trailer, "Should we send them an invitation? Some flowers? Sing them a song? Is that personal enough for you?"

The unfortunate lieutenant was quick to defend the words he was given, "Sir, I think what they mean by it is… is that air strikes could hurt too many Americans that we're trying to save. But if we were to send in more troops to the surrounding areas-"

"Goddamn it. This is like the Obama administration all over again. You can tell those shit-for-brains back at the SZ that we'll lose just as many people by sending in troops. We have drones for the time being, so we're going to use them. I'm not sacrificing my own men to save some stragglers that are doomed, anyway."

"Sir, the SZ says that the 'stragglers' are our first priority."

"*My* first priority is keeping those bugs away from this convoy. If some survivors come across us, we take them in. But I'm not sending us out of our way for any hopeless cases."

"Sir, what should I tell the SZ?"

"Tell them that I'll stop using drones when I run the hell out." The commander had to stop for a moment to regain his composure. Then, once collected, he gestured to the officer's seat at the far end of the trailer, "You're dismissed, lieutenant."

Commander Pullano was by no means new to the prospect of operating in lands controlled by the enemy. He had served two tours in Afghanistan in the 2010's, back when he was young and naïve enough to believe that war was a hunt for glory. Those years lived on in his memory as nothing but a blur of endless caution and fear, being ambushed at random by people that he never saw and thinking that every day was to be his last under this sun. Pullano had always said that those were the years that made him a true man. Even there at the convoy, his body aged and his mind losing its razor edge, these experiences from a generation ago still kept their hold over him. This time, he knew there would be no glory or honor. All that mattered was the convoy, and he would keep it intact no matter what the cost.

The lieutenant hadn't been gone for more than a moment before Pullano heard another voice beside him, "You wanted to see me?"

With a slight jump, Pullano turned and met the mesmerizing, blue gaze. The man before him stood tall and pale; a familiar face with a distinct, almost otherworldly voice and mannerisms. Athriel had helped the commander and his men since the fall of Fort Drum. He was the very man who came out of nowhere and secured them all working weapons and transportation. He had organized the convoy and placed Commander Pullano in charge. If he was honest with himself, which he most certainly was, Pullano would admit that he felt more like a pawn in Athriel's big game than a high-ranking US officer leading refugees to safety. That didn't matter for the moment, however.

"We've got some important matters to discuss, regarding our supplies." Pullano told him, "But first, I've gotta say that you had some nerve making us take that detour last night."

The otherworldly man was quick to dismiss such resentful words, "I had to pick something up. It doesn't concern you, I'm afraid."

The commander's temper flared, "You added time to our journey. You went off with my men. It *is* my business. You're lucky that no one died. One small family is not worth losing trained soldiers over."

"This family is."

"Oh yeah? And why is that? What's so goddamn important?"

"One of them is valuable, commander. You needn't know any more."

Pullano leaned inward, making a clear effort to intimidate this mysterious agent, who stood tall and unaltered before him, "Listen, kid. I don't care about what the hell you are or who the hell you represent. If you endanger *my* men like that, you'd better be ready to tell me why."

"Next time." Athriel nodded, giving a slight smirk, "Promise."

Although the commander held obvious, growing disdain for this kind of arrogance, he chose to move onto other matters, "Anyway, let's get down to the real problem at hand."

"Which is?"

Pullano took a seat on the steel bench that doubled as his desk, "Well it appears that we have no shortage of people. Two hundred and fifty soldiers and over a thousand civilians. Supplies? Well that's another story. I hate to admit it, but it's going to take more than a few days to reach DC at this rate – especially if you plan to make us stop for every family along the way. Meanwhile, we have a pretty scary amount of refugees who need food and clean water, with more finding us all the time. Medical supplies are running short, too."

"So, we have two options, as I see it." Athriel said without so much as pausing to think.

"My thoughts, exactly." The commander nodded, "Either we haul ass to DC, which would present some major problems, or…" he let out a long groan with his suggestion, "…or we stop outside of the nearest city and scavenge around."

"So, you called me here, first to reprimand me for acting upon my own judgment, then to grace you with some words of wisdom. You see the flaw in your logic, yes?"

"I never said that I was a people person." By now, Pullano had lost his animosity, but was still feeling far from apologetic, "I just need direction from someone who knows a bit more about these creatures than I do. I want to know what we're up against."

Athriel's eyes brightened, "Ah, now you're starting to utilize my strengths." He folded his arms and gave a slight nod as he considered the options, "Well if we 'haul ass' as you put it, we wouldn't be able to send scouts ahead to look for clear routes. We'd be running the risk of reaching an impasse or falling into a trap."

"But if we stop to resupply, we'd be making ourselves an easy target for those goddamn bugs. So, what do I do?"

"Do what you feel is right." answered the blue-eyed man. Though, when he could tell that the commander wasn't satisfied with such an answer, he added, "If I were in charge of this convoy, I would stop at the outskirts of a nearby city. Yes, it would give them time to close in around us and set up their own devious traps, but it would also give us time to think."

"To think?"

"The minitia are not mindless. They've been doing this for far longer than I'd care to explain. They know how to keep their prey blind with fear – how to make them run off without a thought. That's precisely how they hunt. If we sprint on towards DC with reckless abandon, we'll be playing the game by their rules. We'll reach some impasse of their design and find ourselves cornered. But if we stop and take a look around, we can figure out how to outmaneuver them."

For a time, Commander Pullano said nothing. His eyes remained distant as he thought through every twist that he could imagine life throwing at them, should they stop along the route. Then, with a slow nod, he opened his mouth. A second of hesitation later, words came forth, "I'll have the scouts figure out where to stop."

"Smart man." Athriel grinned, "Don't get me wrong, though. Many of your people are likely to die. This option is merely the lesser of two evil paths that we are faced with."

"Sir, Mister Athriel, sir." came a rather loud voice, too loud for the echoing confines of a crowded, metal trailer. It was one of the lower-ranking officers.

Athriel told him. Athriel whirled around, piercing the young soldier with his blue stare, "Speak more quietly."

"Sir, I'm sorry. But there's news from one of our medical trucks. A man named Victor Roberts wants to speak with you. He claims that he knows you, sir."

* * *

With the first rays of dawn peaking over the horizon came the painful realization. He laid in bed, anxious and afraid. His mind raced. The little news that he had heard about the outside world told him of the dangers that would await him and Jane. Yet he was also relieved to finally be leaving this dreaded house. When Jane stirred next to him, he knew it was time.

They ate breakfast in silence. Jane's mother was making a vain attempt to keep herself composed while her father darted his eyes from person to person, seemingly deep in contemplation. A fleeting thought in the back of his mind told Travis that this may be his last time seeing either of them. It was a thought that he wouldn't let himself dwell on, but would nonetheless tinge these final moments with a sort of precious longing. After breakfast, the couple went back to the guest bedroom to grab their bags.

It was at the front steps, when they were saying their goodbyes that the tension in the household finally broke. Missus Greene held her daughter close and sobbed into her shoulder, "Be safe, honey." she said, "I love you."

"I love you too, Mom. And I will. Don't worry." Her

daughter answered, and then adding, "It's these two guys that you have to worry about."

"These two?" Travis asked, befuddled.

As if on cue, Tom chimed in, "What, did you think you two could just take my car and leave me here with these geezers? I'm comin' with you." Travis felt embarrassment. He hadn't thought of that. Of course, Tom would be joining them.

Mister Greene stood leaning against the edge of the doorway. When his brother took his place in the departing group, he at last decided to speak up, "So, where do you guys think you're gonna go?" He seemed restless, and Travis wanted to give him reassurance.

"Don't know. Perhaps north for a bit, towards the Canadian border. Lots of open wilderness out there. There has to be some place safe around there."

"Just stay away from the cities."

Travis nodded, "Will do."

"Why can't we go near cities?" asked Jane, looking from her boyfriend to her father.

"It's a long story, hon." Travis answered, "I'll try to explain in the car, but I'm afraid it'll sound rather loony 'til you see for yourself."

Russell's voice grew stern, "And if all goes well, then none of you will see it for yourselves." To that, Travis could only make himself nod.

What came next, though, surprised him. Mister Greene stepped from the doorway and onto the front steps, reached out his arms and took Travis in a hug. No one knew what to say. Travis, feeling himself put on the spot, decided to reciprocate. With hesitation, he put his arms around the aged man. Then, just as fast as it happened, Russell pulled away with the parting words, "Keep her safe." Then he took hold of his daughter and planted a fatherly kiss her on the cheek.

"What are you and Mom gonna do?" Jane asked her father.

"We'll hunker down and keep this house protected for

as long as we can. When we can, maybe we'll make our way north to you." He and Travis could see that Jane had so many questions. What were they protecting the house from? What the hell was going on, anyway? she trusted that Travis would explain it all in time, but the mystery still burned her.

Having said their farewells, Travis Norwich, Jane Greene and Thomas Greene made their way to the car. The house was behind them. Now they departed into the terrifying unknown.

* * *

About ten minutes had passed since they had spoken with the nurse. Victor was growing anxious. What if this 'Athriel' person didn't know what was going on, either? He must have known something. Anything. Would he explain why he broke into Victor's house? Or why he saved them from the cataclysm that took Boston? What Victor needed more than anything – more than water or gauze or rest or even his own family – was answers.

The semi-truck rolled to a halt. Before he could ask why, one of the nurses stood up and shouted above the commotion in the trailer, "You all have one hour to walk around, stretch your legs, get where you need to go, and get done what you need to get done. After this hour, the convoy will start moving again! If you're not in a vehicle at that time, you will be left behind." A moment later, there was a tremendous scratching sound. Someone at the far end of the trailer was messing with the door. It lifted open to a pale, stinging light and the forms of several armed soldiers. Among them was a tall man dressed in a thin Kevlar body suit – the kind that Victor usually saw on those SWAT team shows. The unmistakable eyes gave him away immediately. He was staring directly at the man in the gurney, the hint of a smile arching across his face. Neither he, nor Dan, could look away as Blue-Eyes climbed into the truck. A sense of awe had come over them both.

"Hello, Victor." he said, "My name is Athriel." It was strange to hear this voice again. For the longest time, Victor thought of it as a figment of his mind – an ominous part of an eerie dream and nothing more. Part of him wished that this was still a dream. However, for a reason that he could not explain, hearing this voice again somehow seemed to calm him.

Victor wanted to respond, but there were so many questions. What should he ask first? What should he say? There were too many words buzzing around his head for any coherent phrase to find its way out.

Athriel apparently sensed this and took the initiative himself, "I see that you've brought a friend." His glowing eyes and disarming smile turned towards a stupefied Daniel. The latter forced his jaw closed and held his hand out to meet Athriel's.

"I-I'm Dan." he stuttered, "Dan Emerson."

"I'm glad to see that you've both made it this far." said Athriel, "But you both have much farther to go."

"Why?" asked Victor, at last remembering the concept of speech, "What's going on?"

"Yes, I suppose that I owe you both some sort of explanation. Especially you, Victor. Honestly though, I did not expect you to last this long. If I had foreseen this conversation, I would have prepared some eloquent speech. But I guess that I'll just have to wing it. Be ready, because this explanation will be long. If I lose you at any time, just speak up." With a nod from the two friends, Athriel began, "Well we have to start somewhere… What do you know so far?"

"All I know is what happened to us." Victor began, trying to put into words all that had happened, "You came by six months ago and told me to get out of Boston on April seventh. Then I saw you on that exact day. Seeing you kind of freaked me out, so I left. I took my family with me. Danny came along, too. But when we drove off, every other car was broken down. But not just that, though. Streetlights and cell phones didn't work, either. It was so… eerie. We had to drive around all of these broken-down cars and have their owners move them and stuff."

"And when you finally got away from Boston?"

"We saw missiles in the sky. They hit somewhere east of us, off in the distance."

Athriel's face hardened as his voice lowered, "I am very sorry that you had to witness that. To see your home city destroyed – it must be painful." Those words struck Victor like a punch in the chest. It was true. Those things had actually hit Boston, after all. His home, his city, the place where he'd grown up and spent his entire life was gone. Vanished in the blink of an eye. In this confirmation, he lost his train of thought. Athriel, though, showed no lasting change in mood. He at once returned to his strangely nonchalant state, "But anyway, moving on. What happened after that? What did you experience next?"

Victor was able to find himself again and quickly continued his story, "We were attacked by these... things. These creatures. The nurse over there called them minitia."

"Is that all?"

"Yeah. Then I woke up here. That's it."

"Okay, so let's summarize then, shall we? You saw all electronics except for your old car stop working, you saw your city get struck by missiles, and you were attacked by bipedal, insectoid creatures that looked nothing like anything from this Earth." said Athriel.

"Don't forget about the guy with the glowing eyes." Dan added.

"That, too." Athriel nodded, pointing a finger at the giant of a man, "And all of this information is swirling around your little head as you try to make sense of it all. Tell me, Victor, what do you make of all this?"

"I didn't get a good look at the minitia, so I didn't know what they were like until now." he admitted, "But yeah, it's all been so confusing. And scary. I thought that maybe those things caused the blackout and the missiles – like they were attacking us or something."

100

"Well you are a smart one." Athriel told him, "There is a lot more to it than that, but you have the basic idea."

"So, you know what's going on?" Dan interrupted.

"Of course, I do. That's why I'm here."

Victor took a moment to analyze Athriel's description of the monsters. Insectoid creatures that didn't look like they belonged on Earth. A question came to him, "These things aren't from Earth, are they?"

"In a way, they're natives to this world – much like how you're a native to this land. If I remember my history of this place correctly, that is. You're of European descent, are you not?"

"Yeah."

Athriel nodded, "Well you were born on this continent, but your ancestors originally came from another land. Your relationship with the Americas is much like their relationship with Earth. Their ancestors came here long ago, but these particular minitia were born here, right underneath your feet."

"Under my feet?"

"I'll explain their subterranean culture some other time, if you make it that far. For now though, just focus on what's going on around you."

"And how do you know exactly what's going on?" asked Dan, "What's your story?"

Athriel smiled him, "Well, if we're going by the same analogy, then I'm here with a work visa."

Dan raised an eyebrow, "So, you're an alien, too?"

"Oh, I've always hated that term. In your culture, calling me an 'alien' puts me in the same group as one of those little gray things that probe drunkards and mutilate cows. Using that word in your society it makes you sound like a couple of half-brained conspiracy theorists."

"Okay…" Dan's brow furrowed as he tried to make sense of this, "So, then what are you?"

"Oh, don't get me wrong. I *am* an alien. I just hate the term, is all. And before you ask, no. I'm nothing like the minitia. Those things are locusts." Athriel groaned, his

101

expression turning sour, "They find a planet with life, bleed it dry, and move on. They only care about swarming and feeding. They'd be a real empire if they had the mind for it."

"And what are you here for?" asked Dan.

"I'm here to keep you all safe while they harvest your planet."

"Uh, what?"

Athriel sighed, "Perhaps you'd like a more in-depth explanation. Sometimes, I forget how primitive this world is. No first contact or anything. Not until now, that is. Anyway, it's all simple once you look at the big picture." He took a seat beside Victor's gurney, facing the two humans, and continued slowly, "Your Earth is turning into a battleground. Your people, you *humans*, are getting caught in the crossfire of a conflict that you have nothing to do with."

"Why are they here, then?" asked Victor, "If we have nothing to do with what's going on, then why are they going after us? Are we just another world for them to bleed?"

"In a way, yes. But it's not you that they want. It's something else. Something crashed into your little world on April seventh – something that the minitia want – and they've been swarming the surface world to obtain it. What do they want with this thing? Well they're quite an aggressive species, as you've seen. They believe that the stars are theirs. If they had the mind to, they could be an empire out there in the stars – and that's exactly what they want to do. And with this thing that landed here – if they obtain it, it'll help them gain a good chunk of the Orion Arm of the galaxy, or maybe more.

"Meanwhile, I represent an opposing group of more advanced races – more advanced than yours, at least – that aim to keep these creatures from getting what they want. And tell me, what is the result of two powers with opposing viewpoints clashing on controversial matters?"

"War." Victor muttered without a thought.

"Exactly. Meanwhile, you humans are getting caught in the middle of it. You see, these minitia don't just want what *fell* to Earth. That's part of it, but an empire has to start somewhere. They want to claim this planet for themselves. It's an important part of their plan. But they can't have any sentient apes running around, disrupting all of their work. So… cue the genocide."

"Genocide?" Victor repeated, his voice raising, "They're committing genocide?"

Athriel shushed him and continued, "Isn't it obvious? They've rendered your technology useless, destroyed your largest population centers, and have been hunting you all down ever since. It's systematic extermination."

The three of them were quiet as Athriel let his words sink into their heads. Finally, Dan spoke up, "It sounds so crazy. If I hadn't just gone through these past few days, I'd say that you belong in a psych ward. But it does make some sense. I just have one question, though."

"Ask away, my friend."

"What exactly are they looking for on Earth? What could be so powerful that the minitia would massacre an entire planet just to get it? It's obviously a kind of super weapon, but what is it?"

"It's no weapon." said Blue-Eyes, "More of a rallying cry. I can't tell you every detail about it. The people that I represent are very secretive about it. But I'll at least tell you its name." He leaned in towards the men. As they moved closer to him, his voice dropped to a whisper, "Linious."

* * *

"When is Daddy coming back?" Sammy asked. She sat with her mother on the back of an open trailer, her feet dangled off of the edge, swinging and kicking at the air. They were entertaining themselves by watching all the commotion around them. People hurriedly walked by, random strangers talked amongst each other, Zack was playing tag with the other children.

"Soon, honey." her mother answered, "He'll be here soon. Just be patient." Sammy found it difficult to heed her mother's words, but nevertheless held her tongue.

In truth, Marceline found it far more difficult than her daughter to stay in the realm of patience. She could hardly focus on anything. Was Victor alright? He was bleeding so heavily when the soldiers took him away. Since then, she and her children had been locked in a dark, crowded semi-trailer full of musty air and filthy people. There were perhaps thirty others trapped with them, all trying to remain calm or find their families or get enough personal space to lay down and sleep. Marceline was relieved that her small children didn't have much trouble with that last part. If they were awake to hear what she heard, there would be no calming them. Much of what people talked about revolved around what they saw. Dark clouds above cities, entire towns set afire, monsters roaming through the dark. One woman in particular told another faceless listener about the day that she found the convoy. That morning, she apparently awoke and found that the man lying next to her had gone missing. She eventually found him – or what remained of him – at the end of a trail of blood. The man that she spoke of was her own husband; a thought that pulled at Marceline's imagination and tortured her with 'what ifs'.

Her concern grew with every passing moment. Since the trucks stopped, nearly fifty minutes had passed. Fifty painfully long minutes. The break was almost over. There were only a handful of minutes left before everyone had to pack themselves back into transports. If Victor was still alive, then his window of opportunity to find her was quickly closing. If he was alright, then he would have met up with her by now. Right? Did this mean that he was too far gone by the time that the soldiers showed up? Was she a widow? If he didn't show up soon, then how would she explain it to their children?

While she was entangled in her thoughts, she lost focus on the world around her. Only the voices of her beloved kids brought her back to reality. They were excited, yelling and running off somewhere. Marceline took off after them, calling out their names, but there was no stopping them. When she caught up, they were gathered around their bruised and bandaged father. Victor laughed as he picked his daughter up in a bear hug. Dan stood tall beside him, rustling Zack's hair and making some bad joke. When he noticed Marceline, he nudged his elbow into Victor's bandaged arm. Victor's glistening eyes met his wife's.

"Oh my God." she gasped, "You're okay." Now, it was her turn to run to him. With tears beginning to well up in her eyes, she threw her arms around her husband.

"Nothing that some gauze and stitches couldn't fix." Victor told her, fighting the urge to cry out in pain.

"Does it hurt?" his wife asked, looking him over.

"Only when I move. Or breathe."

"Could be worse." Dan said, "Could've been one of those other guys back at the med truck. We had it easy compared to them."

"True." Victor agreed.

"I'm just glad that you're both okay." Marceline admitted as she embraced him tightly, planting a long kiss on his forehead.

"I take it, this is your family?" asked an unfamiliar voice. Marceline looked up. She had been so swept up in the moment that she didn't notice the soldier standing directly behind Dan. He was young, probably just out of high school, with buzzed hair and a tall, lanky frame.

"Oh yeah." Dan laughed. It was clear that he had forgotten this important introduction. He turned to face the young, uniformed man, "This is Vic's wife, Marceline. And these are their kids, Zack and Sammy."

Victor put an arm around his wife, "Marci, this is Private John Athens. A friend of ours assigned him to protect us. He'll be keeping us safe."

"A friend of yours?" she asked.

"It's a long story."

* * *

"Looks like we're gonna need to stop for gas soon." said Tom. He'd been driving for at least an hour, perhaps more. No one in the car could tell for sure, since the clock on the dashboard was electric.

"How much do we have left?" asked Jane, watching the road from the back seat.

"'E' stands for 'extra fuel', right?"

"Funny." Travis sighed, "Do you know if there's a gas station nearby?"

"I saw a sign a couple of miles back." said Tom, "Says there's a place coming up off the next exit."

The road so far was quiet, with theirs being the only vehicle around that could still move. Hundreds, perhaps thousands of others dotted the road. Sometimes a car would be by itself or with one or two others. Sometimes they came in colorful clusters that blocked most of the road. Tom found himself maneuvering his car around endless obstacles, and then at once being granted a few solid minutes without a single problem. The cycle repeated on and on.

When they eventually found the gas station, it seemed more desolate than they had imagined. It was small, with a scarce handful of pumps and a generic convenience store standing at the far end of the lot. The windows of the store were all smashed in. The door was off its hinges. Broken pieces of brick and glass littered the parking lot. As they pulled in, they saw the back end of a small sedan sticking out from one of the walls. The driver must have lost control when the EMP hit, Travis thought. When the three got out of the car, he took a closer look. Glass was everywhere, all over the ground and the interior of the car. The driver's door was ajar, with small pools of blood underneath. This redness moved off in dried, thick drops towards the front of store, where the door once stood.

"Some accident." said Tom.

"There may be someone inside." Travis warned, "They've lost some blood."

106

Tom led them into the store. It was dark – too dark for Travis to follow the trail of red. They would have to search at random. Jane looked around the site of the crash, analyzing the rubble and the trashed car for any clue. Her uncle went up and down the handful of aisles in the store, stepping over bottles, snacks and other items that had fallen from the shelves. In the refrigerated section, he nearly slipped on a spilled jug of spoiled milk, catching himself just as he was losing balance. Travis checked behind the counter. When he saw nothing there besides broken glass and an opened, empty cash register, he turned his attention to the back room. Through the faint light in the store, he saw that the sign on the door read 'EMPLOYEES ONLY'. He pushed, but it wouldn't budge.

"Hello? Is anyone in there?" There was no answer.

Using his shoulder, he shoved harder. It gave a little, but not enough to let him in. It opened just wide enough for him to see the far corner of the room behind it, illuminated by the light of a broken window on the opposite wall. Something was blocking the door – something that could have been moved if he'd pushed hard enough. He backed up, preparing to kick the door down, but stopped. Travis noticed that his shoes were sticking to something on the floor – some kind of residue. Every time he took a step, he heard a coagulated squishing noise. He wondered what it could be. His curiosity, however, turned into disgust as he noticed the scent of iron in the air.

"More blood." he said, backing away from the site. Far less than comfortable with his discovery, he turned and started towards Jane, "I think we found the driver, but-"

"But blood?" asked Jane, gesturing towards the jammed door.

Travis nodded, "Yeah."

"Well," Tom began, "I hate to say it, but there's nothing we can do for them now." He paused for a moment, pondering the real meaning of his own words. Discontent with the answer, he opted to change the subject, "I'll go fill

107

the car outside."

"Sure." said Jane, "We'll get some snacks for the road."

When Tom was gone, the two got to work. Each of them grabbed a handful of paper shopping bags from the checkout area and began passing through the aisles. They decided to focus on grabbing canned goods. After all, they could be on the road for a while. It wouldn't do them any service to have rotten food. Before too long, they had filled a couple of bags to the brim with soups, beans, ravioli, corn and whatever else they could find in a can.

They were scavengers, stealing from someone who was likely already dead. This thought came to Travis with uneasiness, but may well have never occurred to Jane. He decided that he would tell her everything – he would explain every little piece of what was going on – as soon as they had made it to a safe place. For the moment though, he wanted to keep her in the dark. The less she knew, he figured, the safer she would feel.

Tom's voice bellowed from outside, "Hey, guys. I could use a little help with something. Could you two come out?"

Travis and Jane exchanged brief glances. Travis expected that Tom maybe needed help figuring out how to siphon gas. However, when he walked through the doorway and directly into the line of a pistol's fire, he knew that something else was going on.

A small group stood before them. The one with the gun, a tall, skinny man in shredded clothes, stood at the front with his weapon raised at Tom. A woman stood beside him, with a young girl close behind. They were a family. A terrified, armed, morally defective family. "Hands in the air. Both of you."

Travis' hands shot up.

"Now, whatever you've got on you, you're gonna give over."

They were scared. Unsure of what to do, Travis looked to Tom for guidance. The aged man didn't return his stare, but the stranger's pistol did.

"That means the bags. Drop them. Slowly."

Travis felt petrified. His pounding heart made his body shake with each beat. With effort, he bent his torso and forced his arms downward, slowly placing the shopping bags onto the concrete. Without turning his head, he could hear Jane doing the same.

"Look, you're scared." Tom noted, "I get that. We'll do what you want. Just please don't point that gun at them. They're kids."

"You don't get to tell me what to do."

"You're right. You're the one with the gun. Just please take it easy. We're no threat to you."

"Shut up. Shut the hell up." The assailant's quivering voice betrayed his fear. Travis saw that the pistol shaking somewhat in his hand. He wondered what this man was so afraid of, recalling what Mister Greene had told him the night before. Those things. The minitia. This family here must have seen them.

With the dreaded hand of death still trained on the trio, the marauder's wife scurried over, snatched the bags and withdrew back to her husband and child.

"Okay," Tom began, "now you have the food. Leave me and my kids alone."

"Sure." The man gave a jittery nod. His mouth hung open, his breathing audible in the stressful silence. His wild eyes were distrustful, darting from person to person. He took a step back to leave, but then seemed to change his mind, "Empty your pockets."

"Josh…" his wife whispered.

"No, shut up. I want to make sure that these guys aren't carrying anything else we need." He pointed his weapon at Tom, "You first."

"Okay." Tom nodded as he slowly turned his pockets inside out, placing his wallet and long-dead phone at his feet. He dropped his keys last, letting them hit the pavement with an untimely jingle.

Next, the gun moved to Travis, "Now you, kid. Nice

and slow." Travis followed Tom's example, emptying his pockets and placing his belongings on the ground. When the pistol went to Jane, the wielder didn't even have to speak. She turned her pockets as far out as they could go, showing that she had nothing at all.

"Grab their stuff." said the gunman. When his partner stood motionless, he hissed, "Do it."

"No, Josh." she finally said in a low, hushed voice, "It's not right."

"Damn it." He groaned, "Do I gotta do everything myself?"

The assailant lunged towards the small pile at Travis' feet, grabbing it and tossing it back to his family in one motion. The Brit's wallet and phone skidded along the pavement, the latter making a cracking sound. He didn't care, though. He only wanted this pistol out of his face.

It granted his silent wish, but only to face Tom instead. The gunman went for his belongings, but jolted back as a hard boot met his face. Tom lunged for the assailant, who yelled in pain and held his broken nose with his free hand. He grabbed the gunman's pistol and they grappled together for a time. Travis stood there, watching like a scared child. He wanted with all his soul to jump in and help, but his body wouldn't move. It wouldn't matter, however, for the scuffle ended in seconds with a loud boom. The sound rang out, leaving the onlookers in a state of shocked awe. The gunman kicked his attacker's bleeding body away and scrambled to his feet. Tom slumped to the ground, holding his abdomen in silent agony. Jane let out a yell, her hand moving to cover her mouth. All eyes were on the assailant.

"Damn." He hissed, more to himself than anyone else, "Goddamn it!" Wide-eyed and panting, he held his bleeding nose and looked around, "We have to go. There's no way they didn't hear that."

His wife stood behind, holding their daughter close. Travis heard her muttering to the child, telling her not to look. Then she looked back up at her husband, "Get the keys." She was shaking, her voice quivering, "Josh..."

The man stared around for another moment, as if deciding what to do. Then, as if resolving himself, he locked his gaze with the two standing captives, staring one in the eyes, and then the other. Travis, terrified as he was, could see all the conflict in this man's stare as he stepped over and grabbed the keys off the pavement. Within half a minute, the whole family had gathered in Tom's car and driven off, along with everything that Travis and Jane had scavenged. The young couple was left stranded in the lot, with one of their own collapsed on the cement below, painting the pavement with pooling red.

* * *

As the day grew darker, the people of the convoy grew quiet. Victor took notice from his place on the floor of the transport. The vibrant voices and endless commotion that flooded everyone's ears began to fade. After a time, all one could hear was a series of soft whispers beneath the grumble of all the engines. These trucks and transports seemed to be the only ones who held onto their nature, roaring away in unison as they moved forward along the road. Soon however, those too were silenced.

"We're stopping here for the night." the driver told them. This particular vehicle was topless, allowing for everyone inside to gaze at the world as they passed by. For the longest time, Victor had watched as they drove by endless fields and forests and houses. When dusk drooped over the land, the area began to take on a more urban aesthetic. Plenty of red brick and gray concrete began to replace the seas of green and brown. He wondered if they were heading towards a city. Was it even safe to go near one? By the time they made their stop, a sheet of darkness had blanketed the landscape. After that, there wasn't much left to watch for. That is, aside from hurried shapes and whispers of orders.

It became clear to Victor that the soldiers were setting

111

up a sort of perimeter. Military vehicles, such as tanks and personnel carriers, formed a rectangular barrier around the civilian trucks and semis. They were a border of metal, a claim to this small stretch of highway and a dare to anyone who with the mind to take it from them.

Even nestled inside this vast ring of metal and guns and soldiers, Victor couldn't bring himself to let his guard down. How could he feel safe knowing that those things – those minitia – were out there? The only one to bring him any comfort was the private who acted as his guard. Still though, Private Athens was young – fresh out of high school. He still had a face of innocence. There was no possibility that he had seen any combat before these last few days.

Through the night, Victor had learned a bit about this guard of his. He found out that this Athens boy was a New York native, raised in a small town near Buffalo. His parents owned a little café near the center of town called 'The Greek House'. He worked there through high school, along with two of his three sisters. Apparently the third one, named Jennifer, had never gotten along with their mother and utterly refused employment. He seemed to enjoy talking about her the least.

"What about you?" Athens had asked. They sat with Dan, Marceline, and over a dozen others in a huddled group, all gathered around the light of a single lantern. There were many of these 'camp fires' scattered inside the makeshift highway encampment.

"Well what about me?" returned Victor, "You already know the basics. We're from Boston and Blue-Eyes has his weird, blue eyes on us for some reason."

"Yeah," said Athens, "but what about stuff that wasn't in the briefing?"

"Like what?"

"Well do you have anyone waiting for you in DC? Any family or friends?"

Victor shook his head, "Anybody that we knew was back in Boston, for the most part." said Victor.

112

"Oh," Private Athens paused, unsure of whether or not he'd touched upon a rough subject.

"What about you?" asked Victor, "Is your family waiting for you there?"

"Yes, sir. I mean, I hope they are. I don't know. It's not like I can just call them and ask if they're alright. Right?"

Victor could see the worry in the young man's eyes. It was clear that he had forced a thought that Athens had been avoiding. With all that was going on, both of them knew that it would be unlikely that his family was unharmed. Victor wanted to comfort him, "I'm sure they're alright. Who knows? Maybe when we get to DC, they'll already be there, looking for you."

While Victor was conversing with their new bodyguard, Marceline watched the children with Dan. In all honesty, their actions shouldn't have taken her so aback. It was just that she hadn't seen them play since everything began. For days now, she and her husband had kept them crammed in one tight space or another, whether it be her van or a bus or the back of a semi-truck. Now, out there in the open, they could be kids again. They could run and play games and laugh and yell. It was a warming sight to their mother, who wanted nothing more than to keep them safe and happy.

They were playing tag with a handful of other kids. Her face took to a smile as she watched the little silhouettes dance around each other in the night. They were playing tag. Marceline could tell through the giggles and laughter that Sammy was 'it'. She was running after another girl, lost in the thrill of the chase. Her prey ducked in and out of small clusters of people and under and around trucks, always with Sam following close behind. There was no getting away from her. At one point, the little girl took a chance at leaping into a circle of people gathered around a lantern, perhaps hoping to lose her pursuer in the crowd. It was of no use, for as soon as she made it to the center of the group, Sammy came right in after her. Her prey jerked and whirled to get away from her little hands, but it was too late.

113

"Got'cha!" Sammy cried, "You're it!"

"Hey, shut up!"

Shocked, Marceline watched as one of the adults grab her daughter and the other young girl, shoving them both. They shrieked and collapsed on the ground.

"I said shut up! Shut your goddamn mouths!"

Marceline ran to her daughter's side. That man yelled at her kid. He swore at her. He laid a hand on her. Why? Why would he do this?

"Are you okay, baby?" she asked, helping Sammy to her feet.

"He pushed me."

"Take your friend and go back to Daddy. Okay? I'll deal with this."

With a nod, Sammy took her friend's hand and led her away. When they had gone, she turned her attention towards the man, fueled with the rage of a mother bear, "What the hell is your problem?"

The silhouette of a tall, portly man loomed over and barked back, "Your kid needs to learn to shut her mouth. Those things out there could hear her."

"And they could hear you screaming at her."

"I did what I had to do. They had to keep it down."

"So, you tell them to keep it down. You don't scream at them and you absolutely don't push them."

"You're lucky that all I did was push them. If my wife was here, she'd have slapped them senseless."

"Well I hope your wife made some good dinner!"

Marceline couldn't keep the words in her throat. She didn't mean to say something so horrid, but she was furious. He had hurt her daughter – swore at her and pushed her. She had lost control of herself. The crowd around them had gone silent, taking in what she'd said. Those horrible words. Those evil, cruel words. How could she have said that? She was about to apologize when the looming silhouette in front of her threw a fist. Instinct took over. With a forearm, she guided his fist away and took a long step backwards.

"Say that again." growled the man, "Say it!"

"Okay, that's enough." Private Athens' voice roared in as a handful of figures came between her and the great, portly man, "This woman is under the protection of the United States army. Same with her kids."

"Did you hear what she said?"

"Yes, sir, I did. And if you don't want to be taken into custody, you'll do absolutely nothing about it. Have I made myself clear?"

There was a small pause, then a heavy groan, "Sure, whatever. Just get her out of my face. If I see her again-"

"Don't finish that sentence." Growled her husband's deep, threatening voice. The portly man glared at the smallest of the silhouettes, but did nothing. Soon, the figures turned to leave, the shortest one taking her hand.

"Come on." called Private Athens, beckoning them to follow.

When some distance had come between them and the scene of the confrontation, Marceline turned to the shape of what she figured was the soldier, "I didn't mean to say that. I was just so angry. I didn't know what I was saying."

"Tensions are running high." he answered, "Everybody here's a refugee. Most have lost somebody close to them. All of us are afraid. We just gotta try to get along until we get to DC."

* * *

"We have to stop." Jane whimpered, "He's losing too much blood." She'd been helping to hold Tom up as they stumbled down the road. By now, his weight had started to take a toll on her. It didn't help that her uncle was a good deal larger than the young woman. Her muscles burned like fire. Parts of her clothes stuck to her body, drenched in her sweat and the red of her uncle's wound.

"I'm fine. I'm alright." her uncle moaned, struggling between pained breaths.

115

"No, I'm with her." Travis agreed, holding Tom up by the other side, "You'll bleed out if we keep this up. Let's stop here." They shambled over beside a nearby car and set him down, leaning him up against the front tire. When he was settled, they seated themselves around him.

Travis took a long breath. There was the unmistakable stench of smoke in the air. Something was burning a ways off from the road, too far to be seen but close enough to be smelled. Dusk was steadily dimming the world around them. Soon the trio would be left in total darkness. It was a fact that seemed to only worry Travis, for the Brit was still the only one among them who knew what was out there with them.

"Why did you do it?" Jane asked.

Her uncle was out of breath, seeming to struggle for air. The lower half of his shirt was soaked in a redness that seeped down his pants and stained his hands. Yet through such a grim look, a stubborn, albeit weary smile still stuck to his face, "Couldn't let him take the car, could I? We'd have to walk." He then gave a small, strained laugh.

"Oh ha-ha." said Travis, letting the sarcasm drip from his voice.

"I wonder what my parents are doing." said Jane, "And Olivia."

"Your dad probably has that house under lockdown, and your mum is probably trying to talk him out of his craziness." answered Travis.

Tom sighed, "You talk like you grew up with them."

Travis nodded, then added to his speculation, "And they're probably wondering what you're doing, too."

"I just hope they're okay." Jane muttered, drawing her legs to her chest and wrapping them in her arms, "What the hell is going on, anyway? Does anybody even know?"

Now seemed to be as good a time as any, Travis thought. She deserved to know at least something about what was happening. How would she handle it, though? Her father's story seemed insane at best. How much should he tell her, and how should he say it?

"Well your dad did say something before we left," he began, thinking through his words before speaking, "but he didn't sound like he was... all there. I really don't know what to think."

She raised her head from her lap, coming to rest her eyes on Travis' uncertain face, "What did he say?"

"That we're being... hunted. All of this – the outage, the bombs, the Lewis family – it's all connected. Something's hunting us like animals. At least that's what he said." Travis waited in agony for a response. He wanted them to disagree, to scoff at such an idea. More than anything, he wanted one of them to stand up and rant about how idiotic a theory it really was, and how all that was going on was nothing special at all.

"That would explain why the hijacker was so scared." Jane finally conceded.

"I'll say." Tom murmured.

"One question, though." said Jane, "He said *something's* hunting us? Not *someone*?"

"He's your dad, sweetie. I wouldn't know his brand of crazy."

"Maybe he's not crazy, though." Tom commented. At that, he had their attention, "I mean someone or something is causing all of this. And whatever it is, it's pretty intent on killing us. For all we know, something could be out there, hunting us down like he said."

As he finished with his words, two shots rang out from a distance. All three of them jumped. A shapeless struggle in the night was not too far off.

"Speaking of." Travis muttered.

"I'm guessing you heard that, too." said Jane.

Another distant boom sprung forth from the darkness, followed by a shriek that made Travis' hairs stand on end. One would imagine that such a yell could only come from something trapped and doomed to suffer. A sinking feeling brewed in his stomach.

"Well consider me scared." Jane mumbled, inching

closer into his arms.

"Wish I had a gun about now." said Travis.

"Aren't you British?" Tom responded. Travis' disapproving eyes darted in his direction.

"Now's not the time for jokes, Uncle." Jane warned. The group listened intently, searching the silent night for any sign of danger. The tension among them was almost too much to bear.

"Maybe we should hide." said Jane.

"Where could we go?" asked Tom.

"In one of the cars, maybe?"

"Unless you've got a key on you, we'd set off the alarm."

"It was just a suggestion.'"

"Shh." Travis shushed the Greenes, bringing them back to the uneasy quiet from before.

The crackle of breaking glass pierced the silence. This one sounded far closer than the other noises. Much closer. Then a noise rattled in the dark – a fast, raspy *"tk tk tk tk tk"*. At first, Travis couldn't place where he'd heard it before. Then it hit him: the night when Mister Greene shot that intruder. The chirping he'd heard in the distance. That was it. He knew this creature lurking in the veil of darkness. Russell had warned him about it the night before, and fought one off the night before that. This was a minitia.

"We have to hide." he whispered.

Jane had either sensed his terror or felt some kind of her own, as her shaking voice erupted from her black silhouette, "Under the cars. Now."

Chapter 6

"Travis!" Jane called, making no attempt to conceal her voice.

Her boyfriend came to life at once, rising hitting his head on the underside of the car. He peered around, taking a moment to remember his situation. At last remembering, he rubbed the back of his head and called back, "I take it they passed us by." Then he asked, "Well how's Uncle Tommy? He alright?"

Tom was under a car in the next lane over from Travis, laying on the cold pavement next to Jane. She had a bloody arm around him. "He's really not doing well." She said, her voice shaking, "I tried waking him up, but... Travis, he needs help."

Travis looked around as best as he could from his place on the ground, "Are you sure those buggars are gone?"

"Would we be here talking if they weren't?"

The Brit pulled himself out from under the car and peered around. Only when he was sure that they were safe did he draw himself to his full height and stretch off the previous night's stiffness. He scanned the horizon, trying to find something, anything, along the road that could help them. He found was nothing but open road, littered with broken cars and an impenetrable forest on either side.

He looked back at Jane, her uncle lying limp over her shoulder. Her small frame seemed engulfed by his heavy body. Tom was pale and silent, with large patches of dried blood coating him all over. The sight was nauseating. It scared Travis to admit it, but Tom needed help soon or it might be too late to save him.

Travis noticed something in the distance – a faint, familiar rumble that slowly drew closer. "You hear that?"

"Hear what?" asked Jane.

Travis was silent, listening with intent as the source of the sound came ever closer. His heart filled with hope.

"Oh, I hear it now." Jane exclaimed, "Cars! Someone's driving!"

Before long, they could see what was causing all the noise. A massive line of vehicles, some bulky and covered in camouflage paint, others only simple trailer trucks. They rolled on, military vehicles keeping to the outside, protecting the semis on the center. The sight seemed to be something out of a dream. Other people? Working machinery? Were they finally saved?

"We need to get their attention!" Travis exclaimed as he grabbed one of Tom's arms and slung it over his shoulder. The couple picked lifted him and moved down the road towards their hopeful saviors.

"Help!" yelled Jane, "We need help! Please!"

"Oi, over here!" called Travis, "Over here! We need assistance!"

"Somebody!"

"Our friend is hurt! He needs help!"

The fleet of trucks and trailers began to pass by, showing no sign of slowing down. Were they being ignored? Could these people even hear their cries?

"Help! Please!" Jane shrieked.

"Please stop! We need help!"

But the vehicles didn't stop. They drove on, never slowing down, never breaking ranks. After a few moments, all that was left was a long mass moving further in the distance.

"Damn it!" Jane screamed, "Mother-! Ugh!"

They were panting from the movement, their throats sore from the yelling. The convoy didn't stop for them – didn't even acknowledge them. They were alone. Abandoned.

Then they weren't. At the back of the convoy was a collection of a dozen or so vans. One of them peeled off from the rest of the group, circled around and made for the three civilians.

* * *

Marceline laid awake, sleepless and contemplative. The warm, limp bodies encircling her and the quiet groans and snores did nothing to calm her mind. There were so many people. She didn't mind Victor being so close. In fact, she had missed the times when they would always fall asleep in each other 's arms. However, having so many people packed into one small metal container was horrid. They were like cattle. The place smelled of human filth. Not a moment went by without sounds of shifting or coughing or snoring. She had given up any hope of sleeping through the noise and claustrophobia, and had instead given her mind to her thoughts.

She pondered what could await them after... after everything. Boston was gone. That much, she knew. As much as she didn't want to admit it, it was true. So, where would they go now? She did love cities. New York, maybe? Was New York even still around? Was any city? The young soldier that Vic and Danny brought along – Private Athens, was it? He said that a number of cities had been bombed. Some, though normal means. Some with... nuclear force. She shuddered at the thought.

What was this deal with Private Athens, anyway? From what Marceline had seen, very few of the families in the convoy had personal guards. For most of them, it was because they had the money or were relatives of soldiers. She and her family had neither such luxury. So, why was he assigned to them? Not that she was complaining. No, not at all. She appreciated the extra protection. Athens served as another pair of eyes to watch the children.

The children. She wondered about Sammy and Zack sleeping beside her, and if they could ever forget all that had happened. So much blood and fear. So many long days on

121

the run. They saw their father and Dan run out of a burning barn, covered in blood. They survived an attempt on their lives in a stolen bus. After all of this, would they be alright? How would she explain everything that's changed? How could she tell her kids that they couldn't go back home to Boston? Or that they couldn't see their friends anymore?

Their friends... Marceline didn't want to think about those poor children back in Boston. Sammy had a best friend. Alyssa was her name. She and her mother would always be over at the apartment or taking Sammy out on some fun play date. The two of them were inseparable. Now it appeared they would never meet again. She was eight years old – a third grader, and now... Now she's gone. Forever.

A scream. A terrifying shriek in the night brought Marceline's attention to the world. She shot up and whipped around, not knowing what to expect. The inside of the trailer was pitch black for the most part, the only real light coming from tiny holes along one wall of the trailer. The cage lit up further as other people were beginning to shine flashlights around. These illuminating beams danced around the metal room until several of them, all at once, landed on the culprit.

The young woman at the far end of the trailer was inconsolable. Her small body was arched over as she held her face and cried again and again. Her screams and rang throughout the cage in an ear-splitting screech. The metal walls did nothing to ease the harshness of the noise, instead only seeming to amplify it. It took a couple of minutes for the person next to her, a woman in her early thirties, to begin to calm her down. She cradled her in her arms like one does to a loved one in grief – like Marceline would hold her children, or like Victor would hold her.

It didn't take any thought for Marceline to realize what this poor girl had seen. The woman must have had a nightmare – some awful reenactment of what happened to her in these past few days. She turned her attention to the small, shrouded shapes by her side. Marceline was relieved to see, through the faintest of lights, that Sammy and Zack were

122

still asleep. Two precious little angels. Angels that would hopefully get through this mess without being too tainted.

* * *

The van was packed tight with people and supplies, but nevertheless kept pace with the others at the back of the convoy. From what Travis could tell, this convoy was being organized and run by the military. Was this a government response to all that was going on? If so, why did it seem so... thrown together? And what was in those semis? Weaponry? Soldiers?

The new arrivals were more than relieved to be there in the van; to have their feet off of the pavement and to be on the move. To be part of a convoy of soldiers who, from what logic could tell, were under orders to protect civilians. Still, they somehow felt unsafe with their new friends. Unwelcome, even.

They talked about Tom. He still hadn't woken up. His face, normally warm and bright, had given way to paleness and cold. Jane and Travis were telling their saviors that he needed a doctor, the former being a bit more forceful. One of the soldiers, a corporal in his early thirties with two nasty cuts across his forehead, told the them that members of the convoy were not meant to break formation except at designated times, "We already disobeyed orders to get you three." he said.

"I know, sir, and we're very grateful." Travis answered, "But our friend here is in a lot of trouble. He needs assistance."

"He's going to die!" Jane shouted. Her eyes glistened, wet from coming tears.

The soldier quickly put a finger to his lips, his eyes darting around at the rural scenery outside the van, "Don't bring those goddamn bugs here, girl. I'll radio the med trucks. I'll tell them the situation. One of them's gotta pull over and help."

123

"Sir, are you sure that's a good idea?" asked one of the other soldiers.

"It's my call. I'll take the heat for it."

The corporal did just as he said, and soon the trio found their way into one of the semis. The place was relatively quiet for an enclosed metal box full of people, with the only noise coming from the movement of the nurses. Tom was by no means the only one there who looked hopeless. Blood was a common sight, staining the floor, walls, clothing and skin everywhere.

Tom was taken by a group of men and women in camouflage uniforms, each with a red cross on a white background placed on their upper arms. They seemed frantic, but tired – and judging by the scene around them, Travis couldn't blame them. They'd probably operated on half of the people in this room over the course of a few days. No sleep, scarce rest. He could tell that tensions were high among them, and they were coexisting for the sake of their patients. Travis couldn't help but wonder if Tom would have been better off in different hands.

They worked for a time in the far corner of the moving trailer. Travis didn't know much about treating injuries, but he knew that such a place was terrible for operating. The room was too dimly lit and any sense of sterility was nonexistent. What's more, the whole place was moving down a highway, rumbling and shaking as it went. All that aside, however, even operating in cringe-worthy conditions was better than keeping Tom out on the road. Travis hoped that the risk would pay off rather than seal the man's fate.

After a while, the team working around Tom got especially quiet, their words almost inaudible to the waiting couple. Before long, one of the nurses came approached them.

"I'm sorry." she said, "There's not much that we can do here. It's not just the bleeding. That bullet did a lot of internal damage. If we got to him sooner – just after it happened – then maybe things could have been different."

124

"What are you saying?" asked Jane, her voice quivering.

"This man is dying." said the nurse, looking to her feet rather than Jane's eyes. They were quiet for a moment, trying to digest the news. Travis put an arm around his partner. He tried not to show the great pain that he was in, watching such a great man doomed to pass. As much as he was hurting , he knew that Jane had it far worse. This was her uncle. A close one, at that. When she grew up, Tom was always around, helping her and having fun. All of the stories that Jane had ever told Travis about him were flooding back into his mind. He taught her to swim, to ride a bike, to stand up to bullies. They watched movies and talked about everything from politics to boys. Growing up, he was her best friend when no one else was.

"I'm sorry." The nurse said, yet again.

"We understand." Jane whispered.

"He doesn't have long. And honestly, it'll be painful for him if he wakes up again. It might be best to... well..."

At that, both Jane and Travis broke. She let out an agonizing wail and buried her face into his shoulder, while he held his face and whimpered.

"You might want to say your goodbyes to him now."

"We don't have to, if you don't want." Travis assured her, rubbing her arm.

"I have to." Jane responded, nodding her head and wiping her eyes.

Travis kissed her on the forehead and they went over to the makeshift operating area, the former holding onto his partner.

The two looked upon the pale, broken body of their loved one. His skin was white from blood loss. The nurses had removed his shirt, revealing the horrible wound in his abdomen His lower torso was drenched in blood, to the point where the nurses' attempt to wash it away only left the surface with thick streaks of red and pink. He was still unconscious, a fact that Travis felt was for the best. He didn't have to experience his pain. Or watch them feel theirs.

125

"I'm sorry, Uncle Tommy." Jane said, forcing her words through a voice that wanted to quit, "I'm so sorry." She leaned in and kissed him on the cheek, "You were like a father to me. I love you."

When it was clear that she was done, it was Travis' turn. What was he supposed to say? Apart from the past few days, he had spent so little time with this man. He wasn't related by blood, nor had this man helped raise him from a young age. Yet he still felt such intense sadness for his passing. It was clear that Tom meant something to him. Something that could be translated into words. "Well," he began, "this is goodbye, I guess. I wish I got to know you more. You…" His voice suddenly gave out under the choking sadness, and he could say no more. After a moment, one of the nurses led them away to the other side of the trailer and sat them down. Within minutes, it was over. Thomas Greene was gone.

* * *

The morning went on, but things didn't get brighter. The sun, even when in full frame across the sky, couldn't get past thickening clouds that drifted, large and slow in the sky. The clouds had taken on a strange color, sickly and pale.

At noon, the convoy stopped and its inhabitants got to stretch their legs once more. A handful of people were given small duties around the encampment, passing out food or reporting information to their assigned officers. The rest were left to wander or talk amongst themselves. Some were still optimistic, almost cheerful, but the overall atmosphere and weariness seemed to be seeping into the crowd. Most conversations, no matter how they started, would soon enough drift back to their current situation.

It was in this scene that Victor and Dan were sitting on the open back of their trailer, conversing with Private Athens. They were talking about what they had done before getting to the convoy. The two of them had already made their story

126

known, and now it was Athens' turn.

"Before it all," the young soldier began, "I was in Fort Drum, about a stone's throw from the Canadian border. I was supposed to finish my training in two weeks. That... well that never happened." He was snickering at first, but then his expression grew colder, "We knew something was wrong when all the lights went out. Phone lines were down, so were radio signals. No vehicles, either. We pretty much lost all contact with the outside world. Our CO's put us on alert. We didn't know what was going on, but we knew what an EMP looked like." Private Athens took a moment before continuing, "That's when Athriel showed up. We didn't know where he came from. He was just there all of a sudden. The whole base went crazy. There was an intruder, they said. But before we knew what that was about, the commander came out and announced that the US was under attack. We had to pack up and get down to DC. A lot of our more high-tech vehicles weren't working, but Athriel fixed a good handful of them. I don't know how. I saw him work on one of them, but he didn't really work on it. You know? He just stared at it like he was trying to see through it. Tapped on it a few times. Then after a couple of minutes, it was running again." The color in his face was fading now, and his voice was losing its restraint, "They attacked around dusk. With Athriel, we were able to fight them off. The things he could do. God, what I'd give to do the things he does. I'm still not sure if I imagined some of it or... But anyway, we still lost most of our men. And when we finally got moving out of there, it was the next morning. The bombs had already dropped."

"That's... heavy." Dan admitted, "I don't even know what to say."

"But enough about all this bullshit." Athens said with a wave of his hand, "I wanna hear more about what happened before everything."

"Oh?" Dan raised an eyebrow, "Like what?"

"I don't know. You're both old. You've got to have some stories."

"I'm twenty-nine." said Victor, "And Danny's thirty-two."

"You're still old in my book." Athens exclaimed with a playful sneer, "So how about a story?"

"Well there's not really much to say." Victor admitted.

"You mean to tell me that you went your entire life without doing anything interesting?"

Victor's mind was blanking. He wasn't very keen on being put on the spot. "Nothing that I can think of right now."

"What about one of your college stories?" asked Dan.

The young private's eyes widened, "Oh? I'd like to hear one of those."

"What about you?" Victor inquired, turning to Dan.

"I didn't go to college." Dan countered, "One of us used to party every night and it wasn't me."

"And you did?" asked Athens.

"You could say that." Victor answered, feeling at the bandages on his arm. His face grew warm.

"Well there is this one story…" he began, feigning enthusiasm, "I was nineteen or so. College age. Danny and I were in a bar together."

"A bar at nineteen?" Athens asked him, "I'm guessing you had a fake ID?"

"You guessed right, my friend." Victor nodded, "Anyway, Danny and I were just hanging out, having a few drinks – the usual. Then, out of nowhere, he spots this gorgeous woman across the bar. She's this German exchange student with wavy, blonde hair and a lot of curves. Now, I'm already with Marci by then, so I'm not interested. Danny, though." He threw his elbow, playfully nudging his friend in the ribs. Dan let out a slight groan, while everyone else laughed, "This guy just had to get to know her, but she's already getting a lot of attention from two or three other guys. She enjoyed it, don't worry. But anyway, I tell Danny, 'hey, I'll help you' and he starts getting excited. I'd taken a couple semesters of German, so I told him that I could teach him a phrase or two. I explained that if he walked up and said something cute in German, then he'd stick out to her."

"I can't believe you're telling this." Dan laughed. It was clear that he felt a slight sense of embarrassment, but he appeared willing to let the story continue.

"So, I told him to walk up to her and say, 'du bist ein kartoffel.' I said that it means, 'you look like an angel.' And so, he takes one last sip of his beer and goes off to talk to her. He gets to her, makes his way past the other guys, puts on this whole smooth act of his and says, 'du bist ein kartoffel' in the worst impression of a suave German accent I've ever heard."

"And what happened?" asked Athens.

"He got slapped right across the face. 'Du bist ein kartoffel' actually means, 'you are a potato.' She was pissed!"

The group erupted in laughter.

"And it didn't end there." Victor exclaimed, "I never let him live that down. For years after that, I'd keep reminding him of it. Just every once in a while. A sideways remark here, a text message there. Sometimes I even left potatoes around his apartment. He'd wake up and find one just on his pillow, a pencil replaced with a fry, mashed potatoes in his toilet… Stuff like that. Our other friends thought it was because he's Irish, but we knew the truth."

"Sir," Athens said after he'd regained his breath, "No offense, but you were an asshole back then."

Victor couldn't keep from laughing even harder, "Well, you know, I kind of still am."

At that moment, another soldier came by. This one seemed to be a couple of years older than Athens. "Private," he rumbled, "A moment."

"Yes, sir." They walked off to the point where they were just out of earshot. Victor and Dan watched as the other soldier gave Athens some long speech, followed by Athens saying what must have been another "sir, yes sir," and being dismissed.

When the young soldier came back, he had a curious

look on his face. It wasn't of fear or anger, but nor was it of happiness either, "Well I just got debriefed." He stated, "Looks like we aren't moving from this location anytime soon."

"What?" Victor questioned.

"Don't we kinda need to get to DC?" asked Dan, "I mean, that's what I heard."

"I guess DC can wait." Athens answered, almost as unsure about it as the civilians, "But if the commander wants to stop, then we stop. Now isn't the time to question authority."

"Well do you know why we're stopping?" asked Victor.

"He told me a bit of it, but I feel like he took me away from you guys for a reason."

The two civilians weren't satisfied with his answer, but they decided not to press the matter.

* * *

At about mid-afternoon, the Roberts family was growing stir-crazy. Sammy was especially vocal about it, begging more than once for her parents to let her go explore the camp. Marceline was against the little girl walking around alone, but Sam was adamant. Her parents knew that, if she truly wanted to do something, no amount of rejection or discipline would stop her. At last, they came to an agreement: she was allowed to go wherever she pleased for an hour, so long as her father kept a close eye on her.

It was a nice deal for Victor, too. He was going insane inside his own mind, and needed a minor change of scenery. Perhaps, while they were out, he would find someone who knew more about what was going on. As they went, he saw families setting up tents and cooking meals over electric stoves. Soldiers gathered for patrols and children played by the trailers. By the look of it, people were getting ready to settle down here for the time being. Victor wondered why. They were still in Pennsylvania. Weren't they supposed to get to DC?

Just as this thought was buzzing through his mind, Victor caught sight of none other than the blue-eyed man himself. Athriel approached from the opposite end of the lane, walking with resolution towards some unknown goal.

"Sweetie," Victor asked, "Do you mind if we stop to talk to this man, real quick?"

"Urgh, fine." Sammy groaned, "I thought this was my time, though."

"We can have an extra ten minutes, after this. I just need to see this guy for a moment."

"Promise?" The girl looked up at him with skepticism and hope.

"Of course." Her father ruffled her hair for a moment, causing her to retreat and fix her locks. When the blue-eyed man was close enough, Victor waved him down and called out, "Hey, Athriel."

"Good afternoon, Victor. How is your family. Are you adjusting well enough?"

"Yeah," he said, "I'd say so. I mean it's not easy to get used to being refugees, but we're trying. While you're here, do you have a moment to talk?"

"I really have to be somewhere. The commander wants me... but I think I could spare a moment. What would you like to discuss?"

"I have all these questions." Victor said. To be honest, he didn't know which one to lead with. After all, Athriel seemed in a hurry. Whatever he asked, it would likely be the only answer he would get, "I guess I should start with the most obvious one." He took a breath, "Why'd you choose me? Of all the people on Earth, why me?"

"I was in the area." Athriel stared at him with those piercing blue eyes, unmoved by the query, "No, truly. That's where I landed. I had no time to contact anyone in power, so I went through the nearest neighborhood. I visited as many families as I could before my people found out. Several of your neighbors also saw me. Honestly, I'm surprised they didn't gossip."

"You think anyone would have believed them?" Victor asked, "I mean, my own family thought you were just a dream. And what? Your people didn't want you coming here?"

"My people were preparing to storm the planet and get Linious into custody. Most didn't care about the local populace. Humans are too young of a species to join us, so why bother saving them? That was the mentality."

"But if your people were against you coming here, then why'd you do it?"

At that, Athriel's face softened, "We are shepherds." he said, "We're meant to guide our flock, not throw them to the wolves. I knew that, if I made a preemptive move and leaked information to Earth, then it might motivate my people into action."

This caught Victor by surprise. What did he mean when he said that his people were shepherds? Were they guiding other races? Just how powerful were these people?

"When I was found," Athriel continued, "I was brought before the royal spymaster of my people, Amelatu. I told them that I had contacted an Earth government. Of course, I hadn't. Still, the lie was enough to get the gears moving. Now that Earth supposedly had an official first contact with the tiavan, they were more worthy of defending."

"What does first contact have to do with it?"

"Politics. Protocols. Now if you don't mind, it's time that I headed to the commander." The blue-eyed man began to set off down the convoy.

"Wait." Victor called, bringing Athriel to another reluctant stop, "One more question. Why is it that you're going out of your way to protect me and my family? You saved us in that bus, you gave us Private Athens, and I know you had something to do with our van still working after the EMP. Why all of this help? Are we special or something?"

"I had nothing to do with your vehicle working. Perhaps it lacked the electrical components that an EMP affects. That would be my best guess. It looked rather old, to me. Or perhaps there was enough metal in its shell to act like a makeshift faraday cage. In the end, I do not have a real answer for you, and there are more important things to research, at the moment. As for the other instances… yes, I do often ask myself why I did them. The best answer is that I feel responsible for you. I saved you from Boston. You would already be dead if it weren't for my intervention. Now I guess that I feel some sense of responsibility for keeping you safe." When he was finished, Athriel thanked Victor and turned to take his leave. He got a couple of yards before stopping. It seemed that a thought had occurred to him. The blue-eyed man turned to Victor one last time and smiled, "Perhaps, if we make it to DC, you can be a part of my work. Would you like that?"

"Uh, sure." Victor answered, less than confident, "Depends on what that work is."

"All will be clear, my friend." At that, Athriel turned back around and headed off. As a final goodbye, he snapped his fingers and let off a small burst of fire from his hand.

Victor still had so many questions. So Athriel was something called a tiavan? Just who is Linious? And what was Athriel trying to recruit him for? He despised having so many unanswered thoughts pressing at his mind. However, he decided that time would provide what he needed, just as Athriel had said.

"Come on, Daddy." Sammy whined, "I wanna go explore some more. And you said I could have ten extra minutes."

With her words, Victor snapped himself out of his thoughts and looked to his daughter with a smile, "Sammy, would I lie to you? Let's go."

* * *

"Well, we stopped like you wanted." rumbled the gruff voice of Commander Pullano, "Just outside Harrisburg." He

133

and Athriel were coming upon a tent that his soldiers had set up as a new headquarters. They were setting up camp along a stretch of highway, having found an open stretch of pavement that could house the long convoy.

As they ducked into the tent, Athriel stopped and turned to him, "Have your scouts been able to tell how intact the city is?"

"Word is the place has been torn to shit, but many buildings are still somewhat intact. It's possible that a couple of warehouses are standing strong. We can probably stockpile a lot of goods from them."

"No nuclear devices detonated in the area?"

"Just paranukes."

"Then there is still the danger of chemical fallout."

"It's better than radiation." said Pullano, before adding, "We work with what we can get. If God gives us lemons, we scavenge those lemons for all they're worth. When acid rain comes down, we'll do our best to stay dry. In the meantime, we all have work to do."

"God." muttered Athriel, "I have to say, I wasn't expecting such a word from you."

"Let's get down to business." said Pullano, deflecting the statement.

"Right. My apologies."

The commander took his place at his desk, sitting in one of the few metal chairs they had in the camp. On the other side of the desk were two stools. Pullano gestured for Athriel to take a seat. The latter declined, prompting the commander to simply nod and move on with their discussion, "So the scouts have found something else. Something that you might want to know about."

"Oh?" The blue-eyed man raised an eyebrow, letting his curiosity show, "Is that so?"

The commander leaned back in his seat, tossing the words in his head before deciding how to explain, "There's a horde of minitia moving through the area."

"A horde?" Athriel repeated, the intrigue in his eyes

fading.

"They estimate between two and four thousand. But there could be many, many more."

"There always are."

It seemed that Pullano couldn't read Athriel. His advisor seemed understanding, yet somehow let down by the information. Was he hoping for something else? Anyway, he figured it was of no matter. He couldn't give his mind to such speculations and take away from the situation at hand.

"They'll undoubtedly sweep through the city," said Athriel, his demeanor once again returning to its casual, nonchalant state, "hunting for survivors and such. Feeding. Destroying."

"My thoughts, exactly. That's why we can't make a large move for the city just yet."

"Or at all." said Athriel.

"The first of those bugs are probably at least a day out from the city, unless they pick up speed. In the meantime, we have to scout the area and collect supplies."

"That is not a wise decision."

"I'm not sending the whole force in. Only a handful of squads and fireteams. A small group can sneak through territory that an army can't."

"All the same, commander, they won't come back."

"That's a risk we have to be willing to take. It's this or waiting around strategically blind."

"Yesterday, you scolded me for jeopardizing the lives of a handful of men. Yet now you throw them away yourself."

"This is my decision, Athriel. And it's the right one."

At that moment, Athriel seemed to rise higher, an intensity coming across him that the commander wasn't prepared for. What's more, his voice had grown harder and more authoritative, "You come to me for my advice, commander. That is why you call me your advisor, correct?"

"That's right." said Pullano, ready for a fight, "You're my advisor. Not my CO. Your point is to help me with my decisions. However, the actual decision making falls to me,

135

and me alone." The commander let his words set in before continuing on, "Now, you're the one who said that we should stop. I went along with that. But having a few tangos in the area can't stop us from making use of this situation. We need to supply, scout the area, and find a usable route to the SZ. But to do that, we need to send men out there, no matter what's waiting for them."

"We can still wait until-"

"No, we can't."

Athriel paused for a moment before giving a short nod. His face never changed expression. He knew that he was defeated, "Suit yourself. Just remember one thing: when you lose everybody that you send into this city, it was by your order. Not mine."

* * *

Hours passed and several scouting groups set out from the camp. Some were sent to surrounding roads and highways in an attempt to find some traversable route to the safe zone. Others were sent to survey the outermost parts of the city itself. The fireteam of Corporal Santino Hernandez, however, was one of the unlucky few. His team was to scour the inner ruins of what was once Harrisburg, Pennsylvania. Along with him were three Privates: Logan Armstrong taking point at the front of the group, Richard Graham, his best rifleman, covering behind them, and Preston O'Connor with his weapon aimed high, watching the charred buildings and rubble for any sign of movement. Like shadows, they worked their way through the ruins. Every step was calculated, every breath hushed. As far as anyone was concerned, they were deep behind enemy lines. Any move that they made could be their last on this Earth.

They made their way down what was once one of the city's main streets. Commerce buildings and centers of civil life lined the concrete and pavement, now all descending into shattered ruin. A smoldering hellfire had replaced what was once the capital of this beautiful commonwealth.

"This place is dead." Graham mumbled, his low, near-whisper voice muffled by the gas mask, "How many people lived here?"

"Sixty k." Armstrong answered from the front of the group.

"Goddamn." muttered Graham, "Bless those poor souls."

"Quiet." Hernandez ordered, "We don't know who could be listening."

"There ain't nothing but ghosts here, Sarge." said Graham.

Twice, Private O'Connor thought he saw a dark shape moving on the second floor of a ruined office building. Both times, smoke blocked his view and, by the time it passed, the figure was gone. His first thought was to inform the fireteam, but he decided against it. He was afraid. His mind could have been playing tricks on him. Besides, what were the odds that someone had survived in these ruins?

They continued on for two more blocks, their sight clouded by the smoky haze left by the paranuclear attack. At times, it left them able to see nor more than a foot in front of their faces. They were forced to feel around with their feet so they wouldn't trip on rubble.

Armstrong raised a hand. The group stopped.

"You see something?" the corporal asked, making sure to keep his voice low.

"Can't tell." Armstrong answered, "Too much smoke." He looked through his scope in an attempt to get a closer look, but he still couldn't see a thing. "Should we get a closer look?"

"Your call." said Hernandez.

Armstrong kept his rifle fixed on the spot across the street and took a step. Then another. And another. A crumbling sound caught their attention. Hernandez turned in time to catch a bit broken rubble tumble forward out of the smoke, stopping right in front of them. Hernandez would have told Armstrong to be more careful, if indeed the piece had come from him. The sound had occurred perhaps five yards away, but was nevertheless incredibly audible above the crackle of the burning city. The sound was unlike any falling debris or settling ruin. The rubble that came into view had a higher velocity. Something had knocked into it to send it flying. Or perhaps someone kicked it.

They weren't alone.

Hernandez and Armstrong took aim at once, while Graham covered behind them and O'Connor watched the buildings. They waited and listened, but nothing followed.

"Civilians?" Hernandez asked.

"Can't tell." answered Armstrong.

The fireteam waited for a moment, hoping for some kind of confirmation. At last, something came. But it wasn't the sound they wanted.

"Tk tk tk tk."

"We need to find cover." said Hernandez, looking for any place that they could go. To his right he saw a small shop that was still partially intact. From his position, it appeared that most of the walls were still standing and the doorway was clear enough for the team to get through. "Into the shop." he said.

They made their way to the hole where the door used to be. A fallen plank blocked the way, but a couple of strong jabs from the butt of Armstrong's rifle dislodged it. Once inside, they could do nothing but watch and wait. They were crouched, with Armstrong's rifle pointed out towards the street they came from, while Graham took aim at the store's ruined back wall, which was open enough for any number of creatures or people could come through.

"Damn it..." groaned O'Connor, "damn it, damn it."

"What now, corporal?" asked Armstrong.

"We shouldn't trust the streets." Hernandez began, taking a moment to think before continuing, "The back wall is down. So is most of what's behind it. Let's work our way through the ruins. Try to stay out of sight."

138

"Sir," O'Connor objected, "We can confirm that there's an enemy presence in Harrisburg. Are you sure we shouldn't make our exfil now?"

"A sound is just a sound." answered Hernandez, "We need visual confirmation. Is there just one, or are there hundreds? What are they doing here? A sound can only do so much. We need more information."

O'Connor hesitated before concurring, "Roger."

Hernandez looked around, deciding on their course of action, "I'll lead. Graham, take point around corners. Armstrong, cover our six. O'Connor, watch the ruins. Let's go, boys."

They climbed, one at a time, through the hole in the back wall. Graham first, then the corporal, then O'Connor, then Armstrong. They made their way through the dense remains of devastated buildings, moving from cover to cover, stepping around flames and loose rubble as they went. The scenery they found themselves in looked even more like a war zone than the street. Ash-colored air laid thicker than ever above the smoldering wreckage. At times, they were almost feeling around in the haze, trying not to stumble over broken rebar or shattered concrete. They said nothing, but they all knew they were getting closer to an impact site.

After a time, the sky began to darken. Through the thick haze of smoke and columns of wrecked buildings, they could make out that the sun was starting to drift back down towards the horizon. The day was coming to an end – and with it, any sense of safety. The fireteam abandoned its slow method of moving from cover-to-cover. Instead they walked openly back towards where they supposed their exfil point was. In truth, they were more than a little lost among the ruins. Any rubble and decay that they passed, while familiar by nature, was nevertheless new to their eyes.

"Two o'clock." said Graham, stopping in his tracks and bringing the whole team to alert.

"What is it?" the corporal asked.

"Some hole in the ground, sir."

There it was, a great crevice that plunged deep into the Earth. It appeared as if the ground itself had ruptured, leaving in its very skin an open wound – a hole that tunneled deep into a far abyss. The group could do nothing but stare in awe at the magnificent sight.

"I suppose this wasn't an entrance to some subway." Graham said.

"It could be a sign of the enemy." Armstrong commented, "Should we check it out?"

They stood in silence, waiting for the corporal to make his decision. All were anxious to leave the city before it got dark. Nobody wanted to find themselves here in this war zone overnight. At the same time, however, they had a mission to fulfill. If this great hole was made by the enemy, then it was their responsibility to know.

"Armstrong, Graham. You two make your way down there." Hernandez motioned to the hole with the sight of his rifle, "Get a sense of how deep it goes and what could have made it. If it goes on for too long, just come back to this position. We can't take too much time here."

"Sir." Armstrong nodded.

"O'Connor and I'll stand guard. Keep our eyes and ears peeled. You two do the same. If you make contact, fall back to this position. Do not engage."

With that, they were off. Graham sparked up a flare and tossed it into the abyss below. The green hue didn't make it more than ten feet before hitting ground. Beyond that, the tunnel turned to a forty-five-degree angle, still burrowing deeper and deeper under the city. Privates Graham and Armstrong disappeared into the unnatural tunnel, leaving only footsteps that grew faint and echoed until they too vanished.

Now, it was just Private O'Connor and Corporal Hernandez. Two silent watchers in a place of endless fire and ash. This landscape, desolate as it may have been, still held some kind of life within its scorched interior. The crackle of dancing flames, the rumble and crashes of settling rubble, the hearts beating like drums in the soldiers' chests. They witnessed and experienced a city of blackened death and empty life. As the sun continued to fall from the sky, these crackles and rumbles became all that they knew.

Aside from that, the city was otherwise silent. It reminded O'Connor of the night when the minitia struck Fort Drum. The radios and intercoms that usually blasted away had given way to eerie silence. Even the voices of people around him had fallen to a dismal whisper. All they talked about, if anything was the mysterious stranger who had showed up in the base, warning of something to come. Then only hours later, the stranger's nonsensical words had a terrifying meaning. By dawn of the next day, less than half of the men in the base were still standing.

Hernandez and O'Connor kept checking their watches, never letting more than a minute go by without their knowing. Seven forty... Seven forty-one... Seven forty-two... The numbers began to add up. All the while, the land got even darker and more unsettling.

"Armstrong and Graham aren't back yet." said O'Connor, making note of the obvious before asking, "Should we wait much longer?"

"Either that or we go in looking for them." Hernandez told him, "I'm not leaving them behind."

The corporal's response, while noble, did nothing to ease the growing dread in young O'Connor. Those things were all around – he had no doubt in his mind. Every shadow, every noise, every pulsing beat of his frightened heart – they were behind everything. They were playing with him, trying to drive him mad. He needed to get out of the city – away from any place where they could ever reach him. The last thing he wanted was to be trapped down in that hole.

Without warning, a crashing noise hit the air. It was the scratchy thud of rock on rock. A piece of debris rolled carelessly out of a pile and towards O'Connor's feet. With a panicked jump, the young soldier's finger squeezed two rounds out of his rifle.

"Hold your fire!" shouted Hernandez, "Damn!"

"Sorry, sir." said O'Connor.

"If those things didn't have us pinpointed before, they do now." said Hernandez, "We're retreating to the others."

"Sir."

"I'll take point."

Hernandez made his way into the gaping wound in the Earth, sliding into the hole on his side until the ground leveled out enough to stand. O'Connor followed, stumbling along as he went. It was far too dark. As much as they wanted to avoid drawing attention to themselves, they had to light the way with flares.

The tunnel continued on for perhaps two hundred feet before turning into a spiral. It was so sudden that, even with a flare in his hand, Hernandez almost landed himself face-first into a wall.

"Watch out." he whispered, warranting a nod from O'Connor.

They kept going, working deeper into what was turning into an elaborate maze. Passages kept splitting off and joining together, twisting, climbing and falling all through the underside of the city.

"How long does this place go on for?" O'Connor asked, more to himself than to his superior.

Hernandez let out a hushed groan, "Graham and Armstrong are down here, somewhere. But I don't know how we're gonna meet up with them. For all we know, they're lost."

"What if we get lost too?" asked O'Connor, "How do we get out?"

"Who's to say we aren't already lost?"

From then on, they were quiet, too cautious to make a sound, lest they'd be discovered. All they could do was to continue on and hope to find their compatriots intact. However, no matter how far into the labyrinth they delved, no such thing happened. O'Connor became convinced that they weren't ever going to find the others. They were lost to the maze, never to return again. No matter how many twists and turns they tip-toed around, he and the corporal would never find anything.

This thought came over him as they were about to round a particularly sharp corner. Hernandez in front, O'Connor close behind. The corporal made disappeared his way around and out of view. O'Connor was about to follow when he heard the tap of a rock ricocheting off the wall behind him. He turned, his forwardmost hand grasping tight at his flare and his forearm propping up the front of the rifle.

Nothing.

He turned back around and, not wanting to fall too far behind, at once made for the corporal. He rounded the corner, but found only an empty stone hall.

"Corporal?" he called, "Hernandez?"

There was no answer, save for his own echoes.

"Graham? Armstrong?"

Nothing... Then something. A return of some sort. Something calling back to him through the darkness. The demonic shrieking came from everywhere, bouncing off of the tunnel walls and around corners and into the deepest, most primitive recesses of his mind. He squeezed the trigger of his rifle, and in the light he saw a large shape rushing for him with inhuman speed. Fear took him and he ran. He didn't know where to go, only that he had to get out. He rounded corner after corner, sprinting through the passages, working his way out of the black maze from panicked memory. When he finally got to where the exit should have been, he saw nothing but more rock and darkness. He must have taken a wrong turn somewhere. But where? Could he retrace his steps?

O'Connor began to shake. He was alone. He was lost. He was deep in a place that, for all he knew, could have been the entrance to Hell itself.

Another dreaded screech. The private took off once more, but soon found himself at a dead end. He whipped himself around, rifle at the ready, and retraced himself. When he found another passageway that he had missed before, he decided to try his luck. A minute of walking later, the walls gave way. However, beyond the hue of the flare, the world was dark as ever. He was still underground. It occurred to him that he'd stumbled upon a great cavern. He was out in the open. Exposed. This couldn't do.

He tried to move quietly through the subterranean landscape, hoping to reach a wall on the other side where he could then feel around for another passageway. Before anything came into view, the light of his flare started to die. The soldier dropped it and tried to light another, but a fast, echoing chirp stopped him in his tracks. Even bouncing off the walls, he could tell that it was close. Far too close. If he lit another flare then it would see him.

A footstep. Then another. Then more. All from different places around him. A long, raspy hiss by his side. In the ever-failing light of the flare, he couldn't make them out, but he didn't need to. They were surrounding him and he knew it. A warm sensation came leaking down one of his pant legs. He wanted to scream.

He heard a high-pitched chirp and an unseen force grabbed hard at his rifle. It flew out of his hands, the strap still around his torso. It pulled at the man with enough force to take him off his feet, only parting from him after he had landed face-first on the ground. As he tried to scramble to his feet, more shrieks filled the air. Something knocked into him, tossing him like a ragdoll and leaving a searing pain in his right arm. He grasped the wound as he tried once again to get to his feet. This time they let him. Blood trickled through his fingers. The arm was broken, the bone shattered and the flesh carved away like meat at a feast. Pain screamed in his arm, though not as loud as the shapeless creatures surrounding him. By now, he could see the field of crimson eyes appearing all around him, piercing the blackness. He was surrounded – at their mercy. Another quick flash of pain and his left cheek was slashed open, another and a series of deep gashes appeared across his back. They were toying with him,

144

enjoying every second of it. He could hear what must have been their laughter circling around. Something scraped the side of his head. As his hand reached for the wound, he found that his left ear was gone, swiped clean off. Whimpering, his eyes tearing up, Preston O'Connor placed his hand on the back of his neck, covering it like he would during a bear attack. He tried to crouch down. A sharp stab into his calf brought him to the ground with a pained scream.

As if on cue, his wail was answered by a dozen others. His face was to the ground, but he could feel the bodies lunging at him from all sides. They had played with their food for long enough, and now it was time to end it. And they did. And he felt everything.

* * *

With the deep, rasping chirps and screeches that pierced the night air, Victor knew he wouldn't be sleeping. In the darkness, the minitia had encircled the highway encampment, the only thing keeping them at bay being the scores of soldiers guarding the edges of the camp. The yelling of platoon leaders as they marched up and down the perimeter wasn't helping to ease anyone's nerves, either. He wasn't used to this – being surrounded by men with guns, having to be on guard against imminent danger. He felt like he was at war. Maybe he was. Every once in a while, he heard the chaotic noises of small skirmishes near the edge. Shots and screams, followed by more shots and more screams. Every time it went quiet, he waited and listened, hoping that his side had won and that those creatures weren't swarming through like alien locusts.

Victor stood outside, remaining within a few feet of his family's trailer. Inside, Danny and Athens were asleep with the children. Victor took a step back and leaned against the great metal cage, taking in the night air. He heard the soft voice of Marceline talking with a couple of new recruits. A young couple – in their early twenties, he guessed. One was unmistakably British, but the other wasn't speaking enough for him to make out her accent. They sounded sad, as if in mourning. Victor could only wonder as to what happened to them. Then again, if they had befriended Marceline then he was bound to find out at some point.

He stood out there, continuing to bathe his senses in the strange world around him. Listening to the sounds of a war going on just beyond his sight. Remembering the days that had come to pass. Wondering what the future held for him and his family.

"Can't sleep?" asked a familiar voice. It was Marceline.

Victor reached out and put an arm around her silhouette. "Can you blame me?" he asked.

"Guess not." she said. The couple was quiet for a time. They listened and thought and breathed deep in the heavy, smoky air. For days, it had been getting worse. It smothered their lungs and stung their eyes. From what they heard, the whole east coast, maybe even the whole country, was like this. They only hoped that DC would somehow be a little better, though basic reasoning told them otherwise.

Victor rubbed her shoulder, but she made no response. Was something wrong? Her body was tense. Something must have been on her mind. Perhaps it was about the British couple she had met. Or it could have been about the children. Maybe it was something else entirely. He wanted to know, but decided not to prod. If she wanted to let him in, she would do so when she was ready.

Several shots rang out, far away but still too close. Victor jumped at the sudden noise, but Marceline went without any response. A couple of shouts followed – a soldier giving orders. Then the world was quiet once again. Another skirmish. Another corpse.

Then Marceline leaned in and wrapped her arms around her husband. It surprised him, but he returned her embrace and they kissed a long, loving kiss.

"Just promise me one thing." she said, "Never get yourself caught out there."

"I won't." Victor was taken aback. Why would he ever go out beyond the safety of the convoy? The relative comfort of these trucks and soldiers and Athriel? His family was here. So was Danny. The very thought of leaving, even for a second, seemed ludicrous.

"Promise me." Her eyes glistened, bringing a hint of reflected light to her shadowy figure.

Victor kissed her forehead, "I don't want to be caught anywhere near those things." he said, "Never again. So yes, I promise."

Chapter 7

Three days passed. In that time, Commander Pullano sent out several more scouting teams each night. Fewer and fewer soldiers ever made it back, and those that did were often wounded and spoke only of horrors that no human being should witness. Friends ripped apart where they stood. Shadowy figures carrying people off into the night, leaving behind nothing but cold shrieks and the iron scent of blood. Dark creatures with crimson eyes seeming to cackle in delight as they fed on the flesh of their kills.

More of these minitia showed up with every passing night. They attacked the edges of the camp, mauling scores of its defenders. During those times, Victor and Marceline would hold their children close, wincing at every noise and fearing that every moment would be their last. They would listen to the battle, trying to figure out how close or far the shots and screams were. Every time it seemed as though the fighting was drawing closer, yet it never did make it to their trailer.

One morning, a platoon of soldiers began pushing broken-down cars and trucks from all over the highway into a solid barrier that circled the perimeter of the convoy. After the vehicles were in place, they blocked off the undersides with discarded materials and wood from the nearby forest. The structure made for an effective wall separating the camp from the monsters outside. It seemed to have been built just in time, too. Since that night, the enemy had swarmed the outskirts of the encampment. Not half an hour went by without intense gunfire. Eventually they started harassing the makeshift wall during the day, too. On two occasions, one of those hell spawn got over the defenses and into the camp. Only a single one would get through however, and it wouldn't get too far either. In the first instance, the invader managed to slice into a civilian woman before being gunned down. Its head mounted on a stick and displayed on the wall for its friends to see. The woman lived, but everybody in the convoy got the message: these things were toying with them. Testing them. Finding weak points in their big metal wall. Getting into their heads and keeping them on the edge of panic. These creatures, as savage as they may have been, were masters of their craft. They demanded fear, paranoia, hysteria – and that's exactly what their prey gave them.

It was Thursday, April fourteenth. A full week since the bombs dropped. The convoy had lost too many men in all their attempts to scavenge the ruins of Harrisburg for supplies. What's more, because of all their failed attempts, supplies were starting to run low. Food, clean water, disinfectant, gauze, medications, able-bodied soldiers, weapons. All of these vital resources were stretched to the limit. This convoy needed to resupply and move on before it was too late. Rations were tightened while the civilian population grew. Patrols were smaller and less frequent while the enemy continued to surround their camp. The Northeastern Military Convoy was growing desperate.

* * *

Athriel ducked into Commander Pullano's tent. These meetings, while becoming a regular occurrence, rarely proved to be useful. In his eyes, the officer appeared to care more about asserting dominance than bettering the convoy's chance of survival. He wouldn't listen to a word that his advisor had to say. Countless suggestions and warnings fell upon deaf ears. Athriel wondered to himself if this mission would be better off led by somebody else.

As he entered, he could see how the stress was taking its toll on the commander. He no longer held himself with an air of respectable authority. Rather, he forced everything around him into submission with a tired fury. No longer did he respond to pressure with anything but animosity.

"It's clear that we're being played." Pullano began, "No matter where we send our scouts, they get taken out. We're painfully short on actual intel, but that itself is information we can use. They're cutting us off from knowing anything about their positions, which makes me think they're planning something."

"That is very likely, Commander." said Athriel. He was surprised by his contemporary's deductive skills. It was a welcome reminder of why he placed the man in charge in the first place.

"My goal now is to be out of this place by the time they make their move."

"But it isn't as easy to do as to say." Athriel cautioned.

"Of course not." groaned Pullano. He held a hand to his face and sighed, "Coming here in the first place has been a mistake. We've completely failed to resupply, and now resources are running even lower. Then there's the fact that every man I send out there either doesn't come back at all, or comes back too messed up to be of any use. Now we're running low on everything. We need to get to the safe zone."

"And what would you have your men do?" asked Athriel, deciding not to waste his breath with suggestions.

The commander fell into his chair and thought for a time. Finally, he brought his head up and said, "I'm not leaving here without something."

Athriel expected such a stubborn decision, but it still irked him. "You'd have your men go back into Harrisburg? After all that you've lost there?"

"Well I can't let it all be for nothing." Pullano growled, "Yes, we've lost a lot of men in the city. If I keep sending small groups in, they'll never come out again. That's why we need to make one last push – push ourselves in with a large force, get what we need to get and leave."

Athriel raised an eyebrow, "With respect…"

"Oh, come on. Every time you say that, respect is never what follows."

"Then I'll just say it. Any soldiers that you have left are already stretched too thin across the convoy to be of any use in a large attack. You don't have the men to defend this place, let alone take the city. By now, it's overrun by the enemy. If you care about your fellow people at all, then you'll forget any idea of going back there."

Commander Pullano was quiet for a moment, silenced with contemplation. When at last he spoke, it caught Athriel off his guard. "You're right. We don't have the soldiers for that. We'd have to take civilian volunteers. They wouldn't be well trained or nearly as useful, but it would have to do."

"Civilians?" the advisor asked, "You want to use civilians?"

"They'd have to be led by some soldiers, of course. Say... a platoon of my men, plus twenty or so volunteers... Plus you."

"Me?"

The commander nodded, "Yes, you. I've heard reports of things you've done. My peers say that you can move like nothing they've ever seen before... that you can control electricity." Athriel was silent, prompting his contemporary to continue, "If these rumors are true, then I need you leading this mission."

The advisor wanted to object, but after some thought he decided that he could use this to his advantage. When he's in the city, those people would be under his command. He could ensure that they made it out alive, proving his capabilities to the failing commander. "Where in the city would I take them?" he asked.

"Find a local. They'll tell you where to find something. A warehouse, a supermarket. Something with supplies that we need. Keep some transports on standby to bring the goods back to the convoy."

"Sounds like a plan. A decent one. I'm surprised."

"I knew you'd like it." Pullano smirked.

"I'll get some men to round up volunteers." Athriel turned to leave, but the commander's voice called him back.

"Oh, one more thing. Before I forget."

"Yes, commander?"

"I want that guy to go with you. What's his name? Roberts? Yeah."

"Victor?" Athriel asked. A small look of shock appeared across his face.

"Yeah, him. You went out of your way to get his group here, and you've had an eye on him ever since. Now I don't know why that is, but I don't care. I don't give half a damn why he's so important to you. All I know is, if he's on the mission with you, you'll be more careful. Those people will be more likely to survive."

"That won't be necessary."

"My decision is final."

"Sure, it is." Athriel responded, "It would be." He turned to leave once again.

"That'd better be a 'yes, sir'."

The advisor stopped. He didn't turn back to the commander. Even if he refused to show it, he was infuriated. This human didn't deserve what he asked for.

* * *

A crowd surrounded the Roberts family's semi-truck. Sammy and little Zack were running about, playing tag with their new friends. Marceline would often have to call out and tell them to stay where the adults could see them. They listened for a time, but soon found themselves scurrying off and hiding again.

Their parents and Uncle Danny were talking about this safe zone that they'd heard so much, yet so little about. For how much they heard people discussing their destination, they were still in the dark about what it would be like. They knew it would be some place just outside of Washington DC and that it was guarded by what was left of the military, but that was it. What was life like for the refugees? The convoy was without any sort of information about living standards or their lifestyle. As always, the absence of knowledge gave way to a whirlwind of speculation. It was a haven in a collapsing world. It was run by inhuman beings just like the one with the glowing eyes. Some claimed it didn't exist at all.

"So, what do you think the safe zone's gonna be like?" asked Marceline.

Dan scoffed, "Oh, don't even get me started. I tell you, I've gotten so sick of this trailer park lifestyle. Whatever DC is like, it had better have a hot shower and an actual bed."

"You think that's likely?" Victor asked, raising an eyebrow.

Dan threw his hands up, "A guy can dream, damn it. If my hopes are too far-fetched, then what about you?" He pointed a finger at Marceline, "What do you wanna see there?"

"Honestly, it would be nice to have a hot shower." she laughed, "I mean right now, I think about half my body weight is dirt."

"Pretty soon, the grime will be able to clean itself off." said Dan.

"But I'll settle for just having a good wall to keep those things out."

"We have a wall here, Marci." said Victor.

"No, I'm talking about a real, solid wall. Not some glorified line of cars. Those things can jump over any one of them and get to us. It's already happened before."

"And who's to say a real wall can keep them out, either?" asked Victor, "Who knows how high those things can jump, anyway?"

"Definitely higher than a sedan." Marceline answered, "And that's what I care about."

"And what about you?" Dan looked over to his friend.

"Eh, I don't know." Victor answered.

"You don't know?" asked Marceline, "Come on, there's gotta be something you're missing out on."

"Well yeah," said Victor, "a shower would be nice. Hot or no. I just want to be clean again. And yeah, some good protection would be nice. I don't wanna be killed in my sleep when those things out there decide to stroll in here."

"There's a 'but' in there somewhere." Marceline ventured. Dan raised an eyebrow, prompting her to groan in annoyance, "Oh, grow up."

Victor continued, "But I want something else, too."

"Booze?" asked Dan.

"What's wrong with you today? No, not booze. I want a bit more of an explanation from Blue-Eyes. All he said was that there's some war going on out there in... well, in space... and it made its way here. Then there's that thing that the minitia are looking for. This 'Linious' guy. I want to know what this is all about. What the hell is Linious? Whatever or whoever it is, those creatures think they can give them power. So, what is it? Or who is it? What's so special about this guy? And also, who exactly is Athriel representing in all this? I know he said that he's against the minitia, but I'd like it if he was a bit more specific."

"Vic's got a good point." said Dan, "If we're being put through all of this, then we should know a bit more as to why."

"And what about your part in this?" Marceline asked, looking at her husband, "If this guy, Athriel, showed up in our house to warn you, then obviously he has something in mind for you. I think I want to know about that, too."

"Same." Victor agreed, "To be honest, with all that's been going on, that little detail has kinda been placed on the backburner for the past few days."

Without warning, Daniel's focus turned from the conversation, "Hey, over there. Soldiers."

The others turned and saw a small group of men in camouflage fatigues making their way into the center of the crowd. Marceline called her children back, not wanting them to get too close to the new arrivals. As the children fell back to her, the leader of the soldiers began to recite a speech to the civilians, "Everybody listen up. We're here to make an announcement."

The crowd cleared out at the center, giving some space between them and the armed men in the middle. All eyes were on the speaker.

"Commander Jason Pullano, the commanding officer of this convoy, is preparing a platoon of soldiers for an excursion into Harrisburg. He has ordered us to gather civilian volunteers – people who know the layout of the city or are at least in good physical condition. People with military experience are preferred, but not it's not a requirement."

From the audience, Victor and the others heard a murmur. Why should people volunteer? Wasn't it suicide to go into the city? Why civilians?

"The purpose of this mission is to resupply the convoy enough to bolt for the safe zone." The soldier went on, "I know that many of you have concerns about joining up. I'm here to tell you that volunteers will be rewarded for their actions. First off, more people means a better likelihood of success. We know that you're all probably tired of living in semi-trailers. If we can pull this off, we can get to DC faster and be done with this whole convoy mess even sooner."

The crowd's murmurs changed from discontent to mild curiosity. Still, the soldier went on, "Furthermore, those who volunteer for this mission, as well as the families of those who volunteer, will be given preferential treatment once we reach the safe zone. That means better housing and increased rations."

At this, the crowd erupted in conversation amongst itself. A small handful of civilians, mostly men, came forth and stood alongside the soldiers.

"If anyone else wants to join us," the leader began, "we'll be stationed at that tent over there until oh nine-hundred. After that, we're moving out." He turned to lead his men away, but one of the civilian volunteers put a hand on his shoulder. The warrior turned and listened as he said something into his ear. Then he turned back to the crowd and said, "In case you don't have a working clock on you, it's currently oh eight-fifteen."

The soldiers made their way for the tent, leaving two behind. These young men appeared to have their own, separate announcement to make, "We are looking for a Victor Roberts. Is Mister Roberts here?"

Victor's eyes widened as Marceline and Dan looked at him. What did they want with him? Did this have to do with Blue-Eyes?

"My God, what'd you do this time, Vic?" asked Dan.

"Wasn't me." he responded, raising a hand.

"What are you doing?" his wife asked. She grabbed at his arm, trying to lower it back down.

Victor pushed her hand away, "Hey, they want me for something. Least I can do is find out."

One of the soldiers gestured towards him, "Are you Victor?"

"That's me."

The men in uniform worked their way through the crowd, finding their place with Victor and his family. They looked even younger up close. Only boys.

"What's this about?" Victor asked.

"The commander has selected you to be a part of the mission into Harrisburg."

"Wait, you're drafting me?" Victor looked at the boys, surprised and admittedly horrified, "I thought you were just taking volunteers? I have a family to look after. You can't do this."

"No." Marceline growled, "You're not taking him."

"We're under orders, ma'am." said one of the soldiers.

"I'm sorry." said the other.

"Is there any way out of this?" Dan asked, putting a protective arm around his endangered friend.

"I'm afraid not, sir. This is the direct order of Commander Pullano."

"I wouldn't worry if I were you." said a new voice. The others turned and saw the glowing-eyed man, Athriel himself, approaching them, "After all, I'm going to be part of that mission, too. He'll be under my watchful eye."

The commander had ordered it, the soldiers were enforcing it, and even Athriel was there to ensure it. It was happening. Victor was going. The others were quiet, the man in question asking in a low voice, "So when do we leave?"

Athriel sighed, "Now, assuming you're ready." He didn't seem much more amused by the situation than the others. There was a look of disdain in his eyes, not towards Victor or the soldiers, but towards something else. Something that Victor couldn't figure out.

By now, it was clear that Victor belonged to the will of the commander. Marceline hugged her husband, kissed him and whispered, "Be safe."

"Don't worry, Vic." said Dan, "You got this."

Victor smiled and nodded. Then he turned to his children, "Be careful while I'm gone, you two. I'll be back before you know it."

"Don't worry." said Sammy, "I'll keep Uncle Dan out of trouble."

Victor laughed, "See, Danny? Why can't you be funny like that?" He hugged his children goodbye and then, just like that, he was gone.

He made is way for the soldiers' tent, trudging along at Athriel's side. "Don't worry." said the blue-eyed man, "Nothing bad will come to you."

* * *

By the hour's end, they were off. A battered military transport led the way, three semi-trucks following close behind. The transport was filled to the brim with soldiers. The only people who even had the space to move their arms were the driver and Athriel sitting beside him. As for the trucks, aside from a handful of volunteers, they were totally empty. This left plenty of room for whatever they could find in the city. Victor stood in the back of one of these trailers beside Private Athens, who Athriel insisted would accompany him on the mission. Together, they watched the world through old bullet holes in the side of their cage.

The mini convoy crawled its way past the houses and small businesses, into the city itself. The land was one of concrete and ash, even more so than the encampment. Burnt out cars had to be pushed out of the way by the leading transport, causing sharp groans of metal on metal and the tearing of melted tires ripping from the asphalt. The buildings were no better. Whatever hadn't been blasted away or burned to ruin still stood in pieces. Colorless structures, caked in the dust and debris of their fallen brethren, looked on sullenly at the passing caravan. They were memorials to the people who once called these barren remains their home.

The trailer stopped. A general murmur amongst the civilians echoed in the metal chamber. Then there was the sound of a latch unhooking and the door rolling upward. A bright light stung at eyes that had become accustomed to the dark. "Alright, come on out." called a voice from outside. Victor saw a group of soldiers standing at the end of the trailer. A couple of them had dropped their weapons and were reaching their arms out, ready to help people to the pavement.

They were in the city, but Victor couldn't make out where. A market? An industrial park? There weren't enough surviving landmarks to tell. Looking ahead, he saw that the street was blocked off by a river of vehicles standing bumper to bumper, all in ruin, some still aflame. An impasse, Victor figured. The caravan could go no farther. They would be walking from here onward.

Eight men stayed with the transport and the trailers. Four soldiers and four civilians. The rest followed Athriel. Blue-Eyes was at the front of the platoon, walking side-by-side with a civilian navigator. Victor, being more towards the back of the group, made a point of keeping himself near Private Athens.

Smoke loomed over them in a thick fog. Those with

158

bandanas or spare cloth were saved from the stinging, choking fumes. Most, however, were left to cough and heave. At one point when the smoke seemed dangerously thick, Athens tapped on Victor's shoulder, "Here, take this." In his hand, he held a wrinkled bandana. Victor took it and went to tie it around his face, shielding his nose and mouth. "Don't tell people where you got that." said Athens, "I don't want people begging for 'em."

It was an hour before they got to their destination. Not surprisingly, it didn't look any different from the rest of the city. Bleak and desolate. Wreckage and ruin.

"There ain't nothing here." One of the volunteers moaned, "Nothing but the same old bull."

"Did anybody really expect it to be there?" asked another.

A woman next to Victor asked, "Where are we gonna go now?" He didn't know if she was speaking to him or just thinking aloud. Either way, he didn't answer.

He instead peered at Athriel. The man with the glowing eyes seemed far from phased by the situation, almost as if he'd been expecting it. After a moment of what looked like solitary thought, the alien turned and approached his navigator. Victor couldn't make out much of their exchange, but he had an idea of what they were saying.

"I'd appreciate it if you could make an outline of some other places that we could stop by at."

"I can get you several. Give me a moment."

"They have to be within walking distance. We don't have all day."

Victor turned his attention to the soldiers. They were setting up a small perimeter around the group, on guard against whatever may be out there amongst the rubble. It was a good idea, Victor thought.

With nothing to do but wait, Victor went to sit on a piece of crumbled wall. Before long, he was joined by another group member. Athens. They sat in silence for a time. Victor wasn't sure of what to say, or if he should say anything at all.

"I hate days like this." the soldier told him, "Everything's all about hurrying up and waiting around."

"That your way of making small talk?" Victor asked, "Because, if so…"

"I think I'm allowed to be bored, sir."

"We're behind enemy lines, private."

"And we're armed to the teeth and haven't seen anything since we got here."

"I don't mean to sound rude, but shouldn't you be with the other soldiers in your unit?"

"I lost most of my unit at Fort Drum. Besides, I was brought out here to keep you company."

"Or to be my meat shield if things go south."

"I'm praying for the former."

They fell in to silence for a time. When they returned, it was with Victor's words, "Were you scared?"

"Hmm?"

"At Fort Drum. Were you scared?"

"I'd like to pretend that I wasn't. But in reality, I'm lucky that I used the can before everything went down."

"Is that how you feel now?" Victor asked.

"I…" It appeared that Athens wasn't sure of how to respond, "I'm still scared. Definitely. But it's a little easier." The soldier looked at Victor with curious eyes, as if he were trying to get a read on the civilian, "Try not to psych yourself out. Odds are, nothing will happen. And if something does go down, you'll have all these people helping you out."

"And don't forget Blue-Eyes over there." Victor added. He gave a light smile, trying not to let his fear show through.

"If only half of the stories are true, then we'll be fine with him around."

After another minute of uncomfortable silence, the perceivable tension between the two was broken. A local — the one who Athriel assigned to navigate the mission — returned to him with a map filled with lines, stars and crossed-out patches. "I've got the path laid out." she said.

Victor and Athens watched as the glowing-eyed man

160

came over and took the map in his hands. After a second of study, he turned back to her, "You can get us to all these places?"

"Absolutely."

"Even this warehouse?"

"I used to work there."

"Scouts say that its area didn't burn as heavily as the rest of the city. Good work. You may have just saved this supply run."

Victor and Athens exchanged looks. They knew their break was over. It was time to continue.

"Well, I guess that's it." The latter climbed to his feet. He then turned, smiled and offered a hand to the young father, "Shall we?"

* * *

With Travis gone, Jane was left to nothing but her own thoughts. When he was around, he at least tried to get her mind off anything bad. Now he was away, gone off to the city on some fool's errand. Would he even come back?

Until they got to the convoy, the grave reality of their situation never truly struck Jane. Whatever she saw was like something from a terrible dream. It wasn't real. It couldn't be. Sooner or later, things would go back to normal and everybody that she loved would be fine. She would be fine.

Then Tom died. He died and she watched it happen. Now everything was real. They were in real danger. At any moment, someone that she loved could be torn from her. Someone like her mother or her father or Olivia or Travis. Someone like Tom.

Her mind always went back to the thought of her uncle – all that he had meant to her, all that she had meant to him. As a baby, he would accompany her to the park when her parents didn't have the time. She said her first words to him. It was his own name. She didn't say "momma" or "daddy" or "yes" or "hi". It was "Tom". He would pick her up from play dates and get her to school and take her out to lunch and so much more.

One summer when she was eleven, her parents got into a huge fight. She never found out what it was they were arguing about, but that never mattered to her. What mattered was how her uncle handled the situation. The whole house turned into such a hostile environment and, in response, Uncle Tommy took her and Olivia over to his home. They lived there for about a week. They stayed up every night watching movies and talking about anything that came to mind. He treated them like the children that he never had.

That was it. Jane couldn't dwell on this anymore. She had already spent the past three days in the back of a rickety semi, doing nothing but sobbing and reminiscing. To stay there would do nothing but hurt her. She had to get out.

Jane decided to go for a walk around the truck city. In all their time camped out on that stretch of highway, she had only left the trailer for things like food or when Travis forced her to go out. Never had she taken the time to explore the place on her own.

Her legs were unsteady from lack of use, her eyes red and aching from crying. But one look around showed her that she was not the only one. Several other women and men had looks of their own despair painted across their faces. It comforted her in some strange way to see their sadness. At least she wasn't alone. Some people followed her with their eyes while others looked away, refusing to meet her gaze.

After a time, Jane came upon a scene of commotion and entertainment. Several groups were clustered around each other, all engaged in their own intense discussions. A crowd of children looked to be playing tag, their little feet scurrying from place to place and their laughter piercing the air with high shrieks and bubbling giggles. It was a sight that she desperately needed. One of the children, a little boy of around five years with light skin and brown hair, tripped over the shoe of one of the adults. Jane was expecting him to start crying, but instead he just got up and kept running. An

162

onlooker called out to him, "Go on, Zack! You've got this!"

Jane looked towards the voice. Sitting on the edge of a trailer were two people. Both were rather young, but older than herself. One was a hulking figure of a man, with pale skin and blue eyes. He must have been six and a half feet tall. The other was a slender woman, equally pale, with long, brown hair and hazel eyes. The latter's face struck a tone of familiarity with Jane, though it took a moment for her to place where she had first seen it. That moment was time enough for those hazel eyes to turn and lock with Jane's.

The woman waved with the enthusiasm of a friend, "Oh, hi." Of course. This was the woman from her and Travis' first night in the convoy. Marceline. She had helped them get accustomed to the place and made them feel welcomed. She even listened to the two of them mourn for Tom. How could anyone forget her?

Her greeting compelled Jane to join them by the trailer, "Hello."

"How are you doing?" Marceline asked her.

"Oh, I'm fine." Jane answered, "I'm, uh, doing a little better than before."

"That's really good." said the other woman.

Jane pointed to the man beside them and asked, "And who's this guy?"

"This is Danny."

"Nice to meet you." The man said, extending a large hand. Jane took it, expecting a grip of stone. Instead, he was soft – not something befitting someone of his great stature.

"Is this your boyfriend? Husband?"

"Oh hell no." said Marceline, waving a hand and laughing.

Danny laughed as well, "She wishes." The comment earned him a look from Marceline

"He's just a family friend. Vic, my husband, is out in Harrisburg with the platoon. He was, well, drafted this morning."

"Oh, I see." Jane nodded.

163

"Where's your boyfriend at? The little British kid?"

"He's with the platoon, too."

"And what's his name, again? Trevor? Travis?"

"Travis."

"Sorry." Marceline said, visibly embarrassed by her mistake, "It's just, you know, I haven't spoken to either of you since we first met."

Jane forced a light smile, "I understand. It's fine. I mean I just mistook big guy over here for your hubby."

Marceline smiled back and shrugged, "So neither of us are on our A-game today."

"Who's this?" asked a loud, high voice. Jane turned and saw a little girl standing in front of them. She looked to be about eight years old, with light brown hair a dimpled grin. Jane recognized this girl as one of the children playing in the crowd.

"Sammy, this is Jane." explained Marceline, "She's a friend of ours."

"Hi, Jane." said the girl, smiling at the young Pennsylvanian woman, "I'm Sam." She walked up to the three of them, stopping just short of Jane. Her smile grew malicious as she presented her finger and tapped her new friend on the arm. "You're it!" she shouted, turning and running back into the crowd.

Jane looked up at Marceline, still sitting on the edge of the trailer with her friend. "Well, you heard her." She said, "You're it. Just make sure that Sammy stays where we can see her. Okay?"

Jane nodded, "Of course." Her face pulled itself into its first real smile in days.

* * *

For an hour or so, the group in Harrisburg followed Athriel in relative silence. Eventually, they came upon their first stop – a partially burnt-out warehouse surrounded by rubble. The windows were shattered, the roof collapsed. Fires had destroyed much of its stock, but enough was spared. It took some time, but they managed to carry a good amount of the canned food and other supplies out. They walked the goods over a handful of city blocks, taking several shortcuts through some dilapidated and ruined buildings until they got back to the trucks. Once there, Athriel allotted them a fifteen-minute break. As he put it, there was no use dragging soldiers through enemy lines if they were too exhausted to defend themselves. It seemed he was so certain that they'd have to – at some point, at least.

By the time they got back into the city for another trip, it was early afternoon. This venture, however, proved to be more difficult than the previous one. They came across a number of dead-ends in the twists and turns of the broken city. The burnt-out cars and odd pieces of rubble restricted their movements through this great urban graveyard, at times almost forcing them into the walls of ruin.

Of course, none of this was good for morale. The civilians began to grow weary of these constant detours and backtracking. None of it seemed to bother Athriel, though. Neither did their hushed remarks, which Victor felt the glowing-eyed man heard every word of.

Athriel spent much of the journey talking to his navigator. Every few minutes or so, he would turn his head to scan the crowd behind them, and then go back to their endless discussion. At one point, he appeared to be giving her an order of sorts. She gave a nod and, a few minutes later, got his attention and pointed to a certain point on the map.

The day went on and they worked their way further into the city. As they rounded yet another corner, one of the civilians groaned, "Another dead-end. Doesn't this guy know where he's going?"

A second civilian whispered to the first, "It ain't that easy and you know it. The whole city's collapsed in on itself."

"Not this neighborhood." said the first, "This place is still sorta... here."

This time, Athriel didn't stop and redirect the group.

Instead, he marched them to the very end, where they were surrounded on three sides by buildings, the only open space being the road they came from. There, he stopped in his tracks and began to look around at the fragmented structures around them. Everything was packed in together, with no room between buildings. What's more, the whole street seemed almost untouched by the bombs. While all the windows were broken and small amounts of debris littered the street below, few walls had actually collapsed.

"What are we doing here?" asked a voice from the crowd. Others began to murmur in nervous concurrence.

Athriel turned to address the group, his face as unreadable as ever. Was he annoyed at the constant redirections? Irritated by these civilians and their criticisms? Worried about revealing their position to the minitia who controlled the city? Did he feel anything at all?

He took a breath and began to speak, "If everybody could listen for a moment. I have an announcement." All voices silenced but his own, "Over the past hour, four of our people have gone missing from the group." Uneasy whispers erupted in the crowd, but were again brought to silence when he raised his hand, "And now," he continued, "the rubble around the city seems to have led us to several of these precise spots. Dead ends, cut off from any easy escape route. What's happening here is pretty obvious to me. But in case you don't have as much experience with these situations, I'll explain. We're being hunted. The way I see it, there is no point in retreating just yet. They have no reason to let any of us out of the city alive."

His words made Victor's blood run cold. He figured that they were being hunted since the moment they arrived, but was Blue-Eyes really going to keep them in the city, knowing that they were about to be attacked?

"So," Athriel continued, "that's why we're here on this street instead of halfway back to the trucks. If the enemy wants to have any more of us, then it won't be with our backs turned. It won't be with us on the run. They will take us with nothing less than our full attention."

Athriel had the platoon set themselves up in a perimeter around the civilians. Several men were told to hide explosives in nearby buildings and along the street. He ordered these "explosive experts", as he called them, to detonate their devices on his command only. The way Athriel explained it, threatening to destroy the structures around the group would make the minitia less keen on using them. Also, if the enemy did still use the buildings, he could just as easily bring them down on their forces.

The silence that followed bred a new kind of tension. One that Victor had never before known. The eerie stillness was enhanced by the layer of smoke and ash that filled the city air. There they were, cornered, cut off, unable to see more than a few feet in any direction. Standing, listening, waiting for those creatures to strike. Waiting for death. A level of panic began to take hold of Victor. He looked around, scanning the buildings and the open street in front of them. They all did. Nobody knew where those things were going to come from. Nobody, except perhaps Athriel himself.

A scream. A pained cry coming from inside the group. Then it was chaos. Like a flood, they came forth. Shadowy figures lunging from broken windows and collapsing rooftops. The dark shapes fell like rain amongst the crowd. Shrieks. Screams. Gunshots. The sounds of bodies tearing apart, thrown around like ragdolls.

Athriel turned to his explosive experts. At his command, they detonated their toys and brought down half of the neighborhood. Screeches and wails filled the air with the blasts and rush of debris. Brick and mortar flew out into the street, but somehow stopped short of hitting the soldiers.

It occurred to Victor why Blue-Eyes had held off for so long. He waited for the buildings to fill with minitia, so as to kill as many as possible in the explosions. Then, with debris everywhere and a ring blasted in the enemy ranks, those minitia who made it into the platoon were now outnumbered, surrounded and cut off from their friends. The soldiers made quick work of the stragglers and reformed the line.

As the dust began to settle, Athriel raised his voice, shouting to his fighters, "They are not demons! They are not invincible! They are insects! They bleed like insects! They are crushed like insects!" Victor listened to these words. He wanted desperately to believe him. As he stood there in the crowd, waiting for the inevitable second wave, all he could think of was that night in the bus. How inhumanly strong they were. How they almost tore him and his entire family apart without ever being seen. How, if it weren't for Athriel, he and his loved ones would have died there on that road.

The line was reformed. Many of the people under Athriel's command were inspired by his words. Even more found hope in the wails of dying minitia in the remains of the exploded buildings. These things could bleed. They could die just like anyone else. The thought pervaded through their human minds as they waited with bated breath for the next attack.

Another long silence fell over the place, only to be broken, like the last one, with a sudden burst of shrieks and gunshots. Without warning, the man to Victor's left dropped with a terrifying scream. The dark form of a minitia had taken his place, at once turning its attention to Victor himself.

It was then that he could at last see these things for what they were. The creature before him was human enough, standing on two legs, with as many arms. It had a head and a torso and hands and feet, but that was where the similarities ended. It stood hunched over, with long limbs and an absurd, almost sickly thin frame. Each of its blood-drenched hands held six talon-like appendages, four acting like fingers and two positioned like thumbs. It also appeared to be covered in a sort of exoskeleton – dark, coarse, interlocking plates of some bone-like material that left few openings to the soft flesh underneath. Its features were more monster than man. The beast's face was rigid and cruel. Its mouth laid open, seemingly unhinged, exposing row upon row of teeth. It was a demon, spattered with blood, staring at Victor with crimson eyes that reminded him only of hellfire. Though it was an inch or two shorter than him, it was no less terrifying to look upon. This thing was bred for nothing but fear and death.

Before Victor could defend himself, the creature struck him, sending him toward a pile of crumbled brick and broken cement. He landed on his side, smashing his shoulder and head against the wreckage. Pain screamed through him. As he looked back, the dreaded monster lunged forth. As it was about to reach him, a burst of rounds slammed into the side of its head, breaking the shell and spraying a black fluid over Victor. He peered over, hoping to catch a glimpse of his savior, but saw nothing but a thick, swarming mass of blood and bodies.

By now, the whole street had erupted in battle. Soldiers struggled to hold the line against an onslaught of fiendish monsters. The demons tore into their ranks, throwing people around and cutting them apart like it was a game. Some of them were feeding on their kills, ripping off limbs and faces and gnawing at the meat.

Victor forced himself over broken corpses and stained rubble. His hands and knees became red and gray with blood and ash. The carnage was unimaginable. He had to escape. He looked over among the cracked buildings on the side of the street. One of them seemed to be somewhat intact. Even the front door was still standing, damaged as it was. It didn't matter. Those walls were his protection.

Scrambling to his feet, Victor made a run for the door. A horrid roar came from behind. One of those hellish screeches. Victor turned and, without a moment's hesitation, fired several shots. The minitia dropped in front of him, lifeless. No time to stop, Victor turned back and charged for the door, grasping the handle and praying that it was unlocked. To his relief, it was. He threw the door open and sprinted through, slamming it shut behind him.

Victor crouched down and held himself against the door. He remained there for a time, panting, his heart pounding in his ears, his entire body shaking. Victor tried to take back control of himself as his mind worked to make sense of what was happening. A battle. A full battle had erupted all around him. And he ran.

His head was throbbing. Victor put a hand to where it hit the cement, finding fresh blood on his fingertips. With a hit like that, he guessed that he was concussed too. What could he do? He didn't have the supplies to stop the bleeding. Maybe one of the shelves in the store had something for him. He wanted to look for something to use, but he was paralyzed by the terrible sounds of a war, separated from him only by a simple rickety door.

Victor thought of his family. He wanted nothing more than to see Marceline again. To hold his children. In this time when he was so near those creatures of death, he would have given anything to see them again. A tear began to run down his cheek, but he brushed it away. He couldn't let himself give into this madness anymore. Victor Roberts would see his family again. He had to. No other option could be allowed to remain in his head. This resoluteness calmed him, and after a time he could control his shaking.

After several minutes, the fighting seemed to quiet as though the combatants were moving away from the street. At last, Victor could breathe some semblance of relief. With the gunshots growing more and more distant, his ringing ears could listen closer to his immediate surroundings. There was a sound. A quiet sobbing, seeming to come from one of the aisles in the store. Quiet, but still far too loud. What if those things out there heard the noise? He had to make it stop. As he inched around the corner and into the aisle, Victor caught sight of the culprit.

It was a civilian from the platoon, same as him. He was young; at least half a decade younger than himself. A kid, really. Nevertheless, he seemed to be somewhat taller than Victor, with a slender body, light, Anglo-esque skin and short brown hair. The boy was curled into a ball on the floor with his rifle at his feet, shaking and crying. He could so easily capture the fatal attention of one of those monsters. Victor

170

knew that it had to stop, one way or another. So, raising a hand, he reached out towards the civilian, "Shh, shh. Come on. Crying won't do any good at a time like this. We have to stay focused."

The kid didn't look up at him. He just kept sobbing and whimpering, "We're gonna die. Oh God, we're gonna die."

"No, we're not." said Victor, "We're gonna be fine. You know why?" The kid made no response, so Victor kept on, "We're too damn good to die. No bullshit oversized bug is gonna take us out. We're too good for that."

After another moment of sobbing without any response, Victor asked, "You got a name, kid?"

Through uncontrollable shaking, Victor heard the words, "My n-name i-is Travis."

"Really nice to meet you, Travis. I'm Victor." After waiting for a response, he went on, "Listen, Travis. I'm gonna get you out of this. You hear me?"

"How?" Travis asked, turning to reveal the depth of his fear across his face. Absolute terror had overcome him. Victor felt compelled to calm the boy – to bring him down from this state of panic.

"Well first, let's wait for things to die down a bit out there. Then we'll work on getting back to the others and out of the city."

Travis shook his head and clutched his knees tighter, "T-there won't be any others. They're g- They've killed them all. We'll all die. Just like Tom. Just like Tom. T-they're going kill everybody."

Victor inched closer to his new companion, "Now I don't know who Tom is. But you have one thing that he didn't. And that's me. You've got me here with you. I've got you. Okay? I won't let anything happen to you. Travis? Travis, listen to me. You got a family back at the camp? Someone waiting for you?"

"J-Jane." Travis muttered, "My girlfriend. Jane's waiting. Oh God."

"Just think about her, then." said Victor, "Think about

Jane. Seeing her again. Holding her. You're gonna get through this. I'm not gonna let you lay down and die. You're gonna stay alive. You have to. For her."

Travis voiced no response, but his sobbing quieted. Victor inched his way close enough to put a hand on the boy's trembling shoulder.

"You hear me, kid?" Victor asked, giving him a light push on the shoulder.

"Yes, yes, I hear you."

"Then say it back to me."

"I'll stay alive." Travis whimpered, "I have to. For her."

"And don't you forget that."

They waited in silence for the fighting to die down. The screams and gunshots were further apart. Soon enough, they were only terrible echoes in the hollow streets. The battle was moving away from them as whatever winning side broke and routed their enemy. Victor could only pray that his fellow humans had won.

It was a war zone outside. People were dying. And while yes, the skirmishes were steadily moving away from the scene, Victor still didn't feel comfortable crawling through the ruins with the enemy so close by. While he wanted to leave the store and find Blue-Eyes, he and this Travis kid would have to wait until the time seemed right.

Victor decided that talking would help the time pass by, "So..." he began, "Where are you from? I mean you sound kind of English." There was no response. After a while, Victor figured that Travis didn't want to talk. With a sigh, he readied himself for a long afternoon of silence.

Suddenly, the kid spoke, "You asked if I had someone waiting for me."

Victor raised an eyebrow, "It speaks."

"What about you?" Travis continued, either ignoring or plain not registering the joke, "What do you have waiting for you? I mean, with the way you've been, there has to be something driving you."

"My wife." Victor answered without a moment's

172

hesitation. He then added, "And my best friend. My only friend, really. And my kids."

"Tell me about them." said Travis.

"Well my wife – her name is Marceline. We always call her Marci, though. It pisses her off." Victor gave a small laugh, "She's my one and only. The only one who'll put up with my crap."

Travis furrowed his brow, "You don't seem too bad to me."

Victor scoffed, "Yeah? Get to know me a little more."

"Anyway, go on. Tell me about this friend of yours."

"Danny. We've known each other since we were little. The guy's my best friend – and the godfather to my kids. I got him out of Boston before..."

"Before what happened." Travis finished, his voice low. They were quiet for a moment, silently acknowledging that their distraction from all the ash and ruin had just come back around. It was as if everything anybody talked about would always make its way back to this. It was annoying – painful, really – being reminded of all that was going on when all they wanted was some small escape.

With nothing else to say, Travis decided to move the conversation forward, "And you said you've got kids?"

"Two of them. A girl and a boy."

Travis sat up, "But you look thirty. They've got to be young ones. How old are they? If you don't mind me asking."

"Sammy's gonna be nine in a few weeks."

Victor could tell that his companion's curiosity was growing. Was it strange in the UK as well to have children that young? As it was, it was a somewhat new taboo in the States. With heavy amounts of schooling as a near-necessity, young adults often focused on college or other work. Most held off on starting families until they had the means to settle down, usually in their late twenties or early thirties.

"How old were you when you had them?" Travis asked.

"About your age." Victor answered, clueing him in on the taboo, "Maybe a little younger. We weren't planning on

173

having them that young. I can tell you that. It just- "

"...Sort of happened." Travis finished.

Victor nodded.

"That must have been difficult." remarked Travis.

"I had to give up on a lot of things. College, a career... Marci and I had been together since high school, so marrying her wasn't much of a problem. She went back and got her degree, but it just didn't work out that way for me." Victor sighed, "We were young. We were stupid. I was stupid. I made a lot of mistakes back then."

"Are you implying your kids are mistakes?" Travis asked.

"No, no. Of course not. I'd never call them that."

"Good." said Travis. He realized that he had touched a sensitive topic, but he would be damned if he didn't follow through, "Being accidents doesn't make them mistakes. They need their daddy. And you need them."

Victor nodded and voice went quiet, "I do."

"You'll make it out of this. Same as me. And you'll do it for them. And for your wife."

Victor nodded, letting a soft smile come over his face. After a moment of relative stillness, he realized that it was his turn to ask a question, "And what about Jane? What's she like?"

Travis looked downward, "We're nothing special, really. Been together for a few years. After a while, she came to live with me in London, but we still sometimes come back here to visit her family."

"What brought you here this time?" Victor asked.

"Her sister was marrying some fellow."

"That must have been pretty cool." said Victor, "Was it?"

"I suppose. It gave me a lot to think about."

"Like what?"

"Like..." Travis paused, not knowing how to explain himself, "Jane and I... We just get along so well together. She's always been so down to Earth and intelligent and

174

giving. She's everything that I've ever wanted in a partner. Someone that I can really depend on. And when I saw Olivia in that dress, walking down the aisle like that, it made me think about her... How I think I might want to be with her for a long time."

Travis blushed, finding himself in the situation, hiding in a store and talking about his love life with some stranger, "I don't know why I'm even telling you this."

"No, no. It's fine." Victor assured him, "It's adorable, really. You should do it. Ask her."

"Maybe I will." said Travis, with a red-faced grin.

They talked for a time. Then, when the world outside seemed calm enough, they devised a plan. They would work through the ruins as fast and silent as possible, covering each other along the way. Then they'd try to find either Athriel or one of the soldiers – anybody that could help them get out of the city and back to the convoy. It wasn't much of an idea, but it was what they had to work with.

* * *

Marceline and Dan sat carefree in the back of the trailer, their legs dangling off the edge, watching the few remaining children play amongst themselves. Most of them had stopped playing tag long ago, Zack among them. He had come to his mother in an exhausted state, and spent the past half hour napping by her side, his small head resting on her thighs. She watched him as he slept, his five-year-old face so relaxed and peaceful.

"I can't wait to finally start moving again." said Marceline.

"Same here." Dan agreed, "Do you think they'll have actual beds at the safe zone?"

"This again?"

"Hey, I know we've talked about this before, but I'm really hoping they do. I'm a big guy. Gravity hurts. I need something for my back and these metal floors won't do."

175

Marceline sighed, "Well I hope so, too." Dan said something else to her, but she didn't hear. She had turned her attention back to the children. Something wasn't right.

"Where's Sammy?" she asked.

Dan scanned the area, "No clue."

Before Marceline could say anything else, the booms and echoes of rifles sounded in the distance. The noise went on for some time. After a couple of minutes of ceaseless gunfire, they began to grow concerned. Such skirmishes were common in the past few days, but they normally only lasted a few seconds. This one, however, showed no sign of slowing down. The shots grew faster, more frantic. Somebody at the wall, a soldier, screamed. Another then called out, "Inside! Inside!"

"Where's Sam?" Marceline shrieked.

Zack stirred next to her, "Mommy, what's going on?" She held him close as he tried to get up.

A handful of men and women in uniforms rushed past the trailer, pushing their way through the crowd of civilians. One of them shouted to the bystanders, "Get out of here! Go to the other side of the camp! This ain't a drill! Minitia got over the walls!"

Marceline and Dan exchanged looks of sheer terror. Minitia? Now?

Daniel put a hand on Marceline's shoulder as they both climbed off the edge of the trailer, "Go. I'll get Sam." he said.

"No!" cried Marceline, "She's my baby! I'm her mother!"

"You're Zack's, too." said Daniel, "And he needs you. We can't have anything happen that'll make him grow up without his mom. Go. Take him and find someplace. I'll get Sam."

Marceline wanted to fight, but she knew that he was right. Zack needed her. "Hurry." she told him, her body trembling, "Find my girl."

* * *

"Sammy?" Jane called, "Where are you?" She ambled between two trailer trucks, looking for her little friend. As she gazed around for some clue, an odd sight made her stop in her tracks. Poking out from under one of the trailers were the tips of tiny fingers. Jane smiled and walked further on, calling out in a sing-song fashion, "Where are you?"

When Jane passed, Sammy climbed out from under the trailer. "Here I am!" she cried, leaping onto her friend's back. She laughed as Jane nearly toppled over in surprise.

"You're too good at this." Jane told her.

"Now it's your turn."

Their focus was quickly stolen by a nearby scream. They looked over towards the edge of the encampment just as a dark figure leapt onto the wall of trucks. Another followed. Then another. The guards fired their rifles and a couple of the beasts fell, but more kept on coming to replace the dead. They were swarming the wall.

"Enemy in the camp!" a soldier shouted.

Jane looked back at Sam. The little girl was trembling. A loud, crashing sound in the direction of the shooting made her jump and whimper. They looked over and saw that the minitia had come together and tossed one of the trucks several feet. Now there was a hole in the wall large enough for them to pour through.

Jane knelt and hugged Sam to calm her, "Look at me. Samantha, look at me. I need you to hide again. Okay? Can you do that?"

Sam nodded.

"Okay, just hide under that truck again and be really quiet."

"What about you?" Sammy asked, a tear starting to roll down her cheek.

"I'll find a place to hide, too. Don't worry about me. Just focus on you. Now go."

* * *

Victor Roberts and Travis Norwich kept low as they passed through the crumbling city. They stayed close to each other, lest they become separated in the smoky haze. Time and again, they heard distant shots and faint, echoing shrieks of minitia, always out of sight but ever present. Every time they overheard an encounter between their comrades and those monsters, they would stop and go silent, listening for any sign that their side had won. Often times, it wasn't the case.

Eventually, the two men came upon an entirely demolished city block. Nothing remained but a massive pile of rubble – a hill of broken concrete and brick and steel.

"Should we go 'round?" Travis whispered.

Victor surveyed the area, "No." he answered, "If we go around, it'll make us more exposed. We're already covered in soot. Maybe we can blend in with the debris."

"So up and over?"

"Up and over."

They scaled the hill of shattered brick and glass, making sure not to disturb the countless unstable pieces at their hands and feet. Victor was the first to reach the summit, where he halted and dropped into a prone stance, "I wanna get a view of what's around us." Staying low, he put his hands over the top of his field of vision, blocking out what little of the sun's rays got through the smoke.

Several other buildings had been laid to waste, letting him see a few hundred feet ahead from some angles, but this still wasn't enough. Victor climbed to the highest point of the rubble pile: a mostly intact wall that had fallen on its side, with one end raised high in the air. Travis followed. Now, they could at least see over the tops of some of the remaining structures. Around them, Victor saw nothing but the battered hell that he had spent all day traversing. At first it looked like a still-life of an urban graveyard, but movement soon caught his eye. A lone minitia was crawling through the rubble on three limbs, while holding something long and black in the

178

fourth. In front of the beast, a shape poked out from around a cracked stone block. The minitia ducked behind its own cover as the shape fired off three shots at it.

A soldier. It was a soldier. Victor looked back at the minitia and watched as it took the long, black object and fired a shot back at the human. The creature was using a sniper rifle, probably taken from a human's corpse. How it knew to use it, Victor didn't want to guess. The thought of these beasts possessing human-level intellect scared him to his core.

"Are you a good shot?" he asked.

"I've never tried." said Travis.

Victor nodded and, taking a deep breath for courage, lifted his rifle from the debris. "I'm gonna try to hit that thing."

"From here?"

"It's not that far, and I've gotta try."

"You'll draw them to us." said Travis.

That fact stopped Victor, who was midway through adjusting his aim. He lowered his weapon and looked over to his partner, "You're right. So, what should we do?"

"Let's try and get closer. Maybe distract it. That other guy has a gun."

"Then what if those shots are attracting more of them right now? We don't want to be down there when they show up."

"We'll have a third guy on our side. A soldier who can help us get out of here if things get too heavy."

"You're putting a lot of faith in that guy." Victor thought for a moment, pondering over the options, "Fine. We'll do it your way. I come in from the side. You, from the back. We'll surround it."

With that, the two made their way down the slope of the hill, onto the street below. They jogged towards the site, keeping low and staying as quiet as they could. When the time came, Travis broke off to circle around and catch the bug from behind. It was all going to plan. Victor was no more than ten yards away when the monster turned and saw him. It let out a shriek and took aim. Victor's eyes went wide. He ducked and rolled to the side, out of the rifle's line of fire. The minitia stood up and took aim again, this time with Victor helpless on the ground. As shots rang out, he fully expected to die there, cowering on his knees.

But he didn't. The minitia dropped to the ground, bleeding from its twisted, cracking torso. Travis ran over and helped him to his feet, "You okay?"

"Been better." Victor answered, pulling himself up onto shaking legs.

The lone soldier clambered out from behind his cover. He waved at them. "Thanks for the help." He shouted as he approached. This young, uniformed man looked familiar.

"Private Athens?"

"Mister Roberts?" The Private's eyes widened, "Holy hell, you're alive!" His arms reached out and took Victor in a tight hug, "What are the odds that we'd find each other in this mess? Eh?"

Through his fear, Victor forced a smile, "What are the odds of an alien attack?"

"Good point." Athens' face changed, as if those words had brought him back to the battle at hand. He looked at Travis, then back at Victor. "We have to get out of the city."

"Our thoughts, exactly." said Victor, "Where's Blue-Eyes?"

"Probably leading people back to the trucks." Athens answered, "C'mon. I think I know where we are. I'll get us back."

* * *

It was some time before Victor, Travis and Athens got to the outskirts of the city. By the time they were in sight of the rendezvous point, all but one of the semi-trucks had left. The one remaining was crowded by a number of soldiers and armed civilians. As they drew closer, they broke into a sprint. When faces became clearer, they noticed that Athriel himself was among those waiting.

The trek back to the encampment was a long and quiet one. In the dark, echoing cage of the truck, there wasn't much to do besides think over the events back in the city. The few people that spoke only talked about their injuries or how they wished to see their loved ones back at the convoy. Nobody exchanged war stories. Nobody pretended to be fine. Most of these people had never seen battle before. Even for those rare few who had, it was a difficult thing to grasp. All that chaos. All that death. At least it was over now. As Athriel reassured them, they had delivered enough food and fuel to take the convoy directly to the safe zone.

At last, the truck stopped. The world outside those bleak walls had become loud and frantic. Victor heard people shouting, running, crying. Soldiers ran down the sides of the trailer, their shadows racing over bullet holes in the steel. As the door to the trailer flew open, a soldier at the threshold yelled into the big metal box, "The convoy was attacked!"

A commotion came over the group. "The convoy was hit!" the soldier repeated, "We gotta help! C'mon! Your families are in there!"

Victor and the others sprang to their feet and leapt from the back of the truck. They were terrified, fearing that after all that they had survived they would yet lose something this day. They ran towards the front entrance of the encampment, rifles in hand. Victor's mind raced over all that he'd left behind there. Marceline. Sammy. Zack. Danny. He should have never left. He hated himself for going off on the mission. He hated that officer who drafted him into it. Now, when the only people who mattered had needed him the most, he hadn't been there for them. Above all else, one thing repeated itself in his mind over and over: they had to be okay. They had to have found someplace far away from those things. They had to be okay. They had to be okay.

They crossed the first line of trucks and overturned buses that marked the outer walls of the camp. From the crowd sprinting in, several groups broke off, panning out in different directions to find their own loved ones. Victor and Travis remained close together, followed closely by Athens and Athriel. As one unit, they began clearing lanes, circling around trucks and trailers, weaving through any places that a minitia or a person could hide. They called out the names of Marceline, Jane, Samantha, Zack and Daniel. They shouted until their voices grew hoarse with panic.

They heard a clamor from the roof of one off the trailers. A dark figure raised itself up from above and, with a screech, pounced for Travis. A bolt of lightning dropped the beast before it got close enough to do harm. The three humans turned towards Athriel, who just shouted, "Keep moving!"

As they continued clearing the camp one section at a time, surviving minitia began to stir. Every one of them was brought down, either by a bullet or by Athriel. The blue-eyed man seemed less human than ever. Blasts of electricity flew from his fingertips, jumping through the air and frying bugs in their shells. Victor watched him summon a ball of compacted flame from nowhere. The inhuman man hurled his creation at a line of minitia, where it burst into a deadly inferno upon impact. These creatures, who had proven themselves to be stronger and faster than anything Victor had seen before, were nevertheless outmaneuvered and torn apart by Athriel's physical prowess. If his family wasn't at stake, Victor would have been greatly impressed.

When they passed the trailer that the Roberts family called home, he stopped. "Marceline!" he shouted, "Dan! Marci!"

A sound. Victor turned and watched as the door to the front of the semi-truck opened up. In the passenger's seat were two people: Marceline and little Zack.

"Oh my God." He cried, dropping his rifle and running to them. He helped Zack out of the truck and took him in a tight embrace.

"You're crushing me, Daddy." The little boy said.

"I'm sorry." said Victor, putting him down. He then

hugged Marceline, kissing her time and again on the cheeks and lips, "I'm sorry. I never should have gone. I should've been here."

Marceline hugged him back, "It's not your fault." She said, "Everything's okay. We're okay."

Victor pulled away from his wife and looked around. Tears were streaming down his face, making streaks in the dirt and ash that covered him. "Where's Sam?" he asked, "Where's our girl?"

* * *

"Jane!" cried Travis, "Jane, answer me!" When the others had stopped, he had kept running. They'd found their loved ones. Victor's wife and children were safe, but Jane Greene was nowhere to be seen. No face that passed him by was hers. No calling voice belonged to her. It seemed like she had vanished. Travis passed by his own trailer and called out to her name. Nobody answered. Panting, he ran on, looking in every direction for the one he loved.

He began to give into his most fearful thoughts. What if he never found her? What would he do? The thought of Jane was the only thing that got him through the battle in Harrisburg. He lived to see her again, to be with her. He needed to find her. She needed to be alive.

"Jane! Jane, come on! Where are you? Jane!"

He weaved in and out of lanes, between trucks and trailers, over countless splatters of blood and piles of broken bodies. Every time he passed by a corpse, he looked over its face. Every part of him was terrified that any one of them could have been her.

Travis rounded the edge of a trailer and stopped. In front of him, there knelt a little girl, not even ten years of age. She was crying, huddled over a broken shape on the ground. Slowly, Travis drew closer.

As he came nearer, the girl must have heard him. She turned her head, forcing out a shrill voice, "She hid me when they came... Told me not to come out."

Travis ignored her words. He crept on closer, trying to focus on the body's face. The girl was in the way. His heart beat fast and hard in his weary chest. His lungs dared not catch his breath. As he at last stood beside the crying girl, all doubt in his mind had vanished. In its place was utter disbelief. His throat ached with a pained sadness like he'd never felt before. The broken shape that the little girl was sobbing over was Jane Greene.

Chapter 8

Two days had passed since the battle in the streets of Harrisburg. Two days since the attack on the encampment, and yet the effects of these events still laid like a haze in the air. Even with so many thousands of people in the convoy, nobody shouted or laughed. Hardly anyone felt the need to say more than a few words at a time. Of all things, only the engines kept up their usual chatter. The masses rode southward in a state of quiet mourning.

The commander was by no means apart from this stillness; this stunned silence that had infected the group. Never before had he lost so many people at once. In one afternoon, over thirty soldiers and volunteers died in the city, with more than two thousand lost in the encampment. To the commander, these were two thousand lives that could have been saved if only he had used better judgment. Before, he had pushed for days of excursions into the city. Days that had cost hundreds of lives on their own. Then it was the commander who had demanded the final trek into the ruins, clearing the encampment of most of its remaining strength and leaving it vulnerable.

Their losses would have been even greater if it wasn't for his advisor. Without Athriel, they said that no one would have made it back from Harrisburg. Their losses would have been total. Without those survivors, it would have been that much harder to drive the last of the minitia away from the camp.

Now, Commander Pullano was sitting at his makeshift desk, stuck in the metal cage of a moving trailer. "I just got notification." he said, calling to Athriel, "We're about ten miles out from the safe zone." His voice was sullen. His face, pale.

"I figured you would be happier about that." Athriel commented.

"It's never a happy thing to lose so many people."

"True, but we need to focus on what matters. Because of this convoy, many lives have been saved. Many families left intact."

"Yeah? And exactly how many people did we save? Seven thousand? Eight? There are nearly a hundred million people living on the East Coast alone. What about the rest of them?"

Even against Pullano's irritable growling, Athriel seemed unfazed, "We'll gather them in future expeditions."

"If it isn't too late by then."

"Commander," Athriel began, "there are others like me in the safe zone. Others who share my... talents. Others who will gladly journey out and bring more of your people home." Athriel paused to lean in. He spoke more softly, "I guarantee you that we'll bring those millions in before the enemy can get to them. As many as we can. Whatever the bombs haven't already claimed will be brought to safety."

The commander was quiet for a time, considering the information laid out before him. He supposed that, if another expedition set out with better arms and more direction, then a good amount of those millions could be brought to the safe zone. Still though, millions more would die, without a doubt. Pullano wondered which number would be greater: the number of those saved or of those lost.

At last, the commander turned back to the glowing-eyed man, "So there are others like you."

"And more."

* * *

"Did you hear?" Dan asked, looking over to Marceline and Victor, "The soldiers, I mean." He was talking about the two sitting at the back of the trailer. A lantern sat between them, gifting the cage with light. What's more, one of them was holding a two-way radio.

"No. Sorry." said Marci. Victor only shook his head.

"That one just got off his radio." Dan explained, "We're close to the safe zone."

"Finally." said Victor.

Time passed and the trucks soon slowed to a stop-and-go pace. A while later, they finally halted for their last time. For the first time in days, Victor and the others heard real commotion from outside the trailer walls. There was shouting by the door, and a moment later it buckled and rolled upward. Soldiers stood on the other side, some of them reaching their arms out to help people from the vehicle. "Young, sick and wounded first." one of them called out. Victor and Marceline handed their children off to the men, who took them down from the trailer and onto the pavement below. Soon enough, their parents joined them.

Victor and the others noticed that they were on the top of a hill, allowing them a view of the safe zone that they had been waiting for so long. They looked out, and what they witnessed was nothing short of a bustling city. Many thousands of people scurrying in and out and around cracked buildings. To account for so many lives, every foot of space was put to use. In any place where some structure had collapsed or pieces had fallen off, the debris had been completely cleared out. On every sidewalk, street corner and empty lot, there stood clusters of tents. Each one seemed to house a family – entire communities, whole neighborhoods camping out on the cement. The streets themselves were filled with massive crowds of people and lines of military vehicles rolling past. Soldiers marched in formation, up and down the roads. Some were dressed in standard uniforms. Others were in various suits and full-body uniforms that Victor had never seen before. The place was surrounded by a makeshift wall of buses, vans and displaced rubble, dotted in some places with metal scaffolding and armed guards. From

187

what Victor could tell, this barricade extended around the entire city.

After perhaps fifteen minutes, the semi that carried the family drove off. Soldiers led the crowd of new civilians into the busy streets. One of them, a stocky sergeant with black hair called out over the commotion, "Before you can go anywhere, we have to bring you all to the debriefing center."

"Debriefing?" Victor repeated under his breath.

"Once there, the situation will be explained to you, if it has not already. Then you will be given a tent and a family ID."

Close by, a group of soldiers, all in those strange suits, jogged by. This closer look did nothing to ease Victor's curiosity. The armor truly seemed like nothing that he had seen before. Not Kevlar, not quite metal, yet similar to both. What's more, no two soldiers in these suits were the same. A couple of them were massive – much larger than even Daniel. All their bodies had awkward proportions. Some of them had limb-sized attachments, while others appeared to lack some body parts altogether. Victor wondered if some of them were some kind or special forces or perhaps amputees who were given another shot at the military. In the end, Victor couldn't tell if he was even looking at human beings. Maybe they were extraterrestrial, like Athriel.

* * *

Jason Pullano followed his advisor through the dense streets of the safe zone. He was unsure of where they were going, knowing only that Athriel said they were going to report their arrival.

Soon, they came upon what appeared to be the deteriorating remains of a commandeered house. Cracked windows and rust-colored paint coated the place. A line of bullet holes had torn into one of the walls. Coils of barbed wire surrounded the lawn, separating the property from the rest of the settlement. Two guards were posted by a break in the wire, and two more by the front door.

"Well, here we are." Athriel's words were barely audible over the bustling of the street. He turned and headed towards the property. Pullano followed close behind.

As they approached the wire, one of the guards stopped and raised a hand towards them, "Authorized personnel only."

Before the commander could say anything, Athriel stepped out in front of him and spoke, "We're with the First Northeastern Military Convoy. Fort Drum."

The guard looked into his blue eyes, then stepped aside, "Go ahead."

As they entered the commandeered building, Pullano saw that it had been turned into a command post. The first floor was, for the most part, one large room. A handful of officers were gathered around a table in the center. The table itself was covered with maps and stacks of various forms.

One of the officers looked up. He was a short man, with tough skin, gray hair and pale eyes. He wore the uniform of a US general. He leered at the newcomers, asking in a rough voice, "Who are you?"

Without pause, the blue-eyed man approached the general, "I am Athriel of House Endoraith. My compatriot here is Commander Jason Pullano."

"Ah," the general nodded, "You're one of those people. You just come in?"

"Affirmative, sir." said Athriel, "First Northeastern."

"Good. Forms are over there, on the other end of the table."

Athriel sauntered over and took a small packet of paper from the pile, "Any news?" he asked while searching for a utensil, "I've been relatively out of the loop since the seventh."

"Have you, now?" the General snorted, "Well most of the government is dead. Congress, POTUS. We can't get into DC itself because of the radiation, but that should dissipate in a matter of months."

Athriel, while registering what the man had said, seemed far from fazed, only letting out a, "hmm" as he flipped through the packet. He looked up only to say, "Oh, commander, you'll have to fill out some of this, too." Then he was quiet.

"So, what's going on here?" asked Pullano, feeling that the time was right to say something. The general looked at him with strange eyes. Pullano stared back, unflinching, "Mind telling me?"

The general turned to the man with the glowing blue eyes, "You mean you haven't told him yet?"

"He knows the basics." Athriel began, "I'm not human. The enemy isn't human. We're both from the great emptiness up above."

"Well for God's sake, kid. Tell him what's going on."

"Look." said Pullano, "I'm in way over my head, here. I know that. And I'd like to know what the deal with you is. What those... future-looking soldiers are doing out there. You're all clearly here to help, but I wanna know what exactly you're doing."

Athriel watched him for a time, tossing words around in his head. When he decided on what to say, it came out in his usual matter-of-fact, almost condescending tone, "My people, the tiavan, keep an extensive amount of control across a large number of worlds. Many peoples look up to us and work with us. The minitia aren't those people. They are a smaller, independent power, but they're growing every day. They don't command the same respect that my kind does, but they're the face of fear on every world that's had first contact. When those locusts moved to turn Earth into an offering for Linious, we tiavan and our... vassals... knew that we had a personal stake in the fight."

"And what is this personal stake?" asked Pullano.

"The minitia are here because Linious is here." Athriel answered, "Those bugs have been waiting a very long time for them to crash into this rock."

"Them?"

190

"One person. Gender neutral. Please pay attention to what matters. The minitia want Linious. And why? Because they want to use them. These bugs believe in their ridged little hearts that, once they contact Linious, the bastard will join their ranks and lead their hives to greatness. Intergalactic domination. The problem is that, well, that's exactly what we believe Linious will do if given the chance. And all of us out there know that Linious is perfectly capable of using the minitia forces – their swarms, their armada – to their fullest extent. There is also the fact that Linious has allies. Many allies. If the minitia were to gain them, our locust friends would also gain everyone who is loyal to them. So, we came here to stop this merger from going through."

The commander gave a slow nod, unsure of how to respond, "Fair enough. I'm not even going to ask why this Linious guy crashed into Earth in the first place. What matters is that he's here. Just go on."

"Since my people don't care much for putting ourselves in harm's way, we sent these vassal forces to Earth in our stead. With our coordination, they've formed a relief effort to aid the people of Earth."

The general stepped in to interrupt Athriel, "Not to mention the ground forces you've deployed against those goddamn bugs. And the blockade you have around the inner system. Two invaluable pieces in this war."

"Well the blockade is actually a gift directly from my people. No lesser races there."

"Lesser races?" asked Pullano, "Is that what you… Never mind. And what's the blockade doing in all of this?"

"To stop the second wave." Athriel answered. When his response was met with a strange, uncomfortable look from the commander, he decided to elaborate, "The minitia plan began with keeping forces on Earth in secret. They did so for many years, living deep underground where your people would never venture to find them, as well as keeping small satellites in orbit. When the time was right, they disabled your people with electromagnetic pulses from their satellites, as well as your own nuclear and paranuclear devices. They wiped out your technology, weaponry and transportation, and they surfaced to claim your world for themselves. This much, you already understand. What you might not have known was that this was only their first wave. Reinforcements from their own territories are on their way to Earth as we speak. And I must warn you – this second wave is considerably larger than what's already on the planet, and they'll be using their own native weaponry. Far superior to anything you have faced so far, commander. Long story short, Commander Pullano, is that Earth is becoming a war zone. A lot of worlds are counting on us winning here, and they're all lending a helping hand. You aren't alone in the universe and we're all a hell of a lot more advanced than you. Any questions?"

Pullano was silent, thinking over all that Athriel had said. It was so much information. So much knowledge that shifted everything he'd ever perceived about the world around him. It took some time for him to pull together a response, but after a moment the words came to him, "So, I guess you weren't lying when you said there's others like you."

Athriel rolled his eyes – a decidedly human gesture, considering the circumstances, "Humans, minitia... me. You didn't really think that there were only three kinds of people in this universe. Did you?"

"You'll have to introduce me, sometime."

"You have my word, commander. But for now, I have to report to my own superiors, if you don't mind."

Pullano raised a hand, "Go on. Whatever they have to say is beyond me."

With that, Athriel handed him what was left of the packet, "I already filled out what I could. You have the rest." He then took a small bow and left the clear shelter of the command post, his thin form disappearing into the crowd outside. When he was out of sight, Jason Pullano turned to his own superior, the general, who had since turned back to the sea of paperwork on his desk. "I still don't get it, though."

192

he said, "So those bugs based their entire plan off of one guy? It hardly seems like enough to justify tearing apart an entire planet."

The general looked up from his work, snorted and said, "Our... 'helpers' have been very secretive about what Linious has to offer the minitia. But everyone's certain they're just as dangerous as the bugs are making them out to be."

* * *

Athriel glided with elegance through the crowded streets, weaving by and around clusters of humans with ease. Although he had never been to this part of the safe zone, he knew just where he was heading. After several minutes of this dodging and sidestepping, he turned onto one of the city's few empty side streets. Before long, the civilians were nothing but a low rumble in the distance. In front of him there was only vacant, open pavement in all its crumbling glory. Every few minutes, a patrol of soldiers would pass by in that otherworldly armor. They would watch him with care at first, then ignored him once they noticed the glow of his eyes.

He came upon a small complex of what had once been office buildings, each with its own set of guards in their own odd armor. The complex was surrounded by its own wall, with a great field in the center full of armored soldiers running drills. Athriel heard one of the instructors, a tall character with the frame of an obarosi, yell something about accommodating to Earth's gravity while their platoon ran the length of the field.

Athriel ignored these sights, instead focusing on his task. He approached one of the commandeered buildings. The guards out in front glanced over, but gave him no trouble as he passed through the doorway. Once inside, he came to the front desk, stopped and looked around. As he waited, he took in his surroundings. Every color, every sound, every scent. He often did this when he had a moment to himself. The place was musty, the air static and dreary. Every step he took echoed on the tile floor. He imagined what this place must have been like when it was still in proper use.

"Does the Higher deceive me?" a strange voice called in an even stranger tongue, *"Athriel."*

"At your service." The blue-eyed man answered, giving a slight bow in respect.

A figure rounded a corner and into sight. It was human enough in shape, although somewhat androgynous and with features and proportions that invoked the uncanny valley. The sight almost made Athriel flinch. This being's most defining attribute, however, was the brownish red glow in its eyes. The humanoid laid a hand and upon Athriel's shoulder and gave a peculiar smile. Perhaps this person saw some native doing the same and thought of it as a normal greeting. He didn't feel the need to correct him.

"But you are late." said the humanoid.

"My convoy was delayed." Athriel explained. Then his tone changed, *"What news is there from the blockade?"*

"Several minitia vessels have tried to enter the system, but of course they have been stopped. They are only scouts, though. The armada itself is still yet to arrive."

"And how much of the armada has been mobilized against us?"

"As far as we can tell, thirteen hives have joined the cause. But it seems that more are confirmed with every day."

"Terrible news."

"What of your mission, young Athriel?" the humanoid asked.

Athriel hesitated before answering, *"I have several possible subjects."*

"Very good."

"However," Athriel began, *"many of these humans would make for fine additions. I do not see the need in having me choose among them myself."*

"The point is to determine who would be the most reliable. You have formed connections with some of these natives, yes?"

"That is true. Yes."

"Good. If they would make decent enough hosts, then select them. It would be good for them to see a familiar face during their trials."

194

Athriel nodded, *"I thank you for such sound advice, my friend."*

"Exemplary." said the humanoid. The creature then straightened, drawing to its full height, *"Now, I am sorry but our reunion must end."*

Athriel raised an eyebrow, *"You have to leave? So soon?"*

"We will have to catch up on events some other day. The Higher willing, that day will be soon." The humanoid put a hand on Athriel's shoulder, and then turned to leave.

"Nyro." Athriel called, prompting the figure to stop and turned back. He smirked, *"Next time you try to be human, take care to look like one."*

Nyro shook their head, *"Not every tiavan can be as talented as you, young Athriel."*

* * *

"All I'm saying is that I thought we'd be at least a little better off."

Marceline rolled her eyes, "Really, Danny? We finally got out of that God forsaken truck – away from all those things out there – and you're complaining?"

"What can I say? The tent life is not my life."

"You'll get used to it." said Victor, "We all have to."

The day was coming to an end. Daniel Emerson and the Roberts family had spent the past half hour setting up their new home, complete with what little luggage they had left. The group had set off from Boston with a van full of clothes and random goods. They had kept everything with them as they commandeered the bus, and then did their best during their transition over to Athriel's convoy. However, when they joined up it was nighttime and just after a bout with the minitia. As such, it was impossible to rummage through the wreckage of the bus to find everything. What they were able to bring along was then subject to being misplaced, as well as random theft by other refugees. By now, the food was all but gone and half of their clothing had was missing. They hoped that, with a designated space of their own, it would be easier to keep track of everything without wandering hands whisking it all away.

Not everyone reacted the same way to the convoy. Daniel, it seemed, was worst of all. Zack didn't much like the change of scenery, either. He wanted nothing more than to go home, and didn't understand why his parents insisted on staying there. Sammy, however, was never bothered by the dirt and grime around her. Nor did she dread the idea of living in a tent. However, it could be debated whether or not she actually understood how long they would be there. For the time being, though, she was content, directing her attention to an insatiable curiosity about everything around her.

"I like it." Marceline commented, "My family used to go camping all the time, back when I was little."

"I'm just excited to be out of that trailer." said Victor.

Dan raised a hand, "I am, too. Don't get me wrong. I just figured that, since you went into Harrisburg and everything, we'd be getting that preferential treatment they were talking about."

"Aren't we?" Victor asked.

"Well I guess. If by 'preferential', they mean having one more apple to share among us than the other families."

"We have a bigger tent." said Marceline, "There's five of us and we have a ten-person tent. What did you expect? A four-star resort? We're refugees, Dan. Just be glad that you're not in the stomach of one of those monsters." She then turned to her husband, hovering next to his ear, and asked in a hushed tone as to whether the minitia actually had stomachs. Victor shrugged.

Daniel's eyes widened, "Wow, you're harsh."

"I'm just being realistic." said Marceline.

"Maybe there'll be other ways to get better stuff." Victor suggested, "We could work our way up. Eventually get a spot in a real house or something."

Dan looked from Victor to Marceline, and then back to

Victor. They seemed to be in agreement. "Working our way up? That's it, eh? As if that did it for us back in Boston."

"This ain't some dead-end job." said Victor, "We're not working at the office. There's leeway here. They'll need volunteers for things."

"And," Marceline added, "even if we don't make it that far up, does it really matter? We're alive. The kids are alive. We all have a place to sleep tonight and there'll be food on the table for the foreseeable future. To demand more is... well, sort of bratty."

Daniel tossed his hands up, the thought of being a brat being all too much for him, "Okay, fine. You win. Poor ol' Danny is outsmarted by the dynamic duo yet again. We'll try your plan."

"Oh, don't be so dramatic." said Victor, "Get some sleep. You're strange when you're tired."

After that, the majority of the conversation died. When they did speak, it was of their plans tomorrow. Exploring the neighborhood, starting their jobs, looking for opportunities to volunteer, bathing for the first time in almost two weeks. For the most part, though, they listened to the clamor around them. It was the sound of a city drifting to sleep.

Daniel climbed into the tent for as good a night's sleep as he was going to get. Marceline followed soon after, but Victor just sat there outside in the dirt. He stared at the cloudy sky, trying to imagine the stars beyond the veil. He listened as the noise of the city fell into a tired murmur. When a voice called out, exclaiming that it was time for the civilian curfew, he finally disappeared into his new, almost luxurious home.

Chapter 9

Marceline trudged on towards one of the safe zone's many barracks. In the time that the Roberts family had been here, the adults of the family had all been given jobs. These assignments served many purposes. They gave the zone a sense of unity, having everybody work together and around each other instead of keeping them in their own separate tents and neighborhoods all day. It was also a plain fact that the soldiers and defenses needed constant upkeep. Controlling a fortified area the size of a city was no easy task, and everyone had to do their part to keep things moving. These jobs also kept the refugees busy throughout the day, so as to avoid the complications often posed by idle hands. Therefore, every able pair of hands was put to work. No exceptions.

Marceline's assignment was in the transporting of food. She was part of a team that spread rations to barracks throughout the zone. As simple as it sounded, it wasn't something that she was built for. For the first few days, the job was made up of a lot of heavy lifting. The team had to move massive shipments of military rations and water on foot and by hand. It wasn't until the end of her first week that they were given a few trucks and glorified wagons to move things back and forth.

As she went from place to place, Marceline was given an outstanding view into the world of the Washington DC Safe Zone. Soldiers made constant patrols through streets of cracked pavement and pulverized earth. The normal ones would sometimes talk with the refugees when they had the chance. If they had stopped or were stationed in a specific area, they often welcomed human contact and casual conversation. Perhaps it made them feel like things were normal. However, those were only the average soldiers. The ones in the strange suits – the ones that didn't show an inch of skin on their bodies – they didn't seem as open to dialogue. They kept to themselves, the crowds giving them a wide berth as they marched through the streets.

While the soldiers drew her interest from time to time, it was the other refugees that caught the most of her attention. People crowded the main roads like sheep in a herd. The occasional catcaller would whistle or scrutinize her, though they were ignored. Most buildings in the zone had been cleared away, brick by brick, to help build the wall. Only the least damaged had been spared, but even those had begun showing signs of dilapidation. The soot and dirt that smeared the walls also coated the people who passed by. Refugees walked by with marked faces and grimy hair. Children ran around with ragged, lived-in clothes. Everything was filthy.

* * *

Around noontime, the camp stopped for lunch. Victor, Dan and Travis gathered around one of the cleaner tables in the communal area near the Roberts family's tent. Over the past couple of weeks, they had made a tradition out of this.

For once, Dan wasn't as cheerful as usual. On other days, he carried most of the conversation, talking about the women in the camp or making immature, half-bearable jokes about his coworkers in the deconstruction crew. Today, however, he was quiet.

"Hey, Danny." said Victor, "I'm used to Travis not saying much. But you?"

"Sorry." he answered, "Work just got me a bit down today."

"Wanna talk about it?"

"Well the team and I were going through one of the old homes on Elm Street. You know, part of that walled-off neighborhood that's mostly just for the guys in the tech suits. They wanted it knocked down for whatever reason, so we were going through it beforehand to find anything useful. While I was going through the upstairs, I saw this room at the end of the hallway. The door was locked and nobody seemed to have the key. I thought that, hey, maybe I should take the door down and see what we can grab on the other side. You know? But when I was asking around to see if I should do it, everybody just kept saying that I should just leave it be. We didn't need what was in that room I guess – even though nobody seemed to know what was in there. I ended up going in. I put my boot to the door and it came down and I went in and…"

Daniel stopped. He looked past Victor, watching as Athriel approached them.

"Hello, boys." said the glowing-eyed man.

"Hey, Athriel." Victor answered alone.

The alien gestured to the sole responder, an inquisitive expression on his face, "Might I speak with you for a moment?"

"Sure."

Athriel glanced at the others, and then back at Victor, "Alone?"

"Uh, sure." Victor excused himself and left the other two with each other.

They were quiet. Dan went back to his sandwich. Travis didn't touch his food, still staring at Dan and guessing at the end of the half-told story, "So what was on the other side of the door?"

Daniel finished chewing his bite before quietly answering, "A, uh, nursery."

Victor followed Athriel away from the communal area. When it appeared that there was no one else around them, Athriel turned, "I want to talk to you about something."

"I kinda got the feeling, yeah."

"Do you remember back in the convoy, when I offered you a place in something?"

200

"Is this volunteer work?" Victor asked, "Because last time I did that, we got a ten-person tent. Long as it doesn't kill me, I'm in."

"You get ahead of yourself, my friend. You don't even know what it is you speak of."

"I'll admit it has crossed my mind a few hundred times, but I've always figured that you'd tell me when the time was right."

"The time is right, Victor. You're alive and relatively safe, and everything behind the scenes is in place."

"So, tell me."

Athriel paused. It surprised Victor to see Athriel silent when it was his turn to talk. Eventually though, the entity before him seemed to have grasped the right words, "I am here to make you the offer that I told you about. Even now, there are billions of humans in this world. I'm working for a program that needs a select handful from these billions. I need someone who is intelligent, strategic, resourceful, in good health... and has something to lose."

Victor interjected, "You just described half of this camp."

"I don't know half of this camp. I contacted a number of people throughout the northeastern region of the United States, but you are the only one who even made it to the convoy."

Victor took a moment to process this. Then he said, more as a statement than a question, "So out of all these people, you choose me."

"Yes."

"And what did you choose me for? This program? What is it?"

"You have a lot to lose. That means you have a lot to fight for." Athriel paused and took a half step closer. His voice went low, taking on a hushed, almost secretive tone, "What if I said that I could give you the power to fight? To really fight and make a difference?"

"What are you talking about?"

Athriel's arm stretched outward and, at once, Victor felt a shift in the air. Sparks of electricity bolted between Athriel's fingers. A moment later and his entire hand was glowing in an electric hue. A ball of lightning, interwoven with his fingers, crackled in the palm of his hand before, with the flick of a wrist, exploding into the ground beneath. As the ringing in his ears died, Victor's eyes were as wide as could be.

"This gift I have... This gift that all of my people have. We can alter the material world around us, forcing it to our will. I can move objects with nothing more than a thought. I can summon flame or frost by manipulating the heat around me. I can rip electrons from atoms and form bolts of lightning in my hand. I can even alter my own body to look and sound exactly like a human being. This is a unique power. It comes naturally to my people and is found nowhere else in this universe. However," he paused, "I would make it yours, if you so choose."

So many questions raced through Victor's mind and yet he was left speechless, save for one word. "How?"

"Through a bit of an experiment. In English, it translates into something along the lines of the Host Project." Athriel put a hand on Victor's arm. The human jumped, half expecting to be zapped by another hand of white-hot lightning. "I will not lie." He continued, "It would be very dangerous. Very costly. You might die during the experiment. There is a good chance of that. And even if you don't, you would be sent to the front lines of this war, far away from your family. I would not take it personally if you declined my offer. If this is what you want, though, I am ready to hand it to you."

Victor pondered to himself for a moment. He tried to make sense of all that Athriel had told him. This being would be giving him the power to fight the minitia, while also taking him from his family. Perhaps he would even die.

He felt that an answer was warranted. However, he didn't have one. "I'll need some time to think." he said. His voice was low and humble.

202

"Will you have an answer for me within the next two weeks?"

"Maybe, I don't know. This is a lot to process."

Athriel gave a slight smile, "I understand."

* * *

By now, Victor's break was over. Athriel dismissed him and, after he had gone, turned to go about his day. The glowing-eyed man hadn't gotten far, however, before a voice called him back

"Oi, alien." cried Travis as he approached the being.

Athriel stopped and turned, "Mister Norwich?" By the expression on his face, it was clear that Travis had overheard the conversation with Victor. Athriel prepared himself for what he knew was coming.

"I want in."

"You want in… what?"

"I figure you know exactly what I'm talking about."

"What are you saying? I can't seem to understand your accent."

"Yes you can, you tosser. You sound like you're from the other bloody side of London."

"Is that so?"

Travis groaned, "Will you listen to me or not?"

"I probably shouldn't… but I will." It was clear that Travis would not be swayed. This was a conversation that had to happen. Athriel sighed, "So you want in?"

"On the Host Project."

"I don't think you realize what you're saying."

"Listen to me." Travis began, "Those buggers took everything from me. My home. My friends and family. The woman I wanted to marry. Everything. I want to get back at them."

"You're asking to be part of an experiment."

"I'm asking you to make me a weapon. If Victor can use these powers to protect his family, then I can use 'em to get

203

revenge."

"I need people who are up to the task, both physically and mentally." Saying this only seemed to further rile the young man.

"I can do it." Travis said, "I'm smart. I'm fast. I made it to DC just like Victor."

"Even if you're accepted into the program, you are not likely to survive."

"Whatever gives me the chance to get back at those things."

Athriel sighed again, "Fine. I'll have my people come for you in the morning, two weeks from today. If you honestly believe that this is the best decision, then we'll take you."

* * *

The day went on. Soldiers finished their patrols and exchanged places with the next shift. Civilian workers, done with their jobs, went back to their clustered tents and overfilled houses. Evening came.

Victor came back to his family tent, only to see that Marceline was already there, playing with their children. He stood there just outside the nylon home, afraid to set a foot inside, his heart pounding through his chest, his breathing short and quick.

Daniel approached from behind. Victor barely noticed at first, then almost jumped when he caught sight of him.

"Hey, Vic."

"Daddy's back?" a voice cried from inside the tent. Sammy shot out like a wild animal and hugged him close. Victor hugged back, then leaned down to kiss the top of her head. His daughter led him into the tent, where Marceline was waiting with little Zack.

"How was your day, honey?" Marci asked.

"Oh, it was fine." Victor answered, not sure how to say what was on his mind. Soon enough, he realized that there was an uncomfortable silence in the room.

"Is… something wrong?"

"No, no." Victor assured, "Or, well no. Nothing's wrong. We need to talk about something, though."

"What is it?"

Victor looked from face to face, then turned to Dan, "Would you mind taking the kids for a bit?"

"Sure thing, Vic." Dan beckoned his godchildren outside. He might have said something about going for a walk or exploring some new place, but Victor wasn't listening. His attention was focused on Marceline and what he was going to say to her.

"Athriel gave me a decision to make." he started, "He wants to know if I'd want to join this program. It would be dangerous – very, very dangerous – but it could help us end this war more quickly. I don't think I'd be able to stay here, though. I'd probably have to go wherever he wants me to. Maybe it would be worth it, though. You know, if me being gone for a while means the war ends sooner."

Marceline was quiet. Her face went from surprise to concern to anger, all with the sense of pained tenseness. He wasn't sure of how she was going to respond, or how he should have even responded to Athriel in the first place.

"You're not going." she finally said, "You can't."

"Marci, I think I have to."

"No, you don't." she said, "You need to be here with us."

"I know. This family needs to stay together." Victor paused, then added, "But what if the best way for me to keep you safe is… well… for me to go and do this?"

"Victor," Marceline took his hand in hers. The hazel of her eyes met the green of his, "I'm your wife. Sammy and Zack are your children. We're all going through a dangerous time right now. And yeah, we have that Athens kid looking out for us, but that's not the point. The point is that we need to get through this together. That means having you here with us."

"You're right." Victor said, "You're totally right."

"Now I don't want to hear about this again. Okay? You're staying here with us."

* * *

For the rest of the evening, they spoke no further word of Athriel or his offer. They ate what passed for dinner and thought of random games to play with the kids. The whole time, Marceline watched Victor, stealing glances at him whenever he wasn't looking. When night came, they put the children to bed. A while later Marceline joined them, leaving Victor alone with his thoughts.

He stepped outside the tent, taking in the brisk, dead air of the night. At the corner of what they pretended was a street in this conglomerate of tents, he stopped. There, he decided to sit. He closed his eyes and listened. Soft snoring came from behind. A burst of laughter rang out in the distance, soon put down by a sharp hush. Footsteps pattered on the ground, growing louder and louder. Victor opened his eyes and saw two people, a woman and a man, walking by. One of them had a bottle in their hand. By the way they stumbled, Victor knew what it was.

It was sort of funny, he thought. At any other point in his adult life, Victor would have jumped at the opportunity to get some of that taunting elixir for himself. He should have at least been tempted. Now, he was nothing short of appalled by it. The smell, the taste, the very sight of it made him sick. To think of how much of his life was wasted on that poison. The countless fights and drunken rages... How he used it to drown out the family that he'd resented. It was only now, at the end of the world, that his mind had finally cleared. The urge would always be there – he knew that – but his hate would forever outweigh his desire.

"Out past curfew, I see."

It was Athriel.

"Arrest me." Victor countered, "Anyway, I'm not the only one. There's a couple of drunks who went by a minute ago."

Athriel made a small noise, as if holding in a laugh, "I think I'll let it go this time." He stepped forward and took a seat next to Victor, slouching and crossing his legs in the same way as the human's.

"You're gonna ask me about something." said Victor.

"I'll be answering." Athriel responded, "I'm going to answer any questions that you have about it."

Victor shook his head, "This thing... what you want me to do... I can't do it. I need to be with my family."

"Your family needs someone strong to fight for them." Athriel waited a moment. When it was clear that Victor had nothing else to say, he added, "What if I could ensure your family's safety?"

The human raised his head, "What do you mean?"

"If you go through with this program, my people will be indebted to you. I may be able to pull some strings and get your family away from all of this. I probably shouldn't be telling you this before you've agreed to anything, but my people have been setting up relocation centers for your species. Earth is becoming too inhospitable to hold refugees, so we plan to slowly move them to another world. Your family could be a part of that. They would start a new life, free from the war and the minitia."

"All of this, only if I join you and your program?"

"Joining the Host Project could make your family a priority for relocation."

Victor took a moment to think. He weighed all the facts in his head. He thought about every point of view: his own, his wife's, his children's, even Daniel's. At last, he knew what he had to do.

"No 'coulds'." He said, "No 'maybes' or 'mights'. If I do this, I want my family on the first ship off this world. No exceptions."

"I'll see what I can do." replied Athriel.

"You'll do it. That's the deal. If they aren't in that relocation center at the moment it's open, then I'll do nothing to cooperate. Even if I die during the experiment, I want them far away from here. I want them safe."

Through the darkness, Victor could see the faint image of Athriel's smile, "As you wish, my friend."

The glowing-eyed man then stretched out and got to his feet, "Anyway," he said, "I have to get going. You have a wonderful night. Just make sure to get back to your tent before any patrols come by." Then, like that, he was gone.

Chapter 10

Dawn broke over the horizon, barely managing to push its brightest rays through the heavy clouds. With the first hint of daylight, the camp seemed to come alive. Guards changed shifts with fresh eyes and ears. Cooks and cleaners congregated to the mess halls, readying themselves for another overworked day.

Victor noticed all of this from his spot on the corner. He hadn't moved from there once the whole night. Even when patrols came through, he never got up. He never hid. To be honest, it was a miracle that he wasn't caught outside past curfew. Now though, with daylight breaking and the curfew lifted, he would soon have to rise and get on with his day. Knowing this, he decided to grant himself a few more minutes of peace before going back to his tent and his family.

A set of heavy footsteps came up from behind. Even before he spoke, Victor knew exactly who it was.

"Up early?" Dan asked.

"Never went to sleep."

Daniel raised an eyebrow. He looked at his friend for a moment, studying him, before taking a seat next to him. "What's on your mind?"

"Athriel wants me to be a part of something big. An experiment. Something that'll let me do what he does."

"You mean the lightning?"

Victor nodded, "The lightning. The fire. Moving things without touching them. All of it."

"Well why wouldn't you go for it? He'd be turning you into some kind of superhuman. It seems like a pretty good deal to me."

"It's not that easy, though. Going through with this would mean sending me off to fight the minitia. It would be dangerous. I'd probably die. Even if I didn't, I still wouldn't be able to see Marci or the kids much. They need their father, right now more than ever. I can't just abandon them. The problem is... I think it's the right thing to do. Doing this'll help end the war. It'll keep my family safe."

"Vic," Dan put a hand on his shoulder, "You do what you have to do."

"I've already decided." Victor responded, "I told Athriel last night. I'm gonna go through with it. Anything to end this war faster. Anything to keep the kids safe."

"Damn..." Dan muttered, "That's quite the decision."

"I made a deal with him. I go along with this and he saves them all. And you."

They spent a moment in silence, both contemplating the crossroads that lay before him.

"So, you're really gonna do it?" asked Daniel, his voice low and quiet.

Without turning to look at him, Victor gave a nod.

Dan nodded back, then smiled, putting an arm around his friend, "Then sign me up, too."

"You can't be serious." Victor said, his eyes widened, "You don't know what you'd be getting yourself into."

"Neither do you. Nobody would. Either way, if you have to do this, then so do I. Somebody's gotta look after you."

To say that Victor was shocked would have been an understatement. Here he was, about to lay everything on the line to protect his family. He was ready to walk alone into the abyss of interstellar war. Now, perhaps he wouldn't be alone. Maybe this sacrifice could be made bearable.

"So, you're really going through with this." Victor asked.
"I am if you are."

Victor smiled. He couldn't help it, "Danny." he mumbled, tears forming in his eyes.

"There's still one small problem, though." said Dan,

"How's Marceline gonna react to this?"

* * *

"No." she growled, "You're not doing this."

"Marci, please-"

"Victor," she paused, taking a long, tense breath to collect herself before continuing, "You have a family. A family that needs you – that loves you."

"And I love them, too." he responded, "What, you think I don't?"

"Well you've done nothing but drink us away for the past nine years. And now that we actually need you, you want to run off playing hero with that glowing-eyed freak!"

"Marceline," Daniel intervened, "Listen to him. Please."

They were quiet for a moment, waiting until Marceline seemed to concede. She straightened herself out and took another long breath. She stared at her husband with a look of something akin to hatred.

"I love you." said Victor, "I love Sammy. I love Zack. I can't take back the way I was before all of this, but believe me, I'm trying. I'm trying hard to make up for it. I love you more than life itself. I'd do anything for you. That's why I'm getting you all off this world."

Marceline's expression changed. Her voice faltered, "E-excuse me?"

"Nobody is safe here." Victor explained, "I can't sleep at night knowing that something could happen to you or the kids. That's why I made a deal with Athriel. He'd get you three off of this world, away from the war."

"And all you have to do is, what? Be his guinea pig?"

"He wants to put me on the front lines. It doesn't matter, though. He can do whatever he wants with me."

"Victor…" Marceline couldn't find words to say. She felt as if she had been struck by a train.

"I'm not going to argue about it." he told her, "I already told him that I'd do it."

Dan took a step forward, "He and I ship off in a couple of weeks, and you and the kids get to be far away from all of this."

Marceline turned to her friend, "You too?" She was pale, a look of unbridled pain washing over her face.

"That's just how it works." said Dan, "When something like this happens, people have to make sacrifices." He motioned towards Victor, then to himself, "We fight the war so you don't have to. It's for the family."

"This is different." Marceline pleaded, "This isn't the draft. We aren't in Vietnam. You aren't fighting people. Those things... they'll kill you. They'll kill both of you. My babies will grow up without a dad or their godfather."

"It's better than not growing up at all." Dan countered. His words echoed in her ears, forcing her to confront a possibility that she'd been trying so hard to avoid.

When Marceline couldn't respond, Victor took her hand, "Marci, I know it's difficult, but this is how it has to be. When something like this happens, people have to sacrifice."

She was quiet for a long time. Her face began to flush. Her jaw tightened, "I love you." she said at last. She slumped forward into Victor's arms, "I love you so much." she sobbed, "I just don't want to lose you."

"I'll come back when it's all over. We can be a family again after this."

"Don't make me a promise that you can't keep."

"He'll keep it." said Dan, "I'm coming along to make sure of it."

Marceline broke away from her husband to embrace their friend, "I don't want to lose you both."

"And you won't." said Dan, holding her.

"We leave in two weeks." Victor reiterated, "Two more weeks as a family. Then we can all be together again after the war."

* * *

When the day came for the volunteers to leave, Victor and the others awoke to a group of those strange, armored soldiers. Unlike other fireteams and patrols that they had seen, these ones were all the same in stature and design. Averaging at seven or so feet, they were the kind of behemoth figures that made even Dan appear small.

There wasn't time for lengthy goodbyes. Perhaps, in Athriel's eyes, the last couple of weeks counted as just that. So, Victor and Dan were taken away after only a short moment of hugging their loved ones and wishing them well.

"When will you come back?" Sammy had asked.

"It'll be a while," her father answered, "but I will be back."

"You'd better." Marci stepped in, "We'll be waiting." She took her husband in a firm embrace. They kissed, knowing full well that this would be their last for some time.

When one of the armored behemoths grabbed Victor by the shoulder, he knew it was time to go. He and Dan were led through the streets, with two soldiers in front and two behind. It felt strange to Victor, as if they were prisoners being transported. These escorts made the journey a fast one, though. With every step they took, people would clear out of the way like the parting of the sea.

It only took ten minutes or so to get to their destination. They found themselves in a clearing, where no buildings or tents stood and no refugee dared to go. Travis, along with several other armored soldiers were already waiting by the foot of some massive machine. In Victor's eyes, this enormous figure somewhat resembled a dragon in shape and a house in size. It had a long central body that bent and arched at the ends like an animal readying itself to strike. Each side had an almost wing-like side compartment jutting off of it. The whole thing held itself off the ground by a series of artificial legs. It wasn't until the "mouth" opened and a ramp drew out that Victor realized he was looking at a ship. A genuine star ship, spaceworthy and ready to fly.

"Get onboard." One of the soldiers stared down at him.

Its voice sounded almost as mechanical as the dragon ship in front of them.

"Where's Athriel?" Victor asked, hesitant to move on without him.

"The tiavan is waiting at the station."

The interior of the ship looked about as comforting as the outside. The floors and walls were colored in hues of gray, silver, and white. Every now and then, there would be a touch of maroon or cobalt blue on a sign or the rim of a light or a seat, but for the most part it resembled the feeling of an Earth submarine. However, an Earth submarine would be built for Earth's people. In this vehicle, everything had been designed for a species much larger than humanity. These soldiers, no doubt. He looked over to one of the seats and spotted Travis sitting idle.

"You're coming, too?" Victor asked, "You didn't tell me."

The Englishman looked at him with cold eyes, "Didn't cross my mind. Sorry." It was clear that he, more than anyone else here, was on a mission.

Victor had expected to feel more pressure during takeoff. That's what every online video and science class had taught him. The force of leaving Earth – of going so fast so quickly – he thought that it was supposed to pin him to his seat or at least make him feel some kind of downward pull. When none of this came to be, he couldn't help but feel a little lost.

There were no windows for him to look through. Nothing to give him a last glimpse at his family. Nothing to show him what the world looked like as they climbed higher and higher. He wondered what the world even looked like nowadays, now that every metropolis had been erased with nuclear efficiency. He thought of all the ash and debris that must have been kicked up. Would he even be able to recognize his own world anymore?

"How long until we're there?" asked Dan. He had a very different energy than the rest of the group. It seemed like he

214

was almost excited.

One of the soldiers looked up. Through the black visor on its helmet, Victor could feel its eyes scanning over all three humans. Once again, the same strange, robotic voice came out to answer, "Ninety minutes."

Daniel nodded.

Victor wondered how these alien creatures knew what minutes were. Perhaps those words hadn't come from a real voice, but a translator of some sort? The thought bounced around his head, as he didn't know how to confirm or debunk this theory of his.

"Why do you sound like that?" Dan asked the soldier.

The creature within the machination looked at him for a moment, and then said, "I am speaking through a translator."

Victor's face went red.

The flight continued on like that for some time. Dan would periodically ask a question, to which one of the armored giants would answer. When they said that the ship was going to a station in the outer orbit of Jupiter, it occurred to Victor that he hadn't known where they were even going. He'd gotten on a ship full of massive goons and left without knowing where it was even destined to go.

Through Daniel's questions, Victor had been able to find out some other information, too. These bulky, armored figures were known as obarosi – a species that had sworn loyalty to Athriel and the other tiavan. Apparently, there were a lot of species and planets with the same story. Too many for one conversation, as they put it.

* * *

Travis spent the trip without so much as saying a word. He was far too caught up in his own thoughts to entertain the questions of others. His mind was in a place too dark to see and too pained to care. Just a few weeks ago, he would have been nervous to even fly across an ocean. Today, he was going halfway across the solar system, and what awaited him was destined to be far worse than his partner's American relatives.

His mind went to Mister Russell Greene and his wife, Anna. Whatever happened to them? Perhaps they were still holed up in their house in Pennsylvania. More likely, they had followed Travis' words and went north in hopes of meeting up with their daughter. Little did they know that they had gone south instead. With luck, Mister and Missus Greene were still alive. Realism, in all of its cynical ways, hinted at the contrary. And what of Olivia and her new husband, Jordan? What of Beth and Luke? What of that aunt who tried to take his and Jane's picture? Were any of them still alive? If they had made it to the safe zone, would they have joined up with the Host Project too? Or would they have taken up their assigned jobs and waited for the rest of the world to end?

Travis looked around. He knew why everyone here had joined. Victor was there because he was lucky enough to still have a family to protect. Dan? He said that he was coming along to keep Victor safe. Was there any other reason, though? There had to have been, Travis figured. Nobody would make such a decision without a real reason. A reason like Victor's, or like Travis' own.

Revenge.

Victor still had a family to protect. Travis didn't. He had left everything behind in London. Jane was all that remained. She was what was left of his life – all his hopes, his aspirations, his world. She was supposed to be his future. He loved her more than anything.

And then she was gone.

He had fought for his life to get back to her. To stay alive for her. To not leave her alone in this world.

Then she was dead.

Then they killed her.

It didn't matter what happened to him. He was going to hurt those demons the same way they hurt him. He wanted to destroy everything of theirs, even if doing so destroyed himself.

216

When the ramp opened and the humans were led out of the ship and into the docking bay, the first thing that Victor noticed was the view. Almost the entirety of the back wall was made of a series of screens. Each one showed a live feed of the outside of the station. It was like peering through massive windows. Windows that showed the best view in the universe – a view of Jupiter, up close, in all its swirling majesty.

Victor glanced at Dan, who was staring open-mouthed at the vivid oranges and whites of the gas giant. He understood that he was among the first human beings to ever lay a naked eye on something so beautiful, so marvelous. He did nothing to take that moment for granted. Travis, though, seemed unfazed. He just glared at the ground with the same expression as always.

The humans were led from the docking area, through a series of corridors. As they half-jogged to keep pace with the giants who led them, they also noticed the even taller beings passing by. Of all the things that he had seen in recent times, this had to have been the most surreal. These beings must have been nine feet tall, each with a remarkably slender frame and a body of grey of black or brown or white. Many were clothed in long, draping outfits of intricate, beautiful designs. Each had two slender, fragile arms and two long, beefy legs supporting them. The faces looked completely inhuman, save for a couple of sensory features. Surrounding every torso was a series of six appendages that Victor could only describe as having the shape of dragonfly wings, but longer, flexible, and coated in flesh. What stood out most, though, were the etchings across their bodies. Every one of them was marked with a unique design that flowed over their entire form. They were enchanting to look upon, like strokes of paint across the canvas of gods.

They were led to a long room. On one wall, there stood

a line of closed doors. The place was full of grays and silvers like the ship, but it was bright, lit by the light of Jupiter through a large skylight that ran the length of the room. Across the floor stood a crowd of obarosi soldiers, along with seven more humans. Five women and two men. Victor understood that they were here for the Host Project as well.

As Victor walked in and joined the rest of the group, his eyes went to the large entity waiting for them. It was another one of those enormous, thin beings with dragonfly wings. All along its stark white body, its intricate blue pattern enticed those who looked upon it with surreal beauty. They spiraled and flowed, sprawling out across the torso before curling majestically around the left arm and leg. The being stood with its arms folded, wrapped loosely in a thin, embroidered shawl and transparent skirt that both revealed and complemented the markings on its pale skin. This remarkable entity stared at the humans with a pair of glowing blue eyes.

"Gentlemen." said Athriel. His voice was no longer human, but something else entirely.

"You look... different." Victor remarked, still looking the alien over in a kind of disbelief that he couldn't shake.

The tiavan gave a slight nod, "I will not be returning to Earth, so there is no reason for me to keep the form of a human male any longer."

"So, this is what you normally look like?" Dan asked.

"When I am not looking like other species, yes."

Dan studied him for a moment longer, then said, "I've got a question, but it's a weird one." Victor sighed, noticing the familiar look on his friend's face, "You emphasized that you're no longer parading around, not just like a human, but like a male human. Are you even really a guy? Because I don't see anything that human guys have... down there"

Athriel answered without pausing, as if he didn't register the awkwardness of the question, "My people are without biological sex. I only appeared to you as a male because I had to choose and, well, I personally found it more difficult to replicate the body of a female."

218

"So, could you have just as easily been a woman? I mean, it would make a bit more sense, given the way you rock that skirt."

"With slightly more effort, yes."

Daniel looked the alien over one more time. Then he nodded and, acting casually, turned to Victor and whispered, "Athy is a pretty lady." Victor's smirk gave away his true feelings, but didn't stop a playful shove.

Victor felt a tap at his shoulder. An obarosi soldier stood behind him, holding out a small, circular device. Victor took it into his hands, studying it. One side had a flat, porous surface. The other stretched into a thin, malleable strand. The man looked up at the obarosi, who gestured to his ear. He hesitated, unsure if his impression was correct. Then, risking embarrassment, he stuck the device into his ear. Immediately, the strand seemed to come alive as it latched onto the wall of his ear canal, making him jump. He looked back at the obarosi.

"Can you understand me?" the soldier asked. The voice seemed to come from the object in his ear. A translator.

Victor nodded, "Yes."

"Good."

At that moment, another of the obarosi soldiers approached Athriel. After a brief exchange of words, Athriel dismissed the soldier and turned to the humans, "Your attention, please."

All eyes turned to the tiavan.

"I understand that you all must be tired." he continued, "After all, you have just traveled farther than any other human in history. Unfortunately, this is not the time to rest."

There was a slight murmur from the Earthlings in the crowd. Two of Athriel's wing-like appendages shot up, moving in a way as to mimic human hands trying to hush the lot of them. The crowd silenced.

"You have all been gathered here for one specific purpose: to take part in a project that will turn you into a weapon to use against the minitia onslaught. Now, you all have your reasons for being here and I'm sure that you have all thought long and hard about coming here. I sincerely hope that you intend to stick with your decisions, because your last chance to back out was on Earth."

"Fair enough." Dan muttered, just loud enough for Victor to hear.

Athriel went on, "When your name is called, you will be directed through one of these doors. On the other side, you will undergo the initial procedures of the Host Project. Over the course of these procedures, your body will be altered on a genetic level in order to better adapt to tiavan genetic material. Then you will undergo genetic splicing. Once this process is finished, you will immediately be sent to a recovery area."

Victor scanned the crowd. Mixed expressions were all around him. The beginnings of uncertainty poked at a few, as well as the sudden, stinging realization that there was no way out except through the procedures.

"The first name is Vasily Akulov." said Athriel, "Vasily, if you'll follow the obarosi."

One of the armored figures stepped forward, pointing at one of the humans. A tall, lanky man with large facial features and a noticeable limp was led away through the farthest door on the left.

So, it began.

"Next: Anya Petrova."

A woman with dark hair and nervous eyes was escorted through the next door. As she got to the doorway, she looked back at the others. A small shove from her escort pushed her through and the door slid closed behind her.

"Naomi Daskal."

This one was a fair-skinned woman with curly hair and sharp features. Her face was held in a look of stoic resolution. No matter what waited beyond that door, she was ready.

"Levi Baranski."

Levi held himself with the same stoicism as the woman before him. However, he didn't seem to be as resolute –

220

more like he was like Dan, prone to accepting whatever was to become of him.

"Victor Roberts."

It was time.

A smile from his friend wished Victor good luck as a gauntleted hand grabbed at his shoulder. He was led to the doorway of what must have been his designated room. The doors slid open, but he didn't move.

This was for Marceline. For the kids.

Victor took a step. Then another. Then the doors slid shut behind him. He found himself in a white room, with a clear, man-sized tank on the far end. Another one of those winged beings stood before him. A tiavan. This one was a dusty brown, with silver markings on its torso and appendages.

"Sit down, Victor Roberts." it said. The being was clad in ornate clothing, almost archaic in design, reminding the human of the images of early royalty back in ancient Egypt or Sumer. Yet there was something undoubtedly modern and unique to it. The entity was seated, but still far taller than Victor would expect from a humanoid being, "The preliminary interviewing process should take but a moment."

Victor looked at the being, confusion on his face, "You're interviewing me? But I'm already here. I thought this was a sure thing."

"Athriel of House Endoraith has vouched for you. You have earned the trust of a primitive-loving deviant. Not ours. The overseers of the Host Project must form our own opinion of you."

"Well... okay then." He was tentative, but he had already come this far. He took a seat opposite the alien.

"Think of it as a formality. You are already half a solar system away from home. At this point, there is very little chance that we would actually deny you."

Victor almost didn't want to ask, "And if you did deny me?"

"You would be euthanized in order to save ourselves

the trip back to your world."

Victor almost let out a whimper, but stopped himself, "Oh, okay. No pressure then."

"Let us begin." The tiavan made something that Victor felt may have been akin to a sigh, "We will start with something simple. What was your life like before the invasion?"

"Well that's broad… Uh, well I was born in raised in a city called Boston. I guess I had a pretty average childhood. Got decent grades. Didn't get into too much trouble. Went to college to study psychology, but I dropped out halfway through. I worked most recently at an office, doing mostly data entry. Every once in a while I'd… go out and have a drink or two. That's not me anymore, though. I also have a wife and two kids."

The interviewer's alien eyes stared into Victor's own, as if reading his every thought, "They are still alive? Even after all of this?"

"Yeah, they are. I also have this long-time friend who's pretty much a member of the family. He came with me when all of this started. He's actually here on this space station with us. Daniel Emerson is his name."

"And your drinking? Am I to assume that you have an alcohol dependence issue? I hear it is common for your kind to develop such problems."

"That's not who I am anymore." Victor repeated.

"Your brain is still wired for addiction, is it not?"

"I guess so… What does this have to do with my ability to work for you? You probably don't even have booze here."

"We do not. However, we cannot tolerate spending time and resources on a subject that will be hindered in any way."

At this, Victor felt himself becoming defensive. His voice hardened, his eyes narrowing at the tiavan, "Then do your thing and let me show you how unhindered I am."

"Eager. Good. Now here is your next question. What would you say are your best qualities? What is it that you bring to the Host Project?"

At this point, Victor couldn't help but relate this situation to a job interview back on Earth, "Athriel says that I have a strategic mind."

"Do you believe that?" the interviewer tilted their head to one side, no doubt imitating a human gesture.

"All I know is that when I'm in a bad place, I stop and look for a way out."

"Athriel states that your family survived a journey of more than five hundred miles through minitia-occupied territory, largely without his aid, nor the aid of the local military. He says that they owe their survival in large part to you. What do you say to these claims?"

"It wasn't just me. We spent a couple of days on our own, yeah. But in the end, we would've been dead if it wasn't for him."

"I see." The alien adjusted in their seat. It seemed as if they were getting tired of talking to him, "Last question. What is your reason for joining us?"

"Athriel didn't tell you?" Victor asked.

"He told us his version. We want yours. Primitives often know not how to tell a proper lie."

"My family is all that I have. Athy and I made a deal. I go along with this, do my damnedest for all of you, and he gets my family some place safe."

"And how would your work be affected if your family were to perish?"

Victor answered without hesitation, "I'd be useless to you. So, if we're doing this then you'd better keep your end of the deal."

"Keep in mind where it is you are and who it is you speak to. Besides, this is Athriel's deal, not ours. Anyway, it seems that will be all for questioning, Victor Roberts."

"So... do I pass?"

"Just so. I will alert the council to the deal between you two. It seems you will be useful to us after all."

"Okay, good." Victor sighed in relief before standing back up. Even at his full height, he was hardly more than half the height of the behemoth across from him, "Now, what's next? Let's get this done."

The tiavan looked at him with its pale, silver eyes, "Undress." It said, pointing to the tube on the other side of the room, "And step inside the chamber."

Victor had questions, but he knew better than to ask them. Instead, he did as the alien told and, when he was down to his bare skin, he made his way to the tank. It would have only been a few steps for the giant, but it was a walk for him. The whole time, he was struggling to stay composed. He didn't know why, but couldn't shake the feeling that his entire life, as he knew it, was coming to an end.

The tank split apart down the middle, forming an opening for him to step inside. When the sides came together once again and formed that impenetrable, clear wall between him and the rest of existence, everything fell silent. His whole world seemed to be waiting with bated breath as the silver-brown being moved to what must have been the control panel. Two of those thin appendages from its back reached out and flipped a series of switches on the console.

The first switch sealed the tank shut, making it airtight. For the briefest moment, Victor wondered if he would run out of oxygen. The second switch opened a large vent behind Victor's feet. The third released a thick, transparent fluid into the chamber. It began to fill the tank, reaching his knees within a minute, then his waist, then his shoulders. By the time it came to his chin, Victor was ready to panic. He closed his eyes and forced himself to stay calm. The fluid level rose over his head, but still he wouldn't let himself give in to the fear. Athriel wouldn't have led him to a space station halfway across the solar system just to drown him in a tank.

Victor took a shallow breath. With it, he realized that he wouldn't suffocate after all. This fluid, whatever it was, was somehow breathable. This helped to contain his anxiety. He was right. Athriel wouldn't have brought him all this way just to kill him. Whatever was to happen next, Victor knew that he would survive it.

224

Then came the searing pain.

Chapter 11

"How are the test subjects?" asked Athriel. He was standing in the security room of the testing area, watching each of his new hosts through the cameras in their chambers.

"Another has died." answered another, *"That brings the total to four. Four dead, six alive."* Sycura of House Mecurin was somewhat younger than Athriel, although they were still more than ancient by human measures. They stood nearly a foot taller than their superior, with pale skin and lush, teal markings.

"All three of yours are fine, for the time being at least." they added, *"Daniel Emerson is still asleep, but the others are awake. Victor Roberts is almost ready to begin training, in fact. And Travis is already displaying an aptitude for telekinesis."*

Athriel approached the screens, studying them one by one with stoic intent, *"And will Travis be joining us for training soon?"*

Sycura pressed on the control panel, pulling up readings of human vitals. Under the recordings of bodily functions was a bright warning sign, *"DNA tests on the one called Travis Norwich have been… complicated. The splicing took for the most part, but some parts of his body are still fighting it. Namely his central nervous system."*

"Are you certain?" Athriel asked.

"Not entirely. Not yet. Keep in mind that he has only been hosting tiavan matter for six days. We are still running tests, but this defect seems as if it could spread to other systems as well. Smell, sight, hearing, emotional centers. Anything that determines his external environments or controls his temperament could be at risk."

"We can fix this, correct? If he is already showing promise, then

we cannot afford to lose him. Surely this can be fixed."

"That remains to be seen. We are lucky that we found this early on, but fixing it might not be feasible."

"Are you saying that we could lose a fifth test subject?"

Sycura's face contorted into what was akin to a frown, *"It is a good possibility. The threat is severe enough that the lab contacted me."*

Athriel paused for a time, thinking over the details in his head, *"Very well,"* he said at last, *"I understand. Have the lab workers run their tests. If there is no point in fixing him, then I will arrange to have him euthanized."*

* * *

Travis laid there in his white cot, wearing white clothes, surrounded by white walls, illuminated by white light. He laid there in that room and he felt. With his newfound strength, he felt every molecule in the room as if it was a part of his very body. The rigid metal of the cot. Electrons surging through the walls and ceiling. The racing photons pouring out from every light source. The cold, lazy air drifting around him. Everything. He felt everything. It was almost overwhelming.

He had also figured out that he could interact with the world to some degree, if only he focused. More than once, he had felt for something outside the room, later finding out through nurses or guards that he had turned off the hallway lights. He could also feel when someone was walking by or standing at the doorway. It didn't matter if they made noise or shook the floor. He just knew. He always knew.

At this moment, two guards were standing by his door. A third entity, somewhat smaller than the others, approached them. Travis figured it was a nurse. They often approached from the same direction, stopping and talking to the guards before coming in and performing their tests. This one did just the same. It stopped by Travis' door, in front of the guards. Through the walls, he could hear their muffled voices talking in their strange language. He wondered what they were saying.

Lately, he had been getting better with his manipulations. Now, he wanted to try and see if he could move something intentionally, instead of feeling around and waiting for something to happen. Travis focused. Slowly, aspects of the hallway beyond the door came to life in his mind. The shape of the corridor, the flow of electricity through the walls, the lights and machines and nearby gadgets – he could feel it all, to some extent. The nurse was holding something small, though he couldn't tell what it was. However, he felt that he knew what was around the belt of one of the guards. Travis lifted a hand towards his point of focus, feeling for it from behind the door. He squinted, trying with all his might to move his newfound mental muscles with surgical precision.

The translator buzzed alive, immediately spouting the words, "...ready to euthanize –" before the guard realized and switched it back off.

Travis' eyes widened. His heart sank. Euthanize? Did they mean to euthanize him? Why would they want to kill him? After promising him so much, why would they betray him like that? How could Athriel let it end like this? He couldn't believe what was happening, but soon enough a noise snapped him out of his shock. It was the sound of the locks turning as the door readied itself to slide open. Travis leapt out of his cot, landing with a thud on his bare feet.

The door opened.

"You are... standing?" the nurse asked, speaking in English instead of working through his translator. He hid his surprise, albeit poorly, through a human-like smile, "That is great news."

"I've been walking around in here for days." Travis looked the alien over. He wasn't of any species that the human had seen before. Not a tiavan, nor an obarosi or a minitia. He was tall like the first two, with dark skin and rigid plates all over his body. His arms were folded, but there was

228

something hidden behind the thick fingers of his hand. It looked like a syringe, but it was filled with a liquid that Travis didn't recognize, "What have you got there?"

"We have… noticed that you have not been sleeping. I was told to… give you something to help."

"I've slept fine, thank you." said Travis.

The alien continued its forced smile, "Is that so? Well, my superiors still want me to give you this. They must think it will help."

"You're not sticking me with that." Travis took a step back.

"It will be alright, Mister Norwich. After the… splicing, this is insig… nificant." The alien nurse stepped forward, holding the syringe out towards the human. Travis didn't know what to do. He panicked.

"Get the hell away from me." He raised an arm and the nurse froze.

The smile faded from the nurse's alien face. He looked at Travis with fear, as well as a certain level of disgust, "It is against Kingdom law to… manipulate another… sen… tient life form."

"You're not touching me."

"Guards?"

At that moment, the two guards rushed through the doorway, one after the other. Without thinking, Travis pushed on the nurse with all his might, sending him back into the new arrivals. The guards fell to either side of the entrance, creating a hole between them. One of them tried to catch the nurse, who ended up flying through the opening. The other raised a hand and hit the control panel. The door began to slide closed. Travis acted fast and lunged through, propelling himself with his newfound strength.

At that moment, Travis knew that there were two things for him to do. First, that he had to get as far away from this facility as possible. Second, that he needed a hostage to ensure his safety. The nurse would help him accomplish both.

229

"He has not even recovered from the splicing. How is he able to overwhelm two grown obarosi and an uridan?" Athriel stared at the screens, a level of disbelief across his face. It had only been days since the procedure – only a small time since Travis could even begin to figure anything out. Yet somehow, this human being was exhibiting a level of telekinetic control that would take the average tiavan many years to replicate. He'd been able to do something so intricate as activating a translator, yet he could also throw another life form several feet? If Athriel hadn't seen it with his own eyes, he would have called it lunacy. This host was learning faster than he could have ever predicted. It was a shame that he had to go.

How could he do this? Did the splicing procedure make him more receptive than an actual tiavan? Or did it have something to do with being human? Perhaps it had to do with whatever went wrong with his splicing. Whatever it was, it didn't matter at this moment. Travis was already free from his room with a hostage at his side. Next, he would try to escape the facility.

Sycura looked up at him, *"Should we notify the leaders of this breech?"*

"Not yet."

Sycura was surprised. They couldn't understand why Athriel would want to keep any of this a secret, *"An escaped test subject is cause for immediate notification. Our superiors will be furious if we do not tell them."*

"I did not say that we will forego telling them altogether." Athriel turned to leave. As he found the doorway, he hesitated, *"Sycura, you stay here and watch the monitors. I will take security and track down our test subject."*

* * *

"Keep moving." Travis snarled, pressing on the back of the nurse's head. With an outstretched hand and a willful mind, he was in firm control of the situation. He was getting more used to it by now – these abilities, these sensations. He felt the path in front of him, just as he felt the nurse's head in his mental grip.

The nurse, it seemed, wasn't as used to it, "How did you throw me like that?" he asked.

"You lot made me. You should know the answer. Now stop." Travis felt something just around the corner. However, when he tried to focus on it, he was met with just a haze. He couldn't make sense of any of it. "Look 'round the corner, slow like. Anybody there?"

The nurse lurched forward until his head was beyond the wall corner, "You are clear."

"Good. Now move."

Travis pressed on the hostage once again and they circled around. However, the human soon realized that he'd been tricked. The thing he had felt beyond the corner was a group of three obarosi, each suited in that thick full-body armor.

The nurse cried out to the guards in his native tongue, *"Shoot him! Shoot the subject!"* At that moment, Travis knew that he was in for a fight. He grabbed onto the nurse, grasping a shoulder in one hand and his neck in another. He glared at the three behemoths in front of him and growled, "I'll kill him if you try anything."

The obarosi didn't respond with words. Instead, they took aim with their weapons. One of these giants grabbed onto him. Travis' hands were pried from his hostage and forcing his arms out by his sides. Travis struggled to break free, but to no avail. He was at the mercy of these armored goliaths.

"No, no…" he strained, "Get off me… Leave me alone…" He kicked and wrestled and screamed, but nothing worked. When his struggling proved futile, his heart sank again. He felt powerless. Trapped. Soon they would capture him, and then they would kill him.

"Get away from me!"

* * *

"Around that corner." Sycura uttered through Athriel's earpiece, *"That is his last known location. After that, all of the security feeds cut out."*

Athriel raced through the corridor, flanked on each side by half a dozen security guards, *"Something's happened here."* he said, *"I feel trouble."*

"They had captured him, and then the cameras went dark."

The squad rounded the corner and came face to face with an astonishing sight. There was a fissure in the metal along the floor, leading up one of the walls. On the other wall was a splash of red blood.

Athriel studied the cracked metal closely, *"It did not go through the hull. I suppose that is why we are still breathing. I sense that this is an outer wall, separating us from open space."*

"Your senses guide you well." said one of the guards, *"If the test subject had broken through, everyone in this part of the station would be dead. Himself included."*

The first question Athriel had was how Travis knew that he was at he was at the edge of the station – that damaging the wall could kill his attackers. Were his senses that attuned already? The thought piqued Athriel's interest. Then there was his second question, born from an astute observation. The hull of the station was made from a complex alloy that even Athriel would have had difficulty tearing. How was Travis, a human, able to rip into it with a power that he'd only possessed for a matter of days? Was this what hosts were capable of? If so, Athriel figured that a group of them could take down a minitia hive without casualty, given the proper training.

His train of thought was broken when his earpiece buzzed to life with Sycura's voice, *"Athriel,"* they said, *"I have visual on the test subject. He is close to docking bay twelve, approaching from the east side."*

"Clear the bay of all personnel. We are on our way."

* * *

Travis sighed, "No one is there. Maybe it's a trap." He and his hostage stood behind a corner, just before the entry to docking bay twelve. They had been moving for some time, leaving a thin trail of human blood behind them. However, Travis refused to let a shoulder wound keep him from saving his own life.

"Just turn yourself in." the nurse pleaded, "Please. Nobody else needs to be injured."

"Only if they get between me and one of those ships." Travis went silent as he planned his next move. His face was frozen in a look of quiet fury, as if he could explode at any moment, giving the hostage the impression that he was ready to explode at any moment.

"You should figure this out soon, human." said the nurse, "The guards will find us any minute now and I don't know how much they value me. They might shoot through me if it means getting to you."

Travis looked at his hostage, seemingly unfazed, "What's your name? What are you called?"

"Zaatrid."

"Well Zaatrid, you should probably close the hole in your face where all that noise is coming from. Anyway, I know how we'll be getting to one of those ships."

His arms raised in a fighting stance, Travis made his way around the corner and into clear view of everything in the docking bay. As he stepped forward, a metallic groaning erupted on all sides. Across the bay, platforms shook and railings twisted. This was all due to great effort on the human's part, but he was intent on keeping any eyes focused on the other side of the room. When he got close to one of the ships, he tightened his grip on one of the railings from the far end, managing to unhook it from the platform it stood on. He pulled at it with determination, sending the metal skidding across the floor. The sound was painful enough to make

233

anybody cringe. If anybody was hiding at the far side of the bay, they must have been crushed. Anyone else would be searching in the wrong direction.

"Open the ramp." said Travis, pointing to his new ship. It was a box-like contraption with rounded edges and ridges along the center. Perhaps it was designed to hold cargo, but Travis had no way of knowing.

"I would need the key." Zaatrid answered.

Travis grabbed tightly at his hostage's throat, "Do you think I'm simple? Open it with your mind. I know you can." When Zaatrid still hesitated, he groaned, "Never mind. I'll figure it out." With his free hand, he reached out towards the craft. He could feel all its inner workings. Every inch gave in to his will. It was all becoming clear, but he couldn't figure out what mechanism opened the door.

He tried a couple of systems. The first had no electricity going to it, so nothing happened. The second made an intense grinding noise, as if metal was moving against metal. "Let's hope that doesn't come back and bite me in the arse." Travis commented. Finally, he found what felt like a hydraulic system. With a great deal of effort, he searched for what felt like a lever and, at last, the ramp dropped clumsily from the ship. It occurred to Travis just how unlikely it was that he could have just opened the door to an alien craft. Had this been any other situation, it may have been cause for celebration.

"Travis, please stop." It was the voice of Athriel himself.

At the sound of his name, Travis stopped. He turned, not keen on letting his betrayer have at his back, "I heard what your people said over the translator. You won't euthanize me."

Several obarosi guards accompanied the tiavan. They slowly moved to circle the human, leaving him surrounded. However, while everything looked to be heading towards a fight, Athriel appeared as calm as ever, "That was never the plan." he said, "Travis, you are a part of this program. You are a host of my people's matter. Why would I have you killed?"

"I don't know. Why would you?"

"Just let go of the nurse, my friend. Let go and we can pretend as if this never happened. You can go back to your room and in the next couple of days we can begin to train you. We can make you all that you have to be to kill as many minitia as possible." Athriel paused. Then with a voice that was all too human in tone, he asked, "That is what you want, correct?"

"More than anything." Travis had to admit that Athriel's words were tempting. However, he knew a trap when he saw one, "I want to kill them more than anything, which means I'll need to live long enough to meet 'em."

At that moment, Athriel understood that words would get him nowhere. He motioned to the security guards, who began to close in tighter around Travis. The human threw a hand out towards Athriel, who shot back with an electric bolt. His combatant began to collapse as his muscles froze up, but he quickly recovered and charged for the ship. A couple of guards took aim, ready to fire, but the human's resolution proved too much. The floor beneath them buckled, forcing them off balance. This was enough for Travis to get away into the ship, dragging his hostage along with his telepathic grip. The ramp tried to rise, but Athriel's strength kept it down.

Travis was forced to duck and cover when bright red bolts hit the hull. The obarosi had opened fire. "Raise the ship." he snarled, "Get us out of here."

Zaatrid shuddered with fear, "The ramp is down. We would be killed."

"Just do it!"

With no other choice, Zaatrid tapped at the control panel. The great machine around them roared to life. He went to work, flipping switches and pressing on screens until the lights in the ship switched from a sickly yellow to a bright white. Travis felt the mechanical mass buckle and rise beneath him as they began to lift off the ground. Down below, he heard Athriel shout in his own tiavan tongue. At once, the shots ceased and the unseen force pulling at the ramp was gone. The door closed and sealed. The ship moved forward, through the hangar's plasma barrier.

Once they were in open space, Travis gave a long sigh of relief, "Now get us far away from here."

"Do you have a… place in mind, or…"

"Pick a direction."

It was settled. A moment later, something in the vessel hummed to life. The whole craft shook ever so slightly before the whole universe around it went black.

Athriel could do nothing but watch on as the ship prepared for FTL and burst away, taking his faulty test subject with it. Travis Norwich was gone, taking an uridan worker with him.

Chapter 12

After Travis escaped from the station, the other surviving test subjects found themselves closely monitored at all hours. Only a couple of days after the incident, it seemed that all of them were ready to begin training. Athriel had wished for a larger group to work with, but he had to settle for these five. There were the Americans, Victor Roberts and Daniel Emerson. Of course, they already knew each other. Then there was the Russian nurse, Anya Petrova, the former Israeli soldier, Naomi Daskal, and finally Rin Ishibashi, a Japanese native who, unlike the others, refused to talk about her life prior to the splicing. They were humanity's first offer to the long-anticipated Host Project.

Training started off all too unremarkable. The humans had to be in top physical condition, so they spent the majority of their first week and a half in a gymnasium designed for their small, bipedal forms. The regimens were long and difficult. When they weren't slaving away with weights and machines, they were eating or sleeping or even just sitting around, forced to talk amongst each other. Athriel had expressed the importance of these people getting to know one another since they were going to be 'comrades in arms', as he called it. Because of this, they were given two or three hours daily to simply sit in a room together and talk about anything they wanted.

There were also meditation lessons. Every day after their time in the gymnasium, the humans were all taken to a place in the station that seemed like nothing else on this side of the solar system. The floor was lined with wooden paneling. The lights were softer and felt more natural

A small water fountain babbled away in the center of the room. Beside it, there was an assortment of small objects, all varying in exact size and consistency. At first, none of them knew what these items were, but it soon became apparent that they were tools built to be manipulated by their alien telekinesis. Every day after working out, they would gather in this room where a tiavan instructor would be waiting for them. There, they would spend the next couple of hours learning to feel the world around them. The wood in the floors. The rays of light. The particles in the air. Everyone was encouraged to try to grasp the items on the ground or to bend the streams of water in the fountain. By the end of the second week, every human was at least able to do the former.

* * *

The day started just like any other. After eating breakfast with Dan and the others, he got changed and went on his way. After the initial stretching, he spent a good hour on the treadmill to build up his cardio. He hadn't realized how little running he did in the time before the bombs fell. The pains in his legs and chest scolded him for being so sedentary for all those years. He would have cussed himself out under his breath if he was able to breathe.

Next, he went to the punching bag. As a native Bostonian, punching was always something he was good at. He had the form down long before the Host Project. However, he noticed that as the weeks went on he could move the punching bag more and more. Every time he landed his first hook of the day, the bag jolted back farther than it ever had before. It made Victor feel powerful, like he could break one of those bugs with his bare hands.

"Not hard enough." said Athriel. Victor hadn't even noticed him come in. Of course, even if he hadn't been preoccupied, he still probably wouldn't have realized until those words came out. Athriel always had a way of coming and going without making a sound.

238

"You aren't hitting hard enough." The tiavan said plainly, watching on as the human pounded away at his fake enemy, "You need to do better if you want to progress with the others."

Victor stepped away from the punching bag, "If I go any harder, I'll pull something." His breathing was labored, still somewhat weary from the treadmill.

"Perhaps, if you use your muscles as a normal human does."

"If you hadn't noticed, I'm still human. Your little gene therapy didn't give me any macho alien muscles."

Athriel smiled, "Your muscles are matter." He said, "And like all matter, it can be manipulated." He gestured towards the punching bag. Unsure of what to do, Victor gave it a good jab. When he did, Athriel nodded and continued, "Notice how your arms feel as you take each punch. Notice which muscles contract and when. Feel which ones relax. Analyze the precise moment that every movement inside your arm happens. Now you know which matter to focus on. When a muscle is supposed to contract, do not simply contract it like a human. Force it together like a tiavan forces a rock into the air."

Victor frowned. He never thought about what it took to land a punch – to make any kind of movement, really. He stretched his arms, loosening them and feeling everything inside. Every muscle. Every bone and ligament and tendon. He felt them, not only as the owner of his arm, but as a tiavan felt the rocks in the ground. With hesitation, Victor raised his left arm, poised to strike at the punching bag. The fist lunged forward, propelled by human strength. When it struck, the target buckled and came back like it always did.

Next, he focused on his muscles. Not like a human. No. He focused like a tiavan. Like a host. Victor pulled his fist back and let it fly right into the center of the bag. As he pulled back again, Victor gave a pained cry, "Gah! Damn it!"

Athriel appeared unfazed by Victor's agony. He smiled, "Look how much farther the punching bag went. Do you see

239

how much stronger you became.?"

The human, however, didn't seem to care, "I think I snapped something in my arm, you idiot."

"You probably tore a muscle, my friend." said Athriel, "We can get that fixed. Come with me."

* * *

While Victor spent the rest of the morning fixing his arm in the infirmary, Dan was in the oxygen room learning to do something that any other person would call witchcraft.

"Remember the three steps to conjuring flame." The instructor stated, "First you must concentrate the oxygen around your target area. Then you feel for larger particles. Something abundant. Something flammable. Air always has these loose pieces of matter floating around. You must gather them and mix them with the oxygen. Lastly, you must send electrons to light a spark. Spark, plus oxygen, plus flammable material equals fire."

With the other hosts off working on other skills, their audience was made up of only Dan and Rin. They stood beside each other, opposite of their teacher, with their hands cupped in front of them. One of them was at least able to complete step one of the instructor's task. The other was Dan. No matter how hard he tried, he couldn't bring the fuel together. Even if he had been getting better, it wasn't as if he could see any progress in the imperceptible air.

"Feel the particles." said the instructor, "Sense how the oxygen is different from the nitrogen. The carbon dioxide. The water vapor. Separate it from the rest. Pool it together."

Dan sighed, "Yeah, that's real easy to do when you can't see what you're doing."

"Miss Ishibashi is doing quite well with it." With the flick of an arysthum, one of the six wing-like appendages coming from their back, the instructor gestured toward their more prodigious student, and then back at Daniel, "Perhaps you need more focus."

Dan nodded with uncertainty, "If you say so."

As he said that, Dan felt a sudden burst of warmth from his side. While everyone else was talking, Rin had been ready and focused. And now, while he couldn't even gather the air for such a feat, she had made fire.

The instructor looked on excitedly. First, they muttered something in their own tongue. Then they stammered, "By the Higher. It looks as though we have a natural pyromancer in our midst."

Meanwhile, Dan could do nothing but stare in amazement. Hovering just above Rin's hand was a contained ball of red fire. It was no larger than a baseball, but it burned with an intensity that could have matched the heart of a furnace. While it didn't last long, the sight left an impact on Dan that he hadn't expected. It occurred to him that this was, in fact, the first time in which he'd seen a real human being perform such a thing. He would have expected it from Athriel by now, even the instructor, but it was another thing entirely to see someone just like him – an average human– create fire from nothing. So, he just stared. Then, after collecting himself, he gave his rival a warm smile, "Beginner's luck."

* * *

When the hosts weren't in the middle of training they were getting to know one another. They told each other stories from their past lives back on Earth, going into detail about what their own little worlds were like before everything fell apart. All of them, save for Rin Ishibashi, were open about who they were, what they did, even teaching each other about useful tricks or concepts. Anya Petrova would go on for hours about her medical knowledge – how to fix basic injuries, diagnose certain illnesses, treat for shock. Naomi Daskal, being a former Israeli soldier, taught them basic military formations and even drilled them on hand-to-hand combat. She was confident in her moves and near ruthless in her discipline, but still showed the softness of a trainer teaching her disciples. After a time, Victor and the others came to think of her training sessions as somewhat therapeutic – a way to forget about the stresses and tribulations of the universe outside and just focus on simple things like movement and breathing.

This day, however, was different. While Naomi and Anya were off talking amongst themselves, Dan was taking more to Rin's approach. Instead of socializing like always, he was sitting off in a corner, all by his lonesome. He hadn't even felt the need to take a chair. Instead, he was planted on the ground, his back pressed against the wall and his long legs pulled up to his chest. Victor noticed and, after a time, decided to come over and take a seat next to his friend. They were quiet for a long time, him not knowing what to say and the other seemingly lost in thought. If nothing else.

Then at once, Dan let out a small laugh and nudged his friend, "Do you remember Richard Eldridge?"

Victor raised an eyebrow in curiosity, but still smiled back, "Dicky Ricky? Of course, I do. Guy was such an asshole." He was amused, but confusion still took him. What did this have to do with anything?

"Oh, he wouldn't leave us alone for a good half of high school. Always stealing from our friends, threatening us, trying to get us all to fight him."

"I don't know what his problem was."

"And then there was the day where we finally got back at him. Remember it?"

"We were in the cafeteria and he threw a milk carton at us. Splattered all over the table."

Dan was grinning from ear to ear, "And you were so mad that you got up and threw one right back."

"Oh, he was pissed." They laughed together, remembering the look on Richard's face, red and covered in milk after Victor's pinpoint accurate strike to the forehead.

"The rest of the day he was going around acting all

tough." Dan changed his voice to sell the imitation, "Hope you're digging your grave, Roberts, 'cause I'm gonna bury you." They laughed again, enjoying the memory of a day long since passed. "How did that end, again?"

"I believe I broke his nose while you filmed it." said Victor, "Don't tell me you forgot that."

"No, don't worry." Dan assured him, "I just like to hear you say it."

They were quiet for a moment.

"Things were so simple back then."

Victor nodded, "You can say that again."

"Our biggest worries in life were grades and bullies. Oh, how were we gonna get to the party across town? Who's gonna buy us something to drink? We didn't have to worry about training for the next big battle. We just studied for tests. We weren't worried about our loved ones, praying night after night that they made it to the next day. We just worried about whether or not we'd get into college. Hell, we didn't even have car payments or rent." The smile on Dan's face had faded, replaced by a deep look of thoughtful sorrow, "Even then we felt so overwhelmed, but we had no idea what was in store for us."

"We were young." said Victor, "Things were simpler because we were simpler. Our worries were small because our world was small."

"I miss it, is all. Things being so simple."

"The whole Richard Eldridge thing was fifteen years ago. Times change. We grew up. We got lives. Our world expanded. And after this, our world expanded even more. We can sit around and close our eyes and wish to go back to our smaller world with our insignificant problems, but when we open our eyes we'll still be here."

Dan shrugged, "I guess."

"Think about every major crisis in history." Victor began, "When the Nazis were steamrolling over Europe, did everyone just sit down and wish that things were normal again? No. They fought back. They raised armies, started

243

rebellions and fought hard to win. They forced things to go back to something they could sort of call normal."

"I think I see what you mean."

"That's exactly what we're going to do. We're gonna rail against the problem until it backs off and lets our world return to something resembling normalcy. Got it?"

Dan nodded. A hint of a smile returned to his face.

"That's the spirit."

"No, not that." he explained, "I was thinking about the fight with Dicky Ricky. Do you think the video still exists?"

Victor was at a momentary loss for words, a sense of confusion again brewing inside him, "Uh, maybe somewhere."

"When this is all over, I'm gonna try to find it again. We can even show the kids. I bet they'd love to see their Daddy kicking ass."

* * *

More time passed and the test subjects continued their training. The next day, Victor had learned to amplify his strength. From then on, he had joined Naomi in physical combat training. By the end of the week, Dan was tossing fireballs more than a yard. By the end of the month, all five were deemed ready to begin sparring.

The first match was between Rin Ishibashi and Anya Petrova. Over the weeks, Anya had clearly shown the mindset of someone who preferred to sidestep direct confrontation. She was surprisingly timid for a soldier in training, keeping to defensive maneuvers throughout the match. Meanwhile, Rin seemed to hold an unnerving amount of aggression. While it was true that she was the least social of the group, she had a kind of ferocity in her that had only become more apparent since training began. As one could expect, the match between these women was one-sided.

The second match saw Victor going up against Naomi Daskal. Everybody saw the flaw in this pairing. The

244

American, while a hair larger than his opponent, was by no means a capable fighter. Out of all the surviving test subjects, he had the most difficulty mastering his newfound abilities. Sure, he could amplify his strength like all the others, but he was still much slower to react than any of them, unable to focus his senses like they could. Meanwhile, the Israeli had proven herself to be a force of nature. Her military background made her unrelenting at close range and gifted her with the mindset of a true soldier. Even with advanced protective gear, her opponent knew that he would be walking away bruised and beaten.

Naomi stepped into the ring without a second's thought. Victor followed hesitantly. Naomi brought her body into a rigid, intimidating opening stance. Victor raised his fists in front of his chest. Both waited anxiously for the signal.

The bell sounded. Naomi began to pace sideways, circling Victor. Her demeanor couldn't have been more different from the training sessions. She was cold and rigid, without an ounce of mercy in her eyes. As she moved, she inched in closer and closer to her target. The American turned to keep face with her, refusing to give her a clear shot at his flank. After another moment of rounding one another, Naomi and Victor were within striking distance. Every spectator could feel the tension in the air as Naomi waited for the perfect moment to move.

Then it all seemed to happen at once. Naomi stepped forward and threw a jab. Victor deflected it easily enough and leaned forward for a counterattack. Before he knew it, though, she had grabbed his arm and shoulder. Next, he felt something hit his leg, knocking him off balance. The world spiraled around him and the next thing he knew, he was on his belly with a searing pain in his arm. Only then did he realize that Naomi had flipped him. What's more, she still had control of his arm and kept her foot planted firmly on his shoulder. Victor tried to fight back, to wrestle free or roll away, but nothing broke Naomi's iron grip on him. He was at her mercy.

"Damn it, I'm out!" he yelled, "I give!"

The bell sounded and Naomi released him.

"Well that did not last long." Anya commented through her translator, giving the winner a quiet applause.

Dan shook his head as his friend crawled back to his feet, "Damn, Vic." he said, "Couldn't you have at least lasted a little longer?"

"Bitch knows Krav Maga." said Victor. He took his place at the sidelines, next to Dan.

"What the hell's Krav Maga?" asked Dan.

"It's what she used to nearly tear my goddamn arm off." Victor felt his shoulder with his good hand. It appeared to him as if his arm was one twist away from being ripped from the socket. With care, he began to massage the area where it hurt most, "It's a martial art from Israel. That woman's IDF. I knew she was gonna kick my ass, but damn I didn't think she was gonna go that hard on me."

The instructor came by and, after looking Victor over, told him to sit out for the rest of the session. He was hesitant to accept the order, though. It was humiliating enough to be beaten like that in his first real sparring match, but it was another thing entirely to be forced to the sidelines while everyone else continued. He could do nothing but stand there as he watched Dan face off against Rin, then Anya against Naomi, then Rin against Anya. Each of them had a turn to spar with everyone else. All of them got to show off what they had learned throughout their month of training, while also defining what areas they needed to put more focus into. Everyone, that is, except Victor, who perhaps needed it most of all.

* * *

Every moment of their time on Jupiter Station was documented. Every action was looked over and scrutinized. With Travis still fresh in their memories, the tiavan running the station wanted to catch any behavioral problems before they got out of hand. That meant Athriel had to spend most of the past few weeks secluded in his chamber, looking through security footage of the test subjects. As a result, he got to watch how the test subjects interacted with each other. Social habits in primitive species had always fascinated him. That was part of the reason why he spent so long as a changeling before joining the Host Project. He found enjoyment in learning about the cultures and lifestyles of lesser peoples. Unfortunately, it had been some time since he was last sent to assess a planet. Nowadays, watching the test subjects was the closest thing he could find to ease his curious hunger.

The door slid open, letting a familiar face into his personal quarters, *"Do you have a moment?"* It was Nyro.

Athriel peered up at his friend, a look of curiosity on his pale face, *"You are back."* he stated, more to himself than anything, *"Has Noble Endoraith released you from the blockade?"* He waited for a response. When there was none, he began to understand the urgency of Nyro's business, *"What do you need?"*

"I feel that we should discuss one of our test subjects. Victor Roberts. Every other participant has shown rapid improvement in skills regarding a variety of areas. Naomi Daskal in particular is unmatched in physical prowess. She has incorporated her new abilities into her combat style to a degree that no other host has. Both Rin Ishibashi and Daniel Emerson have made great strides in heat manipulation. I have even seen them create prolonged flames. Anya Petrova has been excelling marvelously at organic matter manipulation. She may even be on your level someday, if she can learn to sculpt a form like you."

"And then there is Victor." said Athriel, anticipating Nyro's next words.

Nyro gave a gesture of agreement, *"Victor Roberts has shown little improvement in any of these fields. He can at least match Anya Petrova in basic telekinesis, but he still cannot work with anything too intricate."*

"It has been twenty-nine days."

"And in this time, every other Host has shown significant

247

potential."

"Think of how we had planned for this." said Athriel, *"They were never meant to make this kind of progress so quickly. As far as we should be concerned, the other four are exceeding expectations. Victor is simply meeting them."*

"But he is not keeping up with them." Nyro countered, *"If we plan to use them as weapons against Linious and their minitia, then we cannot have one of their squad falling behind. As I see it, he must either show genuine improvement or be removed from his team."*

At this, Athriel's composure hardened. His voice took on a stern tone, *"His removal will not be required."*

"How can you ensure that?" asked Nyro.

"I can." Athriel stated, his face rigid, *"I will. We simply have to find his niche."*

* * *

Athriel found his favorite test subject in the gymnasium. When he arrived, Victor was pounding away at the punching bag. Since he learned to amplify his strength, it had become a marvel to behold this small creature toss that heavy sack around like it was nothing. Athriel watched him for a time before finally announcing himself, "I assume your shoulder is feeling better."

"I went to the infirmary after practice." Victor said, "Doc fixed me up. I don't know what's in that gel you guys use, but it's better than anything Earth's got."

Athriel smiled, "Well that is what you can expect from a civilization that has been prospering for longer than your species has even existed."

"Is that so?" asked Victor. He struck his last blow at the punching bag, then turned to the tiavan. He was panting and drenched in sweat, with a look of exhaustion weighing on his face, "Roughly how old are you guys, anyway?"

"I'm afraid you wouldn't believe me if I told you." said Athriel.

"Well how old are you, then?" Victor pointed a finger at

248

him, "A thousand years? More?"

"Far more." Athriel watched as Victor folded his arms and stepped away from the punching bag. A bead of sweat dripped down the bridge of his nose, glistening in the light. His breath was still labored. To Athriel's surprise, however, this human seemed careless of the strain on his body.

"But you didn't come here to talk about your age."

"No." said Athriel, "I came to discuss your progress."

"What about it?" asked Victor.

"A colleague of mine spoke to me. It seems the results of your first month of training have been... lacking."

"Why's that? 'Cause I can't shoot fire or do Krav Maga? That Israeli woman learned that on Earth, by the way. You guys had nothing to do with-"

"That is my colleague's observation." said Athriel, "Not mine. You have no need to prove yourself to me."

"But I have to prove myself to your friend, right?"

Athriel hesitated. There was nothing he could tell Victor except, "Unfortunately so. Yes."

Victor's arms tightened against his torso. His expression turned to one of distress. Athriel knew that whatever feelings Victor was trying to conceal were beginning to break the surface, "Well I'm sorry to let you all down." he said, "I signed up for this. I went through that transformation thing like you wanted me to. I made you promise to protect my family, and in return I was supposed to be some kind of guinea pig or weapon or something. Well I'm sorry if, so far, I'm looking like a failed experiment."

It was then that the tiavan saw what emotions Victor was trying to hide. This human wasn't embarrassed to be so far behind the others. He felt that he had let Athriel down. He believed that he had failed – and he was afraid. He was afraid because Athriel had accepted responsibility over keeping his family safe, and as far as he knew his family was safe. Now, in his mind he wasn't able to hold up his side of the bargain. Was he worried that, if he didn't make sufficient progress, the tiavan might turn his back on the human's family?

"I want to try something." Athriel told him, "I want you to try something."

For a moment, Victor looked at him in complete silence. Athriel could tell that he was being studied. Then without warning, the human seemed to come alive once more. He took a short, deep breath and raised an arm to scratch behind his own head. Then, almost nonchalantly, he nodded and said, "Sure, why not? I'm game."

Athriel gave a hint of a smile, "Come sit down. Sit with me."

"Okay…" Victor followed his lead, unsure of what to expect.

"Now hold your arms out in front of you, bent towards each other at the elbows. Have the palm of your dominant hand curled above the other. Keep them close, but keep them separated. That part is very important."

"Okay, I'll bite. What is this?"

"You'll see soon enough, my friend. Now I want you to cup your palms. Position them as if you are holding a ball between your hands. Remember, your palms should never touch." Victor did as he was told, holding himself in the exact way that Athriel had directed him, "Good. Now I want you to close your eyes and feel."

"The particles between my hands?"

"No." said Athriel, "I want you to feel the particles in your hands. Feel the molecules."

Victor was confused. Was Athriel trying to teach him to change organic matter like Anya was taught?

"When you have a good sense of them, go deeper. Feel the atoms. Then, if you can, try to feel for different parts of the atoms."

Different parts? Wasn't Athriel asking too much from him? Victor didn't see how he could ever do that. Feeling overwhelmed, he shook his head and opened his eyes, "I don't know if I can." he said, "It's already too much to keep track of every molecule. I can't go deeper into atoms."

250

Athriel looked at him with a soft expression that Victor was unaccustomed to, "The key is not to keep track of everything. Simply be aware of them. Tell me, when you place your hand in a stream of water, do you keep track of every molecule as it flows? When you touch your finger to your skin, do you know the exact alignment of every particle?"

"No."

"Of course not. However, you are aware of them. You can feel them, even if you cannot differentiate between them."

"So, you want me to feel the atoms without tracking them?"

"When you look at flowing water, you can focus on the entire stream or you can focus on the little bits of earth and debris flowing with it. I am asking you to focus on the bits, rather than the whole."

Athriel watched as Victor closed his eyes again. This time there was something different about the expression on the human's face. He seemed hesitant, but less overwhelmed. A focused curiosity had taken him. The tiavan smiled, "Can you feel the atoms?"

Victor nodded.

"Excellent. Now go even further. Think of the atoms as the stream. Look for the bits flowing along within them."

"I can feel them." said Victor. His eyes were closed, his face rigid with concentration, "Each one is empty, like a vortex. A hole. But there's something in the middle of the hole. Something strong – and it's pulling on these other things surrounding it."

"Focus on the surrounding energy. Now listen very carefully, because my next instructions are vital. Go within the atoms of your top hand. I'd like you to take that surrounding energy. I'd like you to take it and pull it from the core. Take as much of it away as you can and send it to your bottom hand."

Victor's expression became more strained. His hands began to shake.

"Do this for as long as you can." Athriel told him, "And when you cannot do it anymore, you can let go. However, you have to let go all at once. All or nothing. Hold or release."

As soon as the tiavan finished, Victor's grip on these forces gave out. At once, he heard a loud snap pierce through the air while something hot and fast stung his palms with a ferocity that he hadn't felt since he was a young boy. It brought back the memory of a time when he and Danny were trespassing through an industrial yard and they had to hop a fence. He hadn't read the sign clarifying that the fence was electrified. When Victor touched the metal wiring, he received a jolt that sent him flying back. The shock didn't throw him this time, but it nevertheless told him exactly what he had just done.

He opened his eyes and saw Athriel staring back at him, "Congratulations, my friend." The tiavan said, "It seems that you've discovered electricity."

Chapter 13

The ramp dropped, opening a hole in the transport and letting the light in. Marceline had spent so long in the dark that it was both welcoming and painful to see the bright glow of the sun. Only this wasn't her sun. She and her children have been on a transport ship for what seemed like an eternity. The whole time, they were packed in with others like cattle. Now they stepped from their stellar cage and into the light of a new star. Boots touched the ground, but it wasn't Earth beneath their feet. Nonderan was many things. According to rumor, it was a previously uninhabited world under the dominion of the tiavan and their allies. Being rich in minerals at the time, the Assembly had mined the planet for decades before the war broke out on Earth. In that time, they never made the surface habitable, preferring to keep their settlements within the confines of great interconnected domes. These domes were self-sustained cities, finding energy in the rays of the planet's star and food through its small pockets of agriculture. All of this proved useful when Linious came to Earth, followed by his dark swarm. The domes were already built, many of them even connected at this point, and they could have easily been adapted to suit Earthling conditions. As Marceline stepped off the transport with her children, she was surprised to find trees and grass awaiting her. In the distance, she saw fields of wheat and corn being tended by advanced equipment. Many of the buildings were an amalgamation of human engineering on top of alien bases.

Marceline wondered what would happen if any of the domes were to break. If anything were to happen to even one of them, it went without saying that the entire settlement would have been compromised. The argon-rich atmosphere outside was toxic to a native of Earth. What's more, she had no idea what temperature it was out there. The last thing that any inhabitant needed was for the world out there to get inside. She also wondered if there were any problems that the aliens had failed to address. What if there were unforeseen issues for a human living on another world? Would she and her children be able to return once the war was finished? Perhaps they would be trapped on this rock for the rest of their lives. Maybe they would succumb to some illness or planetary anomaly within days of stepping off that ship. Or it could be that their alien helpers have, in truth, considered every factor and planned accordingly. Marceline realized that there was no point in worrying, since these possibilities were well beyond her control.

"Missus Roberts!" cried a familiar voice in the crowd. Marceline turned, her face lighting up with joy.

"Private Athens!" When he approached, she took him in a tight embrace before taking a step back to look him over, "I haven't seen you in a week. I thought you'd been sent to the front lines. I was so scared for you."

"I was assigned to be your personal guard here on Nonderan. I've been here setting things up for when you arrived."

"Thank God, then." She said.

"God's got nothing to do with it, Missus Roberts. From what I hear, Blue-Eyes made the call."

"Well it's nice to know that he's actually looking out for us. Oh, and please don't call me Missus Roberts. Just Marceline will do."

"Yes ma'am." Athens said, striking the warmest of smiles.

They walked together as Athens led the way to the family's new abode. As Marceline took her first steps into what would be her new home, she couldn't keep the expression of disgust from crawling like a spider across her face. The place was horrid. It was only a single room of about two hundred square feet. The air was stagnant and the whole area reeked of unearthly filth. No furniture to be seen, the room was utterly empty save for the inch-thick layer of dirt and grime covering the floor and Private Athens' backpack leaning against the sturdiest wall. Parts of the floor had crumbled under the weight of something that had long since passed, leaving jagged impressions wherever it went. One of the walls was half collapsed, taking a decent portion of the ceiling with it. Marceline surveyed the damage, appalled at the prospect of her two small children spending a single night in this decaying place. It was clear that whoever renovated the building for human use had never actually met a human being. These were not livable conditions.

"It was worse when I first got here." Athens said, "Much worse. There was even more filth, if you'd believe it."

Marceline scoffed, "That so? Well I hope you didn't make those craters in the floor."

"No, ma'am. Mine are the size twelve prints in the dirt."

With hesitation, Marceline took another step into the poor excuse for a house. She studied the fissured floor and the crumbled wall and the caved-in ceiling, trying to figure out exactly what to do with this place, "So… I guess we've got to make this into a home. Shall we get to work?"

* * *

While Marceline and Athens were busy setting up a life in this decrepit place, no adult could spare the time to watch the children. This kind of thing had happened often during their time at the safe zone, too. By this point, they were used to it. When this happened, Zack would find a relatively comfortable place near his mother and wait for her to finish her work. Meanwhile, Sammy would take the time to go for a walk, exploring the tent city around them. Only this time she was nowhere near the tent city of the DC Safe Zone. That was a world away. This day, she had a whole new place to discover. Nonderan Refugee Center A08. It was exciting, really. She had grown to love the unknown. Never in her life had she seen a town or a city built under domes. It was all so alien to her. What secrets could this place hold? She trembled with exhilaration at the thought of walking down any one of the hundred streets waiting just outside that door.

"Is there anything I can help with?" she asked. After all, Sammy didn't want to go off and disappear if her mother was going to need her.

Marceline didn't even look back, only saying, "No, honey. I think you're good. Just try to stay out of the grownups' way."

"Okay, Mommy." Sammy took a moment to make sure that nobody was looking before slipping out of the disheveled shack. She was careful not to make noise, as she wasn't sure if she could roam through the dome city without supervision. Her mother could just as easily say that it was too "dangerous" out there, or find some other boring excuse to keep her in that sorry-looking house. When she was finally in the clear, Sammy took some time to glance around at everything. She looked back and saw a long road leading to the center of town. Beyond that stood the docks, which housed the only place Sammy knew of where she could enter or leave the city. Branching off the main road were clusters of smaller, less developed streets. Each of those, in turn, broke off into several thin, rugged paths. The whole road system sprawled out from this main trunk like the branches of a vast, rust-colored tree.

Rust. Everything below the domes looked like they were carved from thick mounds of rust. The girl could tell that whoever built this place had actually made an effort to recreate the feeling of a real Earth city. The buildings had the same blocky exteriors and many of the roads were complete with sidewalks and the occasional stretch of real pavement. However, half an effort could never be enough to fool even the youngest of minds. The decrepitude and filth, the stagnant air, the dull shadow of a domed sky, the corroded colors of the streets and walls – none of it fit into a real

256

human municipality.

Without hesitation, Samantha made her first steps into the false city. She followed the main road for a time, studying every crack and stain. Everyone passing by had the same weariness and loathing chiseled into their faces. Every intersection with another street meant a new line of dilapidated shacks and filthy huts. After passing by a few of these rugged neighborhoods, she found that one suited her curiosity. In truth, it appeared no different than the others. The girl simply wanted to explore somewhere, anywhere besides the same street that she had taken on the way to her shack home. She made her way down this avenue with wide eyes and darting glances. Many of these sights were new to her. Entire homes made of nothing but poles for walls and tarps for ceilings. Hovels built from the same grunge that she had been walking on. Inside an open shack, an olive-skinned mother with dark hair and her three young children were gathered around something standing near the back wall. They were crying. Sam never got a clear look at what the object was, but could at least tell that it was made of wood and surrounded by a handful of lit candles. Next door, a pale, graying man was nailing a painted wooden sign onto the space above his doorway. It read, "REPAIRMAN 4 HIRE" in large, red print. Sammy's first thought was to question how this man obtained red paint. After all, almost nothing in this filthy, rust bucket of a city had so much as a coat. Two people across the street, a woman and a man, were resting outside their hut. The man, aged and coated with what can only be described as fur, was leaning against the side of his new home while his slender, more youthful counterpart sat with her back pressed on the wall and her legs pulled to her chest. Neither were clothed – a detail that sparked both Samantha's curiosity and repulsion.

Between two of the larger dilapidated buildings, Sammy found an alleyway. It seemed to go far, uninterrupted by any intersections with other streets. From the depths of the passageway came a dense, foul odor – far worse than

257

anything she had so far experienced on this world. How interesting, it was. Samantha was too excited to stop and think. Her curious nature once again got the best of her as she stepped forward into the long stretch of emptiness.

She wasn't more than ten paces in before a noise stopped her cold. She recognized the low rumbling as something all too familiar. This may have been a whole other world, but Sammy knew a dog's growl when she heard it. She turned herself towards the beast. It was large for a Rottweiler and twice as angry. It occurred to Sammy that she must have intruded on its territory. The dog must have named this alleyway its home and she had stumbled in without permission.

"Okay, doggy." she said, not knowing what else to do. She wanted to calm the beast before it lunged at her, "It's okay. I'll go." She spoke softly, making sure not to make eye contact. This was something that her mother had taught her way back in Boston. Marceline had once told her a story about a time when she herself had come wandering into some dog's ground. Through all the details, the lesson of the tale was clear: don't provoke the animal.

Sammy took a step backwards, away from the Rottweiler. The dog stepped forward, following her. She took another step back and the same thing happened again. Next, it drew its body into a lower stance, readying itself to lunge.

* * *

There wasn't too much to unpack, as the family could only bring what they could carry. For the most part, they were setting up sleeping areas and unloading all the miscellaneous gear that Marceline had brought in her backpack. Matches, eating utensils, toiletries and a single cooking pan were strewn about on top of the sleeping bags. Nothing but those bags could so much as touch the filthy floor. They decided to furnish the place with any random junk that they could find lying around. Until they came across some real furniture, an assortment of discarded crates would make for decent seats. Meanwhile, planks of wood and a slab of some hard, unknown material were coming together to make quite the table. What it lacked in sturdiness or sanitation, it made up for in "personality". At least, that was what Athens had said.

The young soldier lifted his head, scanning the premises for anything else that it might be lacking, and soon noticed that something was wrong.

Zack was over in the corner, drawing in the dirt with a stick. Sammy, however, was nowhere. Where could she be, he thought. A panic came over him in an instant. Soon after, this fear of his molded itself into a plan.

"I'll be right back." said Athens, "I need to find something." His voice was calm, almost nonchalant.

"Need some help?" Marceline asked. She was focused on trying to keep the junk table standing.

"No, thanks." Athens answered, "It'll only take a minute. Just keep doing what you're doing." With that, he slipped out the doorway and began to search frantically for the little girl. First, he worked his way down the main road, checking every face and watching every small body. It wasn't easy, however. The air filtration system in the city had broken down and a bleak, stale haze had once again filled the air and masked anything too far in the distance. In his time on Nonderan, Athens had noticed this occur every couple of days. What a shame that it had to happen now of all times. He squinted his eyes and tried to look past this sun-bleached fog.

Then there she was. Perhaps a hundred yards away, at an intersection between the main road and a smaller, somehow filthier avenue than the one they were on. Athens was about to call out to her when she stopped, turned and ducked into the side street. The young soldier's pace quickened as he pursued. In a moment, he rounded the same corner that she disappeared from. He hadn't gotten far down the road when he heard the growl. Without a thought, he raced towards the sound and came upon the exact scene that he had feared.

"Sam, get behind me." he said.

As soon as the girl took a step back, the beast lunged forward to meet her. Athens launched himself between the two and flailed his leg out with all his strength. The dog squealed as the foot made contact with its face. It fell back, collapsing on its side a small distance from the humans. Athens took a moment to look back and check on Sammy. While startled, she seemed unharmed. A wave of relief came over the young soldier, but that quickly turned into renewed panic when he felt a sudden and sharp pang on his rear.

"Gah! Damn!" he cried.

Athens jerked away from the beast until its jaws released. Then he whirled back around and grabbed the dog, wrapping his arms around its torso and neck. His knee met its ribs over and over and his hands squeezed around the animal's airway. Finally, the thing had had enough. As he let go and let his canine opponent whimper away, Athens turned back to the little girl.

"You got bit on the butt!" she exclaimed.

Athens looked at her with what could only be described as a look of pure shame, "Let's agree to never speak of this again." he said, rubbing the pained area with his hand, "You didn't sneak off. You didn't piss off a dog. I didn't get bit by a dog."

"Except you did."

"Keep trying me, girl." They stared at each other for a moment with tense, stern faces. Then without warning, Sammy broke into another laugh.

* * *

As day turned into night, work gave way to festivity. After all, these thousands of people had escaped a war zone. What's more, they found themselves among the first human beings to set foot on an alien world. A world that was given to them, nonetheless. Nonderan, as dirty as it may have been, was their new home away from the dark minitia swarm. This was more than enough cause for celebration.

Marceline hadn't expected so much food. She assumed that people would have been too busy fixing up their new homes to do much of anything else. So, when she came upon the gathering and found tables full of pies and cakes laid around cut fruit and even meat platters, she was more than surprised. Taking her kids along, she approached the table of delicacies, the likes of which she hadn't seen since before the swarm. After a long day of unpacking and cleaning, she was famished.

"Enjoying yourself?"

"I love this." she answered, with half-chewed roast beef in her mouth, "How did they get fresh meat here?"

"I hear people smuggled them in their carry-ons. How they got meat from the safe zone though, I'll never know." The man extended a hand. Marceline swallowed her food and took it, prompting him to give a small, unnecessary bow, "Tucker Crane." he smiled.

"Marceline Roberts."

"I see you have a ring. Where's your husband at, if I may ask?"

"He's…" Marceline didn't know quite how to explain it, so she went for the simplest of terms, "He's off fighting in the war."

"A soldier?"

"Yeah."

"What branch?"

To this, Marceline had no answer. Victor wasn't with any branch of any human military. Rather, he was part of the Host Project – something that she was advised to never discuss outside the confines of her family.

Tucker must have sensed her hesitation, as he changed the subject, "Are these your children?"

"Yeah. Sammy is nine and Zack is six."

"What's a beautiful, young mother like you doing now

that her husband's away?" he asked, "If I were him, I'd be afraid that someone might snatch you away."

"I... have to go. My friend needs me." she pointed to Private Athens, who was standing a decent five yards away, talking with an old couple. For once, he wasn't in his usual military gear. Instead, he opted for jeans and a button-up shirt. He almost looked like a normal civilian, save for the buzz cut and muscular frame. As she pointed, he made a quick glance over in her direction. Noticing her and Crane, he gave a short wave and a light-hearted grin. Marceline took her children's hands and made her way over to him.

"Your children are beautiful, by the way." Crane called out. Marceline didn't answer or even turn back. At this point, the soldier had left the old couple and started making his way to her as well.

When she at last got to Athens, she let out a sigh of relief, "Thanks, Johnny. I needed to get away from that guy."

"That bad, huh?"

"He actually bowed when I shook his hand." she told him, "And that tone in his voice. And the way he looked at me. I haven't seen something like that since college. I almost expected a fedora and a 'nice guy' monologue."

"Stick close to me." said Athens, "If he tries to talk to you again, I'll get in his way."

Marceline shook her head, "I don't need some white knight antics. Just needed to get some distance from the creep."

"Fair enough." Athens shrugged, "Wanna interact some more with the locals, or should we grab a seat?"

"I'm gonna find a place to sit. You can do whatever you want though."

"Wasn't I sent here to protect you? I should probably be close by."

"I won't tell anybody."

"It's the principle."

At that, it was settled. Marceline and Athens took a seat on a couple of folding chairs by the edge of the communal area. There, they watched the celebration continue. People had food and talked amongst each other, making quick friends of their new neighbors. Some pairs danced together as a woman with a guitar filled the air classic songs. A group of children, Sammy and Zack among them, danced around and played tag. It was the most beautiful sight that Marceline had seen in months.

"So, is your mind blown yet?" Athens asked her.

"What do you mean?"

"Come on. We're on a whole other planet. That's gotta be at least a little exciting, creepy guys and dirt aside."

"What's exciting is getting out of that so-called safe zone. Now, maybe I can actually sleep at night."

"That would be nice. Going a full night's sleep without you waking us up, screaming."

Marceline shot him a look, "Well I'm sorry if my pervasive fear and anxiety attacks have been interrupting your sleep schedule."

To this, Athens backpedaled, "I didn't mean it like that... I'm just glad that you feel safe again."

Was that really what he meant? No matter. She was already upset. It was strange. There she was on a whole different world and safe from the minitia swarm, yet she couldn't help the morose feeling that brewed inside of her.

"You don't seem too... festive." said Athens, "What's going on?"

"I just... wish Vic and Dan could see this."

"I'm sure they've seen plenty of cool worlds by now. I mean, here we are with all these races helping us. And these two just get whisked away by them. They're probably off on some badass adventure right now."

"Or rotting in a hole somewhere." Marceline shook her head, "They're fighting a war, John. Don't you get it? They aren't on some tropical vacation. My husband and best friend sold themselves off as test subjects and slave soldiers. I'll be lucky if I ever see them again."

"Hey, hey. You can't think like that. They're strong

people. Smart, too. Especially your husband. You can bet they'll do all they can to stay alive. And you'll see them again. Before you know it, this war will be over and you'll all be one big, happy family again."

"I hope so." Marceline lowered her head. A look of self-pity came over her. Then, at once, the pity left her, "You know what? Screw it. We're on another goddamn planet. Let's party."

* * *

The next morning, Marceline woke to the sound of a deep, unfamiliar murmur. She had trouble placing it at first, then realized it was a voice – an alien voice, speaking through a translator, prattling on just outside her new home. It was asking for someone to answer the door. Groggy after a long night, she pulled herself to her feet and half-stumbled over to the door. What she found on the other side was something she hadn't expected. The creature was an eight-foot monstrosity with four wide eyes along a smooth, noseless face. It possessed huge and repugnant features, with large mounds of stringy muscle and skin.

"Congratulations," the abomination grumbled through its translator, "you didn't scream."

Marceline stared up at the behemoth, blinking a couple times. No, she wasn't dreaming. "Was I supposed to?" she asked.

"I'm actually grateful that you didn't. Most of your people have simply slammed the door in my face. Perhaps they have never seen an obarosi before."

She paused to look her guest over, immediately regretting her gaze, "Well, not a naked one."

The beast took a small step back, peering down to survey its own body, "Is it really that unnerving?"

"Like a flayed man crossed with a fish." Despite her careful tone, she was stunned. It was huge, with a stocky frame and thick, wrinkled skin that stretched along the body

264

in shades of brown and pale yellow. "Anyway," she continued, "you want something?"

"I am going door to door, asking – or trying to ask – how well everyone is settling in. If there is anything we can do to…"

The slow patter of tiny feet caught their attention. Marceline turned and saw little Zack approaching, rubbing his eyes in a tired haze, "Mommy, is someone at the door?"

"Sweetie, don't look. It's…"

It was too late. At that moment, Zack's eyes widened. Total fear came over him, spurred on by the sight of the monster in the doorway. He screamed, turned away and ran to John.

"What's going on, buddy?" the soldier asked, rising with a start to comfort the small boy. When he noticed the giant by the door, he jumped, "Gah! The hell is that?"

Sammy was the last one up, shouted awake by her brother and the young soldier. She looked to the doorway, first in curiosity, then in morbid attraction, "That's so cool!"

"It's an obarosi." Marceline told them, "I guess this is what they look like without their armor. John, please go make sure that Zack is alright. Sammy, you stay here too." With diplomatic calmness, she smiled and turned to their guest, gesturing past the doorway, "Mind if we continue this outside?"

"Of course, Missus… Roberts, is it?"

"That's me."

Marceline led the way. When they were a comfortable distance from the hut, the obarosi continued its practiced spiel, "If there is any way that we can help make your home more comfortable, we would like to know."

"Well you could start by wearing pants." said Marceline, "Or… anything, really. Just wear something, because… god, that's hard to look at."

By what she could tell, the obarosi was unfazed, "Understandable. Different species, different standards of beauty."

265

Marceline shook her head, "Understatement. And anyway, don't get me wrong. We're all thankful to be here. We have roofs more-or-less over our heads. We're away from all the fighting. We have every necessity... but we're still missing a lot. If you want to help, you can start by fixing the holes in the floor. And maybe some sturdier ceilings. This isn't the only hut on the block with a cave-in." She could tell that her guest was confused, so she elaborated, "Humans can't just survive anywhere. At least not forever. We need creature comforts in order to really thrive."

"Noted." said the obarosi, "What else have we missed in renovating this settlement?"

"I went to a block party last night and got some good information about this place. I heard that we have resource mills. Metals, clay, synthetic food. And I hear that we're getting job assignments at the end of today. But what I didn't hear about were farms, schools, construction crews..."

"What use would these be in making things... more comfortable?"

"We need fresh fruits and vegetables. I saw some last night and I know we still have the seeds to make more. I saw someone going around and collecting them. And schools are where human children go to learn and become members of society. It's... It's what they had before it all... Do you understand?"

The obarosi looked at her with four strange, multicolored eyes, "I don't think I could ever understand what it is they have gone through. Perhaps something resembling normality will... maybe it will help them."

"I think it'll do a lot." Marceline told the alien.

"So, I have a question for you, Missus Roberts. You say that all of this should be provided. How, in your mind, can it happen? You are a settlement now. A society. How would a human society deal with these problems?"

Marceline was taken aback. Hadn't this obarosi said their people were going to provide any necessities? After all, they had offered to help make the place more comfortable. If they were going to take care of any problems, then why would they need to know how humans would deal with them? She thought for a moment, "Well first, we'd need tools. If I were in charge, I'd have the steel mill forge them. Then I'd have some able-bodied men and women come together as a construction crew and build the school. Anyone with experience regarding plants can become a farmer, while artisans can use their craft to make everything from windows to silverware. The trading of fresh food and different goods could start up a bit of an economy."

The obarosi stared at her for some time. It was a long and awkward silence, to the point where, when the monstrosity at last spoke, it was almost jolting, "You have been giving this much thought, I see. Only here for one day, and already so prepared. I must say, Missus Roberts, that I look forward to seeing how you run this place."

Again, Marceline was taken by surprise, "What do you mean? This was a job interview?"

"I am naming you a committee member for Nonderan Refugee Center A08. I hope this is a satisfactory position."

"Well…" she searched her mind for the best words, "Thank you. I'll try not to mess things up too much."

* * *

The next day was a fresh start at a new career, on a new world, in a new life. She was up early, about half an hour before the Nonderanian dawn rose over the dome settlement. Perhaps it was sheer excitement that wrestled her from sleep. Never before had she been dealt such an important profession. It was exhilarating, but at the same time it seemed to be quite the daunting task. To be part of the team that was meant to give these refugees some semblance of normalcy, to lead them in creating a new society, to begin the process of rebuilding human civilization – the enormity of her duty was not lost on her.

Why her, though? This was the question that kept

resurfacing again and again in her thoughts. Of all people, why choose someone like her? She had no political experience. She was a toxicologist, not a woman of the people. Were her answers as insightful as the questioner had insisted? Or was the obarosi ready to hand this task off to anybody they deemed half-decent for the job? How many people were recruited for this, anyway? Would she be one of many? Just a voice in the crowd? Or would she hold actual responsibility over what happened under this dome? To be honest, she didn't know which answer she preferred.

The walk was a lonely one, not that she minded. Despite being a Bostonian, she had grown to enjoy short silences and empty streets. She made it to the city hall – or what they called the city hall – before most of the city had the chance to undo the heavy shackles of sleep. Families were only beginning to stir in their shacks when she climbed the oversized steps and passed through the leaden doors of the great building.

Marceline found the committee room already occupied. Two others had gotten there before her, their faces perking up as she made herself known. Who knows how long they had been waiting? As she entered, a pair of familiar eyes met hers, "Good morning, sweetheart."

"Tucker?" she stammered.

The person at the head of the table, an aged man with a beak nose and white beard, looked over in surprise, "Mister Crane," he began, "you know this woman?"

Tucker Crane smiled, keeping his eyes on her while adjusting his glasses, "Miss… Roberts, is it?"

Marceline scoffed, "It's Missus Roberts, actually."

"I met this young woman at the festival the other night. As I recall, she was rather forward with me."

At this, Marceline shook her head, "That's not tr…"

Without letting her finish, the older of the men raised his hand and said, "Well, try to keep the flirting to a minimum, you two. We wouldn't want to have to tell her husband." His taunting smirk made her blood boil.

"Oh, her husband isn't on Nonderan." said Crane, not hiding the attempt to smear the new arrival, "He's off being a war hero."

Marceline was fuming. She had come here to do her job. Not to be put down, "Can we get started, please?"

The eldest man gave a look of agreement, "Of course, Missus Roberts. Please, have a seat." When she took her place at the table, he went on, "I'm Roland Dubicki. Back on Earth, I was a bit of a political man, but never anything this prestigious. My magnum opus was on the town council of Everett in Maine." He smiled and gestured to the other man beside him, "You've already met Mister Crane."

"Unfortunately." she mumbled, taking her spot at the table.

Roland shook his head, "Enough of that. We have a lot to discuss at this, our first meeting."

Marceline was expecting them to get right into it, but it seemed no one knew where to begin. The silence was uncomfortable, but it gave her a moment to study the men she was with. Tucker was a tall, lanky individual whose shifty, mud-brown eyes sat behind scratched, oversized glasses. Even though he had passed middle age, no one seemed to have let him in on the fact. He appeared more prepared for junior prom than an administrative position, adorning black pants, a red button-up shirt and a gray vest. A pitiful beard latched to his face, growing in a handful of long, wispy patches under his chin. It made Victor's usual fuzz look like a full, masculine face of hair.

Roland Dubicki was a different story altogether. He came in this day dressed in a gray suit that fit him to perfection. Marceline couldn't begin to understand why, of all things, he would bring formal attire to a refugee camp, but she wasn't about to complain. After all, the outfit was a crisp, clean contrast to the face above. It wasn't that he was ugly. In fact, he must have been quite a handsome man before... before whatever happened. Nowadays, a thick layer of scarring marred his left side – a grim reminder of a terrible day long passed.

"So, how should we begin?" the scarred man studied the room, waiting for a response.

"Maybe we should start with putting people to work?" Tucker glanced between the others, making sure he had their attention, "The aliens got us these jobs, but they can't interview everyone like that."

Roland considered his words, "And how would we contact that many people? It would take weeks if we just went door to door."

"Maybe they can come to us?" Marceline interjected, "We could announce projects that require different expertise, and offer compensation for people who show up to work on them."

Tucker smirked, "How would we spread the message? We don't have phones or fliers."

"The old-fashioned way." Marceline answered, trying her best not to sound too rude, "We go to the communal areas and talk to people. Spread the information like that."

"And how would we pay them?"

"With food, at first." Marceline gave a wry smile. It seemed she was the only one who actually brainstormed beforehand, "I know we've got seeds floating around. We could start with building farms. With all the space under this dome, we could make enough to feed everyone, at least to some extent. And those who work on the farms can get the first pick of the crop. Sounds like a good bribe, right?"

Marceline could see that Tucker was about to say something, but he was cut off by the sound of Mister Dubicki snapping his fingers, "And when we have enough food to go around, we can use it as a sort of currency. We need someone to build a radio or watch some children? Pay them in food. Housing could work that way, too. We have far more people than homes. I've seen as many as four families sleeping under the same roof. Imagine splitting them up by having the more capable ones build their own houses."

"A wonderful idea." said Crane.

270

Marceline ignored him, instead keeping her focus on Mister Dubicki, "And I've got some ideas regarding the children, now that you mention it."

"Well, let's hear it."

"You see," she began, "our world may have ended, but it doesn't mean theirs has to. I'm all for the idea of having people babysit them until we get things up and running, but I feel like eventually creating a legitimate school system would be in our best interests. They should still be able to learn in a controlled environment, rather than left out on the streets or shooed away into a corner forever."

Roland looked at her with knowledgeable eyes, "I don't see any problem with that. If we plan to be here for a while then we have to prepare for the long-term. For all we know, future generations will call this place their home. Best they're raised properly in it." In a move that confused Marceline, the old man rose in his seat and let out a hearty laugh, "Mister Crane, this woman is full of ideas. Feel free to stop glaring and join in, too."

Chapter 14

His heart beat hard with anticipation. His muscles, loosened and composed, laid anxiously in wait. All was calm and still, ready for the cold silence to shatter. It was time. At long last, the buzzer rang and Victor bolted down the course.

Obstacle after obstacle stood in his way, forcing him to leap and bound around like an animal. He was faster now, more nimble. His muscles were used to this kind of strain. While he was by no means graceful, his movements were decisive and effective. After so much practice, this simulated warzone was a playground for his instincts to take over. Hollow metal targets sprung up all around. Any that looked human or obarosi or tiavan were spared, while those shaped like minitia were shot back down by bolts of Victor's lightning. Sometimes a large, bug-shaped object would be shot at one of the human or obarosi figures. Those, too, were blasted without restraint before they could hit their marks. Rows of turrets rose from the walls, but Victor short-circuited them all before most could fire a shot. Those that did still weren't able to lock onto him, merely peppering the ground beneath him with rounds of training ammunition. All the while, he worked his way through the maze of fake rubble and replicated buildings.

Months of training had taught Victor to feel everything around him. Every turret, every target, every twist and turn of the ruined labyrinth. Almost none of it came as a surprise to him and, as soon as they came up, he always had a plan of action.

Before he knew it, Victor had caught sight of the end. He leapt and twisted his way around every obstruction, dodging and breaking anything that shot at him until he was on the other side of that finish line. As he reached the end, Victor stopped and looked back at what he just made it through. Though he was covered in sweat and his heart was racing, he pulled a confident smirk out through heavy breaths. These displays had made him bold. In moments like these, he almost felt as if he could take on Linious and their insects by himself.

* * *

Elsewhere in the station, two other hosts were preparing to face their own challenge. Daniel Emerson and Rin Ishibashi were in the sparring pit, each preparing to face the other in yet another controlled fight. Meanwhile, two tiavan onlookers watched from behind a thick panel of glass.

The humans paced around each other for a time before Rin made the opening move. Without warning, she forged and hurled a blazing fireball at her opponent. He dodged, but before he could recover she leapt forward, closing the distance between them with another sphere of flame in hand. Dan knocked it away with a strike to her wrist and shot his clenched hand out towards her throat. Rin moved to the side but couldn't clear the fist before it made its smoldering mark on her shoulder.

"The male has improved." Nyro commented.

By now the two humans were engaged in an aggressive melee. Each landed blow was enhanced by an intense barrage of excited molecules, burning the victim as they struck. Every now and then, a spark or a whirl of open flame would erupt from their bodies. Before long, it was clear who would be victorious. Rin countered every move of his with something faster and harder. In time, she managed to break away from the sparring and laid into him with wave after wave of heat and cold. The wild sensations of furnace-like hotness and icy chill disoriented him, taking him out of the moment. That was all the opening Rin needed to pounce in one last time and punch him square in the jaw. No more burning. No more enhancements. Just a clean strike to the side of his face. At last, her punching bag could take no more. As Dan's seared and exhausted body slumped to the floor, a bell declared his foe the winner.

Athriel smirked, *"It seems that Rin is still the better fighter. However, neither of them would stand a chance against our star pupil."*

"You really must tell me your secret with Naomi Daskal." said Nyro, *"I am most impressed by her."*

"Her talent is not mine, I must say." Athriel admitted, *"She fights with training that the others were never given. On her world, she is from a people called the Israelis. In their culture, everyone must learn to fight. It came to her naturally then, just as she excels now."*

"You know much about human cultures, my friend."

"Remember, that it was my profession until recently. I know much about these people. It is to my knowledge that the Russians were never known for their stellar medical work, and yet…" His eyes left the humans, turning instead to Nyro, *"How is Anya doing anyway? I hear that she is focusing on her organic manipulation."*

"That is true. She is training to be a field medic."

Athriel gave a small nod, *"That makes sense. Our data on her states that she was a nurse back on Earth."*

"What was that?" asked Nyro.

"A nurse? You know what a nurse is."

"Of course, I know that. I ask about that thing you did with your head. What was that?"

"Have you never seen a human nod before?"

"I have never seen one of our kind do that. Why do you still perform all these human acts?"

"I can't say I know." Athriel shrugged, *"Perhaps I find their mannerisms interesting. Even intuitive, to some degree."*

Nyro wasn't pleased, *"Humans are primitive, Athriel. Hardly even spacefaring. They are below us by nature alone. Especially you."*

Athriel studied his critic with a skilled eye, *"They are young, yes. But I am not convinced that their primitivism is much to look down upon. Perhaps in another few generations they could have advanced enough to join the Assembly on their own terms."*

274

* * *

At about midday, Marceline Roberts was free to break for lunch. She found a spot in the local dining hall by the end of the room, near one of the windows. It wasn't her usual spot, but they were all pretty much the same anyway. All the tables were rusted and rugged, with jagged edges and rickety seats. By now, she was used to the squalor that she had been living in. Not to say that it hadn't gotten better in the months since she'd moved there. Things were, in fact, coming together in a manner that looked much more like an actual human town, rather than the repurposed, ramshackle mining settlement of an alien race.

In the days since the Roberts family arrived, the air filters had been almost fully repaired. Now the smog that had once been a hallmark of their life under the domes was a sort of rarity, only appearing for short times and passing through small, unremarkable districts.

Partway through finishing her lunch, Marceline felt the table sag and creak under the weight of a new guest. It was Athens. "Hey, Marceline." he said.

"Afternoon, John." she answered. It occurred to her that he was at last taking to calling her by her first name. Perhaps he was getting used to her and the family. After all, over the past few months his mannerisms had become far less wooden. What's more, he was talking about more than just the day-to-day life on Nonderan and what led him to joining the army back in what used to be the United States. For a while now, they had talked about deeper, more meaningful subjects, like human nature and existentialism. Were humans violent by nature, or did something like society make them that way? What meaning could life have if no religion was right? To be honest with herself, Marceline had dearly missed having someone to talk to on such a personal level. Before, it was only Victor that she could speak so profoundly with. However, her husband had been gone for

275

nearly nine months by now and she was in dire need of another brain to pick.

Athens settled down and opened his food pack, revealing a simple supplement block. Those bricks of stiff brown were at becoming less popular now that livestock had been brought over to Nonderan. However, it seemed that the city's soldiers and guards were always the last to enjoy new luxuries.

After a few bites of what he called food, Athens looked up from his meal. With a mouth full of chewed sludge, he asked, "How's the committee?"

"We're still focusing on basic infrastructure and Tucker's a pretentious dick." said Marceline, "So nothing's changed. How's the caravan?"

"We're moving a shipment of steel tonight. A13 needs it to build some tenements."

"A13?" Marceline's brow furrowed, "That's pretty far. How long is the trip gonna be?"

Athens shook his head, "I don't know. No more than a day, I hope." He went to take another bite of his supplement block, but stopped when he saw the look of disapproval on Marceline's face.

"Didn't Athriel send you here to guard my family?"

"He did. The people running this place don't know how to keep to a deal."

"I know that I've said this before, but you need to find a way to transfer. Find a job that keeps you in A08."

"I'm trying. You know that."

"You should be allowed to do what you came here for." Marceline told him, "Besides, the kids are really starting to like you. Especially little Zack."

"Maybe it's because I'm a sarcastic prick like his dad?" Athens asked, a joking look on his face.

Marceline shook her head, "You two are really good together. It's like you're becoming a big brother to him. He misses you when you aren't around." She was going to continue, but the overhead alarm went off. Her lunch break was over. As she got up from her seat, she leaned over and tousled his hair, "I've gotta go. Good luck on your field trip."

* * *

"Hey, Vic." came a voice in the night, "You awake?"

"Trying not to be." Victor turned in his bed to face the whisperer. It was Dan, who sat idle in his bed, wide awake in his rationed sleepwear.

"What'cha thinking about?" he asked.

"How ripped you look in that outfit." Victor smirked. False flirting aside, he meant what he said. Daniel had always been in shape, but never like this. They had all gained a substantial amount of muscle since training began at Jupiter Station. Even Victor, who was somewhat pudgy before the swarm, was now in the best shape of his thirty-year life.

"You two lovebirds need some privacy?" asked Anya. Victor hadn't noticed that she was awake as well, lying in bed with her eyes jumping from one man to the other.

"Oh, you know it." Dan joked.

"I think I need some alone time." Naomi muttered from under her covers, "So I can get some sleep."

"Sorry." Dan returned. After a moment of silence, however, he seemed to have forgotten his apology, "I just really can't sleep."

"Well the door isn't locked." Naomi growled, this time in accented English rather than translated Hebrew, "Go for a walk. Let me and Rin have some quiet. I'm sure she'll appreciate it as much as me."

"I'm up for that." Victor told them.

"Me too." Anya joined, rising from her bed, "Anything to end the boredom."

The three left the bed chamber behind and wandered the ring-like halls for some time, continuing along their path until they were right back where they started. When they ran out of space to explore, they would choose a new floor and repeat. Victor led the way for most of it. He often went for walks on the nights when his insomnia dug in its heels. As such, he knew his way around areas of the station that the others never had reason to explore. Tonight, he was leading them on a grand tour.

One floor that he showed them was what he called the tiavan lounge. It was an entire level dedicated to the comfort of the Ancients who ran the station. Each room held its own brand of excitement. In one, an assortment of enormous chairs surrounded an amorphous statue. The structure itself couldn't be described, as it never remained stable enough to define with clarity. It shifted from one shape to another, never holding one posture for more than a moment. This was the beauty of tiavan art. Ever-changing. Evolving from one form to the next, molded like wet clay until the end of time.

Another room held what appeared to be a great planetarium. It was enormous, perhaps a hundred feet from one end to the other. Holograms of galaxies circled the air with magnified stars and worlds dotting the spiral arms. Of the galactic images, two stood out most of all. They were tremendous, sailing at opposite ends of the map with all the other celestial forms falling into orbit around them. The smaller of the two goliaths housed a light blue field that stretched over half of its surface. According to Athriel, most of the worlds and people under tiavan influence were in the Milky Way. The Universal Assembly, he called them. Perhaps Victor and the others were looking at the extent of their territory. Perhaps it was something else. There were other colors as well, from the largest galaxy's distinct golden glow to a pair of white clouds below.

"This is beautiful." said Anya.

Dan called out to them, "I think I found a control panel." He was pointing to a gold-tinted screen on the wall, "Should we try it out?"

"I didn't know you could read alien." Victor said, his voice coated with sarcasm.

"It looks simple enough to me." Dan answered. He poked at the screen, causing some hexagonal image to come up over the galaxies, "A lot of pictures. Maybe we don't need to know how to read it."

"What would you even do?" Anya asked, "What would you look for?"

"I don't know. Maybe it can show us Earth."

At that moment, the great map of galaxies and colors shrank away. In its place stood the transparent, holographic rendition of a solar system. Eight worlds circled a single star, a ring of asteroids separating the small, rocky spheres from the gas giants. All three recognized the system as their own.

"Well that was easy." Dan mumbled.

"What's that?" asked Anya. She pointed to a sphere of golden dots surrounding the outermost reaches of the system. Victor was quick to tell her, "That's the Kuiper Belt."

"No, it isn't." she returned, "That's this ring out here. I'm talking about these."

"I heard there's a tiavan blockade around our system." said Dan.

The room went quiet. They had wanted to forget, even if just for a moment, the situation they were in. This reminder of the war was unwelcome to their eyes.

"So gold means tiavan." Anya said at last, breaking the silence, "Good to know."

"Let's move on." Victor suggested.

"Good idea." she answered, "I've had enough of this room."

They moved on, trekking through the immense hallway with their small, human steps. After a time, they came upon an area unfamiliar even to Victor. The doors there were locked, without a doubt meant to keep unwanted eyes and ears away. One of these forbidden rooms had a bold insignia on the door. It was an elegant, black figure that looked to Victor like a rising flame. He reached with his mind, but couldn't budge it open. He decided not to press further. After all, anything with some level of security must have had reason to be off limits. It was clear that the humans weren't meant to know what was beyond the door. At peace with his defeat,

Victor continued with his companions close behind.

"The runaway still hasn't been found."

The voice came so suddenly. It was tiavan in nature, translated into English through Victor's earpiece. Who could it have been?

"You hear that, too?" he asked.

"Hear what?" Dan returned.

"Come here" Victor whispered, "And be quiet." They gathered around the locked door, their ears pressed against the metal.

"That could mean a number of outcomes. He could be dead."

"That is most likely. It is what we must hope for."

"He could also be in hiding. However, with how little he knows of the universe, this would prove most difficult."

"The human could also have fallen in with the enemy."

"Do you think that likely? The minitia have destroyed his world – slaughtered his people."

"Even so, we cannot deny the possibility. Besides, Linious is not our only foe. Only the most present. Others may seek to benefit from what we have made."

"Your words are true. If his power fell into the hands of those who would misuse it, then he could be as dangerous as a rogue tiavan. Many of our enemies would want that. However, while Linious gave motivation to this weapon, they are perhaps the only one who could not benefit from our work. After all, they already possess the power with which our subject has been imbued."

Victor had heard enough. With a soft growl, he detached from the door and marched off. Dan followed in pursuit, "What's wrong?"

"How can they talk about him like that?" Victor hissed, careful not to be overheard, "How can they talk about Travis as if he's just some sort of... some sort of weapon? They're talking about him as if he's a thing. They hope he's dead."

"They don't know him like we do." said Dan, "They didn't survive with him."

280

"Not to mention they're tiavan." Anya added, "We are insects compared to them. If an insect signs its life away to you and then runs off, why should you care about its wellbeing?"

Victor could feel his face growing red with anger, "It's not right. Travis is a human. One of the last."

Dan put a hand on his friend's shoulder, "Let's hope he's okay."

"Let's hope he's just in hiding." said Anya, "He can't be dead, and I don't believe he would join the enemy."

"We don't even know what enemy they're talking about." Dan reminded him, "Anyway, we should be getting out of here. Who knows what they'll do if they find us here."

Victor gave Dan a long look. His breathing slowed as he regained control over himself, "I guess."

Anya approached them, a look of growing concern on her face, "Come on, boys. We should get back to bed."

* * *

With the council meeting concluded, Marceline's day was almost done. All she had to do was pick up some food from the market and hand it over to John and Sammy. A quick meal later, and she'd be off to bed. Tonight, they were having chicken and carrots. The Olsen family had just killed two of their roosters, and offered to save the smaller one for the Roberts household. It was at a sizeable discount, so long as she claimed it before dusk. That was the benefit of having such gregarious children. Whenever Sammy or Zack made a friend, so did she.

The only problem was that the market stood far from her workplace, in the opposite direction of home. She would have to walk to the market to get the chicken, and then double back to get it to her chefs. By then, it would surely be dark, and she often heard stories of what happened on these streets once night fell.

The first leg of the trip was rather uneventful, as she

hurried through the lit, crowded streets of A08 and made it to the market in record time. A short conversation and an exchange of food currency later, and the chicken was hers. At last, she was on her way home, along a route that took her past her point of origin. In fact, she was coming upon the city hall when she saw him. There, at the edge of the steps, was Roland Dubicki. The elder stood there, a look of caution etched across his charred face. What was he afraid of?

"What are you still doing here?" Marceline asked, approaching with the still-feathered, freshly-bled chicken wedged under her arm, "Our meeting ended a half hour ago."

"I could ask you the same thing." Mister Dubicki answered with a tired smile, "That's a nice bird, you've got."

Marceline laughed, not knowing how to react, "Either way, I'm on my way home now. See you tomorrow, Roland." She continued on, waving to him with her free hand.

"Eh, wait... please..." his voice trailed from behind, stopping her with its nervous cadence, "I hate to ask, Missus Roberts..."

"Please," she interjected, "we've been working together for months. It's Marceline."

"Marceline..." Dubicki corrected himself, "I hate to ask, but it's a rather long way home and I'm not as... capable as I used to be. I'd feel a great deal more comfortable if I had someone to walk with me."

Marceline was taken aback. No one had ever asked her for something like that before. Perhaps it was because of her feminine nature, or maybe her small stature. Either way, she wasn't what the general public saw as the archetype of physical strength. So, why did Mister Dubicki want her as his companion? Her first instinct was to decline on the grounds that, if something were to arise, she may not be able to help. She wasn't a soldier. It was her curiosity, though, that eventually won her over.

"I'd love to." she said, a nod and a reassuring smile backing her words.

The first few minutes of their walk was spent in silence.

282

It seemed that neither of them knew what to talk about outside of work. He was decades older than her, with an entire life of differences. What could she have said that would resonate with someone like that?

With Marceline tongue-tied, it was up to Roland to start any conversation. When he did, it came as somewhat of a shock to his companion, "I wouldn't normally ask this. It's just, I've been feeling less safe lately. Too many stories of what happens at night."

"Well, we're the ones in charge." Marceline told him, "If there's anyone to complain to, it's us."

"Yes, but it can be hard to enforce the laws we've made. Tucker always says he has some grand plan to clean up the streets, but it never happens."

Marceline flinched at the mention of his name. Roland must have noticed, because his next words were directed at the source of her annoyance, "If you don't mind my asking, what do you think of him?"

Marceline answered without a second thought, "He's a creep, if you ask me." Then, at once, she remembered who she was talking to, "I don't mean any offense. I know you two talk a lot."

"We do." said Roland, "And yet I find myself agreeing with you. The way he looks at other people... It's concerning. I don't understand why our overseers chose him, of all people, to lead with us."

"Do you think he's underqualified?" Marceline asked, her brow furrowed with confusion. Over the months, Mister Dubicki had seemed fond of Tucker. Was she wrong to assume they were friends?

"I feel that others may have been more qualified than him. So, in that sense, yes. I'm surprised you don't have more to say about him, giving your history."

Marceline stopped, "My history? What are you talking about?"

For a moment, Roland appeared self-conscious, "Why, Tucker says that you two were almost an item before this assignment."

At that, Marceline couldn't hold in her annoyance, "That couldn't be further from the truth, Roland. First off, I'm married."

"Many who are married still wander." Mister Dubicki began, "Though, I must admit that I've never seen you as that type."

"Good catch. Anyway, when we first got here, my kids and I went to a block party. That's where I met Tucker. He flirted with me, I rejected him. That's all that's ever been between us. If he says otherwise, then he's a liar." She was seething, enraged by falsehoods. She had to clear herself of anything Tucker may have said against her.

"I believe you, Missus Roberts." he said, "Trust me, I've caught him in a number of lies, myself."

The rest of the conversation took a turn that Marceline hadn't expected. Roland had seemed to be a friend of Tucker Crane – she believed as much for all these months – but his stories told another tale. As he went on, Roland confirmed every nasty thought she had of Crane. The man was a weasel. A snake who did nothing but lie and manipulate. The aging man's testimony gave a second voice to her concerns, that Crane was a poor leader and a horrid man. It was cathartic, in a way, to be validated by someone who she had grown to respect.

It was dark when the two finally got to Roland's home. To Marceline's surprise, it wasn't all that different from every other shack in the dome city. No extravagant decorations or makeshift additions. Just a square hut with clay walls and a metal roof. A single window stood to the right of the dilapidated door.

"Here we are." Roland turned to her and, with a warm smile, laid a hand on her shoulder, "Thank you, Marceline." he said, "Really. I feel a lot more comfortable knowing that you're looking out for me."

Marceline smiled back, though not knowing what to say. After a moment, she came up with, "I'm happy to help."

"I hope it wasn't too out of your way or… boring."

"Actually, I kind of liked it." she told him, "And we're not too far from my place. Just a couple blocks down." That last part was a lie, of course, but she didn't want to make him feel bad for taking her so far from home. Also, if she was being honest with herself, she really did enjoy the time with him. He was, at his heart, one of the gentler souls that she'd met on Nonderan. He made her feel valued and wise in ways that she hadn't felt in months. Plus, it was good to know where he stood with Tucker. As it turned out, even Crane's own friends didn't harbor any good feelings for him.

"Well, I'll let you go on home." Roland took a step towards his door, "Your family is probably wondering about you, and that chicken isn't getting any younger."

"Oh, right." In all the talking, she had almost forgotten the bird wedged under her arm, "I'll see you tomorrow, Roland."

"And I, you. Good night, Marceline."

* * *

"How's the grub today?" Dan asked as he took a seat. It was mealtime for the hosts of Jupiter Station. As usual, Dan and Victor joined Anya and Naomi at the smallest of the tables. Around them were uridan workers and obarosi soldiers, all congregated into their own groups and talking amongst themselves while eating their fill.

"Almost tastes like real meat." said Naomi, "I swear, these alien cooks are improving every day."

"Thank God, too." Victor remarked, "Remember what it was like when we first got here?"

Dan smirked, "I couldn't tell if it was cow shit or ground cricket."

"Gee, thanks for the image." Naomi stuck her tongue out. Then, clearly wanting to change the subject, she shifted her focus to Anya, "So how was practice? Learn how to shapeshift like Big Blue?"

285

The Russian shook her head as she finished a mouthful of fake meat, "Not yet. But I made progress on medical training. I learned how to mentally differentiate between various types of tissue. Tomorrow I should be focusing on repairing myocardium on a cellular level."

"Okay," Dan interjected, "even with these translators, I don't know half of the words you just said."

Anya laughed, "It only makes sense that the American doesn't understand his own language."

"Hey, I resent that." Victor exclaimed.

Anya raised a dismissive hand at him, "You know that I didn't mean you."

The table went quiet for a short time as everyone took a few bites of their meals. Then, as Dan swallowed a chunk of the mystery food, he looked up at his friend, "So, Vic, how was your day? Do anything fun? Shocking, maybe?"

"Funny." Victor said, "Actually, yeah. I went through one of Athy's obstacle courses. Set a new record."

"A record's easy to set when you're the only one running it." Naomi remarked, "When is he gonna let us take a stab at them?"

"When you all can charge a battery with your fingertips." Victor joked. His deadpan delivery made the rest of them laugh, "Anyway, how was your fight, Danny? I hear you and that Rin girl got into a bit of a scuffle."

As if waiting for his cue, Dan dropped everything, cleared his throat and began what seemed to be a decently rehearsed spiel, "Oh, it was amazing. Tons of fire and punching. The whole thing must have been cool to watch. Especially the part when I won. I guess it could be said that she gave me a good run, but in the end, I was just a little faster. In fact, afterwards one of those tiavan came up to me and said that it was the most impressive thing they'd ever seen."

The table was hushed by thought. Anya gave a small giggle, "Really? Because I heard that you didn't even last two minutes." At this, everyone but Dan laughed.

286

"And where'd you hear that?" he asked, accusingly but with a hint of concession. Dan looked around at the group, expecting someone to make some playful and snide remark. When nothing came, he paid mind to their faces. They were all looking past him, their eyes fixated on something else. He turned around and saw Rin approaching, a tray in her arms and her head hanging between her shoulders. Dan thought that she was joining them for once, but she passed by and found her place at an otherwise empty table.

"Is anyone else a little worried about her?" asked Anya.

"Maybe she's just introverted." Victor pondered, "Doesn't mean she has to treat this like high school, though."

"Perhaps someone should talk to her." Anya suggested, looking to the others.

When her eyes came to Dan, he was still staring at the lonesome woman in the corner, "Maybe." he repeated, right before pushing his chair back, standing up and making his way over to her.

"That match earlier was pretty fun." he said. He waited for a time, eager to hear any words she might have to say. Nothing came, prompting him to try again, "How about you come join us? We've all made friends with each other." Still, there was no answer from her. By now, Dan was getting irritated. Not only because she was ignoring him, but because she had ignored them all for so long, "Listen, kid." he told her, "It's been months. You'll have to talk to us at some point."

Finally, it seemed that Rin had found a response. Without looking at him or otherwise acknowledging his existence, she said, "This is not high school. We are at war. It is best not to make friends with those who will only die in battle." Her words were plain, with no hint of expression. It was almost like listening to a machine.

"Well I tried." Without another word, Dan pulled himself up from her table and went back to sit with the others. When he found his old spot, every eye was on him. He could do nothing but shrug and tell them what she said.

"This is worse than you realize." Naomi insisted, "Rin is supposed to be our comrade. When people fight alongside one another, they must trust each other. How can we trust her if we don't know her?"

Dan let out a long sigh, "We still have time. With luck, it'll be a while before we're thrown into a real fight."

* * *

Did tiavan sleep? He almost never saw one during quiet hours. Even when he did, it was someone that he'd never seen during the day shifts. Perhaps a few more nights of this wandering would give him an answer.

Victor walked aimlessly through the halls, traversing the sleek, wide corridors like a phantom in the night. Over the months, he had grown accustomed to the high ceilings and polished, decorated interior of Jupiter Station. Nowadays, he explored these chambers a couple nights every week. This area in particular was new to him. It was several levels above the sleeping quarters, in a place where the hosts seldom went, but from which they weren't barred.

At some point, Victor started to get the feeling that somebody else was nearby, though he couldn't tell who. He followed his new sense, tracing the halls along the way and peering into any open room that he came across. All the while, the feeling grew stronger. He could tell he was getting close. At last, he came to a stop in front of a large door. It was immense by his standards, but small as far as tiavan architecture went. There were no windows, but he could tell that, whomever he was sensing was on the other side. The sign overhead was in the tiavan language, the glyphs unrecognizable to his human eyes. However, the bold green text didn't look like anything important, so perhaps it wouldn't have been such a big deal if he stepped in to see. Victor approached the door, pulling with his mind until it slid open.

There was a circle of seats large enough for the beings

288

who built them, as well as some small enough for human beings. In the center of the ring stood a platform that held a metallic fluid within a transparent barrier. The substance seemed to move freely, swirling with elegance and shaping itself into one design after another. It wasn't until it took the form of Victor's own face that he remembered there was someone in there with him, sitting relaxed in one of the seats.

"Good evening." said Athriel, "I believe that's the term."

"Mind if I sit here?"

"Please do." The alien gestured with an arysthum, "You're the only one who will fit, after all." Victor smiled and took his place across from his friend, "Cannot sleep?"

"Nah," the human shook his head, "I've had insomnia since I was young. Sometimes I like to wander the halls around here. I hope that's alright."

"Insomnia?" Athriel's gaze held a look of intrigue.

"Don't tell me that you don't know what insomnia is."

"I'm afraid that I don't know everything."

Victor gave a small laugh, "Is it bad if I'm actually surprised by that?"

Athriel stared at him for a time, as if trying to see through the human. Victor studied the alien's peculiar expression, his relaxed and vigilant posture. He noticed the way those blue markings danced across his skin, showing through the thin, loose fabric of his garments. He was so familiar now, but a sense of mystery never left him. It was as if, no matter how well he knew his alien friend, Victor would never truly comprehend him.

Victor came to notice the long silence between them. With a feeling of awkwardness, he asked, "What are you looking at?"

"Someone who is far more lost than he realizes."

"Why? Because I'm out of bed? Or because I'm in a space station halfway across the solar system?"

"A bit of both, I presume."

"I can get behind that, I guess. When I was a little kid

dreaming about being a grownup, this wasn't exactly what I had in mind. I don't really have another choice though, so I'll take it."

"Where is it that you saw yourself being?"

"I don't know." Victor admitted, "Just... doing something. Something different than this. I think you can understand how much of a curveball this whole minitia thing has been. I thought I'd be on my own world, living with my own family, working at some decent job and living a decent life. Until now, I've only ever known Boston. I'd never gone travelling to any far-off places. I'd never been in the military. I was only in college for a while before dropping out. My whole life was pretty much just in Boston. A bit of the surrounding area too, but I'd never been farther than New York. All of this now is like... it's like living another life."

"How about the other side of the coin?" Athriel adjusted in his seat, as if readying himself for discussion, "Hmm? What is it you see when you look at me?"

"A shapeshifting genius with an ego the size of Texas."

"No, Victor. I'm serious."

"So am I." By the calculated expression on Athriel's white-blue face, Victor could tell he was looking for a better answer. This must have been a question that the tiavan had been mulling over for some time, "You seem like you know so much." said the human, "We're two different species, you're from a whole different world – another galaxy, I think – but you can read me like a book. Our brains probably couldn't be more different, but you're an expert on everything human. Our emotions, our history, our language – you probably speak English better than I do. The way you look at things, it's like you've seen it all before. It's like everything is old to you. It's like you've lived a hundred times a normal human life."

"It's not simply that I've lived many lifetimes." he began, "I have also lived many lives. The worlds I've seen, the people I've known... For millennia, it has been my job to survey emerging species – to integrate myself into their

290

worlds and see how they function. Over my career, I have been to three hundred and thirty-eight planets. Each had its own assortment of people and societies. Each was at its own level of social development. Most of them, I visited multiple times. In fact, I've been to Earth on a total of four occasions. My first time, you lot were hardly out of the stone age. I was in a place – an early city-state in the desert. I lived as a farmhand, then. The second time, I integrated myself into the mainland of Europe. I posed as a merchant, going town to town selling feed and cheap tools."

Athriel smiled, his voice rising like a human reliving an old, fond memory, "I actually obtained my starting supplies from a real merchant that I found on the road. He had passed from the plague some days before I came along."

"You were around for the plague?"

"The Black Death. That is what your historians call it, I think. I journeyed from village to village, city to city. At first, they were bustling, full of life. Perhaps not the happiest people, but they made do with what they had. Then, as I kept on for month after month, people began to vanish. Some cities were cleared out, everyone either dying in their homes or trying to outrun the damage. More than a few places refused to let me in. Even if I had something that they needed – feed for their animals, shovels, fresh fruit – they were too frightened to let me near. They thought I would pass this 'curse' onto them."

"Were you even able to get the plague?" Victor asked, "I mean, you're not exactly from here."

"That only means that I had no natural immunity, my friend. I can guarantee that I would have gotten the illness if my people weren't such masters of their bodies. Don't forget, a tiavan can feel and control anything, if they only set their focus to it. Perhaps you can too, given a few millennia of experience."

Victor's eyes widened, "Millennia? You don't think I'm actually going to live that long now... Am I?"

"Who knows?" the tiavan answered, shrugging with a

couple of arysthum, "You could deteriorate in the next month, for all I know. No known humans have taken part in the Host Project before."

"Have other species?"

"A handful, yes. Most of those hosts are on the front lines right now, fighting in place of real tiavan."

The conversation came to a pause. Talking of the ongoing battle reminded them of the reality they were facing. Both thought of how, someday, inevitably, they would have to be on the front lines, fighting alongside the others. It was a dark feeling for one to live in the quiet before the storm.

"May I ask you something?" Victor asked, breaking a silence between them that was becoming unbearable. Athriel's face perked up at the sound of his voice, eager to talk on, "Go ahead, my friend."

"Who is Linious, really?"

Athriel's excitement began to fade, "He is our enemy. I've told you this."

"No," Victor shook his head, "That's what he is. Not who. Humanity is going down this path. We're becoming a part of this huge universe around us. This universe that we know nothing about... I wanna learn about it. Linious is obviously a major figure, otherwise we wouldn't be fighting a war over him. So why not start with him?"

"That seems fair enough."

"So... who is he, really? Why is he so important? Why did the minitia take over an entire planet just to get him onto their side?"

"Linious is... one of the Kingdom's mistakes." Athriel said, his alien voice for once losing its solemnity, "He was a powerful figure, a sort of warlord in the early times. Sovereign Mecurin eventually bested him, but not without grievous loss. Then, instead of disposing of him and being done with it, we all made the mistake of letting him live. We believed that a prolonged punishment would be more suitable than a quick death."

"And he got out?" Victor asked, "He got away from

wherever you had him?"

"From what we've gathered, his prison collided with Earth. He and his cell went through the atmosphere like a meteor, but a tiavan isn't an easy thing to kill."

"So, he survived on Earth and the minitia caught wind of it."

"Indeed, they did. They view him as their greatest chance to best the Eternal Kingdom itself and to spread into every territory that we protect. When they found out that his prison was set to hit Earth, they formed a plan to be there when he arrived."

"...I think I understand now. I have so many more questions, but..." Victor didn't know how to continue, or if he even should have.

Athriel's demeanor was noticeably enervated. After a moment, he began to rise from his seat, "If you do not mind, Victor, I believe that I'll be heading to my chambers now."

"Oh, okay."

"Good night, my friend." As he passed by, an arysthum reached out to Victor, stroking him across the shoulder.

Victor turned, giving the tiavan a light smile, "Good night, Athy."

* * *

Victor awoke to the soft, warm sunlight sneaking through the bedroom window. He was back in Boston, in his old apartment. Cars rushed along the street outside. Marceline slept soundly next to him. He heard his children playing together in the living room. They must have heard him stir, because within a moment they were in the room, pouncing on the bed. Bright, wondrous smiles painted their faces in the color of happiness.

"Daddy's awake!" Sammy chanted, "Daddy's awake! Get up, get up, get up!" She stood on her hands and knees, bouncing on the bed with a kind of energy that could only be found in a young child. In past times, Victor would have yelled at her for barging into the room like that and messing up the bed. Then when she cried, he would have gotten an earful from Marceline. Those days were gone, though. For once, he didn't mind. Not even a little.

"What day is it?" he asked, rubbing the sandman's dust from his eyes.

Marceline rose from her spot of slumber, looking at him with loving eyes, "It's Friday, sweetie. The eighth."

"We're in Boston?"

"Of course, we are."

Victor was in disbelief. Could it be that he was home? Last he knew, he was halfway across the solar system. All these memories – the missiles, the bus, his first sight of Jupiter, his training on the space station, the tiavan, Naomi, Anya, Rin, Athriel – it all felt so real. So genuine. Was he really home, or was it...

"You have to wake up, Daddy." Sammy crawled over the sheets until she was a foot away from her father's face. Her bright demeanor changed, a ghoulish tone sinking into her voice. The smile on her face twisted into something more akin to dread.

"What?"

"You have to wake up." she repeated.

"We're dying without you." Those words from Marceline stabbed into him like knives, "Where are you, Vic?"

"I don't understand." he pleaded. He was shaking, unnerved by the sudden shift. The sun was gone. The smiles had faded. Even the air had become cold and bitter.

Little Zack looked at him with sorrowful eyes, "I want my Daddy."

Marceline put an icy hand on his shoulder. Her skin was blue, her face bloated and bruised, "We just wanted to see you one more time before..."

Chapter 15

A loud screech jolted Victor from his sleep. In his dog-tired haze, it took him a few seconds to recognize the alarm. At once, he and the other hosts scrambled from the bed chamber and, still in his sleepwear, made his way to the common room. There, they met with a line of obarosi guards clad in full battle armor. It was clear that something unexpected had happened.

After a brief survey of the room, Victor fell in with the other hosts, "What's going on?" he asked them. Their faces were just as puzzled as his.

"No clue." Dan shrugged, "Maybe we're under attack?"

"It's possible." said Anya, equal amounts curious and scared.

"Wouldn't we know if we were being attacked?" Victor asked, "Like, wouldn't the station shake if we took hits?"

"Quiet." Naomi hissed, motioning for the others to stand at attention.

Anya looked to the front of the room, by the main doorway, "Ooh, the tall boys are coming. This should be good."

Victor and the others looked on as the main doors slid open and three tiavan made entry. Though he should have been used to their great height by now, the sheer size of these beings still made Victor breathless. They towered over the humans like the gods of old. On the far left was Sycura, who Victor somewhat knew from past interactions. Sycura had overseen the station's security and, to a lesser extent, the well-being of the hosts. As a result, they had inevitably encountered each other on a few occasions. On the right was a dark, pale-skinned tiavan. Victor had never said a word to them, but he'd heard the alien called by the name Nyro. The entity between the two was none other than Athriel.

"I assume you're all wondering why you've been called here." Athriel stated, his voice more alien than human. His face was paler than normal, his expression icy and bitter, "Approximately four minutes ago, we received word that the blockade around the inner solar system has been breached by the minitia armada. As of now, our retreating forces have regrouped and are trying their damnedest to keep the minitia from reaching Earth." A few hosts exchanged glances with each other, "However, it's clear that they're only delaying the inevitable. I assure you that the Eternal Kingdom's fleet will fall and the armada will reach your world. When that happens, they'll be sure to formally declare for Linious and kill off any resistance. That includes your human refugees."

Athriel paused to let his words sink in. The room was seemed to have been stricken mute. Not a word – no noise of any kind – broke the unrelenting silence of the chamber. At last, the tiavan saw fit to continue, "Our mission today is simple. We shall be taken to Earth and sent to whatever safe zone needs our help the most. We are to aid in the evacuation of any noncombatants in the area. No heroics, no tide-turning maneuvers. This is simple damage control. Each and every human being rescued is another step away from extinction. Now, I realize that this will not be an easy task. However, this is exactly what you have all trained for. You've been given the lifeblood of the Ancients. I expect you all to use it well. Dismissed."

The congregation began to clear, but while everyone went off to prepare for what was coming, Victor made straight for the being with blue eyes. His heart was in his throat as he called out, "Hey, Athriel."

The tiavan looked at him with softened, yet judging eyes, "You should be readying for the battle ahead."

"I plan to." the human said.

"Whatever you have to say, please make it fast."

Victor was taken aback by his bluntness. Never before had he seen Athriel so straightforward and demanding. Not even in Harrisburg. "It's about my family." he said, "I'd like to know how they're doing."

"This is not the proper time to be asking such a thing."

"Well you're gonna have to make time." Victor asserted, "I need some answers."

"We are about to enter a combat zone." Athriel extended an arysthum like a hand, almost touching the human's shoulder, "Victor, my friend, I'm afraid I have no time for this."

"I let you play with my genes." Victor spurted, shocking both himself and the tiavan. It was the first time that he'd ever raised his voice to any of Athriel's species, "I'm about to walk into a battlefield – maybe even die there. All I want is to know if my family is still alive and well. I want to know if I still have a reason to die."

At this, Athriel's eyes faded, "In the interest of transparency... I should tell you that I do not entirely know what has become of your family. Last I heard, they had been moved to a world called Nonderan. The planet has many refugee centers, designed to give shelter to those who otherwise have no homes or safety. Millions of humans and other earthlings have been sent there, your family among them. That was some months ago."

"So that's it? They got sent off to, what? Nonderan? And that's all you know?"

"If you come back from this, Victor, I will find out whatever you want to know. I promise you."

Victor took a few seconds to digest the alien's words. For all he knew, his family could be dead. Marceline, Sammy, Zack... Any of them may have been hurt or killed, and there was nothing that he could do about it. All that was in his power was to trust Athriel. At last, the human gave a nod, "Deal."

"Now please let me be. We both have our own

preparations to make. You'll be in orbit around Earth within the hour."

* * *

Though there were no true windows in the transport, the video screens on the walls told Victor and the others anything they needed. These "windows" were strategically placed around the inside of the ship, showing in real time every detail of the battle raging on the other side of the hull.

Cold monoliths drifted over a desolate Earth. They reminded him of old children's tales and adventure films, where towering mountains floated high above their fantasy worlds. Sleek, flowing hills stood side by side with jagged peaks, the spaces between them alive with eagles and vultures swirling and dancing around one another. It was like a great show. All those bolts and blasts illuminating the black above and cutting over the brown and blue below. Each one that met its mark sent fire and metal in all directions, like feathers scattered in the wind.

This was the hell that they found themselves in.

Were they prepared? Perhaps. Did they feel as such? Far from it. Everybody in the transport was about to enter a warzone, the likes of which they had never seen before. As if that was bad enough, they were being forced to go in with little information as to what was happening. They didn't know where it was they would be touching down, only that it was on Earth and that, when the doors opened, they would be fighting for their lives. They didn't even know yet what it was that they would be doing on the surface. From what they gathered, the battle was hectic, with every available officer and tactician hard at work. Nobody seemed to pay mind to the hosts, not even bothering to give them real orders. At this point, they had settled on the idea that Athriel would oversee them. Whether that meant they would stick together or split up was not yet known. Not even to Athriel himself. Either was possible, really. Their battle suits were equipped with

298

radio transmitters, so they could contact each other across the field of combat. If it came to it, they could coordinate with each other across some distance.

The ship rattled in the air as it descended, beginning the moment they entered the atmosphere. Soon though, it grew into an intense shaking that nobody could ignore. Was this normal? Victor didn't remember anything like this happening when they took off from Earth all those months ago.

"Calm down, Rin." Naomi warned, "You're going to tear a hole in the ship."

At that, the ship began to calm, the stress on the hull withering as if some unseen hand had released its grip. All that was left was the humming of whatever this craft had for an engine and roar of the wind ripping by as they shot like a bullet through the atmosphere.

"Is this your first battle?"

Victor realized that it was him Naomi was talking to. He looked up, his eyes meeting hers through the visors of their battle suits, "Second." he told her, "My first was in a place called Harrisburg."

"My first was in a village in Palestine." she said, "Believe me, it will get easier."

Victor pondered the smile on her face, "Aren't you scared?"

"Of course. But it will not control me. Fear can be just as big an enemy as the ones shooting at you."

Those were words for Victor to dwell on. He thought about his actions back at Harrisburg. He had acted out of fear, running and hiding while the rest of the group was ambushed. It saved his life, yes, but what if that was not all it did? What if he hadn't run? If he had stayed and fought, perhaps more people in the party would have survived the fight. It was a concept that Victor had tried not to think about – that he may have been at least somewhat responsible for the bloodbath that crippled the convoy's militia.

"Hey, Petrova." Dan called out above the background noise. Victor was expecting some cheesy remark or foolish statement, but the look on his friend's face showed only severity, "You worked in a hospital, right? What's it gonna be like down there?"

Anya turned to him, speaking just loud enough for the others to hear, "Back when I was a nurse, back in Russia, I saw much carnage. People were brought in because of car accidents, muggings, random violence, freak incidents... They came in torn apart, with holes in their bodies and pieces missing from themselves. It was the worst thing I've ever seen in my life... Whatever awaits us out there... It must be worse."

The passengers kept to themselves for a time, silently digesting her words. Victor thought back to the worst thing he'd seen in his life. It was in the early days of the invasion, back at that barn, where he and Dan had found the farmer tied up and bleeding, chunks of flesh and muscle missing from his body. The memory still kept him up at night.

Dan inched his way closer to Victor, "You ready?"

Victor shook his head, "How could anybody be ready for this?" He took a long breath, the words on his tongue desperate to leave his lips. With solemn resolution, he looked up at his friend, "Listen. If, for some reason, I don't make it out of this... see to it that Marci and the kids are taken care of."

"Vic..."

"Promise me, Daniel."

The look on Dan's face was one of shock, "I-"

"Look alive, soldiers!" came Athriel's voice from the front of the craft, "We're about to touch down!"

After so much time away, it pained Victor to see the world he called home. It was even worse than he remembered. Everything was coated in filth and building debris lined every road. The terrain was shrouded and bleak, the sky itself darkened by the ash of a long-extinguished nuclear fire. The air was frigid, the cold of January further burdened by the sun's absence. Steam filled their faces with every breath stolen from the icy air. Even if he had been to

300

this part of the safe zone before, there was no way to recognize the area. After all, most landmarks look that same when they've crumbled into pieces. All Victor could gather was that it used to be a more urban area. Rows of scorched brick and collapsed shells outlined what once stood as offices, clinics, markets and homes, all wiped away by paranuclear blasts. Twisted metal and melted glass marked the graves of countless vehicles engulfed by the fires that had blazed through the streets. This was a cemetery for a civilization – an entire city full of thousands, perhaps millions of people, all burned away to nothing. It made Victor think of Boston.

Once they arrived on Earth, the hosts were split into teams. Victor and Anya stayed in port with the order to guard the evacuees. Dan, on the other hand, was sent off with Naomi and Rin to stop the minitia ground forces from advancing any further towards the refugees. It was a task that Victor was relieved to not be a part of. Still, he worried for his friends – Danny especially. They were going to the place where the fighting was at its thickest.

Some kind of projectile burst through the sky, singing in the air before landing a fatal blow on a descending craft. Debris fell like hail, forcing the soldiers and the hosts to take cover.

"Hope that didn't have anyone important." Victor quipped, earning a dark look from Anya.

"Not funny." she told him, choosing to speak in plain English instead of talking through the translator.

"No, I suppose not."

The improvised port was itself nothing more than a clearing in the dead city. From the appearance of the ground beneath the ash, it looked to have been a park. This day, however, it was a battlefield. Strategically placed sandbags and rubble walled off otherwise easy access points to the clearing. Anybody who wanted in, be it insect or human or tiavan, had to make their way through a bottleneck crawling with obarosi and human soldiers. Victor and Anya exchanged looks, agreeing that this was where they were needed most. What better to keep the unwanted out than with two human weapons? They kept low to the ground as they moved for the chokepoint. As they drew near, they could make out the alarm in the faces of the civilians pouring in. Many were running, almost trampling each other on their way past the guards. The reason for their panic became clear when a dark form shot over a barricade and into the crowd. Razor-like claws tore into clothing and flesh. Screams rang out, followed by gunfire. In no more than three seconds, the event was over. The monster lay crumpled on the ground, motionless in a growing pool of dark fluid. A number of civilians were down as well, either from malicious claws or misguided bullets. Several spots of crimson stained the ash on the ground.

Victor realized that he had frozen in his tracks, paralyzed by the chaos. "Come on," Anya pulled at his arm. Her face was bathed in mortal terror and stoic resolution, her voice high and beseeching, "We have a job to do."

* * *

The minitia advanced into the safe zone, ripping apart everything and everyone in their path. Their jagged ships soared overhead, burning the ground with their bolts and cutting apart friend and foe alike. The military struggled to halt the enemy's advance into the core of the safe zone. Anyone trapped in the outskirts of the city was destined to be left behind and left for the savage beasts. Acceptable losses, they were called. All for the greater good. All except for one man. In all this chaos and bloodshed, it wasn't a crowd of civilians or a check point that Lieutenant Holt was tasked to save. It was one man – a commander pinned deep behind enemy lines.

There were twelve men left under Holt's command. Taking point was Private Campbell, who was one of the calmest and easily the fastest shot they had left. Under the lieutenant's direction, Campbell led the way through the smoke and ash and blood. They were moving low, racing with the upmost caution from cover to cover along their path.

"Here." Holt pointed, "Along the wall."

Echoing shots pierced the distant air. The soldiers could sense that the bulk of the battle was moving away from them for the time being. Still, they couldn't risk letting their guards down. As far as they were concerned, the enemy could be around any corner.

"Watch your step." Campbell warned the others.

Holt looked down and realized the bloody remains of a skirmish were lying at his feet. Americans and minitia corpses sprawled out in the road. As they drifted through the killing field, they saw in detail just what had happened. A number of men were positioned between a collapsed bakery and an overturned SUV. They must have been on the defensive, forced to find whatever cover they could. It goes without saying that it wasn't enough. Flesh was shredded apart, bones were exposed, heads were caved in. It looked to be the scene of a slaughter. A handful of stragglers laid face down in the debris, having attempted to rout from the area.

Murphy, one of the privates under Holt, knelt down to turn over one of the bodies. His shaking hand fumbled for the dog tags resting around the fallen soldier's neck.

"Leave them." The lieutenant ordered, "We can't waste time picking through the bodies."

"Yes, sir." Murphy answered.

One of the other men kicked a piece of exoskeleton down the road. He was Private Gilks, the youngest of the soldiers under Holt. He looked around, scratching at the burn mark across his cheek, "This whole district is a dead zone." A handful of others grunted, either agreeing or attempting to dismiss

"Stay low, boys." Holt told the others, "The walls have eyes here."

They continued on, stepping around battered corpses and pools of red and black blood. One of the men, a young private named Stevens, couldn't help but stare at the faces of his fallen brothers on the battlefield, "It's damn eerie out here." he said. It was becoming clear to them which side won this skirmish. Only one of every five or so bodies were minitia.

"Where'd all the bugs go?" asked Corporal Belichick. It wasn't clear to the others if he was talking about the lack or alien corpses or the absence of all life besides their own. They were deep in the enemy's territory, yet there was no sign of continued life outside the bursts of distant gunfire and mortar shells.

"This place has got trap written all over it." declared Stevens.

The point man, Campbell, couldn't let his comrade's assumption go without adding his own take, "There's no way they aren't watching us right now." he announced, "Nothing we can do about that."

The lieutenant must have agreed with his men, or perhaps he wanted to end their postulations. A moment after Campbell finished, Holt turned to the bulk of his men and grumbled, "Just don't think too hard about it."

"Yes, sir." Belichick affirmed.

"Oi, look at the rec center over there." Campbell pointed with his rifle, "It's got the star on it."

"Let's hope our VIP's still in there." Stevens commented.

The rendezvous point was nothing more than a broken shell of a building. Most walls had already collapsed, leaving only the ballroom and part of the atrium standing with any certainty. The men approached the structure from several angles, covering each other in case of minitia attack and keeping away from any wall or half-standing rubble that appeared too unsound.

Private Campbell was the first to enter what was left of the interior, followed by Turing and Stevens. A moment later, Holt got the signal they all needed, "Clear."

"Friendly spotted." said Turing.

304

Corporal Belichick lowered his rifle as he approached the uniformed man. Even in the shadow and haze of the room, he could make out the insignia on the man's uniform, "It's our guy. It's the commander." Holt came in for a closer look. He was an aged man with hard features. The name on his uniform read 'Pullano'.

"Where's the rest of 'em?" Stevens asked, more to himself than anyone.

"First Lieutenant Adam Holt, here to get your ass out of this shit storm, sir."

"These your men, Lieutenant?" asked Commander Pullano.

"I don't have any more men, sir." Holt admitted, "These brave soldiers joined me when their own contingents fell."

Pullano looked from face to face. Perhaps he was surprised to see so many men this far out beyond the front lines, or perhaps he was surprised at how few. He had the kind of face that was almost impossible to read.

"Well," he began, grabbing his rifle from the edge of the table and walking towards the front of the room, "I'd like to thank all of you personally for coming to get me, but let's save the sentimental shit for when we're out of here."

Holt turned to the men and signaled for them to follow, "You heard the commander, folks. Move out."

The tilted forms of shattered buildings threw shadows all around the street. Every point of darkness could have held their deaths, but death never came. Each step they made as they trudged through the ruins was met with nothing but its own echo. The hellish sounds of remote combat grew even further away as the group distanced itself from the enemy's land. Holt and the others couldn't shake the feeling that things were about to take a turn for the worse.

The group came to an overpass. On one side were the soldiers, standing in the open like the easy targets they were. On the other was the way out of the dead zone. The road it passed over was charred and deadly, with twisted, sharp

305

frames of burnt vehicles littering the path. One by one, they made their way across. Campbell in the lead, followed by Stevens, then Belichick, then Murphy. Gilks and Turing covered the rear while Lieutenant Holt and Commander Pullano stepped onto the overpass.

A burst of rounds split the air. Two of the soldiers, a private and a corporal, slumped to the ground. Someone or something at the far end of the bridge had opened fire on them.

"Contact!" cried Private Campbell.

Everything happened too quickly. The remaining men returned fire. Before they could reposition themselves, another rifle opened up on them, this time from the end of the bridge they'd just passed by. The enemy must have been laying unseen, waiting for the moment to strike. Never before had he seen the minitia plan their attack so well.

"Behind us!" warned Belichick.

"To the roadblocks! Go!" Holt roared.

Those closest to the cement barriers took cover and laid suppressing fire down the ends of the bridge, giving the rest time to find some relative safety. Holt thought they could take a moment to collect their thoughts and contemplate of their next move. After all, the overpass was far too narrow for them to be outflanked any further. Then, as if the world itself wanted to prove him wrong, he caught the sight of his men fighting hand-to-hand with a minitia behind one of the roadblocks. The beast must have climbed over the side of the bridge to catch his men off guard. Now more were leaping over, ready and waiting to lunge forth and tear apart everything in sight.

"There's a semi under the bridge!" cried Stevens, "We can use it to step down off the overpass!"

There was no time to weigh any other options. Either they acted now or they would die on this overpass. "You heard the man!" Holt shouted, trying to keep his voice above the hailstorm of bullets, "Move your asses! Stevens! Turing! You two cover us! Campbell, take point!"

306

One by one, they made their way to the front of the truck and slid off, tucking and rolling onto the ground. As they hit the charred pavement below, metal rained at them from all angles. This, too, seemed to have been part of the trap.

"Damn it!" roared the commander, "Find some cover!"

It was a mad dash for the nearest alleyway, overturned car or anything else that could put something solid between them and the endless rounds singing through the air. Crimson blood sprayed the survivors as men dropped all around. There was no time to think, no time to help one another. It was everyone for themselves.

* * *

"Stay low!" Naomi roared, trying to keep her voice above the commotion, "Hurry!" An air of wary confidence, born from relentless practice and training, enveloped them. This was the place where all their work would come to fruition. Either they would make it through this day or they wouldn't, and it all depended on if they could utilize what they had learned. They were confident. They were ready. Above all else, they were determined. They had to be, for they were running straight through the front lines.

They were wearing a combat skin that was not so dissimilar to the training fatigues they wore at Jupiter Station. It was the same black and gray design, helping to camouflage the wearer into the surrounding ash and mortar. These, however, were far thicker. While providing more protection, they also somewhat restricted the movement of whoever wore them. The headgear came equipped with a visor that protected the eyes, while simultaneously giving the user access to battlefield information. Allied positions, directional warnings of unidentified bodies and a top-down map of the explored area were all there, ready to use without so much as the touch of a button.

It only took a couple minutes of earnest searching

before they found their first targets. The hosts rounded a corner into an old lot for what was once a strip mall. A pack of minitia were scurrying through the open area, making a move for the source of some far-off shouting. They stopped when they caught sight of the three humans standing. A handful of them carried weapons, military grade rifles that undoubtedly came from US soldiers. The rest, a good ten or so, had nothing but their claws and hooked teeth. They looked hungry, their twisted bodies ready to lunge and feast upon their prey.

"Contact!" Naomi cried, "Take them out!"

A wave of terrible howls rang out from their foes. This was what they had trained for. Dan and Rin shot for the armed ones, hitting them with waves of fire while Naomi took it upon herself to deal with the rest.

One of the unarmed creatures seemed to ignore its challenger and instead lunged for Dan. Before the host could react, he was knocked square onto his back. The fiend tore at his suit like a rabid hound, cutting rugged marks in to the mesh in its ravenous bid for blood. Thinking fast, Dan blocked his face with his arms. He worked them forward against the onslaught until his hands were around the beast's throat. At once, the monster was off him, making distance between itself and the foe it had, until now, taken for a normal human. A bolt of fire volleyed forward, charring its shell and forcing it to retreat.

Dan stared down at his arms, surveying the damage to his suit. Scratches and tears littered his front side. Even with such advanced material in the way, the creature had managed to draw blood at a couple of points along his forearm.

"You okay?" Naomi asked. He could tell what she meant by the tone in her voice.

"I can keep going." Dan nodded. This was his first real fight with a minitia. Of course, he had plenty of experience seeing what it was they could do. He witnessed it back at the farm in New York, where owner and animal alike were slaughtered without mercy and their home set ablaze. He had seen what happened to Victor's arm when they tried to pull him from the bus that night. He was there for the devastation in the convoy. Still, these monsters had never gone after him like that before. It occurred to him that he had never actually combated one of those monsters. Not until now.

"Should we go after it?" asked Rin.

"No," Naomi shook her head, "We're going after clusters, not chasing down stragglers. Let's keep moving."

Further into the city, the three noticed that a once-distant patch of gunfire was beginning to grow louder. As they progressed along a sidewalk and cleared another street corner, it all became clear. A group of soldiers, outfitted in American combat gear, were ducking behind pieces of a fallen wall, pinned by enemy fire. They were outgunned and a moment from being outflanked. At several points, minitia would try to converge on them from the sides. They knew that if they were to get close enough with their human prey, they could win the fight with ease. Fortunately for the humans, most of the monsters were gunned down long before they got within claw's reach of the defenders.

Daniel watched on as the other hosts closed in. One of the soldiers let out a cry of panic, and all of a sudden, the group went up in a blast of fire and dirt. The survivors were retreating before the smoke had even cleared, screaming and crying along the way to their new cover. Two were shot in the back as they turned face. Another found the claws of a monster that was waiting behind a pile of debris.

Naomi kept moving forward until she was at the site of the explosion. Then she grabbed one of the smoldering bodies, slung it over her shoulder and raced back to the others. The soldiers covered her as she went. When she returned, she gingerly lowered the charred figure onto the ground, "He's still alive, but he needs help."

The commanding officer, a skinny lieutenant with a torn lip and a swollen, brown-eyed face, turned and shook his head, "Negative. We can't get any medics out here. It's too dangerous."

"I will take him to the medics myself if I have to." she told him, "We do not leave our comrades behind."

"Yeah, and what would you know about that?"

"I'd listen to her, if I were you." Dan warned, "She's a former commando for the Israelis."

One of the soldiers, a young private with a burn mark seared across his left cheek, seemed to have been caught off guard by the words, "Wait, she is?"

"She doesn't even have a weapon." said another, "None of you do."

"If that's true," the lieutenant declared, "then we need her here with us."

"Then get this man help!" Naomi growled.

The lieutenant motioned to a couple of his surviving men, "Stevens, Campbell, get Belichick somewhere safe. Find him a medic tent. Check the inner roads. They might not have fallen yet."

"Move when I tell you to. Do not stop for anything… Ready?" Naomi signaled for Rin and Dan, who conjured balls of flame and hurled them at the enemy position, "Go now!"

The soldiers froze in amazement. It occurred to the hosts that these people had never seen something of this sort before. "Go, damn it!" Naomi roared, shoving Campbell out from his cover. That seemed to do the trick, as he and Stevens snapped out of their confusion and bolted away with Belichick.

"What now?" the lieutenant asked.

"Our mission is to stop the minitia advance into the inner parts of the safe zone."

"We were sent to evacuate a person of interest."

"Where is this person?"

"Around the corner, laying by a bridge. Last we saw, they were turning him inside out."

"Well, lieutenant," Naomi shook her head, "You have two options. Either catch up with your wounded and retreat, or help us keep the bugs off the civilians."

"Most of us have family in the safe zone." The

310

lieutenant announced, "We ain't going nowhere. How can we help?"

* * *

"There's an opening! Do it now!"

At the order, Victor whipped around from behind the barricade and let loose a tremendous bolt of white-hot lightning. All the electrons that he had gathered, all the ions he had formed were unleashed in a magnificent ray of stinging plasma. The current tore through his body, shocking his muscles and searing his very flesh. It was a blinding sight. When the spell had passed, all he could do was drop to the ground and hope that he was behind cover.

"You hit a car!" one of the soldiers cried, "Didn't get a single one of 'em!"

"Damn it!" Victor cried, his mouth somewhat numbed by the shock. His body was shaking now, drained and injured in ways that he hadn't thought possible. He had been fighting for what seemed like days. The shifting sun, masked as it was behind the haze of ash and ruin, told him that it had at least been a few hours. It was longer than he had expected to last in this hellscape. It wasn't the claws that scared him the most. As long as they remained as far from his flesh as possible, they couldn't harm him. No, it was the bullets that made him fear for his life. The enemy had been practicing their aim. Rifles and handguns commandeered from the corpses of men and women found themselves used by minitia on the front lines. They fired until they jammed, or the wielder died. Then they were tossed aside for the next set of claws to snatch up. They seemed to have an endless supply of guns and bullets. It made sense, as soldier they killed provided more resources for them to utilize.

Hour after hour, the pressure never ceased. The minitia rushed them time and again until their bodies piled in the street. They hid behind their fallen brethren, using the dead husks as sandbags to catch and oncoming fire. It was an effective method for gaining ground, Victor had to admit. However, it was a tactic that could only be implemented if the attacker had near endless numbers. The fact that they were using it meant only the worst for the handful of men guarding the port.

their plan culminated in a grand advance on the makeshift wall, eventually landing themselves beside a nearby tower. To be honest, it would have been too generous to call it a tower. It was more like the shell of a building that collapsed just right to form a sort of tower structure. The creatures knew that such a formation wouldn't hold up against much force, so they opted to help it along. After a few minutes of chipping brick and the squeaking of bending girders, the tower-like structure gave into its own weight and tipped over toward the soldiers. Its impact with the street shook the wall hard enough for some smaller bits and pieces to come tumbling off. When the debris cloud bellowed up and masked the battlefield, the minitia made their move and swarmed for the wall. A volley of rounds couldn't slow them. It was an electrical storm from Victor that kept them from simply slamming into the wall and knocking it over.

Victor peered over, glancing down the safer side of the wall. Anya was tending to a crying soldier. The corporal was bleeding from his temple and eye, where two razor claws made their marks. He would never see from that socket again, but perhaps Anya could rebuild his tissue fast enough to keep him alive. Beside her was another patient, one who could never again claim to have luck on his side. It was clear that the stress was getting to her. Holding onto their lives, clinging to them with everything she had, only to watch them melt away between her fingers. Her face was rigid, her eyes wide and her jaw tense. It was clear that she was doing everything in her power to keep herself together. Not that Victor could judge her, for he was in the same place.

Every soul could feel the pressure mounting. With every moment, more of those hell spawn swarmed into the choke point. Machine guns and grenades and lightning could only

312

do so much against such a wave of hunger and fury. They were almost shoulder to shoulder now, pushing and shoving against each other to break down the barricades. Obarosi pressed themselves up against the sandbags, trying to keep them in place against the onslaught. Little by little, the wall separating the monsters from their prey was beginning to crumble. Echoes of shrieks and the rampant patter of claws on cement rang all around. It was clear that they were searching for another way into the port. In time, they surely would find one. Everyone knew that it was not a matter of if, but when they would be outflanked and overwhelmed.

Without warning, Victor's earpiece sparked to life. He looked over to Anya and saw that she had paused as well, waiting anxiously to hear the message. "This is Athriel." It said, "Orbital defenses have been overwhelmed. The ground you stand on will belong to the enemy within the hour. Any host hearing this message is hereby ordered to retreat to their transport and prepare for their own evacuation."

Finally. These were the words that Victor had been waiting for. It was time to go. His family wasn't in the field of fire. They hadn't been for the better part of a year now. Nothing that he did here on Earth could save or condemn them. Moreover, he and Anya had already bought time for countless people to make it to the transport craft. So many had made it off world because of them. As far as he was concerned, their work was done. Now he wanted nothing but to follow his orders and get the hell off this God-forsaken rock.

"You heard the alien." he said, "Let's go."

"We can't." Anya protested, grabbing him by the arm as he readied to move from the wall.

"Like hell!" cried Victor, pulling himself free of her grasp, "We did our job here."

"There are still people in the safe zone."

"We already got hundreds, maybe thousands, to the ships. We've done all we can. Now it's our turn to get out."

"Not while there's still one soul left here."

"These are our orders, Anya!"

"And where are theirs?" she cried, gesturing to the soldiers by their side.

"Hey, Russian!" barked the voice of a captain, "Don't worry about us. Everyone here knew what we were getting into. If we get the order to retreat, we'll retreat. Until then, we're ready to fight to the last man."

"Then let us fight with you."

"No can do, ma'am. You have your orders. Besides, I've seen what you two can do. You're both worth more to the cause alive than dead."

Victor watched Anya's face as she worked through her inner struggle. At last, it seemed that she had conceded, "I wish you luck, Captain."

"Let's go." Victor repeated.

"After you."

They hadn't made it halfway across the park before a section of the makeshift wall collapsed. The soldiers who weren't hit by falling sandbags and debris were swarmed by minitia. Victor grabbed Anya by the arm, forcing her to keep moving. She was never able to look back – he didn't allow it – but he saw everything.

* * *

Jagged teeth and razor claws lunged at Daniel Emerson. The host acted without thinking, using his strength to catch the beast by its arms and throw it onto its back. A short burst of amplified punches to the creature's chest broke the exoskeleton and laid the monster to rest.

"You heard the message!" Naomi shouted.

"Well let's get the hell out of here, huh?" he returned.

"Come on!" Naomi grabbed the lieutenant's shoulder, "We're getting back to the port!"

The hosts led the soldiers in a long sprint for the park. In time, the bursts of rounds became more and more sparse. Perhaps the enemy was running out of ammunition. On any other day, that would've been a wonderful sign. Under normal circumstances, the army with the firepower controlled the field. These, however, were not normal circumstances.

They ran for maybe half a mile before one of the soldiers, the young man with burns across his cheek, broke into a trot, "How much farther?" he asked them between heavy breaths.

The rest of the group slowed down, both to accommodate him and to rest themselves. Dan's visor told him that they were just under a mile away, after taking into account all of the twists and turns of the ruined streets. He was about to tell the soldier, but a black figure, quick and agile as a shadow, lunged forth, seemingly from out of nowhere. Before anybody could react, the boy's bones were crushed and his neck was open. The monster reared its head upward and let out a hellish cry before turning its crimson eyes at the others. A burst of rounds befell the beast as it went for the lieutenant, leaving the thing bloody and squirming on the ground. It tried to get back upright, but only managed to crawl. A gnarled, bloody limb stretched out to Lieutenant Holt. Dan could see the hideous black blood oozing down its inhuman hand. Four fingers, forward-facing with razor-like talons, and a thumb on either side of the span. Deep cracks along the wrist let blood and inner matter drip out onto the pavement. Dan looked at its twisted face as it let out one final cry. Then utter silence took over. The minitia, stuck in an empty stare with its jaw wide open, seemed to accept its fate, not giving so much as a flinch as Naomi came forward and put her boot through the shell of its head.

When the deed was done, she turned to address the crowd, "We're a little under a mile from the evac site. If we're going to make it, then we have to be fast. Can't let these things swarm us."

Dan looked from face to face, watching the men before him try to fight off the panic. He could hear more of those bugs coming just beyond the rubble at the end of the street. The clacking of hard feet on broken pavement sounded to

315

him like a fast-approaching wave of death. There was no fighting a force that great. Naomi was right. If they were to have any hope of surviving, then they would have to stay ahead of the swarm. However, the minitia were easily twice as fast as any human being, and they were so far from any place that could be considered safe.

At Naomi's command, he and Rin raised a wall of fire from one end of the street to the other in a spectacle that made more than a few soldiers look on in disbelief. Then, working together, the three hosts pushed the heated air and towering flames forward into the minitia onslaught, cooking everything in their path. Perhaps that would slow them down. In the end, all they could do was hope. Then they ran. They ran and they prayed for the best.

"I'm going to signal the others!" Naomi shouted above the growing roar of their impending death, "See if they can come to us!"

"The other what?" Lieutenant Holt asked, "There's more of you supers?"

The roaring around them grew louder, even starting to shake the ground beneath their feet. "What the hell is that?" cried one of the soldiers.

A long darkness swept over their path as a jagged ship carved low across the sky. The figure was enormous, larger than anything that humanity had ever forged, like a mountain of black and crimson floating in the sky. Its very presence made the ground quake, shaking apart any half-standing structures and knocking people off their feet. Its dark, twisted shape cast an even darker shadow over the land below. Nobody said a word, but they were all thinking the same thing. How could anyone fight that? The battle was lost. Earth was lost. Now there was nothing else to do but try to get away, to clear the grasp of death and live to face another day.

It wasn't long before Dan could hear the scraping of claws on concrete again drawing closer to the group. Fiendish calls from behind gave word that their predators were never far behind. Soon now, it would all be over – for better or worse. That much, they knew. All of a sudden, Dan felt something collide into him, sending him face-first onto the ground. The beast turned him over and tore at his abdomen, shredding at his combat suit. He threw a frenzy of fists and elbows at its face, but they didn't stop the creature from sinking its claws into his flesh and dragging them along the inside of his ribcage.

* * *

"Distress signal." Anya warned, motioning to her helmet, "Naomi."

"I see it, too." Victor nodded.

"The others must be in trouble."

It wasn't lost on Victor that Dan was out there, too. He looked to the display on his visor, spotting three golden dots moving together less than a mile away. One of these icons, the one with Dan's name etched over it, blinked to a sickly yellow. Panic struck at Victor's heart. What was happening over there? Was his friend okay?

"Please tell me we're getting them." he begged, trying to keep a solid voice.

Anya looked at him, her understanding eyes showing through her transparent visor, "As if that was a question. I will tell the pilot."

She disappeared and, a moment later, the engine hummed to life. The ship rose sharply from the ground before furling off like a bird in flight. Its movements were erratic, the pilot taking evasive action against anyone who thought it wise to raise a weapon to the sky. A couple of times, they were hit by small arms fire. Victor couldn't tell if it was from minitia trying to bring them down or humans who saw the craft and didn't know any better.

By now, the park-turned-port was long behind them, the scenery below transforming into the burnt city that Victor had grown to know. Under a haze of smoke, he saw

American soldiers and minitia hordes gunning and ripping each other down in the streets. Rounds of metal bit hard into concrete and armor and flesh. Swarms of teeth and claws carved into those who dared to run. Blood and body parts had been scattered all over the roads, the creatures of torment piling the remains of their victims into crimson mounds. Victor would have sworn that he could almost hear their screams. Perhaps he would have, if they weren't drowned in the shrieks of a thousand demons crying out in exuberance. This was no longer a battle. It was a feast for monsters. The one thing that terrified Victor more than anything was the knowledge that Daniel was trapped down there, waiting to die.

Something moved under the smoke. The transport slowed into a hover and began to descend. Was this the place? Victor checked his visor and saw that he was right on top of the yellow marker.

"Danny!" he cried into the street below. He couldn't control himself.

The craft came within a couple feet of the ground. Anya rejoined him and together they leapt from the ship. It appeared that they had come at a break in the chaos. Dark shapes laid about the road, black blood pooling around them. Between the bodies and the hosts were nearly a dozen figures, most of them clad in American fatigues. Victor and Anya joined them at their cover – a crushed and overturned SUV.

"Who are the soldiers?" Anya asked.

Naomi came forward from the crowd, keeping low to avoid being spotted by the enemy they all knew was out there, "They have wounded and need evac. Get them on the ship. I will get Daniel."

Where was Dan? Victor looked around at all the faces. Soldiers in camouflaged gear rushed past him and climbed through the open hatch of the transport. Several rounds from an unseen foe forced him to drop for cover. There, below all the yelling and senseless commotion was Daniel Emerson, lying against a piece of concrete. His face was paler than

318

normal, his eyes red from the smoke and his skin and hair as filthy as everything else. A deep redness took over his abdomen, spilling onto his lap and hands. All that blood made Victor's heart jolt in his chest. Naomi was attempting to get him to his feet. Without another thought, Victor joined her and helped lift him into the craft.

Just as Victor himself was about to get onboard, a flash of movement came in from the corner of his eye. The side of the transport went up in a scream of shredding metal and roaring fire. Before he could pull himself back to his feet, another missile flew their way. This one was stopped by Naomi's invisible hand forcing it into the pavement. Pieces of road pelted the side of the ship, a bleak reminder of what could have been everyone's demise.

Anya's translator buzzed to life, barely audible above the noise, "We cannot take another hit like that!"

"Take off!" Naomi called, backing away from the transport, "I will keep them away!"

"We will not leave without you!" shouted Anya.

"I will catch up! Just go!"

Victor stayed silent, looking back and forth between the two women. He knew what it was that Naomi was doing. With a look of defeat, Anya told Rin to inform the pilot before moving herself to Dan's side. She didn't even say goodbye.

The transport then rose up, drifting almost frictionless into the sky. Victor, still laying on the floor of the vessel, looked out of the side of the craft and watched the ground slowly disappear below. No more missiles hit them. Naomi Daskal made sure of that. Each one that flew their way was knocked off course by the same invisible hand. The last thing Victor saw was a circle of minitia standing under the craft with Naomi in the center, ready to fight to the end. They lunged together, piling onto their prey just as the smoke blocked his view. Only her killers would know if she put up much of a fight.

"Close the hatch!" Anya shouted. Victor looked at her,

then Dan. He heard the voice of her translator, but couldn't process her words. He just sat there, motionless, unbroken from his spell. "Victor!" she cried again. This time, Anya's command got through. He rose to his feet and closed the hatch to the transport, sealing them off from the smoke and fire and chaos outside.

"Help me with Daniel!"

His body didn't want to move, but Victor forced himself forward. When he was by her side, she took his hands and placed them over Dan's abdomen.

"I need you to hold right here." she said, "Keep pressure on the wound." Anya held her hands flat over Victor's with an inch of space between them.

"What are you doing?" he asked.

"I am trying to build a cell barrier in the openings. See if I can stop the bleeding long enough for us to get him some real help."

It was then that Victor noticed what was happening under his palms. The soft, torn matter exposed by the shredded armor started to change. It was as if a film was developing over the wounds. Soon, the flow of blood began to slow.

"Oh my God, it's stopping." he said, in disbelief.

"Keep the pressure on."

Through tears in his eyes, Victor watched Dan's pale face. He wanted the color to come back. He wanted those icy blue eyes to open again. Danny had always been his brother. A life without him wasn't a life at all. Victor didn't even want to imagine it, let alone live it. He just had to be okay. He had to.

"You can take your hands off now." Anya told him

"Okay." Victor sniffled as he tried to force the tears back.

"Slowly... There. None of the matter I built got stuck on you, did it? I tried to keep it to his cells."

Victor looked at his hands. His shaking, filthy, crimson-stained hands, "No, you're good. All clean."

"I will keep maintaining the barriers until we make it to safety. At this point, if we survive the flight out of here then he will probably make it. Weaker men than him have come back from losing more blood. I have seen it."

"Oh, thank God." Victor's voice cracked as new tears ran down his cheeks. He couldn't keep himself together. All he could manage to do was to sit back, pull off his helmet and cry. He cried over Dan and the thought of losing someone who he'd spent so much of his life with. He cried from the stress of all that he had just been through. He cried for Naomi, for the soldiers back at the port, for everything. He was overwhelmed.

"Over there." Anya nudged him, trying to shift his attention to the screens on the wall, "Take your last look at Earth."

He looked up, wiping his tears on his forearm and peering at one of the screens. He watched as black ships descended into the cloud below, ready to reap their spoils of war. This was it, Victor thought. This was how the world ended. Just a small rock caught in the way of an unstoppable force. A force that nearly took away everything that he'd ever loved. A force that would only be emboldened now that it had tasted the sweet blood of victory.

Chapter 16

So that was how the world ended. Not with a bang or even a whimper, but with the victory cries of a hundred million monsters. He could still hear their terrible shrieks and screeches ringing like sirens in his ears. He could still see the wall breaking down, unleashing the flood of teeth and claws and bullets onto the defenders he was so willing to abandon, lest he'd join. Still in his head was the last look of Naomi Daskal, a look that was now seared into his retinas, perhaps for all time.

As soon as the hosts got back to Jupiter Station, everybody was rushed to the infirmary. For most of them, it was just an examination combined with some basic first aid. When the doctors saw Dan, though, they were quick to wheel him to an operating table. Victor wasn't allowed to join. His immediate dismay came from the fact that he couldn't stay by his friend's side. Later it turned into a morbid curiosity about how tiavan performed surgery in the first place.

That night, Victor knew that he wasn't destined for a moment of sleep – not that he wanted to, anyway. One of his tiavan caretakers offered to sedate him, but he was quick to turn it down. To witness the dreams of his mind, the way they would certainly twist and mutate all that he had witnessed, was of no priority to him. Instead, he opted for the nightmares of reality. Memories of his hours spent on the ground played over and over, every detail as clear as a photograph in his mind's eye.

After a much-needed night of sleepless reflection, Victor was called in to give his report of the battle. At the order of the interviewer, he went through every moment of the previous day – or at least the moments that would have mattered to any higher authorities. Before he knew it, the questions were over and he was free to go. As he left, he found Anya waiting just outside. She was paler than usual, but appeared more alive than himself.

"Hey, Victor." she said, "How are you holding up?"

He looked at her with distant eyes. After a moment, his vacant expression shifted into something more present-minded, "I'm managing. Still just processing it all. How about you?"

"The same."

"How's Danny? Is he… any better?" He almost didn't want to ask, fearful of what the answer could be.

"They are still keeping him sedated. His wounds were grievous. It may be a while before he is awake."

"What's a while?"

"A few days. A week, maybe." Her tone changed as she spoke. Victor could tell that she was making a conscious effort to avoid seeming too dour, "He will wake up, though. He is getting better medical care than either of us could have dreamed of… It's weird." She shook her head. Then, for reasons Victor could not fathom, she gave a quiet smirk. She looked at him with glistening eyes, "All this death and gloom and that's all I can really think of. My inner nurse is in heaven."

Victor made his best attempt at returning the smile, "At this point, I'd say your inner nurse is just you."

"That may be true… But anyway, I need to get going. The tall boys want my report next. We will talk later, yes?"

Victor nodded, "I'll probably be with Danny. Stop by there whenever."

"You are a good friend to him." she said. Then, in a gesture of amity she took a step forward and placed a hand on his shoulder. They looked into each other's eyes, his a deep, mournful green and hers a vibrant blue, almost reminiscent of Danny's.

When she had gone, Victor remained for a few minutes.

His hand rose and grasped at his shoulder, where her palm had laid. He felt the scars – shallow dips in his skin just underneath his shirt. Their first encounter with the minitia had left him with marks that he would carry for the rest of his life. Now the same could be said for his friend. Victor couldn't help but feel terrible. If only he had told Dan not to join him in the Host Project. If only he had fought to stay by his side in the battle. If only... No, none of that mattered. What happened had happened. There was nothing that wishful thinking or 'what ifs' could do to change cold reality. His best friend was fighting for his life on the other side of the station. After a moment of contemplation, Victor pulled himself from the introspective haze and began his journey to the medical bay.

* * *

These were the great halls of the August Palace, where the higher levels of tiavan government met to conduct their work. Its gilded halls and ornate décor had seen the discussion and planning of every major event in the Eternal Kingdom since before the reign of Mecurin. At any other time, this place would have been quiet and organized. Silence in these halls was a clear sign of peace across the Kingdom. The last time he'd been here, it was to discuss his secretive actions on Earth several months before the fighting. Today was a different story. Today, the Kingdom was preparing for war. It was something that Athriel had thought – and hoped – to never see again.

Noble Endoraith permitted him to sit in on the meeting, but forbade him to speak. *"You are a captain on a research team."* the admiral had said, *"Nothing more. Your house name does not grant you rank."*

The meeting began when Sovereign Mecurin entered the chamber, surrounded by their usual escorts. As they claimed their seat in the back, it was at last time to begin. Asanur of House Urun, High Speaker of the Council opened with less than stellar phrasing, *"This could not have been more of a disaster."*

Noble Endoraith was quick to their own defense, *"It was inevitable. We all know it. The blockade should never have covered so much space. We were stretched too thin to properly counter a multi-pronged assault."*

"You have done far more with far less, High Admiral." joined Faratheyn of the August Guard, *"Perhaps it was a mistake to trust a hero of the past with an action of the present."* Those words stirred a sort of restlessness in Athriel. A restlessness that made him want to object, to outright counter this profanity. He refrained, however, knowing full well what his place was in this meeting. Still, he couldn't help but wonder why Faratheyn had a right to speak either. After all, their only call to glory had come from their ability as a bodyguard.

As it was, Endoraith was more than prepared to defend themself, *"Would you say that you could have done better, Faratheyn? I invite you to try."*

Another councilor, Spymaster Amelatu of House Anur didn't hesitate to add to their words, *"Noble Endoraith has more combat experience and versatility than the rest of us together. To blame them for losing an unwinnable battle is to denounce our ability as a species. Surely you do not mean to do such a thing, Noble Faratheyn."* Amelatu had questioned Athriel back when his actions on Earth first came to light. They were always collected and dignified, only electing to speak or act when they deemed it necessary. When Athriel had undergone questioning at the Gateway, he'd expected some level of torture. The fact that he'd been given such hospitality gave him a respect for the spymaster that would not soon subside.

"Why are we spending our energy on assigning blame?" asked Sirnerin of House Uthulen, Master of the Domain, *"It is pointless to reflect in such a pointed way. We are above this."* Those words brought a silence over the chamber.

It was Amelatu, the spymaster, who broke the silence, *"Noble Sirnerin is right. This is not productive. At the end, the situation has not changed. Countless sentients are dead, including many of our own kind. The minitia have won their first major victory against the tiavan since the Reclamation."*

"Linious has their armada." declared a voice from the far end of the chamber. It was none other than Sovereign Mecurin, sitting tall and rigid in their throne, *"One that already defeated our High Admiral without their new master's aid. There is no telling how far they can press us now. We had hoped that the war would end on Earth. Now it will undoubtedly spread through the stars. So now the question is... how do we defeat this? If we could not contain the swarm, then how do we conquer it?"*

* * *

"Initial scans seem to be accurate." said Zachen, "Most of the ship's systems are down. Air filtration, temperature regulation. However, there still seems to be some residual heat left in there."

"Could there be life aboard?" asked Aeriz.

"If there is, it's done a great job of staying quiet."

These uridans were part of a three-person salvage team. A local government had sent them to investigate a mysterious object seemingly trapped in orbit around their world. The figure was first noticed by observers close to a dozen rotations ago. Satellite images showed that it was small and sleek, consisting of some unknown metal. It was a ship of alien origin – that much was clear – but who could it have belonged to? The obarosi? The felisks? Perhaps even the gel'mas? The general design, as vague as it was in the images, showed a distinct tiavan inspiration in the craft's architecture. Any of these species could have been responsible. It wasn't uncommon for such ships to enter orbit around Uriid Ei, but they usually came with some kind of purpose. They would dock with a trade port or make landing on the planet's surface. Very rarely did they remain in open space for long, and even then, they would still use their engines to keep a solid trajectory. By now it was clear that, whoever was inside, they had either no desire or no ability to move from its current aimless drift.

326

Aeriz, the closest thing this crew had to a captain, watched on as Zachen as studied the vessel.

"It's definitely tiavan." said the latter. "Look at the etchings on the hull. Only the Bright Ones would take the time to make those."

"Watch this be another junk ship." said Tiri, the ship's second-in-command, "If it is, I say the first one aboard gets first pick of the loot."

Aeriz shook his head, not taking his eyes off the screens, "My concern is that it's a shuttle from the Glowing Masters, but there appears to be no life onboard. Anybody on that ship must be dead, and only the Masters would be on there."

Tiri laughed, "Nothing could kill a tiavan, Aeriz. The shuttle must have launched through some malfunction and drifted too close to the planet."

"Could be a solid theory." Zachen joined, "Except for the fact that the ship appeared here through faster-than-light travel. An accidental launch wouldn't bring it to that kind of speed."

The team studied the ship until they were certain of its safety. Then it was time to dock. Zachen maneuvered their own ship to match the angle and rotation of their target. When they were aligned, they moved in and connected the airlocks of both vessels, sealing the craft together. Once all was clear, Zachen restarted the directional engines, bringing the ship back to its original rotation, with the mysterious craft attached. This was how they liked it – boarding on their own terms, with the spin of the ships summoning forces to simulate their own gravity.

When it was safe to move again, Aeriz and Tiri prepared to board their target. They donned rugged atmosphere suits. They were older and more primitive in design than most, but it was all the crew could afford. Of course, they still had shortwave communication with each other, but the range was rather limited and the signal could have been stronger. Furthermore, the suits didn't come with their own lights. Since sight was a necessary sense for their mission, each of them had to carry their own external light source.

After another moment, they heard Zachen's voice call

from around the corner. *"Airlock secure. Atmosphere on the other side is breathable. You're all set to go aboard."*

With the press of a button, the airlock doors opened, greeting the uridan salvagers with a gust of wind. Beyond their own ship, the new vessel was dark and still. Tiri and Aeriz looked at each other, neither of them strong enough to admit to the strange sense of foreboding gestating within them. The latter gave a slight hand gesture towards the mysterious craft, *"After you, friend. Good looting."*

"If you insist." Tiri answered with more than a hint of sarcasm. She took care in each step as she walked, light in hand, across the threshold between ships. Aeriz followed shortly after, disappearing with her into the dark unknown. Once together, they began to divide the area between themselves. Aeriz would go right as Tiri went left. It was a small enough ship that they were unlikely to fall out of sight with each other.

After a moment of looking over blank walls and empty compartments, a strange form came into Aeriz's view. A bipedal figure, a little over seven feet tall, was lying lifeless on the ground. It was leaning against the far wall, its head and torso angled towards the airlock. It was an uridan. Barely even full grown. His face was sunken, the flesh drawn tight across his bones. A look of pained weariness had frozen across his face. Whoever he was, he had died exhausted – perhaps starved and suffocated, too. Without some sort of autopsy, none of that could be certain. What was certain, however, was that this uridan wasn't alone when he died. The binds around his wrists indicated that he was held prisoner by someone else.

"I see something." said Aeriz, *"It's one of us. An uridan. Zachen, we have eyes on a dead uridan. Male. Unclear cause of death."*

Tiri came in close to get a good view of the find, *"Could be the work of caravins, the menace they are."*

"Why would caravins be on a tiavan ship?" Aeriz asked her.

"Why is an uridan?"

"Look at the uniform. He must have worked with them."

328

At that moment, half of the light in the vessel vanished. The uridans exchanged looks. Tiri's light had gone out.

"*Strange.*" she said.

"*I thought you had charged it.*"

"*I did.*"

"*We'll use my light for now. If we find something that keeps us here for a while, we can go back and charge it again.*"

They went back to searching, this time remaining in close proximity to share Aeriz's light. There wasn't much interior left to search through, but Aeriz wanted to be thorough. If this craft was important enough to send an excavation team, then warranted more than a basic scan. Aeriz made his way towards the control seat, Tiri following close behind. The screens had long since deactivated and frozen over. Still though, a soft light radiated from one of the panels, casting the opposite wall in a faint, white hue.

"*Give me your light.*" said Tiri, "*I want to check something.*"

"*Here.*"

Aeriz had expected Tiri to at least reach for the light when he offered it. Her stillness… It was unnatural. She was like a statue in a space suit.

"*Tiri?*"

Now he was truly frightened. His body tensed, his breathing slowed. With caution, Aeriz leaned forward to see his partner's face. When it finally came into view, he felt himself coming unnerved. Tiri looked shaken and hurt, as if she was struggling against some great, unseen force. He called her name again, his wavering voice revealing the terror he had wanted to conceal. Then he saw her eyes. Two rust-colored spheres looking straight forward, locked on the darkest corner of the ship. Curiosity bested his caution and Aeriz whirled around to follow her gaze.

As soon as the glow of his light touched the pale creature, he knew they'd walked straight into the nirzhikn's den. At once, it felt as if a thousand hands were holding him in place, pressing on every cell in his body. He couldn't turn his head, but a loud burst at his side told him everything about Tiri's fate. Then the force that ended her veered back and turned for him. Instead of a quick death, though, Aeriz found himself hurled against the back wall of the craft. There he was pinned, trapped while the pale demon lunged for the airlock.

"Zachen!" he cried with every last bit of his strength, "It's in there with you!"

Epilogue

Her eyes opened, staring lazily at the ceiling of the shack. It was a new morning; a bright and warmer-than-usual Nonderanian morning in A08, and Marceline Roberts was feeling hopeful. Rumor had it that there was a great battle at Earth, and that one of the sides was sent scurrying away. Perhaps things were looking up for her. Maybe she would be able to return home – or to whatever was left of it.

The thumping of small feet stole her from her trance. Sammy came bursting in, nearly hitting her arm on the divider separating Marceline's bedroom from the rest of the shack. For a girl of nine years, she was still clumsy as ever. "Mommy!" she cried, "Come here! Look at the sky!"

"In a bit, dear." Marceline answered, pulling herself from her bed of blankets, "I just need some coffee."

It wasn't really coffee, of course, but saying so helped to keep her sane. After all, who wouldn't want to feel normal? In reality, this drink was nothing more than a random collection of common herbs that a trader had concocted into a half-bitter tea. Hazel nuts had been crushed into powder and mixed in to add some flavor. It hardly tasted like coffee, but the look and the slight bitterness made for a satisfactory illusion.

With drink in hand and the first nasty sip brewing in her stomach, she walked over and sat at the dining table across from John Athens. He was already dressed for the day, wearing a buttoned shirt with a red checkerboard pattern and long khakis that bunched up at the bottoms of his legs.

"So, any plans today?" Marceline asked him, "This is your day off, right?"

331

Athens nodded, a playful smile edging across his face, "Well I'm thinking about starting a garden."

"Oh? And where would you put it?"

"Maybe in the dirt by the doorway. I don't know."

"The kids would love that. Especially Sammy. What would you plant, though? And where will you get the seeds?"

"Pretty sure I was joking."

"Not anymore, you aren't. I like where this is going."

"So, what? I'm your personal guard and your gardener?"

Marceline smiled, already knowing what joke would get under his skin the most. Pointing a finger at him, she let it loose, "Hey, it takes a real man to grow tomatoes. Come on, be a man."

"Isn't the doorway a terrible place to plant things anyway? We'd always be trampling over it, and if something did grow, then someone would just come by and steal it."

"Maybe we could use the roof. Since we repaired it, it's been pretty sturdy."

Athens had a look of subtle surprise on his face. For a part of a joke, she had presented a decent idea – one that might actually work, so long as they had an easy way to get on and off the roof.

"We're legit doing this, aren't we?" he asked.

Just then, Sammy interrupted, "Mommy! Look!" This time, she had Zack by her side. The little guy seemed scared, his eyes wide and his lip beginning to quiver.

Marceline took him into her arms and rose from her seat. "Okay, hon." Sammy led her to the doorway. Perhaps something was going on outside? Maybe a parade or a new shipment of settlers?

"Now what is it you want me to-" she never finished her words. Instead, she found herself captured by the haunting sight above. All over the dome city, people were leaving their homes and staring awestruck at the sky. They were fearful, confused, panicked. Long, menacing shadows dragged across the streets. They reached across the troposphere like clouds back on Earth. Oh, how Marceline wished they were only clouds, and not the jagged ships of the minitia armada descending toward the world.

TO BE CONTINUED...